Totally Bound Publishing books by Pamela L. Todd:

Escaping Normal

Beautiful Sinners
Secrets, Lies & Vegas

What's her Secret?
Now You See Me

I0611444

Beautiful Sinners

SECRETS, LIES AND VEGAS

PAMELA L. TODD

Secrets, Lies and Vegas
ISBN # 978-1-78430-516-1
©Copyright Pamela L. Todd 2015
Cover Art by Posh Gosh ©Copyright March 2015
Interior text design by Claire Siemaszkiewicz
Totally Bound Publishing

SECRETS, LIES AND VEGAS

Dedication

First and foremost, for Matthew — will you call my
name?
And also for the best family a girl (and author) could
ask for.
The support from all you guys is truly humbling.
Thank you.

Chapter One

Excitement fizzed in my stomach as I followed the girls, who talked a million miles a minute and barely paused to take a breath. We walked into the restaurant...or was it a circus tent? Soft, floaty material of all colors was our ceiling and the wall panels displayed vintage art from the big tops of days gone by. In fact, the only clue that we hadn't stepped into a 1940s circus was the window that overlooked the world-famous fountain display. It took my breath away even in daylight, but now, lit up against the backdrop of darkness, I could barely tear my eyes away.

Hayley introduced us to the hostess, who led us to our table, the most central in the restaurant. Eve scanned the room, her hunter instincts on full alert as she surveyed her prey. Beth looped arms with hers, giggling in her ear.

The moment our waiter appeared, Hayley ordered a bottle of champagne.

"Well, I think we should make a toast," Hayley announced once our glasses had been filled.

"Here, here," Eve said, raising her glass. "To Marley! For without her, I would never have met that cute investment banker from Chicago."

Hayley rolled her eyes. "Yes, Eve, that was exactly what I was thinking."

Beth giggled, flipping her long, shiny black hair over one shoulder. "Yeah, because it should be about Ken from Kentucky."

I snorted a laugh. "You do remember that his name wasn't actually Ken? And the fact that he only put up with the nickname was because you left your bra pinned to the wall in Coyote Ugly and he could see your nipples through your dress?"

Beth waggled her eyebrows. "Well, I do have very nice nipples."

"You should send that to Hallmark," Hayley said. "Okay, in all seriousness guys, I really do want to make a toast to Marley."

Beth and Eve raised their glasses, eyes on Hayley as they waited for her toast.

"Marley, you know we love you," Hayley said with a smile, "and I think it goes without saying that this trip has been ridiculously overdue. So here's to our last night, and going as hard as we can."

"To Marley!" Beth and Eve chorused, chinking their glasses at mine.

I forced a smile and took a gulp of champagne, which tasted sour on my tongue. That toast, whilst heartfelt, felt like a needle in my heart. It was just another reminder of how different I was from my friends.

Eve tossed back the remainder of her drink. As she placed the empty glass on the table, her eyes darted between us all when she noticed us staring. "What are you all looking at? You said go hard."

"I said hard, not sloppy," Hayley said, shaking her head, the small smile pulling at her lips, ruining any scolding she may have intended. She tugged on the end of Eve's shoulder-length blonde hair. "You might want to pin this up before bed, because no one will be holding it back for you."

Eve leaned closer to Hayley, pursing her glossy red lips. "Honey, I plan on burning all the alcohol out of my system with vigorous exercise."

Beth laughed. "Let's make a toast to that!"

We ordered our food when the waiter returned, Beth and Eve still sizing up their potential prey. I circled the rim of my glass with my fingertip and felt a set of eyes on me. Hayley studied me with her curious blue eyes, a tiny crease between her eyebrows.

Out of everyone, it was Hayley I was closest to, the first out of this group of girls I'd met. They pulled me into their orbit in a blur of cocktails and club music. Beneath the man-eating exterior of these women were big hearts and kinder spirits. I adored them all, but Hayley was the one I felt the deepest bond with. But like any close relationship, it had its perks and its downsides. Like right now, when I knew she could see more than the others.

"Last night blues?" she asked, her tone light.

I gave a swift nod. "Something like that."

Hayley patted my knee under the table. "We'd better make it a memorable one then, hadn't we?"

"It's already been pretty memorable, Hayley," I said, giving her a genuine smile.

And it had.

Surprisingly.

None of us had been to Vegas before and I had been hesitant to come. Sin City... Who wanted to go there?

A city where people flocked to make stupid decisions and change their lives…for better or worse.

Maybe that isn't such a bad idea…

I wasn't altogether sure what I'd expected of this place. When the plane had begun its descent toward the ground and I'd seen the bright lights of this unusual world, a flicker of excitement had rumbled low in my body. I'd all seen the movies, the TV shows, but really, nothing could have prepared me for the intensity of Vegas. I'd had my preconceived ideas, the mental image that was a far cry from the glossy, fluorescent reality. I'd thought I'd known what to expect, but it wasn't until we'd driven down the Strip with the lights reflecting off the windows that I'd discovered there wasn't actually anything—real or imagined—that could have prepared me for Vegas herself.

It felt like I was a Lilliputian in a glittery and exotic setting—only the buildings were Gulliver, and these were my travels. Truth was, I had looked down my nose at the thought of a trip to Las Vegas. I wasn't a snob. It was just the white-trash stories that went hand in hand with the city which made it a less than desirable vacation spot. But when I'd got here, I couldn't have been more wrong.

Wealth and luxury screamed from most places and it was larger than life. A playground for those looking for an escape from reality, even for a short while.

Maybe this was exactly where I needed to be.

After a delicious meal that was served on a plate with pictures of monkeys, the girls tried to decide where to go for the night's activities. Well, Hayley tried to narrow down the options—Eve and Beth were still admiring the specimens on display. I, on the other hand, ogled the dessert tray.

God, I hate diets.

Beth subtly pointed out a target to Eve. "Look at that one, over there."

"Oooh...." Eve crooned.

"Oh! That one!"

"Oh my God, are you serious? What are you, blind?"

"Over there then."

"Mmm-hmm."

"Wait a minute... I've got it... By the bar. See?"

"Dibs."

"You can't call dibs!"

"I just did!"

"But I saw him first!"

"Then you should have called it."

"Fine. Whatever. I don't care."

"You so do."

Beth and Eve's shameful game of man window shopping was a welcome distraction. It was an impressive feat that they found so many desirable men in the restaurant, considering there were only nineteen tables. When I'd first met them, I'd thought the guys they favored were lucky to have such beautiful girls fawning over them. Now I felt sorry for the poor bastards. It was like watching a lioness flirt with an innocent springbok. There was no doubt that these girls were predators – and they were hungry.

They thought of this vacation as a buffet table, and the helpless male habitants and visitors of Vegas were the only meat on the menu. I'd lost count of how many business cards and cocktail napkins with carefully written phone numbers they'd acquired this weekend. With tonight being our last night, they would be bringing their A game...and no one was safe.

Hayley giggled, breaking my reverie, and leaned over the table to whisper, "A guy at the bar is staring at you."

My eyebrows shot up "So?"

She rolled her eyes. "So go talk to him!"

"Yeah. Right," I said, folding my arms across my chest.

Hayley frowned. "Why not?"

"I can think of a few reasons." Maybe it was because Hayley had made me aware, but I felt a pair of eyes on me. The little hairs on the back of neck stood on end and it was all I could do not to turn around.

Hayley gave a slight shake of her head, as though admitting I was a lost cause. "So where are we going?" she asked, the question aimed for no one specific.

"I really want to go back to Coyote Ugly," Beth pleaded, clasping her hands together under her chin and pouting.

Eve arched a perfect eyebrow at our friend. "And lose another bra to the wall? Good thing we're only here for the weekend. Imagine the loss if we were here for longer."

I rolled my eyes. "Please. Like Beth needs an excuse to buy new underwear."

"We are so not going back to Coyote Ugly. Come on, you guys. We need to make this a stellar night." Hayley's eyes flickered to me. "For Marley's sake."

I frowned. "Why for Marley's sake?"

Beth shot me a pointed look. "Like we could get you on another vacation. It was hard enough getting you to come this time!"

I dropped my eyes, unable to look at their accusing faces. Though they were messing around, I doubted they would ever know how much their words stung.

How quickly they forgot the easiness of their own lives.

Hayley cleared her throat. "Guys, focus. Where are we headed next? We've already been sitting in here for more than two hours. And I nominate Marley to be in charge of tonight's festivities."

"Why don't we just stay in the hotel tonight?" I suggested. We were staying in one of the best hotels on the Strip, yet we hadn't even experienced its nightclub yet.

Hayley nodded her agreement. "Vault? Yeah, I heard it's meant to be one of the best. We're staying here anyway. May as well keep close to home."

Beth looked disappointed at being outvoted, but when a group of well-dressed and devastatingly good-looking men walked past our table voicing their own plans to visit the same club, she soon perked up.

Beth wriggled in her chair. "You guys done?"

* * * *

My spirits soared as we took the escalator to the club. The bright purple lights of the entrance loomed into view as the steady beat of the music pulsed through my body. The club itself was dark — black and gold décor adding an element of luxurious mystery with strategic floor and ceiling lighting providing enough illumination to see. The brightness of the bars shone into the large space like beacons, above the DJ box a frenzy of flashing colors. We walked past booths and tables stocked with bottles of Cristal and slender flutes — wealth and elegance dripping from every sconce, every detail. It was a club full of secrets and I couldn't help but wonder how many indiscretions it witnessed.

We progressed into the main room. Eve grinned before disappearing into the thick of the crowd, headed toward the bar. The rest of us found an unoccupied area at the railing overlooking the crowded sunken dance floor. I perched on a stool and leaned on my elbows to watch the dancers.

One couple in particular caught my attention. They looked extraordinary. *Isn't everything in Vegas?* It wasn't until a person took the time to scratch the surface, that the true beauty of someone could be seen. Who would do that here?

The couple looked like a painter had dreamed them up to complement each other. The man was taller than the woman and she slotted perfectly into his chest under his chin. He bent to whisper in her ear and a slow smile pulled her full lips. I wondered what he'd said. He raised her hand to his lips and kissed it. She melted into him, her body becoming visibly boneless and languid as they melded together, becoming one inseparable unit.

I wish I could be as free as them.

A desperate wave washed over me and I couldn't pull my eyes from the beautiful couple and their indisputable happiness. I wasn't sure what it was about them that sparked such a reaction in me, only that as I sat observing them, an anxious feeling clawed up my throat and I wished I had any other life than the one I did.

Eve returned with a tray of Cosmos, which we greedily consumed. With the first round gone in record speed, Beth was the first to storm the dance floor.

"That guy from the restaurant is here and staring at you again," Hayley shouted in my ear.

I sighed. "And again I say — so?"

"There's no harm in talking."

"Isn't there?"

"What happens in Vegas stays in Vegas!" Hayley said, raising her cocktail glass in a toast.

I lifted my eyebrows at her.

She laughed, unperturbed by my less than carefree attitude. "Oh come on, Marley! You never relax! How often do you take a vacation?"

"Uh, never," Eve said, overhearing our conversation.

"So just relax. Just because you talk to a guy doesn't mean the world's going to end. You're on vacation. You should be having fun," Hayley said.

A bright light from the dance floor flashed and stung my eyes. Taking the opportunity to look away from Hayley and eager for the subject to be dropped, I turned from them and scanned the bar. My heart gave a jolt as the light once again flashed and I looked into a pair of eyes that were so intent on mine that my heart thumped. It was impossible to look away. The music seemed to fade to a whisper and all I could hear was the blood rushing behind my ears.

"Marley," a faraway voice murmured.

"Marley…"

"Marley!" A none-too-subtle nudge to my ribcage followed.

I jerked in surprise. Tearing my eyes away, I turned to look at Hayley with a frown. "What?"

Hayley gave a nod to the right. "Are you going to ignore this gentleman all night?"

There was a short cough beside me. Twisting in my seat, I was faced with a tall blond man wearing a shit-eating grin.

"Hello," he said, that grin widening, as though he'd already won whatever he thought this was.

Oh, God…"Hello."

"Would you like a drink?"

"No, thank you."

"Dance then?"

"I'm fine, thanks." Something told me my manners would run out in approximately four seconds.

He leaned closer. "Oh, come on. One little dance won't kill you."

I frowned. Make that two. *Hasn't he heard of personal boundaries?* He was a centimeter away from eating my nose. "No."

The corners of his mouth twitched, and he pressed closer. "It's a shame to let that dress go to waste. You should show it off."

Leaning away from him, I wished my new black Armani dress wasn't so flattering. I glanced at my friends but they conveniently turned away, ignoring my silent plea for help. An aggravated sigh escaped my lips. Their efforts to force me into an innocent flirtation possessed all the subtlety of a New Jersey mother-in-law.

I twisted back around to try again to get rid of the perv, only to find a different man stealing my attention. Over the blond's shoulder I saw the man who owned the piercing stare stride toward me, his gaze somehow both determined and casual...and still fixed on me. My breath caught in my throat and my pulse roared behind my ears.

The crowd parted to let him through, and I could finally take him all in. He had the darkest hair and olive-toned skin, only making his eyes look greener and his hair darker. He wore his hair short, though it didn't lie flat or straight against his head, making me think it would curl, were he to wear it any longer.

He was tall and lean, with broad shoulders and narrow hips. Though he wore a well-cut designer black suit, complete with black shirt and silk tie, and therefore completely clothed and covered up, his strong and toned physique was evident. The man moved with a grace that clearly came from honing his body to optimal performance, treating it with care and respect to gain absolute control and physical strength. He maintained constant eye contact with me on his slow approach, as though afraid that if he broke it I would bolt like a frightened animal. His mouth pulled into a picture-perfect smile that widened as he grew closer. And just as he was about to finish his approach, he winked at me.

The man, who should have been the scale that all hotness was judged by, placed a hand on the small of my back and planted a delicate kiss on my cheek, intoxicating me with his scent. It wasn't the usual guy cologne. It was something else, some scent that belonged to only him and no one else—a sharp citrus smell tinged with pure masculinity that made me feel primal. He pulled back, allowing me to swim in his eyes startling green eyes. It was the emotional equivalent of a drive-by. One that sparked a dull throb between my legs.

"There you are," he said, his voice soft and strong all at once. "I've been looking all over for you." He turned to face the guy who didn't know what a hint was. "Can I help you?"

"No, *you* can't," he shot back. "I asked the lady to dance."

My enthralling rescuer cupped my elbow, gently raising me to my feet. "I don't think she wants to."

"Why don't you let her speak for herself?"

"I believe she already said no. Besides, she's busy." He snaked his arm around my waist, pinning me to his side.

Every thought fell from my mind as he pulled me in the direction of the bar. All that mattered was his rich, silken voice that rang in my ears, making my heart thud that little bit faster. As we reached the bar, he dropped his arm and leaned his side against the counter so he could face me. I avoided his eyes, feeling incredibly self-conscious.

"Can I get you a drink?"

Tearing my eyes from the floor, my breath left me in a rush as our eyes met. Those eyes... They penetrated my body, everything that I was made of, until I was sure that he could see my very soul. His lips twitched as he gave me an amused smirk.

Great. I'm staring at him like an idiot. I managed a nod and a meek gesture in return.

"Cosmo, right?"

I nodded again, wondering how he knew what to get for me. "Thanks," I said, as I found my voice.

He slid the drink closer to me as the bartender placed it down.

"For the help — and the drink," I said.

He grinned. "You looked like you needed an escape route."

The smile was infectious and it took a beat for me to realize I was imitating him. "Yeah. That guy did not know how to take a hint."

He studied me. Somehow I managed not to squirm on the spot and sipped my cocktail for lack of anything else to do.

"Feel like a dance?"

My cheeks burned and I cursed myself, the yes already formed in my mouth. *What do I think I'm doing?* "I should get back to my friends."

He leaned an inch closer, as though about to reveal an important secret. "I don't think they'll miss you."

I frowned. "Why?"

He nodded to the railing where my friends and I had been sitting. I followed his gaze and saw that the area was now occupied by a different crowd of people. Hayley and Eve must have found willing dance partners, leaving me alone...with this guy...who was still staring.

"I don't feel like dancing right now," I said in a rush, wishing my cheeks would cool.

"Would you like to sit?"

There was no harm in sitting, was there? "All right."

His eyes softened with warmth and his hand once again found the small of my back. A rush went through me as I thought how perfect it seemed to both fit and feel there. He guided me through the throng of people in such a way that I knew he was familiar with the layout of the club.

Does he do this often? Rescue women and play the gentle yet oh-so-heart-stoppingly sexy green-eyed god?

We reached a roped-off area. A bouncer nodded to him and unclipped the rope to let us through. I arched an eyebrow at my new friend. "VIP lounge?"

He smirked. "I find it more comfortable. Allows for a certain degree of privacy."

Gulp.

He motioned to an unoccupied booth away from everyone else. I've no idea how he did it—the club was wall to wall with bodies, yet he secured a decent-sized booth where it didn't feel like people were falling on top of us. I slid in, clutching my cocktail glass as though it contained all the answers...because I sure as hell didn't know what I was doing.

"So," I said, watching him as he slid in beside me. A little thrill went through my body as I realized I was trapped. "You seem like a big deal around here. Can I ask what you do?" I asked, avoiding his eyes.

"You can, although the answer isn't very interesting."

Glancing up I smiled, encouraging him to go on.

He laughed. "I work in the hotel, that's all. I suppose... The job comes with good perks."

I gave him a look. "Oh, come on. Everyone seems to bow down to you. Somehow I'm not getting the impression you're just a bartender on his night off."

He grinned. "No, I'm definitely not a bartender. I'm kind of like the manager."

"Of the club?"

"Of the hotel." He shrugged in an 'I'm trying not to make this a big deal' sort of way. "Executive vice president, if you want to get technical about it."

So he was like the most important person in the room and he was talking to me... If I thought about that too much I'd choke and look even more stupid than I already did. He really didn't look old enough to have such a high-powered job. If I were to guess, I'd have said he was three or four years older than my own twenty-three.

"Did you enjoy dinner?"

I blinked at his change in conversation. A nervous flutter began in my stomach. *This is the guy Hayley was talking about?* "My friend saw you in the restaurant."

He shifted in his seat. "All part of my job. I came in to see how things were going."

"Do you need to come into the club every night?" I asked, smiling.

He chuckled. "No, I felt like getting a drink. Tonight is meant to be my night off. I prefer the lounge downstairs. It's quieter...more intimate. But the vultures find me and don't leave me alone. Here, on the other hand, they tend to give me space."

"Oh." At least he hadn't been following me — not that I thought that highly of myself. I was so glad I hadn't said that out loud. How big-headed would I have sounded? "My friend said —" A blush burned my cheeks. "You were watching me."

He lowered his eyes for a moment before meeting mine with a steady gaze. "Your table was most central in the restaurant. And you did catch my attention."

"You knew what I was drinking." *When will I learn to shut the hell up?*

He chuckled again, eyes dropping. "Would you buy it if I told you knowing what keeps the customers happy is all part of the job?"

I giggled. "No, but it would be a good shot at an excuse."

A smile tugged at his lips as he observed me. His eyes seared into me, making me anxious.

"So are you from Vegas?" I asked, nerves getting the better of me. Crap small talk, it seemed, was the only thing I could think of to say.

He shook his head. "God no, I'm from back East. What about you? I'm guessing you're on vacation."

"Just a girls' weekend. We go home tomorrow." I felt a pang in my stomach as I said the words.

He grinned. "Last blow-out before you have to face reality again?"

I glanced down and mumbled, "Something like that."

"Do I get to know your name?" He ducked his head to force me to meet his eyes.

"Marley."

"Pleased to meet you, Marley. I'm Blake." He extended his hand.

I was sure I jumped. The jolt that coursed through my entire being as he slipped that hand into my own was sheer electricity. *The guy should come with a health warning.* I didn't know how long I stayed like that, staring and holding his hand. A long time — too short a time.

When he released my hand, Blake slid his arm behind me along the top of the booth, bringing his body closer to mine. My heart rate picked up speed and I wondered if this was it — the moment he would make his move. But instead of tracing my shoulder with his fingertips or leaning to whisper in my ear, he picked up his drink with his free hand and settled back in his seat…looking a million times more relaxed than I felt.

"You already know I'm not a native and what I do for a living. Call it simple manners, but I really want the answers. Tell me, Marley, what is it you do back home?" Blake asked. He wore an open, relaxed expression.

It hit me, then, that he had figured out how nervous I was, and was throwing me a bone by taking it easy on me.

My shoulders eased out of the tension that had held them a fraction higher than usual. "I'm an assistant to the owner of a mid-sized PR firm."

He nodded. "Is it administration? Or do you work events too?"

"Both, usually. It's a lot of fun."

Blake jerked his head to the side, in the vague direction of the dance floor. "So this is your usual scene? Clubs, parties, making sure the beautiful people are at your events?"

I smiled. "Something like that."

His eyes skimmed over my face. "I can picture you there. But, at the same time, I can't. I'm not getting the impression you're the kind who gets off from power trips — a beautiful bitch who looks down her nose at the poor unfortunates trying to get in."

A laugh bubbled in my throat. "Not in the least. There's a lot of competition between PR girls from different firms. It's never great when our paths cross."

"I'm guessing you have more class in your pinky toe than the rest of them do in their entire body."

"How do you know I don't have a pinky toe to rival Bigfoot's?" I asked, a small smile pulling at my lips.

Blake leaned a fraction closer. "Because I can't believe there's a single inch of you that's less than perfect."

His words, coupled with the silken roughness of his voice, warmed my body from the inside out. It took every smidgen of self-control I possessed not to close the distance between us. I cleared my throat and took a sip of my drink, flushed from the way I was very obviously responding to him. "I suppose that makes two of us. I can't picture you the hard-ass Vegas boss controlling the gangsters in the casino."

He laughed, full and throaty. "What would you expect — something right out of a movie set in the twenties?"

"Yeah, something like that."

"Sorry to be a disappointment to my cliché, but times have moved on from those days." Blake shifted in his seat. "I know a lot of people don't like Vegas for whatever reason, or they do like it, but only so they can act the complete opposite of themselves. But I love it here. There's so much more to this place than meets the eye — especially the people, the ones who make it what you see now, and the people who are so far removed from the Vegas stereotype you'd be embarrassed to have ever considered placing them in that category. Yes, there can be a lot of phonies, but it's also one of the most frank and honest places I've ever come across."

It was clear from the way he held his body to the passion in his voice how much he cared about this city, and his job. He wasn't making this easier for me. "I think it's great you care so much about the place you live in. Happy people make for happy places."

A small smile touched his lips, as though he were pleased that I understood his passion. "I couldn't agree more."

I shrugged. "I grew up in an average-sized town. The people there look out for each other, support one another. It's a great community."

"What made you leave? Because I can't see a PR girl getting much in the way of work in a place smaller than a city."

"I left because it was what was right for me. I love where I'm from, but I want to see more and experience way more than what it can offer."

"Are you an adventurer at heart?" Blake asked.

Ordinarily I would have laughed at the question—I didn't think I possessed a single adventurous bone in my body. But here I was, poised on the brink of what felt like a life-altering adventure, and all I wanted to do was fall head first into it. "Deep down, I think I could be."

"I think there's more to you than meets the eye. You're an enigma, Marley."

"Right back at you, Blake."

He sipped his drink. "So tell me about this town of yours. I've known nothing but the chaos of cities."

I laughed. "How provincial do you think it is?"

"I don't know. Does it have a Walmart?"

"And a bowling alley."

His eyebrows shot up. "Then it's already doubled in size from what I imagined."

A shocked laugh burst from me. "What? Did you have me down as a country girl or something?"

Blake smiled, his face open with amusement. "Or something."

"I'm not sure if I should be offended or not."

"Don't be." Blake gestured toward me with his hand. "Seriously, tell me about it."

"Okay," I said past a laugh. "But don't blame me when I get to the end and you wished you'd never asked."

"Try me."

"Where would you like me to start?"

"At the best part, where else?"

I smiled. "Okay. My dad's store."

"What kind of store is it?"

"Hardware. I used to spend so much time there as a kid. I would help customers find stuff, getting to the point where they'd ask me which products I'd recommend." A warmth bloomed in my chest as I remembered the days of my childhood—the light that filtered in from outside and sparkled off various shelves of stock. The smell of piles of timber, the noise of the key-cutting machine, my dad's overalls covered in grease when he'd been fixing something or other.

"Now that I can picture," Blake said.

"We had this old RV that was always breaking down and falling apart but Dad refused to part with it. Every family vacation we took was in that thing. God, I hated it—and now I miss it. How stupid is that?"

Blake shook his head. "Not stupid at all. I always wanted to do a road trip when I was a kid. Closest I got was flying across the country to visit some obscure relative. My family always did overseas trips, but all I wanted was one of those driving vacations where you hit those 'World's Largest Weird Thing To Be Proud Of'. Though when I visited family, they did take me to this cool town with cheesy museums and oddities."

"Sounds like this place we visited once in Ohio," I said.

"Where in Ohio?"

I frowned, trying to recall the name. "I can't remember — it was somewhere outside of Toledo."

Blake grinned. "Me, too."

"No way," I said in disbelief. That was the thing I loved about fate — two random strangers could share the same experience, just at different times. Memories in the same place.

"Did you ever go to... Damn, what was it called?" Blake frowned, his forehead puckering. He gestured with his hand as he tried to remember. "That uh...diner thing? That was —"

"A converted bus?" I asked, not expecting the reaction it caused in Blake.

"Yes!" he exclaimed, laughing. "They ripped the interior out and turned it into a tiny diner. Shit, what was it called?"

"Greyhound's," I said, smiling. "God, I loved it there. The milkshakes —"

Blake's eyes widened, his face opening up. "The milkshakes! How could I forget about them? They were the thickest — the best goddamn milkshake I ever had. Ever."

"Tell me about it." I nudged him. "I've got a serious jonesing for one of those now. Thanks a lot."

"You brought it up." Blake chuckled, rubbing his stomach. "Oh, man. I had some of the best sugar rushes of my life with those. How long do you think it'd take to drive up there and grab a few? Think we could be back before daybreak?"

I laughed. "I doubt it. And I think I'd miss my flight if we tried."

"Ah, come on," Blake said in a voice that was completely and utterly seductive. "Can you look me in the eye and tell me whatever real life waiting for you is even half as good as those milkshakes?"

I smiled, and for the first since I'd met him it didn't feel genuine. If only he'd made any other comparison. "No, I can't. And as much as I'd like to, we still can't go."

"You're killing me." Blake smiled and rested his hand over his heart. "Why is it always the beautiful ones that break your heart?"

I looked down, his words affecting me more than I would have thought possible.

Blake touched the hand I clutched my empty glass with. "Settle for a Cosmo? It's no Greyhound milkshake, but it's something doable."

* * * *

When Blake returned with another drink each, my melancholic mood had disappeared. My worries fell away a little more with each sip. I wanted to forget about home and real life and just enjoy myself for once. Maybe Hayley was right— *What happens in Vegas...*

I was swimming in dangerous territory. That wasn't me. I was a good girl, a sensible girl. I didn't go to party central every weekend to meet cute guys. Really cute guys...with amazing green eyes...

What the fuck am I doing?

Blake started as I jumped from my seat.

"I'd better find my friends," I squeaked. "It's getting late."

He glanced at his watch. "It is late."

I hurried to the railing to look out over the dance floor. It was damn near impossible to try to make out a single face among the sea of bodies from this distance. I dug out my cell phone from my purse. No service.

"You can never get reception in here. Do you want to try outside?" Blake's voice by my side made me jump.

I nodded then followed him as we headed toward the exit of the club.

"Some people like to get a drink in the lounge after being in the club. Would they have gone in there?" Blake asked.

"I'm not sure. They aren't really the type to leave a man behind, so to speak." I frowned. "But they also aren't the type to *worry* about leaving a man behind."

Blake smirked. "How about we go in and look?"

"All right."

I felt more than a few sets of eyes on me as I walked through the club with Blake. Two women by the railing overlooking the dance floor raked me from head to toe, their eyes flooding with venom. *Previous conquests? Or did they never even get that far?*

Leaving was slow going. Blake was stopped by a bouncer, two men in suits and a panicked bar manager. It seemed everyone had a question, that 'no, it couldn't wait', to ask Blake. By the second person, he stepped to the side to accommodate me, his arm sliding around my lower back as though to reassure himself that I was still there and wasn't going to ditch him the second his back was turned.

Shivers crept up my spine at the contact and at the very nearness of him. I couldn't hear whatever problem the men in suits had, but Blake dropped his gaze to mine. Blake rolled his eyes and smiled as if to say 'so much for a night off'.

When we were finally free of people and hateful glares from pissed off women, we progressed to the exit. Blake's hand didn't move from my back and I couldn't help but walk a little taller, knowing that it was me he was leaving with.

On the escalator heading into the club, I had been excited and had had a rush of anticipation. Can't say my body was reacting all that differently on the way down.

Hayley and the girls weren't in the lounge and I couldn't help feeling almost relieved. I looked out of the two-way mirrors that showed the busy casino on the other side. Again, there was no sign of my friends.

"Any big wins?" Blake asked as he nodded toward the casino.

"Me? No. I'm not the gambling kind." *In every single sense.*

"Why not?"

I shrugged. "Maybe I don't have a very adventurous heart after all."

Blake smiled. "You mean to tell me you haven't even played the slots?"

"Not a dime." I blushed. "I don't think I would be very good."

"Gambling is all about chance. No skill involved, especially with the slots."

I raised my eyebrows. "None at all?"

He shrugged. "The card games take skill, but then you're into high-roller territory."

"Does cheating take skill?"

Blake laughed. "Why, are you thinking of learning?"

I leaned in a little and dropped my voice down low. "Do you really break cheaters' legs?"

Blake's laugh was more raucous this time. "Nothing quite so sinister. Two large men may politely ask them to leave if they catch someone cheating."

I wrinkled my nose. "That's it?"

He smiled. "They get a life ban and we alert all the other casinos on the Strip, so they can kiss goodbye to the chance of gambling in this town again — anywhere decent at least. Why, are you disappointed?"

"A little. It's not as exciting now."

"So, do you feel like giving it a try?"

"What?" I asked. "Gambling?"

Blake nodded.

I arched an eyebrow. "I really don't feel like losing a ton of money on my last night."

He rolled his eyes and offered me his hand. "Just because you gamble, doesn't mean it has to be big."

I blinked at his words. Wasn't every gamble a big one? Surely 'big' was the definition of gambling. My whole world felt like one huge gamble — every choice I made I could only pray the other player's cards weren't as good. Just looking at Blake's outstretched hand felt like a gamble in itself.

He smiled. "We'll keep it to the slots. How about that?"

With no further thought, I slid my hand into his.

Blake guided me out of the lounge and into the casino, walking purposefully toward the slot machines. As in the club, he seemed to ignore all the looks he got. A few people went wide-eyed for a moment and tried to look busy. He clutched my hand so gently my skin tingled. The only thing different from walking through the casino and walking through the club was the expression on Blake's face. It was stern, his forehead puckering and his lips a hard line. The result was that no one bothered him. A few people opened their mouths to ask him something but quickly closed them again. We stopped at the change booth and the cashier's mouth dropped into a little 'o' of surprise before she handed over twenty dollars' worth of quarters to Blake.

"Now what?" I asked, as Blake handed me a plastic cup of coins bearing the hotel's logo.

"Now choose your machine."

I turned to face the rows and rows of neon flashing slot machines. The casino wasn't as busy as it had been when I'd walked through it with the girls earlier in the day, but it was still noisy and hectic. *Probably due to the lateness of the hour.* A few people seemed to be trying to figure out the patterns of the machines and sat with notebooks in their laps. Maybe what I was looking at now was the darker side of Vegas — the side you didn't read about in guidebooks.

I picked a machine at random and settled myself onto the stool in front. As I dropped the coins in and pulled the handle, I had to admit that it was fun, even if I wasn't winning anything. My coins dwindled away until I was left with only one. I gave Blake a pointed look before dropping it into the machine and pulling the lever. Three identical symbols rolled into place and a musical tune bleated from the machine, followed by the chink of coins falling into the tray at the bottom.

"*Ohmygosh!*" I jumped up and down on my stool, taken aback by my sudden win.

Beside me, Blake grinned. I scooped out my winnings, counting them in my hands.

"What did you win?"

"Ten dollars!"

"Do you want to play your winnings?"

"Are you kidding me?" I hopped from my stool and backed away from Blake, grinning from ear to ear. "I'm quitting while I'm ahead!"

He smiled and followed me. "Technically you're down ten bucks."

I laughed. It didn't matter it was only ten bucks. It could have been ten million and it wouldn't have felt so good. "I don't care. I've never won anything before." I hadn't been prepared for the rush I got when I won. "Did I do good?"

The corner of Blake's eyes crinkled as he smiled down at me. "You did better than a lot of other people. But...I don't think I'll be adding you to the Big Fish list quite yet."

"Whatever. I bet I could take 'em." Using my thumb and index finger, I pinged a quarter at Blake.

He caught it and arched an eyebrow.

"What? Didn't think I'd give you your cut?"

Blake smiled and dropped the coin into a pocket. He dropped his eyes to the floor before raising them to look at me. "Have you seen the gardens yet?"

"No."

"Would you like to?"

I smiled. "Are they even still open?"

"Twenty-four hours."

"Sold."

Chapter Two

There wasn't a soul in sight. This wouldn't have surprised me when I first arrived, but now that I knew *this* was the city that never slept, it was a shock not to see another person in the gardens.

"This place never ceases to surprise me," I whispered as I walked along the wide marbled courtyard, my voice quietly echoing around me. I thought the gardens would have been cloaked in darkness, perhaps only the light of the moon to guide us. Instead the exhibits were lit up, all the displays and flowers coming alive in colors I'd never experienced before. Enormous flowers and butterflies loomed above us, the glass ceiling of the conservatory twinkling with reflective light, making me feel like I was under a bright blanket of the heavens.

Blake smiled. "This is my favorite place in the hotel. I never get tired of walking around here."

"You always do it this late?"

He grinned. "Not usually. But it does feel like another world at night."

I wrapped my arms around my body. The early March air was crisp, but not as fierce as the cold weather I'd left at home.

Blake shrugged out of his suit jacket and draped it over my shoulders. The warmth from his body sent a shock down my spine. A delicious waft of his scent teased my nostrils, overpowering my senses. I gave him a shy smile. "So what else have you seen on your trip?" Blake asked, jamming his hands into his pockets.

I laughed. "I'm almost embarrassed to tell you." And I was. After tonight, the past few days felt mediocre. How could I compare shopping, which I could do anywhere, to seeing giant ladybugs and caterpillars covered in flowers, Venus flytraps, and watering cans sprinkling water, all poised in motion, frozen in their peculiar perfection.

He grinned. "I'm intrigued. Why?"

"Friday my friends and I were shopping. All day. Then we went for dinner at Chin Chin before having drinks at Coyote Ugly."

"So Friday was a New York oriented day then, huh? What about Saturday?"

"Saturday we were at the spa. Again, all day. We had dinner at Michael Mina but I went back to my room straight after."

"Not up for another night of partying?"

I shrugged. "I just didn't feel like it."

"What about today?"

"Today the girls hit the casino. I stayed with them for a while but ended up going to look at the art gallery."

"Did you like it?"

I nodded. "I thought it was really interesting, especially since it is all about female artists."

Blake smiled. "Why were you embarrassed to say that's what you'd done?"

"It's hardly noteworthy, is it? I haven't done anything I couldn't have done at home."

"That isn't the point of a vacation. The point is to come and have a good time. Have you?"

"I guess. To be honest, I didn't want to come in the first place." I glanced up at him. "But I'm glad that I did."

Blake's smile widened.

"There's so much more I would do if I came back."

"Like?"

I paused to admire a snail with an elegant flowery shell beside a small pool of water. It was lit from underneath with purple lights, the water flowing into the pool off a luscious green leaf. My mind drifted to all the wonders I'd heard about since coming here. The rush of wanting hit me hard and I struggled to force it down. "I'd see everything."

"Truth is…you could live here your entire life and still find something new. Construction is always going on all over the city. What a lot of people forget is there's so much more as you head off the Strip."

"What would you do? If you were only visiting?"

Blake gave me a lopsided smile. "I'd see more than two hotels."

I nudged him with my elbow. He guided me toward a bench in front of a fish pond where dozens of koi fish were twisting in the water, the moon a pale white orb reflected in the glassy surface.

Blake twisted his body toward mine as we sat, our knees touching. "Even if I were only visiting, I'd come for a good chunk of time, at least two weeks. I'd see O, their displays… The only word to describe them is magical. I'd see every animal and fish at Mandalay

Bay. I'd eat at all the restaurants you read about, but I would definitely go to the one in the Stratosphere. I'd ride the rollercoasters till I threw up. I would take a helicopter ride—at night, just to fully appreciate the sheer scale of this place. And you can't come to this part of the world without checking out Hoover Dam or the Grand Canyon.

"The history here too, it's incredible. I mean, for a city that's only a hundred years old, it's seen a lot. I know most of the museums can be tacky, but some are pretty great. You get to learn about old Vegas, what it was like in the times of Elvis and the Rat Pack. You can go to the Tropicana and see Bugsy Siegel's death certificate. *Bugsy Siegel!* He was the original Vegas gangster, from the times when they really *would* break your legs for cheating. You can go to Luxor and see the tomb of Tutankhamun, or head out to the Primm Valley Hotel and see Bonnie and Clyde's car, even Clyde's shirt! Where else in the world could you come and see *anything* like all that?" Blake paused and took a breath. He dropped his gaze and stared at his hands as though embarrassed about his passionate speech.

In the moment of silence that hung in the air, all I could think about was how different this trip would have felt if I'd been with Blake, which was ridiculous. I didn't even know him, but it didn't stop it from being true.

In the long run, I knew that was for the best. God only knew how long it would take for me to push Blake from my mind when I was home again.

I forced a soft laugh to lighten the mood. "You sound like a guidebook."

Blake looked at me and grinned. "If I wanted to sound like a guidebook I'd tell you that if you laid out the concrete used to make Hoover Dam, it would be enough to make a two lane highway from San Francisco to New York."

My smile widened. "I appreciate the trivia."

He held my gaze for a moment, his eyes seeming to look straight inside me.

Tearing my eyes from his face, I fished my cell phone from my purse and tried dialing Hayley again.

"Hey, this is Hayley, leave a…"

I flipped the phone shut, not bothering with a message. "Damn," I muttered. "She has my room key."

"Would she have gone back to the room?"

"Maybe."

"I'll walk you up," Blake said, taking my hand and placing it in the crook of his elbow.

We remained silent during our walk back through the gardens and toward the golden elevators. With the conservatory at our backs, I darted one last glance over my shoulder, sad to leave it behind yet a knot of anticipation brewing with each step I took with Blake.

I walked close to him and snuck glances at his profile from under my lashes in the elevator. He barely even looked at me. Maybe that was a good thing. Maybe saying goodbye to someone I'd known only for a few hours would be easier without eye contact.

The noise from my heels was muffled by the carpet underfoot in the hallway toward my room. I kept my eyes focused on the intricate designs under my feet and the soft pastel colors on the walls. We stopped outside my room, and I pounded on the door with my fist. Nothing.

"Do you think she's still out? Gone to a different club maybe?"

"We said we were staying in the hotel all night. She's probably in there. The girl sleeps like the dead."

Blake glanced at the floor. "You could come to my suite. Call your room from there? Maybe the ringing would wake her."

My stomach flip-flopped.

"I don't mean anything funny," Blake assured me. "If she doesn't answer, I'll get someone to bring you up another key card."

I let out a slow breath. The thought of spending more time with him, even if it was only another half hour or so, was too tempting to resist.

"Plus my room has an amazing view."

Not trusting my voice, I nodded.

* * * *

The only sound I could hear was my thudding heart. I wasn't afraid of Blake, but he made me nervous. It was as though I was hyperaware of my body and everything about it. There was possibility in every breath I took and every step to his room I made.

Blake opened his door and stepped inside, flipping switches. Light flooded the room and a shocked laugh caught in my throat. I followed him in and looked around. Who knew what I'd expected to see. A room similar in size to mine, maybe. But I definitely hadn't expected to be stood in a gargantuan suite.

"Home, sweet home," Blake murmured, closing the door.

"You seriously live up here?"

He nodded, and I let out a low whistle.

"Nice."

The thick gold carpet was soft, almost spongy underfoot. I had a sudden urge to remove my shoes and bounce on the balls of my feet just so I could fully appreciate how good it would feel. Trailing my eyes across the lounge, I drank in the rich colors the room was doused in. I spotted a few closed doors that I could only assume led to a bedroom. *Bedrooms*? Who knew in a place like this? On the far away wall rested an enormous flat-screen TV with two large couches facing each other. A fully stocked bar was in the far corner behind one of the couches and to the side was a curved staircase — where it led, I had no idea. The room screamed wealth and I felt overwhelmed by the lavishness of it all. And this was only what I could see on first sight.

Directly in front of me and covering almost the entire north wall were floor-to-ceiling glass doors, separated by pairs of thick golden curtains. I walked across the enormous lounge to peer out. Blake followed me and opened one of the doors. An icy draft ruffled the curtains and tickled my face. Ignoring the cool air, I stepped out onto the balcony. I leaned over and marveled at the extraordinary sight.

It was as though Paris herself was directly in front of me. The smaller-sized Eiffel Tower demanded attention across the lake of the Marebello. Its waters were normally a perfect aqua blue but now shone black from the night, lit only by a few under-water lights. It made me wonder what this city wasn't capable of. All the famous landmarks, hotels and lights could be seen from that balcony. The Strip looked magical. It was easy to forget that beneath the blinding lights lay a city of darkness and greed.

"You said you had a good view, not *the* view!" I exclaimed.

Blake grinned. "I didn't want you to think I was just trying to get you to my room."

I snorted a laugh and stepped back inside. "You cannot call this just a room! The lounge in this room is bigger than my first apartment."

He smirked. "I find that hard to believe."

"I used to live in the East Village."

"Maybe not so hard to believe."

"Told you."

Blake hooked a thumb in the direction of a phone unit on an end table. "Do you want to call your room, or would you like a drink first?"

My stomach dipped, and I waited a beat before answering. "I'll take a drink."

"Make yourself comfortable."

I moved across the room and sank onto the softest couch I had ever sat on. Blake followed close behind with two Scotch glasses. There was an appropriate space between us that I itched to close. "You seem normal," I said, studying his face.

He blinked. "Thanks. I think."

"I'm sorry—I don't want to seem rude. It's just, you live in this incredible suite in one of the world's most famous hotels, yet you seem so grounded."

Blake shrugged. "I guess I am. I only do a job, just like everybody else. Sure, mine may pay a lot better and come with way more advantages, but it's all just material at the end of the day. None of it is real. *Nothing* in Vegas is real." There was a bitter edge to his words.

Maybe Blake and I weren't so different. Maybe we were both searching for that realness.

"You seem to be."

Blake grinned. "Maybe. You seem pretty real yourself."

His words shook my core. *If only he knew the truth.* "I'm only here for the weekend."

"Thank God for that. The city would corrupt you."

I arched an eyebrow. "You don't think I could take care of myself? Not allow the corruptness to steal me?"

He leaned closer and the intensity and seduction of his eyes made my heart pick up speed. "The thing about the corruptness of Vegas is it sneaks up on you. It charms you and whispers pretty things in your ear. You don't even know you've been corrupted until you are. Then it's too late."

I laughed at the seriousness in his voice, mostly to conceal how much he affected me. "Okay. So how do you fight the evil forces of the corrupt men of the city?"

His smile was boyish. "The suite comes with an awesome hot tub. An hour in there and all my stress dissolves."

My eyebrows shot up. "There's a hot tub in here?"

Blake nodded.

"Can I see it?"

He took my glass and placed it on the coffee table. Blake reached for my hand and pulled me to my feet. I brushed against him as I stood up. A heat tore through my body, unfamiliar and unexpected.

Blake guided me to the curved staircase, my heart pounding every step I took. We climbed to the loft level where there was another flat screen mounted on the wall as well as the same tall glass windows as downstairs. Of course, these things held my attention for oh...a nanosecond. Huge, marbled and bubbling, the hot tub begged to be occupied.

"Feel like a dip?" I asked. There no sign of nerves in my tone, though I was sure I was trembling.

Blake glanced at me. "Sure. I'll get our drinks." He let out a breath and turned to jog back down the stairs.

Before I could talk myself out of it, I unzipped my dress and let it fall to my feet. Stepping out of my shoes, I was thankful I'd worn my favorite La Perla black lace set. I dipped a toe in and shuddered at the warmth of the water.

Blake returned with our drinks. He sat them on the edge of the hot tub and cocked an eyebrow at me. I was already fully emerged in the water. He spied my puddle of clothes, but didn't comment. I turned away from him and leaned on the edge of the tub, staring at the bright view.

There was the soft sound of his clothes dropping to the floor. I turned in time to see him lower himself into the water and drank in the sight of him. Though he had a lean physique, his body was powerful and well honed to hard-muscled perfection. I skimmed my eyes over his shoulders, his chest and stomach. His skin had a natural olive tone that I guessed would only deepen with extended time in the sun.

He's beautiful.

Blake rested his elbows on the lip of the hot tub, his piercing gaze never leaving mine.

It was as though I had been taken over by a foreign entity. I did not recognize this Marley. This Marley had never been seen before, nor was she likely to be seen again after tonight. I'd spent my life abiding by the will of others, putting everyone else's needs before my own.

Not tonight.

This night I was going to be free and live without regret. Life was about impulse and desires. Even if it was just once, I would know I had lived.

I stood up. The water cascaded over my body, dripping down me. Blake swallowed hard. He visibly struggled to keep his focus on my face. As I inched slowly toward him, my heart thumped almost to the point of pain. It only made me feel more alive. I slid next to him, allowing our skin to brush.

Blake raised a hand to push a lock of hair from my face. He tucked it behind my ear, his finger stroking my jaw. "You're not who I thought you were," Blake murmured, his voice thick and throaty.

I moved again, this time positioning myself in front of him. Blake reached for me and pulled me onto his lap. I wrapped my legs around him, pinning my small body against his powerful chest.

Sliding my hands up his abdomen, I relished touching this man…*this man*…and twined my fingers in his hair. "You don't want to know who I am," I whispered. That desperate feeling of need for him ripped through my body.

Blake cupped my face in his hands. The hunger blazed in his eyes before I shifted closer and gently pressed my lips against his.

Electricity coursed through me, igniting every cell in my body. It wasn't just because he was the hottest guy I had ever seen. It wasn't because we were in this amazing suite. It wasn't even because this was the last night of my mini-vacation. It was him. Every inch of him made me *feel*.

I was a different person. I was confident and impulsive with no inhibitions. I trusted him, crazy as that sounded. I needed him. Needed him more than food or oxygen. More than life.

Blake's hands drifted from my face. He rested one on the side of my neck, caressing and sending delicious shivers down my spine. With his other hand he traced tiny lines up and down my back. My skin burned under his touch.

Our kiss deepened and he parted my lips. He teased the hollow contours of my mouth with his tongue. I pressed tighter against him, wishing somehow our bodies could fuse as one. Blake ran a finger over the clasp of my bra. With one hand he unhooked it. The straps slid from my shoulders. He broke our kiss, his shaky breath tickling my face. I shivered as Blake slowly pulled the straps down my arm. He tossed my bra away, his stare roaming over my bare flesh.

My breathing spiked as Blake ran his fingertips over my sensitive breasts. He lowered his head and took the flesh in his mouth. His teeth grazed the pebbled nipple, and I fisted my hold on his hair and moaned in anticipation.

Blake released my nipple and his eyes shot to my own as though the sound awoke him from a trance. He pulled my face down and caught my lips in a feverish kiss. There was a new, hungry edge to him, as though he wanted to devour me.

He kneaded my hip, the motion bringing me forward on his lap, and I gasped at the delicious friction he created. His length thickened under me, and I rocked more firmly on his erection. He slid his hand into the water and teased the edge of my panties.

I made a pleading noise in the back of my throat and shifted against him once more. Blake shoved my underwear aside and stroked one long finger against my swollen folds. I cried out, and Blake groaned, pushing that finger inside me.

He primed my body to the brink of insanity, my temperature soaring as the arousal consumed me. He circled my clit with his thumb, and I came undone.

Blake slowed his hand to a gentle caress as the effects of the orgasm faded. He lifted me, his dick poised at my cleft. "We need a condom."

My head swam. I was safe. Clean and protected, but really, as much as instinct told me I could trust this man, how did I know I really could? I grasped his forearm, my blood racing and desperate to feel him inside me. "*Now.*"

Blake swooped his head and captured me in a hard, fast kiss. He stood up, the water sloshing at the walls of the hot tub. Reaching over the side, Blake picked up his pants. He fumbled in the pocket and pulled out a condom.

As he made to rip it open, I touched his hand, stilling him. I stood up and took it from him, never letting my gaze drop from his. Blake tensed as I opened the packet with my teeth, his forearms corded with restraint as he let me take the lead.

My heart thumped as I took his dick in my hand and slid the condom on. Blake made a noise low in his throat as I squeezed him at the root. He plunged his hands into my hair, holding me in place as he slammed his mouth down on mine. Blake spun me around, urging me onto the lip of the hot tub. He nudged my knees apart, slotting his body into the space he'd created.

He skated his hands up my thighs, his touch featherlight and breaking my skin out in goosebumps. I gripped his shoulders, impatient and about to tell him so.

As though he sensed my growing frustration, Blake shifted his hips until his cock met the silken wetness of my cleft. Our eyes locked as he eased inside my body, Blake letting out a low, guttural noise that sent shock waves to my core. For a moment I was still as my body stretched to accommodate him, the blissful bite of pain present as he was just that little bit too big.

Blake held me there, our bodies connected as we adjusted to the feel of each other. He kissed me again and lifted me, his strong arms gripping my hips. I locked my legs around his waist and he lowered us into the water, taking up our earlier position on the bench.

He wrapped an arm around my lower back, his free hand curving over my ass. Lifting myself up, I slid back down his length. Blake's grip on me tightened, his fingers biting into my flesh. He helped guide my movements, taking control and making my head spin. I thought I would die from the fireworks that tore through my body. Nothing had ever felt so good, so real, so…so…

I threw my head back and Blake pressed his lips to my throat. I increased our speed, torn between wanting to draw out my release and desperate to feel it right that second. He sucked on my roaring pulse, and I squeezed him with my inner muscles.

He let out a bark of pleasure and used my hips to slam me down on his dick even harder. I kissed him, thrusting my tongue into his mouth as another orgasm ripped through my body. He held me tighter and gritted his teeth until he gave one final, powerful shove and came so ferociously he roared.

Every thought fell away from my mind. There was only him—him, his touch—his very being. I never wanted it to end. I wanted to stay in that bubble forever and never think of the real world waiting for me.

** ** ** **

It had to end — and it did. Tears pricked my eyes as I snuck from his suite in the soft dawn light. For a moment I considered waking him, but he looked too peaceful — too happy. I didn't want to leave his warm bed where he'd made love to me a further three times before giving in to sleep. The second time hadn't been as rushed as the first time in the hot tub. It had been tender and sweet. So sweet I was sure I would remember his taste on my lips should I think about it hard enough in the future.

That was dangerous, of course. I shouldn't think about him.

As I closed his door behind me with a soft click, I struggled to force him out of my head. The farther away I walked from him, the easier I thought it would be to push him out of my thoughts.

It wasn't.

I resembled a sitcom character as I tried to sneak into my hotel room after sneaking out of Blake's. Once I'd bolted down to reception to beg and plead for another key card, I tried to silently enter the room without waking my gossip-mongering roommate for fear of her never-ending stream of questions. Thankfully I thought to remove my shoes before entering the room, since the marbled floor would be a definite giveaway of my late or, rather, early, entrance.

I tiptoed across the room and flipped the bathroom light on. After I turned on the shower, the room began to fill with steam. Hot water cascaded over my weary, aching body, and I felt a little like crying. *You're only tired… That's all…*

A fluffy white towel hung on the rail beside the shower. I wrapped it around me and opened the bathroom door. Hayley leaned against the door jamb, arching a perfect eyebrow.

A shriek caught in my throat. I placed a hand over my racing heart. "Damn it, Hayley."

"So..." she said, smirking.

"What?" I asked, pushing past her to towel dry my hair.

"Have a good night last night?"

I shrugged. "It was okay, I guess."

Hayley nodded. "Last I saw you were in the VIP area with the hot guy who couldn't take his eyes off you."

My cheeks burned. "Yeah, so?"

"I'm just saying. You go to his room?"

"What? No—no of course not. I...You know...went to another party. Got pretty wild." *Liar, liar, lace panties on fire.*

Hayley threw back her head and laughed. "Fine. You want to live in Denial Land, go right ahead." She sank onto the couch and kicked her feet up on the coffee table, nudging my purse and spilling the contents.

With a firm grip on my towel, I swatted her feet. "You mind? Do I even need to say *Marc Jacobs*?"

She sighed and moved her feet onto the floor, watching me with a smile as I shoved all my paraphernalia back into my purse.

"What?" I asked at her look.

"Why do you have so many quarters?"

My cheeks burned. I kept my eyes down. "I played the slots last night."

"Uh-huh. And what was it you said to us yesterday? Something about gambling being a waste of money, 'you may as well buy a pair of shoes—at least then you'd have something pretty to look at'?"

"Depends what shoes they are. Last pair you bought were totally questionable— *Ow...*" I glared at Hayley

48

and tossed the pillow back at her. "So what if I played the slots? Can't a girl change her mind?"

"Depends what girl she is," Hayley said with a smug smile.

* * * *

The cabbie managed to fit all our bags into the trunk of his cab. The other girls were already inside, giggling and discussing various events of the night before. I paused with my hand on the cab door and twisted around to look up at the gleaming windows. He was in there, somewhere. Would he be awake yet? I couldn't help but wonder how he would react to the empty space beside him.

The balcony I'd stood on the night before couldn't be seen from here. There was a hint of longing in my heart as I tried to force my eyes to see it.

Eve called my name and broke my trance. I slid into the cab and shut the door, drawing a big black line under my trip to Sin City.

Chapter Three

Hayley shot me curious looks on the plane as I gripped the arm rest so tight my knuckles turned white. She didn't ask me any questions and she didn't say anything to the other girls, thank God.

My beloved city was cloaked in gray as the plane landed at JFK.

Was Vegas really as great as I remembered? Or was it one memory in particular that made the whole city shine in my mind? Whatever it was, it was enough to put a sour edge on my return to the city I was in love with body and soul. It made me long to see the theatrical and overstated throbbing lights rather than the giant buildings stretching up to meet the heavens in the concrete jungle I was so much more familiar with.

Grudgingly, I forced my weekend in Vegas into a little box in my mind and locked it up tight. The others were sharing a cab home but there was a sleek black Mercedes waiting for me—the driver lifting a hand to give a small wave before getting out to help with my bags. He smiled, his face relaxed like it always was when it was just me he was picking up. The girls hugged me goodbye, and I thanked them for an awesome weekend. Hayley mumbled something, but I didn't catch it.

We pulled away from the airport and I began to feel like myself. In other words, I no longer felt so alive. The excitement and uninhibited happiness that had come so easily to me in the presence of Blake were long since dead.

* * * *

The apartment was quiet as I opened the door. The stark white walls, though bright, held no warmth. The noise from my heels echoed as I walked down the long hallway, pale hardwood flooring underfoot. I wheeled my suitcase into the bedroom and abandoned it in the walk-in closet. I could deal with it later.

Somewhere in the heart of the apartment, the soft murmur of a voice grew louder, closer.

My stomach dropped as Theo came into the room. His face flickered briefly with surprise as he saw me he but didn't rush to end the phone call. He tossed his BlackBerry onto the bed when he was done.

Theo pecked me on the cheek. "I wasn't expecting you till after eight."

"It's almost nine," I said.

"Time must have gotten away from me." Theo's Blackberry vibrated on the bed and he walked back to retrieve it.

I nodded. The brush-off even quicker than normal.

"Are you hungry? Why don't you order some food?" Theo suggested, replying to his email.

"I'm tired."

Theo looked at me briefly and did a double take. "You do look different."

My heart pounded. I was sure the guilt was all over my face.

His smile was so condescending it set my teeth on edge. "Did the girls keep you out late last night?"

I looked down. "Yeah, something like that."

Theo nodded, probably not even hearing me. "The florist sent a mock-up of your bouquet. If you want any changes, let him know."

"Okay. Did your tux fitting go okay?"

"Yeah," Theo said, already walking out of the door.

"Nice talking with you," I mumbled at Theo's retreating back. I let out a shaky breath and headed into the bathroom to fill the tub. Stripping out of my clothes, I tossed them in the hamper. I stood in front of the mirror and reached up to untie my hair.

Long chocolate waves hung past my shoulders, my collarbones a little more pronounced than they had been a few months ago. Image was everything, and Theo wanted our wedding pictures to be perfect.

Large brown eyes peered back at me, the haunted, almost resigned look held at bay as the remnants of my night with Blake lingered in my system.

There were no outward clues as to how I'd spent my last night in Las Vegas. But to me, they were everywhere. Blake's mouth was on my throat, my shoulders, my breasts. His hands touched every inch of my skin and his eyes devoured me.

On the outside, I was the same old Marley.

Inside…there was a part that no one could ever take away.

After a hot bath, I dressed in comfortable pajamas and lay between the cool sheets on the enormous bed. As I closed my eyes for sleep to find me, I remembered how it had felt lying in bed with Blake. *He pressed his chest against my back and held me tight. Our arms and legs tangled and we slotted together like we were built that way, like I was the only one who would fit that perfectly in his arms.*

Theo had never held me like that.

How was it possible to miss someone who, aside from being able to draw a detailed map of my anatomy, was little more than a stranger?

* * * *

The next morning, I resolved to throw myself into work and wedding plans. With the wedding only four and a half months away, details were being finalized. The clock was ticking louder each passing day.

Theo wanted me to quit my job once we were married. He'd said there was no need for me to work — why not take it easy? Do the things that make me happy and remove an unnecessary stress from my life.

But I loved my job. I worked for an event planning firm on West 28th Street that owned a few nightclubs in Midtown, did its own PR work and promoted various events for clients. I was the assistant to the boss — not the most glamorous job in the company, but I still adored it.

It was a lot of fun hanging out at the parties and helping at the club and I couldn't get enough. It was long hours, but that was half the appeal. At least if I was working I wasn't sitting around waiting for Theo to come home. It was because of my job that I'd met Theo. He worked for a prestigious law firm and his company had hired mine to throw them a bash for one of the partners' birthdays. I'd caught his eye and the rest, as they said, was history.

Theo worked ungodly hours. He was always pulling all-nighters at the office and jetting off around the country to other branches of his firm. Theo left me alone a lot and I struggled not to feel neglected.

I had already talked to my boss, Henry, about my impending nuptials and he had said he would be sad to see me go. Of course he would! Not only was I a good employee, but when Theo and I had announced our engagement, all his friends' wives and girlfriends had taken me under their wings and included me in their affairs. The plus side? Henry's client list had rapidly expanded.

As much as he understood, I knew Henry didn't want me to quit. Not because of the clients I brought in, but because our office was like a little family. We were all happy together and it was a great dynamic of people.

The thing about Theo was he liked control. Theo controlled everyone in his life and I was no exception. The second the Tiffany diamond had been lodged on my finger, he'd terminated the lease on my apartment and moved me into his penthouse on Park Avenue. He'd given me a black credit card and made sure he knew everywhere I went and everyone I talked to.

Which was why it had been such a surprise that he'd been open to the Vegas trip. I'd turned down countless invites from the girls for long weekends or vacations because of the distasteful look Theo gave me when I brought them up. Of course, in this instance, he didn't have time to worry about little old me—his firm was handling a huge case right now—his most recent catchphrase.

'Sorry I'm late for dinner, we're handling a huge case right now.'

'I've got to go to the Chicago office for a few days for this huge case.'

'Damn, did we have plans tonight? It's this huge case. It's messing with my head.'

And my personal favorite—*'Marley, won't be home tonight. I'm in the middle of a huge case. Forgive me? Theo xxx'*—a note on a colossal bouquet of flowers delivered to my office. The stinger was I knew he hadn't contributed to the note. It had his secretary all over it. Theo would never, ever ask forgiveness.

Underneath everything he was a good, kind man. And he loved me as best he could.

No woman in her right mind would think she was settling for Theo Lorimer.

* * * *

Oh my God. I'm going to die. I'm going to drop down dead in this ridiculously expensive boutique and forever be known as the girl who died during a fitting for her wedding gown.

"That's it! Come on, you can breathe in more than that!"

Hateful bitch. Either I'm going to die or she is. One of us is leaving this store in a body bag. I squeezed my eyes shut and figured that if I didn't breathe, it wouldn't hurt so much. The wall in front of me was cool under my hands as I braced myself against the forceful tightening. Surely she couldn't tighten it anymore. She was a millimeter away from breaking bones. It would be just my luck for a rib to puncture my lung or something.

What I really wanted to do was let out a long, deep breath and go to my happy place but I didn't dare.

Instead I wondered why the boutique bothered with the calming neutral colors and soft lighting, no doubt intending to put the client at ease, when all the staff really did was test the durability of said clients' bodies.

The severe woman—who I was sure was a dominatrix in her spare time—tugged again on the lace of my corset, making my already small waist even more miniscule.

I should have known she would be Satan in a dress. Her thin lips had curved more into a sneer than a smile when my bridesmaids and I had entered the boutique for our fittings. She wore her black-as-night hair scraped into a high ponytail, pulling her skin tight over the bones in her face. The woman looked evil, and I was pretty sure she was trying to make sure I stopped breathing.

How had women dealt with this torture every day when this godforsaken corset had been all the rage? No wonder some of them had actually died, all their insides being mushed together like that. With one final tug, she tied the ends and we were done. I stepped into my white dress and pondered my reflection in the mirror.

I looked terrified.

My face had taken on an unhealthy pallor and my eyes seemed too big for my face. Looking down, I thought—not for the first time—that this wasn't my wedding dress. I was never the kind of little girl who tied a pillowcase to her head and fantasized in magnificent detail about her wedding day. Whenever I thought about it, I always just assumed I would be in a vintage frock, not even floor-length, and maybe even barefoot.

I would not be wearing a high-fashion seventeen thousand dollar couture gown.

It did no good to ponder what could have been. Here and now was my reality. All I had to do was calm my nerves, talk myself off the edge and we would be good to go. Oh, and figuring out how to breathe might also be useful.

Hayley and I stepped out into the biting cold, though it was fresh and rejuvenating after feeling so claustrophobic.

"She was the most terrifying woman I have ever met!" Hayley laughed as we escaped the portal to Hell on Madison Avenue.

I laughed with her and winced at the sharp pain. "I think she cracked one of my ribs."

"Come on. I'll buy you a coffee and an ice pack," Hayley said with a grin as she led the way.

We sauntered through Central Park, sipping our low-fat mochas, warming our hands on the insulated mugs. Spring still felt like months away and winter hadn't gotten the memo to start retreating.

"So....are you ever going to talk about Vegas?" Hayley asked, her tone suggesting casual, her eyes shrewd.

I was instantly on my guard and fussed with the collar of my new Burberry cashmere trench jacket. Theo's latest gift. "What is there to talk about? You were there. It's not like I need to tell you about the sights."

Hayley nudged me with her elbow. "Marley, we've been back for nearly two weeks! You know I know you did something — or someone."

I choked on a mouthful of coffee. When my coughing was under control, she wore an amused look. "Drop it, Hayley."

She rolled her eyes and turned to stand in front of me, stopping me in my tracks. "I'm your best friend. My loyalty is to you, no one else. You can trust me with anything."

I looked down, a sudden lump forming in my throat. I hated lying to her, but I was also lying to myself that the weekend was pretty much forgotten. Talking about it with Hayley would give new life to the memories and I couldn't afford to linger on what I couldn't have again. "I know. There just isn't anything to talk about."

"You stayed out all night. The last any of us saw of you, you were all snuggled up in the VIP area with that guy. That *hot* guy, might I add."

I laughed. "I was not snuggling with him! He rescued me from that creep. That's all."

"Mmmhmm." Hayley turned her head away, shifting her attention to the ice rink nearby.

Wollman's Rink was a favorite of mine, an indulgence I looked forward to every winter. "Beautiful, huh?" I asked, jumping on the chance to change the subject.

"Yup. Every winter I say I'm going to come down here and finally make use of the rink, but I never do."

"There's still a week before it closes for the season. You still have time."

"Maybe next year." She linked her arm through mine and started walking again. "I really love this jacket. Where'd you get it?"

"Bergdorf's."

"Ooh…I have a sudden craving for some Louboutins. You in?"

"Always." The warmth of Bergdorf's and the beauty of Christian Louboutins were sure to chase away the unpleasant memories of the hateful dress-fitter and this chilling day.

She chatted like always, cheerful and perky as we salivated over the shoes, giving every sign that our conversation was forgotten. But I knew I wouldn't be able to hide the truth from Hayley forever. She was ruthless. When she smelled gossip, she didn't rest until she knew every last juicy detail. I was a rotten liar and stood no chance against her. Thankfully for me, Theo paid little attention and I doubted he would even be able to tell if I were to lie to him.

Maybe I should tell him. He would cancel the wedding. Kick me out. Make sure my name was trash in Manhattan. Was that a bad thing?

I didn't care about the repercussions of my actions, but I did care about his feelings. As cold as he could be, there was a good heart somewhere in Theo. Though I had only seen it a handful of times, I knew it was there. I couldn't embarrass Theo. It would cause more harm if I told him.

I would continue on as I had been doing long before Vegas. My path was unchanged by the indiscretion. My priorities were set and nothing would distract me.

* * * *

I was reminded of my soon-to-be wifely duties when a few weeks after my dress fitting, Theo came home from work and told me about a benefit we were attending that night. His firm had three tables at the event so they were out to show their charitable side. Theo had already confirmed our attendance, and it was blind luck that I wasn't working, so at least I didn't have to stress over trying to get out of it. Theo handed me a Versace garment bag and told me to be ready by eight.

My acting skills had been finely honed during my relationship with Theo. Most of his colleagues were arrogant and thought no one was as smart as them. But the wives... Those women cared about shopping, jewelry and real estate—and not much in between. Theo encouraged me to spend time with the wives and girlfriends of his world. Like he thought they would be good role models and would mold me into the perfect Stepford wife.

* * * *

The benefit was for child leukemia and was being in held in the ballroom at the Waldorf Astoria. Decked out in all its finest, the ballroom fell nothing short of spectacular. Tables that seated ten people at each were covered with pale pink tablecloths and stunning pinky-purple orchids for the centerpieces. The ceiling danced with different colors as the lights ebbed and flowed, changing so subtly it took a moment for me to realize. Four colossal screens were mounted in each corner, every one showing a picture of a sick child before morphing into a new picture of another.

I loathed coming to these events. Not because I was a closet Scrooge or whatever, but because the whole thing brought back horrible memories and unnecessary pain.

As Theo led me inside the ballroom, I couldn't help but notice how the people were interested in each other and what they were wearing, yet not one person glanced at the screens or showed any sadness for the reason that they were there in the first place.

After sitting through a ridiculous five course meal of edible wealth and being ignored for about ninety-five percent of it, it was time for the speeches. Up on stage, framed by a silky red curtain, doctors, recovered patients and representatives from the charity gave speeches and begged everyone to be as generous as they could.

A long table ran the length of one wall holding pictures in gilt frames of things to bid on. It was a silent auction to raise money for the kids, but I couldn't help wondering if the people would be more generous if they were bidding out loud. What good was being charitable and generous if no one heard it?

I saw Theo bid on a romantic getaway for two to Rome. I also noticed he didn't bid high enough to worry about actually winning.

"Marley! Sweetheart, you look fabulous. Has Theo been treating you again?"

I choked on a fog of perfume as Helen Yates double kissed me and admired my dress. Stupidly I had thought now that dinner was over and people were milling around looking at the items to bid on, I could blend in and disappear.

"Yes," I said, making an effort not to cough. *Who the hell needs to wear that much perfume?* It couldn't be good for our atmosphere.

"It suits you." Helen linked her arm with mine and led me toward the bar. "Now, you have been away in hiding far too long. Where have you been?"

"Around," I said, cringing. My acting skills were on the fritz. "I've been busy working."

Helen tsked. "Never mind. It won't be long then you won't have to bother with such a chore."

I felt my hackles rise. "I like working."

"You'll enjoy *not* working even more!"

I smiled thinly. There was no arguing with this woman.

She frowned as much as Botox would allow. "I'm not the only one who missed you, you know. All the others did too. Brunch isn't the same without you!"

"Oh, I've missed it too. It's too bad I'm always working and can't make it." Would she catch the false note in my tone?

"If you explained to your boss, I'm sure he would understand and let you join us," Helen said, as though the real world were so simple.

Right. I could see how well that one would go down. *'Henry, can I have a few hours off every Tuesday?'*
'Why, Marley?'
'Why? Oh, so I can go to brunch with a bunch of sycophantic and narcissistic women.'
'Hahahahahahahahahahahahaha. Ahem. No.'
'Okay. No harm in asking, right?'

"Maybe." I smiled.

Helen handed me a champagne flute. "So. Theo tells me you're back from a weekend in Vegas." She said 'Vegas' like it left a taste in her mouth.

I nodded, keeping my eyes on the floor.

"I suppose it is good for shopping, but so is L.A. Next time you feel like a break, give me a call and we'll arrange something." Helen grinned.

Oh my God. A whole weekend with this woman? I'd rather shoot myself then go swimming in the ocean.

Helen's eyes widened. "I just remembered! Have you met Kimberly Rose yet?"

Probably, but I had no idea. "I think so."

"Well she told Caroline, who told April, who told me...that she is putting together a spa weekend! We *must* include you!"

Really? Must you? "Oh, that would be...super."

Helen beamed. Damn, did she have to look so pleased with herself?

"Get back to me with dates. Work is hectic at the moment." I had a funny feeling I was working an event that weekend — whatever weekend it happened to be.

"Of course."

"I'd better go find Theo," I said. It was really saying something that out of everyone in this room, it was Theo I was trying to escape to.

Helen winked at me. "All right. I'll find you later!"

I sincerely hoped not. It took forever to find Theo, and he was flushed looking when I did. He strode across the room like he was intent on being somewhere.

"Theo," I called to him when I was within earshot.

Theo whipped around and actually had the nerve to look surprised to see me. Then again, it wouldn't be the first time he had forgotten he'd brought me to a party. "Are you enjoying yourself?" Theo asked, slipping an arm around my waist.

My best fake smile was already in place. "Of course."

"Good. Would you mind getting me a drink?"

I nodded, positive that if I bit down any harder on my tongue it would come clean off. After Theo had been attended to, I snuck away from the crowd and found a secluded spot where I could stand and people-watch in peace. From where I stood half encased in the shadows, I could see all the sins and secrets of the party. There was the wife of a senior partner hanging off every word from the bartender. The alcoholic secretary binging on yet another Scotch. The blonde shark circling the party, sizing up her prey.

Glancing down at my watch, my stomach fell when I saw that it was only eleven-thirty. I sighed. No way could I stand to be in this room for a minute longer. I pushed my way through the throng of people until I found Theo. "I'm going to take off," I whispered in his ear. "I'm not feeling well."

"You'll miss finding out who the winning bidders are."

"I don't mind," I said, knowing neither Theo nor I would be wining anything.

"Okay. Take a cab. I don't know when I'll need the driver."

"Fine." The instant I was outside in the crisp night air I felt the chains vanish from my shoulders and I was able to take a deep, clean breath. Now that I had my freedom and was no longer suffocating, I figured it was a shame to waste a nice night like this. I walked around the block, trying to make my mind settle on something to do. Late night coffee? Not a chance, I had enough trouble sleeping. Food? No. Then the penny dropped. Movie.

With my destination front and foremost in my mind, I charged forward. A gory action movie was about to start. *Perfect!*

I sat alone in the darkened movie theater and lost myself in the magic. Therapists should totally recommend going to movies alone. It seemed to work for me. So much of the stress that had accumulated on my shoulders for months—the last few weeks in particular—began to dissolve and puddle around my feet.

By the time the movie finished and I was in a cab going home, I had managed to convince myself that things would work out just fine.

Chapter Four

Theo appeared behind my reflection in the mirror as I glided clear gloss over my lips. He straightened his collar and fixed his already perfect tie. "Are you free for lunch today?"

"Today? Sure," I said, unable to keep my forehead from creasing at Theo's request. *Stranger things have happened, I guess.* It really wasn't like him to ask.

"Great. My best man is flying in today."

The elusive best man from Theo's prep school days that I had yet to meet.

"But the wedding isn't for another four months."

Theo frowned. "Yes, I know. He's in town for business. So. The Garden at the Four Seasons, one-thirty."

"All right," I said, turning around to face him. "So how come I haven't met this friend of yours?"

He brushed invisible lint off the skirt of my pencil dress. "He's hardly ever in the city anymore. I've told you about him, haven't I?"

"I can't remember. Is it the one you got hammered with at your senior prom?"

Theo smirked. "One of the same. Hammy, remember?"

"Right." Couldn't wait. All I could picture was an overweight ex-football player who loved to relive the glory days—or worse, someone just as arrogant and conceited as Theo.

He kissed the top of my head and left for work.

* * * *

I was running late for lunch. Henry had wanted to go over a few details about an act playing at one of the clubs that night and I'd swear I'd been invisible to every passing cab when I'd finally escaped. After hauling my ass for twenty minutes, I was out of breath and red-faced as I stumbled into the Four Seasons.

Theo didn't often ask me to meet him during a workday, so I figured it must be a big deal for me to meet his friend, and therefore a bad idea to piss him off. I massaged my side, willing the cramp to go away. A nasty side effect of rushing. Maybe I should work out more. Yoga didn't seem to be cutting it.

"Can I help you, miss?" the hostess asked, raising her impossibly fierce eyebrows.

I tried to rub the prickling of sweat away at my hairline. "I'm meeting Theo Lorimer in The Garden."

She smiled. "Of course. Right this way." The hostess led me to Theo's usual table by the window and thankfully my breathing seemed to have returned to normal.

Both men were seated when I arrived. Theo rose to greet me, his friend still sitting with his back to me.

"There you are," he said, his smile too sharp to be considered friendly.

"Sorry," I mumbled.

Theo planted a cold kiss on my cheek. And trust me — it wasn't cold because of the weather.

The friend stood up. Theo moved out of the way, allowing me to see him.

Oh, God... I think I'm going to hurl. The green eyes that had danced with excitement and held my gaze so easily just weeks before stared at me, cold and angry. I felt the blush creep up and stain my cheeks, branding me the liar I was.

"Hammy, this is my fiancée, Marley. Marley, my oldest friend, Hammy," Theo introduced, his voice faded in the background. I barely heard him.

"Nice to meet you." Blake's voice was empty as he shook my hand, dropping it quickly as though I'd stung him.

"You too," I said, my voice strained and high-pitched.

"You all right there, Marley?" Theo asked as I sat down beside him.

"Yes. Why?" I asked. Had he noticed my panicked state?

"You look a little pale," Theo said, scanning the menu.

"I'm fine." I was anything but. My hands were shaking, my heart was racing and it was a good thing I'd sat down when I had because I couldn't rule out a good fainting spell. Coward that I was, I hid behind the safety of my menu while trying to silently get control of my breathing. I closed my eyes and counted to ten. Then twenty. I just didn't stop after thirty.

I jumped about a foot in the air as a hand curled around the top of my menu and pulled it down. "What?" I asked, startled.

"What are you having?" Theo asked, and it took a moment to realize three pairs of eyes were staring at me.

I glanced at the waitress who wore a patient smile. "Oh, um," I mumbled, looking back at the menu. "Caesar salad, thanks."

She snatched the menu from my clutches. I shot daggers at her back for stealing my shield.

"What was the work emergency that kept us waiting?" Theo asked. To anyone else his tone was joking, but the hard set of his eyes told me he wasn't pleased at my tardiness.

"No emergency. It just wasn't possible for me to drop everything and come running," I said, swallowing the biting remark that pooled on my tongue. Provoking an already angry beast was unwise at the best of times, least of all when the object of my infidelity was right in front of us. "Henry wanted to go over a few details for tonight."

"You're going out tonight?"

I gritted my teeth. "No, I'm working tonight."

Theo laughed and winked at Blake. "Hanging out at a club, keeping the customers happy. That sound like work to you, Hammy?"

Blake smirked but remained silent.

"Speaking of, how is work treating you?" Theo asked him, taking a sip of club soda.

"Oh you know, the usual. Hanging out at clubs. Keeping the customers happy. Can't complain." Blake raised his piercing eyes to mine, and my insides jolted.

Oh, come on! My fingers twitched over the fork and it was an effort not to stab him with it. Ass.

Theo snorted a laugh. "I think your job is slightly more stressful than Marley's."

Blake shrugged, dropping his eyes.

"Seriously, though, how is the hotel?"

"Good," Blake said. "Keeps me on my toes."

"I still can't believe some schmuck trusts *you* with their hotel."

Blake grinned. "What are you trying to say? They trust me fine. I'm a rare breed in Vegas. It's not often you stumble across an Honest John like me."

I felt his eyes on my face again. My cheeks burned darker. This time there was nowhere for me to hide.

"Ever been to Vegas, Marley?"

The air around me became thick and toxic. I nearly choked on the mouthful of water I was drinking.

Theo saved me from answering. "She was there a few weeks ago! I should have set up a meeting between the two of you. She could have stayed at your hotel. Where was it you stayed again, Marley?"

"The Marebello," I murmured, knowing full well where this horrific, bloody train wreck of a conversation was headed.

Theo's eyebrows shot up. "Oh! She was with you after all, Ham."

This time it was Blake's turn to choke. Serves him right. Ass.

"Hope you gave her a good room."

My stomach twisted as Blake flickered his eyes over to me. "The best," Blake said in a gravelly tone I'd last heard when he'd been inside me.

"I'll bet you could have shown her all the spots you like." Theo chuckled. "Although, our Marley isn't one for excitement, so I doubt she would have been a good companion."

Blake kept quiet.

I released the death grip on my fork.

Normally I would have gotten a kick out of watching the salad being prepared table side, but my concentration wasn't quite up to par. At least it stilted the conversation, which was a thankful break.

Either God had rendered me temporarily deaf, or I somehow focused hard enough on not hearing as Blake and Theo finished catching up. I chewed my salad slowly, not really tasting it. Theo was halfway through his tuna *Niçoise* when the shrill ringing of his cell interrupted his long-winded speech on some case or other. I wasn't listening.

"Hello?" Theo answered. He sighed. "I'm on my way." He tossed his napkin on the table and rose from his seat.

My heart jumped into my throat.

"The office needs me. I'll see you tonight." He kissed the top of my head.

"Wait! I'll come with you!" I shrieked.

He frowned. "Don't be ridiculous. Finish your meal." Theo turned to Blake. "We'll arrange another time, Ham?"

"Sure thing," Blake said, giving Theo a tight smile before he left the table.

My eyes dropped to my salad, my appetite a fleeting memory. I snuck a look at Blake's plate. He had pushed around his salmon for most of the meal. Seemed he wasn't too hungry either.

"A heads-up would have been nice before I agreed to this ridiculous meeting," Blake muttered.

I gasped. "I had no idea who you were! Or what I was walking into."

Blake lifted his head to look at me. Pain flooded his striking green eyes.

A moment passed and I hissed between my teeth, "Ever been to Vegas, Marley. *Seriously*?"

His lips twitched. "I couldn't help it."

I sighed and picked up my purse. "I have to go."

"No, Marley, wait," Blake rushed, struggling out of his chair. It was too late. I was gone before he could catch me.

* * * *

Henry had let me go home early that afternoon. It seemed I was a little distracted. I welcomed the chance to think uninterrupted. I paced back and forth in the apartment for what felt like eternity. I didn't know what I was going to do. Was Blake going to tell Theo? It wasn't getting caught that frightened me. I didn't want to hurt Theo. The embarrassment of the situation would haunt him forever if it got out.

I couldn't do that to him.

Theo had been so good to me. Yes, he might be a control freak, but he was a kind control freak. No one deserved to be hurt the way Theo would be if he found out. After dining alone, I changed for work. I pulled my long hair into a high ponytail and wore a tight black fitted suit. No shirt.

* * * *

Working in the club helped lift my spirits. The band was awesome—a chick rock band that ensured everyone jumped around like crazy people in time to their lyrics. Afterward I even managed a full two hours of sleep before getting up to start the day all over again.

My friends, Hayley especially, didn't understand my need to work constantly. I worked all day at the office and three nights a week at one of the clubs. I didn't need to sleep a lot and found I functioned better with a hectic lifestyle. Hell, I'd probably end up an alcoholic after the wedding when I had nothing to fill my days with — or become an insane hobby-whore.

Concentrating was easier at work the following day and I actually managed to do my job. The better part of the morning was spent calling catering companies and relaying messages. During my break I perched on the edge of Kelly the receptionist's desk, the only one in the whole office that wasn't translucent.

Henry had a thing about see-through stuff. He said he didn't have any secrets and his staff shouldn't have any from each other. Therefore every door was completely glass including the handle, and every desk was a kind of über-thick clear plastic with chairs to match.

Kelly, originally, did have the same desk as the rest of us, but the girl had a penchant for micro-mini skirts and Henry thought she might scare away the more reserved clients. He'd given up a long time ago trying to encourage her to dress more conservatively, and he couldn't seem to bring himself to flat-out tell her to add an inch or two to her hemlines. So she had a white desk that prevented any accidental flashings.

"So what's the dirt?" Kelly asked.

"No dirt," I said, swinging my legs as I devoured a protein bar.

"I haven't seen you since your Vegas trip. You have to have a few stories!"

I looked down. "Nope."

Kelly laughed. "Everyone has a Vegas story."

"Not me," I mumbled. None I could talk about, anyway.

Kelly whistled under her breath. "Check it out."

I followed her dazzled stare. *Shit! Shit! Shit!* Blake was talking on his cell phone in the outer lobby, thankfully not looking in this direction. He was dressed in another tailored suit like he'd worn the night I'd met him. For a moment, all I could do was stare — and stare some more. Then I remembered myself and did the first thing I could think of.

Hide.

From my concealed spot under Kelly's desk I heard the door open with a squeak and I silently thanked her obsession with minuscule skirts.

"Hi there," Blake's smooth and alluring voice washed over me.

I couldn't help it. I closed my eyes and remembered exactly how it had felt when he'd whispered in my ear.

"Hi," Kelly said, a little breathlessly. "Can I help you?"

"I hope so," Blake said.

God, I could imagine the gorgeous smile that would be on his beautiful face.

Kelly giggled, and I rolled my eyes.

"I'm looking for someone. I'm not sure of their surname," Blake continued.

"Oh, that's not a problem. We're a very intimate group here. I'm sure I'll know who you're talking about."

Do you have to be so helpful, Kelly?

"Great. Her name is Marley."

"*Marley?*" Kelly repeated.

"Yes. Is she free?"

"Um…"

I peeked up at Kelly and saw the confusion on her face. She glanced around her for a moment.

"She was right here." Kelly chose that moment to look down and clock me. "Oh! Yeah she's —"

I flashed her a warning look and pinched her leg.

"Ouch!" Kelly jumped and rubbed her leg.

"Are you all right?" Blake asked.

"I'm fine. I guess something stung me." Kelly shot me a venomous look.

"So...is she free?"

"Um, I think she's out on an errand."

"Do you have a number for her?"

"Yeah sure, let me —"

I pinched her again.

"Shit!" Kelly exclaimed. She sighed. "Actually, I'm not supposed to give out employee details without their consent."

Blake chuckled. "I understand. Do you mind if I wait for her?"

"No problem."

This time my pinch was a little harder than I intended.

"Damn it!" Kelly jumped out of her seat. "I'm not paid enough to put up with this!"

"Are you sure you're all right?" Blake asked.

Kelly took a deep breath. "I'm fine. Thank you for asking. We're experiencing a pest problem in the office today."

"I'll get out of your hair then. Could you let Marley know that Blake stopped by?"

"Sure." She shot me an amused look. "Will she know which 'Blake' you are?"

He chuckled again. "Yeah. Just say her friend from Vegas stopped by. I'll see her soon."

"Will do."

The door squeaked again, and I felt safe to crawl out from my genius hiding place.

"No Vegas story my ass," Kelly said, as I righted myself and brushed the dust from my skirt.

"Dude, your desk is disgusting under there."

"I'm the receptionist, not the cleaning lady."

"Whatever. The dust bunnies are starting to colonize."

The door squeaked once more and I spun around.

"I forgot to leave my...card..." Blake's voice trailed off. He arched an eyebrow at me, no doubt wondering how my hair had turned gray with fluffy stuff to match. "Let me guess. You're the pest?"

Kelly snorted a laugh. "You have no idea."

Blake leaned on the desk, his palm cupping his chin, looking decidedly amused. "Did you hide from me?"

"No."

He gave me a look.

"Maybe."

"So, if you're finished playing hide and seek, do you have time to take a walk?"

"I'm actually in the middle of something...important."

"I can take care of that for you." Kelly smiled sweetly as I clenched my teeth.

"That settles it then." Blake grinned.

"Five minutes," I agreed.

My head swam with too many thoughts for me to muddle through as I walked outside with Blake. I had no idea what he wanted. Okay, so I did have a slight inclination as to what things we might discuss—our nakedness in Vegas could be one—but I chose to ignore any ideas that popped into my hyperactive mind.

Blake walked close beside me. It was as though he expected me to make a bolt for freedom or throw myself in front of the first homicidal bike messenger I saw, so he positioned himself close enough to catch me.

I picked at the lining of my coat pockets as we walked and stared at the sidewalk passing under foot. How odd this feeling was... We shared the sidewalk with hundreds of other people, the traffic was its usual loud and honking self, yet the whole world seemed to shrink to just the two of us.

"Are you okay?" Blake asked.

"What? Yes, I'm fine," I said quickly. Too quickly. Avoiding his eyes again, I tightened my Burberry jacket around me and burrowed my face lower into the high, soft collar. The March air stung my nose and cheeks, yet I still felt as though I was burning from the inside out. Blake's watchful gaze ensured my heart rate stayed spiked. I looked up as Blake gave me a crooked smile.

"Why are you so nervous?"

"I'm not." I let out a breath I'd been holding.

Blake chuckled.

My shoulders slumped as I gave up all pretenses of normality. "What do you want, Blake?"

"I just wanted to see how you are."

"Oh, I'm swell." I laughed.

"I figured," Blake muttered. "Look, I just wanted you to know. I'm not judging. People do stupid things. They panic. Everyone gets nervous before they get married. And hey, you were in Vegas! Vegas is the capital of being stupid. It's practically law."

I glanced at him and found his eyes sincere.

Blake sighed and jammed his hands in his pockets. "I'm not going to say anything to Theo. You made a mistake. People make mistakes. No need for anyone to get hurt over it."

I knew I should be jumping with glee that he wasn't going to say anything, but all I could think about was how he'd referred to our night together, twice, as a mistake. Did he think it was a mistake? Or was he trying to make me feel better? *Why am I even thinking about it?*

"You're really not going to say anything?"

Blake shook his head.

I took a breath, positive I would regret what was about to come out of my mouth. "Why?"

Blake stopped walking and turned to face me. "Theo is my best friend. I've known him for years. Do you really think he would want to hear I slept with his fiancée?"

I looked at my feet. "No one wants to hear that."

"Exactly. What would it achieve if I told him? Like I said, you made a mistake." Blake's eyes searched my face. "I'm pretty sure Vegas brought out the crazy in you. Even when we were together, I kept getting the feeling that you weren't that girl. You just didn't seem the type to have random hook-ups. So, I trust that you've never done that to Theo before. And judging from this experience, I very much doubt you will ever do it again."

I felt ashamed to the pit of my stomach. Blake was actually a decent guy. I'd created an intricate web of mess and had no one but myself to blame. Why was I such a fuck-up?

"I'm going to be in town for a while. I thought it best to clear the air. No doubt we'll be seeing each other again and I'd hate for it to be awkward." Blake chuckled.

I nodded briefly, trying to swallow the lump forming in my throat. "Yeah, couldn't have that."

"I'd like to try to be friends with you, Marley. Aside from our indiscretion, you seem like a cool girl. I don't see why our mistake should prevent us from being friends."

I nodded.

Blake laughed again, quieter this time. "I'll let you get back to work. I'm glad we talked."

"Right," I said, trying to smile. "Bye, then."

"Take it easy, Marley," Blake said to my retreating back as I did my favorite thing in the world in this city—lost myself in the crowd.

Strangely, talking with Blake had made me feel better. I still felt guilty, but less so. God, I was such a horrible person.

At work I managed to concentrate on the task at hand and push all other thoughts away. There was no point dwelling over points of the past. As Blake had said, what good would it do anyone? Especially Theo. I felt disgusting hiding it from him, but it didn't mean anything. It didn't change how I felt about Theo. I forced myself to look upon the indiscretion with fondness. Even as a teenager I had always been a control freak and had never really let loose. Blake and Vegas was just me making up for a spotless adolescence. I just had to stop picturing him naked, and everything would be fine.

There was a message on the machine when I got home. Theo was working late. Again. I wasn't surprised to hear that he hadn't even left the message. His secretary had.

Chapter Five

I pushed open my front door and an unusual sound greeted me. Laughter. Male laughter. "Hello?" I called out. *Great idea, Marley. Just let the crazy robbers know you're home. Fantastic.* I was probably going to be shot, possibly, stabbed or even impaled any second now.

"Marley? We're in here," Theo called from the lounge.

My brow creased. Theo was home? But it was still light out. It had made more sense that the apartment was being robbed. As I turned into the room, I swallowed a gasp and tried not to show my full-bodied reaction. Theo was sprawled on one long gray suede couch with a beer in his hand, and Blake was his double on the couch opposite. Some sporting game blared from the flat-screen mounted on the wall.

"You're, uh, home early."

Theo chortled. "Yeah. Figured I would make it home in time for dinner."

"How thoughtful," I murmured. It was always odd to hear Theo refer to the apartment as 'home'. He wasn't the kind of guy who was into clutter and his distinct lack of stuff was ridiculous. The actual apartment was classic New York wealth, with penthouse views of the park. Theo was into the modern minimalist approach and every wall was white with each countertop or molding black or steel. No carpets or rugs, just hardwood underfoot.

And not only was it too barren to be considered homey, he was also never in it.

"Go get dressed. We're going out for food soon," Theo said, not taking his eyes from the screen.

"I'm working tonight." I cringed, knowing full well how he would react. My eyes flickered to Blake, whose gaze passed between me and Theo.

"Get out of it," Theo said.

I clenched my teeth and took a deep breath. Heaven forbid my work come before his plans. "I can't, Theo."

His whole body tensed. "Fine."

Great. Just. Fucking. Great.

The hot shower worked wonders for relieving most of my stress. I tried not to think that Blake was in the apartment—in the apartment and I was naked. *Don't think, don't think, don't think.*

Theo seemed to be over his irritation by the time I left for work. He kissed my cheek and said I looked beautiful. I wore my favorite backless black halter with black pants and my beloved stiletto Mary-Jane shoes.

I could have told Theo I was only working half the night at the club. I was only needed till ten-thirty, but he didn't need to know that. A good fiancée would have told him. But Theo expected everyone to run to him at the click of his fingers. He had to learn that I couldn't be like that. No—*wouldn't* be like that. My theories and good intentions were always strong in my head, but never quite materialized in reality.

As I worked the door and ticked off names on my list, I gave Theo my *'I'm your fiancée, not your secretary'* speech in my head, in which I let him have it and swore I would not be the kind of woman who waits around for her man to come home. I had my life and he had his. Okay, so I might not have had that much of a life, but it was something. I had friends that I saw sometimes. I had a job that I loved. *Wow, I need a longer list…*

* * * *

"Marley, isn't that Theo?" My co-worker Angela nudged me with her elbow and pointed with her pen at two figures approaching.

My stomach dropped. "Yeah."

Theo grinned. He'd been drinking. He only grinned when he'd been drinking.

"What are you doing here?" I mumbled as he kissed my cheek.

"Thought I'd surprise you," Theo said. "Blake wanted to go out. Figured we should come here."

Angela sighed as she stared at the handsome men who couldn't look any more different if they tried. "That's so sweet."

Theo grinned wider at her and slung a heavy arm around my shoulders. "So what do you say, feel like covering for Marley for the rest of the night?"

"Theo —" I started.

He held up a hand to silence me and, like an idiot, I let him.

"Actually, Marley finishes in five." Angela turned to smile at me. "Just go now. I've got this."

"Wonderful." Theo's smile tightened.

Great.

He caught my elbow and led me inside the club, dropping it the moment we were out of sight from my co-workers. The music thumped through my body — or was it adrenaline from the certainty of the fight we were about to have?

"Why didn't you tell me you were only working a half-night?" he shouted above the deafening music, leaning over me.

I looked down and cursed my submissive nature. "I forgot. Didn't realize till I got here."

There was a pause before he spoke again, "At least it's only for a few more months."

"What?" I asked, looking up.

Theo's smile didn't reach his eyes. "When we're married I won't have to worry about you out till all hours at a club. You can be at home — with me."

I snorted a laugh. "When are you ever home?"

"More than some men." Theo's eyes tightened and he pressed closer, forcing me to strain to look up. "I can't wait until you don't have any other distractions. You can focus on our marriage with the proper amount of attention."

My blood simmered under my skin, fast approaching boiling point. I fought to keep my face neutral. In recent months I'd become a master at hiding my emotions. I stared into his cold blue eyes and held back every retort that bubbled on my tongue.

Our feud by eye contact was interrupted when an associate of Theo's appeared out of the crowd and clapped him on the shoulder. Using the moment to escape, I pushed through the throng of people to get a drink, my breath catching in my throat as Blake leaned on the bar beside me.

"I have to say, that was surprising," Blake said.

The bartender slid a Cosmo under my nose. I loved knowing the right kind of people. "How so?" I asked, after a monster gulp. Residual energy lingered in my veins from the altercation with Theo and it would take more than one cocktail to get rid of the rest. Not to mention the way Blake made me aware of every single part of me.

Between the two of them, these men were set to wreak havoc on my nerves.

Blake rubbed his thumb over his bottom lip, and I followed the movement as though in a trance. "I know I don't know you all that well, but from what I do know, I didn't expect you to take that kind of crap."

I shrugged, trying to snap myself out of a rather potent memory of that mouth.

"Why did you take it?" Blake asked, resting his forearm on the bar and leaning farther into my personal space.

"I'm used to it," I said, barely above a whisper.

Blake sighed. "You shouldn't have to get used to it."

I turned to face him. "It's Theo. What do you expect? You're his best friend. You know who he is."

His eyes narrowed as he drew himself up to full height. "Yeah, I do. I guess I never expected him to be like that with you."

"What did you expect?"

Blake shrugged.

I sipped what was left of my cocktail, desperate to explain myself to him. I saw my life through Blake's eyes—the quiet, broken housewife who followed orders like a well-trained dog. The spoiled girl who accepted all the gifts he showered her with.

There was so much he couldn't see.

"Are you really quitting your job?"

His question shamed me—more than our night together did, which I still couldn't bring myself to feel guilty about.

Blake leaned closer. "I guess you really aren't who I thought you were."

"Blake, you have no idea who I am," I said, my words startlingly close to ones I'd told him in Vegas. His scent that I remembered so vividly teased my senses and I scowled at myself for being so weak. "I can't talk about this with you."

His eyebrows shot up. "Why? I thought we were friends now."

I laughed. "Seriously? One minute you lean so close to me I can smell you and say I'm not who you thought I was. Then the next you say how great buddies we are. Seriously?" Thankfully the dark lighting of the club helped conceal my burning cheeks.

Blake smiled. "Look, I'm just trying to figure you out. I feel like I've met six versions of you. Which one is real?"

"Maybe none." *Maybe you were the only one to see the real me.*

"I don't believe that."

My heart picked up speed. "What do you believe?"

"That you're better than this…waiting for someone. You're too passionate to be kept dormant." Blake dropped his head then shook it.

I laughed again, more rattled this time by his comment. "That's exactly my point! How can you say something like that to me and at the same time try to be my friend? Friends don't say things like that to each other."

Blake smiled and for a brief moment looked both innocent and full of mischief. The combination was utterly adorable—and completely unrepentant. "Sorry. I'll be good. So what do friends do?"

"They talk." *About safe, neutral things.*

"Then let's talk." Blake turned to the bartender and motioned to a bottle of Bud in the chilled cabinet and hitched a thumb at me, already having picked up how well I was known. *Another Cosmo... Something told me I'd need it.* He paid then guided me to a table with his hand on the small of my back. I tried to ignore the shocks it sent through my body.

"Okay, talking..." Blake said rubbing his chin.

"Where did you grow up?" *See. I can be good. And normal.*

"Right here. I went to prep school and college with Theo."

"What was your major?"

"Architecture."

"How did you get into the hotel business?"

"My dad."

"He influenced you?"

"He owns it."

Okay, that stopped my rapid flow of questions. "He owns it?"

Blake nodded, his lips twitching. "Among others."

"And so he hired you to manage one of them?"

"Yeah."

I laughed. "How can you be so casual about it?"

"How do you want me to be? It's just a job. I'd sooner be doing something else." Blake lifted his beer bottle to his lips.

I shook my head and chuckled at his nonchalant attitude. He appeared so down to earth and laid-back it was difficult to imagine he was probably the heir to an absolute fortune.

"So why are you in New York? Shopping for a new venture on behalf of your father?" I asked, lifting my eyebrows. That sort of business sounded time consuming. My stomach fluttered at the thought of him becoming a more permanent fixture in my life. What a sweet kind of torture that would be.

"Yes, actually."

My cheeks flushed. "Any luck so far?"

Blake shook his head. "I've been distracted."

I felt the presence of someone behind me a heartbeat before they placed their hand beside my cocktail glass, crowding me in with their body. I twisted around in my chair to see Theo loom over me, his eyes blazing with a fierceness that made it clear my earlier insubordination hadn't been forgotten.

"Are you ready to go home?" he asked.

I tried to ignore the sinking feeling in my stomach. "You just got here."

Theo shrugged. "I'm tired. I have an early morning tomorrow."

"You have an early morning *every* morning."

Theo smiled with no warmth. "So do you."

I didn't argue with him and rose silently out of my chair. The untouched Cosmo a weird symbol for everything left unsaid between me and Blake. I glanced at him and saw something in his eyes that made my breath hitch. In that second I could have shrugged off Theo's hand and taken my seat beside him again.

Instead I managed a small smile that I knew betrayed more of my feelings than I would have liked. Blake stayed at the club as Theo and I left. I did my best not to think about him meeting girls and hated the sick feeling I got in the pit of my stomach when I did. That night his easy smile and probing eyes taunted me when I saw his face behind my closed eyelids as Theo made love to me, quickly and devoid of passion.

I managed three whole hours of sleep before I gave up and went running.

* * * *

Blake was everywhere. It seemed like every time I turned around his smile was there to greet me. It didn't feel awkward — instead Blake felt like a friend I'd known all my life. He was such an easy guy to be around. My entire body came to life at the mere mention of his name and I couldn't help the genuine flush of pleasure or smile when he was near. I just hoped no one else noticed. Then again, I wasn't sure anyone else was as aware of him as I was.

The soft ring of the doorbell echoed throughout the apartment as I was getting dressed. Theo padded past the bedroom on his way to answer it.

I heard muted voices, but paid no attention as I pulled on knee-length yoga pants and adjusted my sports bra. Slipping my feet into a pair of thin black ballet pumps and grabbing my yoga mat from a shelf in the closet, I was good to go.

Theo was still talking to someone as I twisted my long hair into a messy bun. The voices grew louder as they approached where I stood in front of the hall mirror. "Are you going out?" Theo asked.

"Yeah, my yoga class starts in thirty minutes."

"Oh. I've got to go back to the office to deal with something. Looks like you're out of luck, Blake. Best make some new friends to go to the movies with you."

I twisted my neck around and saw Blake standing a little behind Theo. My heart gave a little unexpected squeeze.

Blake sighed. "It is sad when my only two friends in the city bail on me."

Theo laughed and pulled his jacket from the hall closet. "You could always go to yoga. See you two later." Theo didn't bother with a goodbye before leaving.

"Did you want to hang out or something?" I asked, rummaging around in the same closet Theo had been in a few moments before as I tried to find a hooded sweater.

"Yeah. I was at a loose end for something to do tonight."

I grinned at him as I pulled on my jacket. "Well, you could always come to yoga."

Blake smiled and narrowed his eyes. "All right. Why not?"

A laugh bubbled in my throat.

He scoffed. "You don't think I could?"

"I didn't say that. It's kind of an advanced class —"

"Pfft." Blake rolled his eyes. "All right, Miss Jacobs, we'll see who can do the advanced class. Give me a minute to change. Theo won't mind me stealing some of his stuff."

We both paused. For a fraction of a second, the loaded sentence hung in the air. It was yet another reminder of the night I'd sworn to forget.

Blake cleared his throat and disappeared into the bedroom, before reappearing a few minutes later in a pair of Theo's basketball shorts and a tight sleeveless Lycra shirt.

Wow. That shirt did more things to his torso than a Wonderbra for any woman's boobs. The difference being Blake's shirt didn't enhance his chest muscles, so much as accent just how...wow...they were.

* * * *

Blake raised his eyebrows at me as the class was about to start. I shook my head at him and tried not to giggle. Faye, the instructor, really hated talking or noise during her lesson.

I shouldn't have scoffed at the idea of Blake doing yoga. On first glance, he would be more at home in a gym—lifting weights or doing mixed martial arts or something equally manly. But here he was in my advanced class, handling every pose with ease and fluidity.

I couldn't take my eyes off him.

Out of the corner of my eye, I saw his muscles move and contract under the skin. I glanced over his shoulders, his biceps and strong forearms. As I moved downward in my appreciation, taking in his flat stomach and endless strong legs, I felt the burn of a craving in every inch of my being.

Squeezing my eyes shut, I took a long, calming breath and forced any thoughts that weren't to do with yoga into the dark recesses of my mind.

Yoga, yoga, yoga. Yoga.

"Your Sun Salutation is beautiful."

I looked up and saw Faye also had trouble averting her gaze from the man beside me.

Blake flashed her a smile and looked at me, his eyes wide in innocence.

"You big cheater!" I mumbled through my teeth.

His smile widened. "What?"

"You made me think you've never done this before. What are you, a pro or something?"

"I have no idea what you are talking about, Marley." He turned his head, but I didn't miss the amused quirk to his lips.

Faye moved into the King of the Dance pose. I was fortunate enough to be graced with good balance. Blake on the other hand now looked a little unsteady.

"What's the matter?" I whispered. "This one a bit difficult for you?"

"Be quiet," he mumbled. "I'm concentrating."

I grinned, absolutely loving the turn of events. "Wouldn't have thought a pro like you would need to concentrate that much."

His wobbling intensified.

I giggled.

"Shh!" Faye shot me a look. "No talking."

"Yeah, Marley, be quiet," Blake said, his lips twitching into a smile.

"I said no talking!" Faye shouted, losing her patience with both Blake and me.

The suddenness of her exclamation made Blake jerk to the side. He tried to regain his balance, and I could see disaster looming. He swayed back and forth once more before losing the battle for balance. I watched in horror as he toppled toward me. There was no time for me to prepare myself — the whole thing only took a second or two. I managed to squeeze my eyes shut before he knocked into me and sent us both falling.

There was a sudden burst of pain in my ankle, and my eyes flew open as I tried to catch my breath. A quick glance around confirmed the only victims of the collision were me and Blake. No domino effect like I'd feared.

Blake was still on top of me, our limbs in a tangle. I became breathless for a whole other reason.

I focused every cell in my body into not moving. If I moved, even the tiniest fraction, then there was a chance my instincts would take over and I would rub against him in a way that was entirely inappropriate for a yoga studio. Or, you know, rubbing on my fiancé's best friend.

"Ow," Blake mumbled, his cheek against the floor.

"You're saying 'ow'? You broke my ankle, you dolt!" I exclaimed. I was caught between wishing he would get off me, so I would be free of the agony of having the weight of his body on top of me again, yet unable to do anything about it, and wishing that he would stay there forever.

Blake pushed himself onto his elbow and peered down at me. A hint of a smile touched his lips. My breath caught in my throat. This was worse. So much worse. Because this sight was achingly familiar.

Faye rushed to our sides to untangle us. Blake jumped to his feet and hooked a hand under my elbow to help me up.

"Are you two all right?" Faye asked in a pinched tone.

Whoops. Looks like I won't be welcome at Yoga Works again.

"Yes," we said in unison.

Blake looked me up and down and clearly saw I wasn't putting any weight on my left ankle. "You said I broke your ankle!"

A blush burned my cheeks and I tried to smile. "I was exaggerating."

He wasn't convinced. "Looks pretty sore."

I took a step and hissed as the pain jolted through my ankle.

"Come on. We're going to the Emergency Room."

"I'm fine!"

Blake's eyebrows shot up. "Oh, you never mentioned you have a medical degree."

I rolled my eyes. "I don't."

"Then you don't know you're fine." Blake swung me into his arms before I could blink and faced Faye. "Sorry for the disturbance. We'll be leaving now." And he carried me all the way outside and bundled me into a cab.

My ankle might have been swelling and turning an unattractive color, but I felt like a goddamn princess.

He kept me occupied as we waited for my ankle to get checked out. Blake read me crazy stories from the magazines he picked up and made me laugh at his running commentary on them. There were worse people to be stuck waiting with.

Theo was home when Blake and I returned from our four and a half hour trip to the Emergency Room. I limped into the lounge and dropped onto the couch.

"What the hell happened to you?" Theo asked, looking at my bandaged foot.

I looked up at Blake. "Someone came to yoga."

Theo glanced between us and let out a deep laugh. "What?"

"The idiot fell on me. Sprained my ankle."

Blake smirked. "You'll be fine in a day or two, Little Miss Drama Queen."

I hit him with a pillow.

* * * *

After the yoga fiasco, Blake was around even more. He would call me as I was leaving the office and ask if I felt like having dinner with him or checking out a comedy club he'd heard good things about. The places we went would never have impressed Theo. They were greasy Chinese restaurants and steak joints where they challenged you to eat almost an entire cow. There was nothing pretentious about Blake and he didn't feel the need to flash his cash around. If we went out for drinks, we didn't always go to the trendiest bars. Sometimes we went to quiet little pubs that had better atmospheres and pool tables where I would beat him shamelessly.

"Feel like a movie?" I asked him one evening. I had no work plans and Theo was—yet again—working. When would I stop being surprised?

"Sure. What's playing?"

I shrugged. "We'll find out once we're down there."

Blake wanted to see some deep movie full of hidden meanings and morals. I, on the other hand, had different ideas.

"You like slasher movies? Seriously?" Blake asked as we walked into the darkened theater.

"What's not to like?"

We found seats, and I dug into the popcorn.

"You won't have any left for the movie," Blake chided.

I shrugged. "I know. I never eat during the movie."

"Why?"

"I guess it distracts me. I get caught up in the story and forget all about it. Plus, I have a really bad habit of missing my mouth and most of the popcorn ends up down my shirt." Glancing down, I realized I was wearing the perfect shirt for stray popcorn. *Oh, God, stop drawing attention to your cleavage, Marley!*

Blake chuckled. "I find it hard to believe you forget to eat the popcorn. This place always had the best in the city."

"I just love movies. You get to be in a different world for a few hours. I think they're beautiful. I mean, movies don't care who you are or where you're from. They're made so people can be someone else, even it's only for two hours. You could be the biggest geek in school and for a little while you get to be part of the popular crowd. Movies make you cry, laugh, can make you inexplicably happy or terrified. Even though they aren't real, I guess they can make you feel alive. So, yeah, I forget to eat my popcorn."

Blake's expression softened and his eyes flickered over my face.

"Why are you looking at me like that? Do you think I'm weird?"

He laughed. "Yes, but that's not why I'm looking at you funny."

I frowned. "Why then?"

"Just when I think I've got you figured out, you turn around and surprise me."

"Aren't surprises good things?"

"Yes." He shifted in his seat. "I like not knowing every detail. It makes it all the more fun when I learn stuff about you."

"Oh," I said, torn between wanting to play on being a mysterious woman and telling him all my secrets so I could see that look again. "Do you want to know something else?"

Blake nodded, leaning ever so slightly closer.

I smiled and looked around, checking no one was listening. "It's really embarrassing. Promise you won't tell?"

Blake held up his pinky finger, and I linked mine with it.

"I'm afraid of tomatoes," I whispered.

He blinked. Then Blake's raucous laughter echoed around the theater, earning us filthy looks from the other patrons. It got him a swift jab to the ribs.

"Sorry," he choked out. "Are you serious? That is the craziest thing I have ever heard."

"I hate them. Especially big ones cut down the middle or sliced and you can see all the inside parts." I shuddered, and not for dramatic effect. "The juice and the seeds… God, I feel sick just talking about it."

Blake continued to laugh until the movie started. And every now and then I would feel his eyes on me and he would chuckle softly to himself.

Chapter Six

The chef shot me another peeved glare and my face burned a darker shade of pink. "Miss, I don't have time for this. Your fiancé is already thirty minutes late."

I smiled so wide it hurt. "I'm aware how late he is. Thanks."

Theo had arranged everything—the time, the place, the sample menu, everything. He'd said all I had to do was show up. It seemed he'd forgotten that was necessary on his part too.

"The dishes are prepared. Would you like them packed to take home?" Though the question was considerate, his tone and facial expression warned against this. Chefs' temperaments tended to run a little high, especially the ones who knew they were talented and in demand and could charge whatever the hell they liked.

"Don't worry about it. Five more minutes, how's that?"

His face turned puce. "Three minutes."

I tapped my cell phone against the table. What was it with stupid useless technology that felt the need to die just when you actually needed it? I swore it was a conspiracy. I used to think in horror movies it was so convenient that the phones would be out of service or just plain dead. Now I knew better.

The chef's face brightened and he stood straighter. Only Theo or the sight of his credit card could spark such a change in his attitude.

"I'm so sorry I'm late."

I paused as I rose from my seat. That voice didn't belong to Theo.

Blake shook the chef's hand and gave him his million dollar smile. "I hope I didn't keep you waiting." He looked in my direction and gave me a lopsided grin.

My stomach flip-flopped with the gesture. It felt like a rare treat, getting to see Blake so unexpectedly. Lately, he was starting to feel less and less like Theo's friend and more like...not my friend—friend was too gentle a word for what we were. But whatever it was, I liked it. And I wanted more, in whatever way I could get it.

"Not at all, not at all. How would you like to start?" the chef asked.

Oh sure, to him you're nice.

"How about you pack everything up?" Blake winked at me.

Shit, am I still gawping?

"It's a beautiful day outside and I can't stand to spend a second of it indoors. Marley and I can enjoy the food at our own pace and we can get out of your hair, save you waiting on us."

I bit my lip to keep from laughing. The chef's smile was so tight I thought it was about to rip his face in half. I sank back into my chair as Blake dropped into one opposite me, saluting the chef as he stormed into the kitchen.

"So did I miss something?" I inquired.

Blake grinned. "You don't like to turn that on?" He nodded to my cell phone.

"It's dead."

He nodded. "Theo called me about an hour ago to say he couldn't get away from work and would I mind coming to a menu tasting in his place. He said he left you a message."

"I didn't get it." If he even left it at all.

"I figured. Isn't the wedding only three months away? Shouldn't the menu be done by now?"

"It was until Theo's dietician put him on some newfangled diet, so now we start from scratch." I sighed. "I don't argue. I just do as I'm told."

"So I've noticed."

Before I could even comprehend that sentence, the chef dropped two white paper bags onto the table between us. He muttered something before disappearing back into the kitchen.

I stifled a giggle and fled outside with Blake hot on my heels.

"That guy is going to give himself a stroke," Blake said as we slowed our pace. "So. Feel like a picnic in the park? We're right beside Morningside. May as well take advantage."

I arched an eyebrow. "What makes you think I have the time? I was waiting for half an hour and my office is all the way downtown. Didn't anyone explain the time frame of a lunch hour to you?"

Blake narrowed his eyes at me. "I have a feeling you banked on something like this happening and have the rest of the day off."

I gasped.

"I'm right, aren't I?"

"How did you know that? Are you secretly a psychic and the hotel biz is just a front?" I asked, nudging him with my shoulder.

Blake laughed and nudged me back. "When you didn't pick up your cell, I called your office. Kelly told me you wouldn't be back today."

I swatted his arm.

Blake found a great spot in the park that wasn't too crowded. I had a huge Hermès scarf in my purse that I spread on the ground as a makeshift picnic blanket. Designers and fashion addicts across the world would faint at my actions, but hey… You've got to work with what you've got.

After a while I forgot what we were eating. I forgot who we were and what had brought us together on this wonderful day. I forgot we were sampling food to be eaten at my wedding – my wedding to Blake's best friend. And, I think Blake forgot, too. Instead we were eating gourmet food from plastic containers with plastic ware in the middle of Morningside Park, not caring that it wasn't really warm enough yet to be eating outside and the ground was still damp and cold. Instead of the labels that weighed each of us down, I was just Marley and he was just Blake.

* * * *

There was nothing more liberating for a woman than feeling sexy and confident in her outfit and dancing with her best friend. Hayley and I danced like no one was watching for what felt like hours until we were exhausted and laughing until it hurt. My favorite band, The Veronicas, were playing at the club and I'd been desperate to go. Henry had given me two free tickets and Hayley had jumped at the chance to come when I'd called her.

After the girls had finished their set, Hayley and I collapsed in a booth.

"I haven't danced like that since I was seventeen!" Hayley exclaimed breathlessly.

I rolled my eyes. "Dude, you're twenty-three. It wasn't decades ago!"

Hayley laughed and fanned her face with her hand. "I know, but you know what I mean!" She paused, a frown creasing her forehead.

"What's wrong?" I asked.

"A guy at the bar looks familiar. I've seen him someplace before. Do you recognize him?"

I twisted in my seat to see if I could spot who she meant. My heart gave a little squeeze when I saw him. It was Blake, of course.

"So? You know him?" she pressed.

"Yeah, that's Blake. He's Theo's best friend," I said in what I hoped was a nonchalant tone. "I'm going to go say hi. You want a drink?"

Hayley nodded, her eyes still on Blake.

Any second now she'll figure it out.

If I were being honest with myself, I wasn't all that scared of Hayley realizing where she had seen Blake before. What I was terrified of was that when she knew, I'd have to give serious answers to the question of just what the hell I thought I'd been doing these last few weeks.

Blake broke out into a grin when he spotted me approaching.

"Hey there," I said.

"Hey yourself." His eyes dipped down my body for a heartbeat and I stood a little taller, thankful that I'd chosen a short, ripped black skirt with my backless halter and terrifyingly high heels.

"What are you doing out tonight?"

"I came to see the band."

"You like The Veronicas?" I asked, waving to the barman and holding up two fingers.

Blake smiled. "You told me they were awesome. I figured I would check them out — see what all the fuss was about."

"And?"

"Not bad." Blake admitted. A wicked look flashed in his eyes. "I saw you dancing."

My cheeks burned red as I laughed. "Oh my God, you were watching?"

Blake's lips twitched. "Couldn't help it. You looked so... I dunno, free and happy."

There was a flutter low in my belly. I liked the thought of him watching me more than I had any right to. "Who are you here with?"

"No one."

"You came to a club by yourself? That's so sad."

Blake laughed. "Gee, thanks."

"Come sit with me and my friend," I said, picking up the cocktail glasses the bartender had placed in front of me.

Hayley's pale blue eyes were sharp as she watched Blake and I approach our booth. I slid in opposite her and handed Hayley her drink. Blake followed behind me, keeping a respectable distance between us.

"I should send you to the bar more often," Hayley said, her attention flitting between us. An open smile stretched her lips, softening the flirty statement. She stretched out a hand to Blake. "Hi, I'm Hayley."

"Blake," he said, shaking her hand.

"Marley tells me you're friends with Theo?"

Blake nodded. "That's right."

"How is it I've only just met you?" she asked, taking a sip of her cocktail.

I laughed. "Inquisition much, Hayley?"

She huffed. "Since when is curiosity a bad thing?"

"There's curiosity and then there's you," I said, grinning when Hayley pulled a face.

"I don't live in New York," Blake said, amusement coloring his tone as he glanced between me and Hayley. "I'm here on business for a while."

Hayley shot me a look as though to say some people didn't mind her inquisitive nature. "How are you liking the city?"

Blake smiled. "I'm from here originally, so I like it plenty."

Hayley scoffed. "And you *left*? Some New Yorker."

He laughed. "Hey, just because someone leaves doesn't mean they don't take part of the city with them."

She rolled her eyes and reached for her drink. "So not the same. Some of us are loyal to our one true love, but whatever."

I bumped Blake with my elbow. "Excuse my friend. She's a little nuts about her home."

"He left New York and *I'm* the nuts one?" Hayley mumbled into her glass.

"Shut up and drink your cocktail," I said, tossing a napkin at my friend.

Hayley didn't stay long after she'd finished her drink. She wasn't a vapid insomniac like I was and actually needed sleep to function properly. But I thought she liked Blake, even if he had committed a massive sin in her book by saying goodbye to the city. It gave me a strange flush of pleasure that my best friend got on well with Blake — not that it should have mattered to me.

"Just you and me," Blake murmured, once Hayley had said her goodbyes.

"So it seems," I said quietly.

He gestured to my empty cocktail glass. "Will you stay for another?"

I'd stay for a dozen. "I'd love to."

Blake gave me a smile and rose to get us fresh drinks. As I watched his back, my heart gave a little tumble. *This is a stupid idea.* Blake...me...alcohol — a sure recipe for disaster. But as sensible as my head insisted I be, I could not make myself stand up and give Blake whatever excuse I could think of and get the hell out of there.

He was back before I knew it, this time sliding in opposite me. "I'm dying to know — how do these Cosmos measure up to the ones in my club?"

I sipped the drink he'd placed in front of me. "It's impolite to ask a woman personal questions like that."

Blake grinned. "Well, excuse me."

"If you must know, these have always been my favorite." I couldn't help but laugh at the look of indignation on Blake's face. "But yours were pretty damn good."

He gave me a cocky look. "I knew it."

"Have I satisfied your ego enough now?"

"For now," he said. "You and Hayley seem close."

"We are. I'm the closest to her out of our group. She's good people, you know?"

Blake nodded. "I can see why you like her so much."

For a heartbeat my stomach pinched with jealousy. I tried to reassure myself that Blake didn't seem like the kind of guy who worked his way around a group of friends.

"Does she get along with Theo?"

I snorted a laugh. "I don't think they've exchanged more than ten words." There was no love lost between Hayley and Theo. But she cared enough about me to never make an issue out of it.

"Did he even try to make an effort?"

"Are you really asking that question?"

Blake smirked. "Fair enough. Another?"

It took a moment to realize he meant another drink. Glancing down, I saw that my glass was empty again. Either these were going down seriously well tonight, or the present company was relaxing me enough to really let loose.

"If you are," I said, already knowing his answer.

Blake flashed me a smile and headed again for the bar. Any more and I'd have a pretty good buzz going. When Blake returned with a tray and shots as well as our usual drinks, I knew I'd be leaving with well more than a buzz.

At my expression, Blake chuckled. "Two for one on shots tonight. It'd be rude not to."

I snorted a laugh. "Well, we'd hate to be rude."

Anyone else might have said that the drinks were enough of a social lubricant to relax the conversation and let it flow. But in all honesty, I couldn't remember when I'd had so much fun just sitting talking with someone. With Blake there was no pressure—no appearances to be upheld, no one to impress and no having to be someone different.

The hours drifted by in a cocktail-induced haze that was sound-tracked with laugher, until we reached closing time. The last thing I wanted was for the night to end. It had been too real, too fun to just end.

Blake scanned my face with his curious gaze. "I have a pretty good bar back in my room. You game?"

Was there even an option?

* * * *

I tucked my legs underneath me as I sat on the thick and luxurious cream rug in the lounge. Blake's 'room' was an enormous suite. I didn't ask if there was a hot tub, but I was dying to know.

Blake brought a bottle of tequila, a salt shaker and a bowl of chopped limes from his bar in the corner. He dropped beside me on the rug and placed his assortment of items in front of us on the coffee table. He put music on and it played softly in the background. I barely heard it, but it was comforting that is was there.

I laughed as Blake filled two shot glasses. "I haven't had tequila shooters in forever."

"College?"

"It was the drinking game drink of choice."

Blake grinned wickedly. "Then we need a game."

I swiveled to face him. "All right. How about Never Have I Ever?"

"Deal. You first."

"Um, never have I ever…eaten a banana."

"That's it?"

I shoved him, but would have had better results trying to bench press a city bus. "I couldn't think of anything. Are you drinking?"

Blake chuckled and lifted his shot glass to his lips. "Wait—aren't you?"

My cheeks warmed. "Um, no."

There was a moment before he collapsed in a fit of laughter.

"You…never…ate…a…banana…" he choked out past the laughter.

"I hate them! Even the smell makes me nauseated!"

It took Blake a long time to recover from his laughing fit, but he eventually wiped his eyes and took a deep breath. "My turn? Uh... Never have I ever...danced like a lunatic for two hours straight."

I narrowed my eyes at him. "Are you trying to say I danced like a lunatic tonight?"

Blake smirked. "Are you drinking?"

"I think you're just trying to get me drunk." I coughed after the shot.

"You're already drunk!"

Our *never have I ever* statements grew more far-fetched and ridiculous. More than once we both dissolved in drunken giggles, from which there was no return.

"I never got wasted at my senior prom," I said, clutching my aching side.

"Oh, that's not fair! I don't know any stupid things you've done in your past!" Blake protested before doing his shot. The bowl of limes was almost bare. "I never streaked around my college campus." Blake tried.

My drink remained untouched, as did his. I smirked at him, enjoying the tiny victory. "I never had a nickname as lame as 'Hammy'," I said, grinning.

Blake shot me a disparaging look before taking another shot.

"Why 'Hammy', anyway?" I asked.

"Theo and I got hammered at senior prom. Hammered turned to Hammy, plus with my last name being 'Hamilton', the guys had too many reasons for it to stick."

"I almost feel bad for you," I said, with mock concern on my face. "Anyway, your turn."

Blake sighed. "I can't think of anything else!"

"And I don't know anything else embarrassing about you. That's not fair." I pouted.

Blake glanced at me. "Okay, I've got one."

I arched an eyebrow, which was really hard to do with my compromised motor functions.

He filled the two glasses and handed me one.

I snorted. "You seem sure of yourself."

Clutching his glass, Blake looked me dead in the eye. "Never have I ever had a Vegas hook-up."

My jaw dropped open and the seconds ticked by. I'm really glad I was as drunk as I was. I probably would have hit him if I'd been sober. But sober was an island faraway in the distance and so I thought it was really funny. I almost dropped my glass from laughing. "You ass!" I exclaimed, wiping the tears streaming down my face. God, laughing was fun.

We both sank our shots.

There was one lime left.

I narrowed my eyes. It had to be a really good one. I refilled his glass and left my own empty. "Okay…" I tapped my fingers against my chin. "Never have I ever…had a crush on my best friend's fiancée."

Blake snorted and was quiet for a moment. The more I watched his face, the funnier I found it all. My stomach immediately cramped up again. I massaged my side and tried to quell the amusement.

"You're the devil," Blake said, shaking his head.

I cackled with glee. "I know. Are you drinking?"

Blake stood up. "I can't. I'll puke."

"Don't be a girl! Drink!"

Blake chuckled and backed away from me. I narrowed my eyes and stood up, taking the shot and the last lime with me.

"No."

"Yes."

He continued to edge slowly away from me and backed himself right into the wall.

"Come on," I said, teasing. "You want the lovely tequila-ness."

Blake chuckled as I raised the glass and held it toward him, still closing the space between us.

"I don't."

"You do. Admit it." I pressed the glass to his lips. He parted them and allowed me to clumsily pour the liquid in. Lowering the glass, I stepped closer, brandishing the lime. I wiped a droplet of tequila from his chin. We were inches apart. I looked up and found Blake's eyes wild.

I rubbed the lime across his full lips as my heart spluttered. It jolted as Blake knocked my hand aside and framed my face with his hands. He pulled me close to him, devouring me with a delicious kiss.

His mouth was bitter from the lime. I didn't care. All that mattered was the havoc he was playing with my nervous system, the crash of our tongues as they met urgently, his lips that felt as good as I remembered. Blake wrapped his arms around me, forcing me closer. It wasn't close enough. I moaned and Blake tightened his grip. The glass and lime fell from my hands. Now they were free, I raised my hands to fist Blake's short hair. He pressed his hips into me and the thick hardness of his erection pressed against my belly.

I had been kidding myself that we could be friends. I wanted him too badly to ever be friends with him. And from the way he was kissing me, he wanted me just as much.

The kiss slowed. Became more intimate. It was a kiss I wanted to drown in and never come up for air.

"Shit," I mumbled into his mouth. I placed my hands on his chest and pushed myself back a little. Blake's breath was heavy on my face.

"Told you you liked me," I said, more to break the silence than anything else.

Blake's lips moved into a rueful smile, and he chuckled with a sad undertone.

"I should go." How was it possible to be so drunk yet feel sober? I didn't trust my balance, yet everything was so sharp and vivid. Especially my thoughts, which focused on the frantic drum of Blake's heart under my fingertips.

"Don't." Blake's voice broke. "Stay."

The temptation was easy to give in to. His fingers trailed delicately down my arms, making me breakout in goosebumps. I sighed. "I can't."

Blake dropped his head onto my shoulder. He traced a line down my spine before ceasing his beautiful touch. I twisted my head to kiss his neck. Blake's body tensed, and I somehow found the will to move out of reach.

He didn't try to stop me leaving.

* * * *

Dawn had barely broken when I went for an early run. The steady thump of my feet slapping against the gray asphalt was therapeutic in a constant kind of way, like counting heartbeats. Somehow the still-bare trees made me feel lonely and isolated, despite many other joggers around. The sky was an unending expanse of gray cloud with drizzly rain that was barely even there yet managed to drench me. I focused on the scenery as much as possible without running into or tripping over animals or people...my own feet.

But no matter how hard I tried, the second I lost concentration, my thoughts were flooded with Blake. I wished the rain could wash away my thoughts of him and leave my mind clean and refreshed. My subconscious allowed me no rest and his kiss followed me wherever I ran.

Stopping at my usual coffee place on the way home, I ordered a triple espresso and drank it at a table outside as the rain had stopped. The bitter edge from the cool air gradually lessened and the pale sun gently kissed my face.

"Marley."

My breath caught in my throat when I heard him. Why did I have to recognize his voice so fast? It had been a week since our drunken kiss and just hearing his voice brought back a torrent of memories.

I ignored the skip of my heart while looking up at him. His normal, carefree expression was gone. There were a million words for faces and how they looked. Melancholic, depressed… But Blake just looked sad — like the world had served him the biggest plate of shit and kicked him in the balls then told him his goldfish had died.

"Hi," I said, swallowing the thick emotion that lodged in my throat.

Blake gestured to the chair opposite. "Can I sit?"

I nodded. How could I refuse him when he already looked so miserable?

"You've been avoiding me."

"You too."

Blake nodded. "I'm sorry. For everything."

I sighed. "Don't be. You didn't do anything wrong."

Blake snorted a laugh and scrubbed a hand over his short hair. "Right."

The first blossom of guilt unfurled in my stomach. Each kiss, each touch with Blake I'd locked in a safe place deep inside my mind that I could cherish for the rest of my life. I couldn't bring myself to feel guilt over it. But this—seeing him so torn and distressed—I hated myself for doing it to him. "I mean it, Blake. None of this is your fault. You didn't know anything about me. I knew my commitments and it was my choice to betray them."

"I kissed you."

I waved the statement off. "We were drunk. Just leave it at that."

He lifted his pained eyes to meet mine. "You would forget all about it?"

I forced a smile on my face, though smiling was the last thing in the world I wanted to do. "Already have."

Blake looked down. "Right. Of course."

"We're still friends, right?" Because I needed him however I could have him, even if it felt like purgatory.

"If you say so." Blake let out a breath and rose from his seat. "I'd better get going."

I nodded and refused to allow myself to look at him.

Chapter Seven

Sometimes I felt like I'd spent my whole life waiting. Waiting for the bus, a cab, a favorite show to come on, a cute boy to call...or as was the case right now, waiting for my fiancé whose middle name should be 'I'll Be Right There'.

After the menu tasting fiasco, I had hoped that Theo would have had the courtesy to show up on time to his tux fitting. It had been lost in the dark and misty corners of my poor exhausted mind and had only come to the surface when Theo's secretary had called to make sure that I would be there with him.

I didn't understand why Theo needed so many fittings. He was a guy! But then again, Theo was no ordinary guy. He was obsessed with staying in shape and his dietician made routine drop-ins to his office, always eager to impart her wisdom on how to eat better and get the most out of his body. As a direct result, Theo was way more figure conscious than I was. Hence the numerous tux fittings. *Sheesh.*

Henry understood when I informed him of my pressing appointment. Of course he did. Henry was the world's best boss. You could tell him you were feeling a little sleepy and he would let you take a nap under your desk. *'Just don't let any clients see you. Seriously.'* That had happened with an intern last year. As long as your work got done and done well, he was so laid-back he was practically horizontal.

So there I was, on the receiving end of yet more filthy looks from harassed people kept waiting by Mr. Lorimer. It would be easier if he came with his own time zone and we all just switched to his.

The bell above the door chimed and in swept Theo, oblivious to the fact that if looks could kill, we would both have been in some serious trouble. His phone was cemented to his ear as always and he dipped to kiss my cheek. He nodded to the woman wearing a measuring tape around her neck and tapping her foot.

"Thank God you're here," Theo murmured to me. "Run down the street to Starbucks and grab me a triple espresso."

"They have coffee here," I said with a tight smile.

Theo wrinkled his nose and shooed me away with his hand. I swore I could stab him sometimes.

With a dark cloud fixed over my head, I marched to Starbucks. But I was feeling mischievous and had a coffee of my own first before ordering Theo's. Twenty minutes would do it. *He should be reaching tantrum stage right about now. Time to head back.*

The seamstress's assistant led me to the back where the dressing rooms were. There were several drawn curtains. She quickly scampered. Poor girl was probably terrified of catching Theo in various states of undress. Not that she should have been. For all his obsession with good health, it sure had paid off and ensured he had a hot body.

There was a silhouette behind the curtain in front of me.

"You done yet?" I asked as I ducked behind the curtain.

It wasn't Theo. *When am I going to learn to stop getting myself into situations like these?*

Blake spun around to face me, his face mimicking the mortified expression on mine. He wasn't naked but he was buttoning his pants and didn't have a shirt on. It was enough for the white hot flame to tear through my body making me feel like my hair was on fire. *Oh yeah, he definitely should come with a health warning.*

I couldn't tear my eyes off him. All I wanted, all I could think about was reaching out to touch his warm skin. Blake's body was a masterpiece that I could study for hours. The deep V of his hips, well-defined stomach and chest, smooth, wide shoulders... I wanted to mold myself against him, I wanted some relief for the ache between my legs.

Blake's hands fell from his pants and the movement drew my attention down. The outline of his hard-on made my breath catch in my throat and I took an involuntary step toward to him. I dragged my gaze up. Blake's eyes were heated. He shifted, bringing himself that tiny bit closer.

As though I was reliving a memory rather than creating a dream, I saw myself lunging to close the space between us, sealing my mouth over his and shoving his dress pants down. Blake would catch the backs of my thighs and lift me, press my back against the wall and push into me.

I could hear the blood rushing behind my ears. We weren't touching, were only barely within arm's reach. But this...it felt more intimate than sex.

Blake closed his eyes, and when he opened them the raw heat had been replaced with something else. Some kind of pleading, an almost defeated look. My heart clenched and I was right back to the moment in his hotel room, balancing on the precipice of right and wrong—duty and desire, loyalty and love.

What am I doing?

My cheeks flushed and I backed away as fast as I could. But me being the klutz that I am, got tangled in the stupid curtain. I started apologizing, though I wasn't sure who to. Blake? Theo? The fabric I was maiming with my fingers?

I whipped around and managed to spill the contents of Theo's coffee down my white shirt. If I had been a child, this would have been the point when I would have thrown myself on the ground and pounded the carpet with my fists, crying angry tears.

Instead, because I am a grown-up, I let the mortification wash over me and avoided eye contact with the small crowd that had gathered due to my antics.

The seamstress handed me some napkins to try to save my ruined shirt. I should probably have been hopping around in agony from the scalding coffee, but I felt nothing through the sheer embarrassment.

Theo popped his head around his curtain and gave me a look before ducking back in. I knew what that look meant—don't embarrass me.

Too late, I was embarrassed enough for the both of us.

"Are you okay, miss? Can I get you anything?" the assistant asked.

Sure. A clean shirt and a time machine would be swell, thanks. I smiled so wide it hurt. "No, thank you."

Theo pulled back his curtain and stepped out. He did look really good in his tux. Theo was the kind of guy that when he walked down the street, it was clear he was going somewhere important. There was purpose in his walk, unlike me, who would happily mosey on through life in a skipping-through-the-meadows sort of way.

Though Theo and his groomsmen would all be wearing the same thing, there would be no doubt on anyone's mind on the day of the wedding who was in charge, the leading man. Theo wasn't purposefully arrogant. It was just the way he carried himself, the burdens and stress he muddled through every day. The success he had made of his life.

My convoluted thoughts on Theo were shattered the moment Blake stepped out of his dressing room—fully clothed, thank God.

But just because clothes covered up that awesome body, it didn't stop the uneven thump my heart gave. He looked stunning in that tux. It was a simple black tux with white shirt and lilac handkerchief in the breast pocket, but it fit him like a glove. It accentuated everything about his body that made me crazy—the swell of his broad shoulders, his narrow waist, his long, long legs.

Blake didn't meet my eyes and instead threw a shaky smile in Theo's direction. "Does this bring back memories or what?"

Theo laughed, a deep barking laugh that I hadn't heard before. "You're right. Senior prom comes to mind right about now."

Blake chuckled.

Theo wiped his eyes. "I don't want history repeating itself, though."

"Aw, come on. We had a great night hanging out." Blake grinned.

Theo laughed again. "As I recall, it was my date you were more interested in that night." Theo turned to me and pointed his thumb at Blake. "My so-called best friend hung out with me for all of half an hour in which we got completely wasted then he sets his eyes on my date!"

"You barely knew her," Blake said, shifting his stance.

Can Theo hear the uneasiness in his tone?

Theo laughed. "True. But I think I feel a little more attached to Marley, so be warned." He looked at me again. "Watch out for him, Marley. I don't think a woman yet has been able to turn Blake down once he turns on that infamous charm of his."

My stomach flipped and rolled and dove and did everything else it could. The guilt washed over me in sickening waves. Theo had no idea what he was saying but the irony of the conversation was all too painful.

"Relax, Theo," Blake said.

I glanced up and locked eyes with him, shocked at the steeliness that had replaced that almost painful look from before. "I wouldn't dream of trying anything with your *wife*."

"Ah, I think she's too besotted with me to notice you." Theo chuckled.

His voice was faint and distant as my heartbeat pounded in my ears. Tears stung my eyes but never would they be allowed to fall.

In that moment I hated them both. I hated Theo for being such an ass, ignoring me all the time, treating me like a trophy Barbie doll and trying his best to turn me into something I wasn't. I hated Blake for being so nice and so annoying and so...Blake. I hated that every other word that came out his mouth could be construed into a different meaning. I hated the silent conversations we could have with Theo completely oblivious.

I hated that he gave me the power to hurt him.

Most of all I hated myself. I could get angry all I wanted at both of them, but at the end of it all, we were having this horrendous conversation because of me.

* * * *

Since I had a night off, I called Hayley to arrange a girls' night out. She told me they were thinking of going to the new club, Red, in the East Village and me having a night off for once just gave them all an excuse for a night on the town.

With my new purple dress and my hair done, I felt excited to be leaving all my worries at home as I planned on dancing the night away. I tried not to be too peeved that the girls had been thinking of going out and hadn't thought of me—my own fault for working all the time, really. They would have assumed I would be busy.

"Oh. Are you going out?" Theo asked as he walked into our room and saw me fastening the straps on my sandals.

"Yes," I said, not lifting my head.

"I have a client dinner tonight." Theo paused on his way out of the room. "Everything all right?"

My heart skipped a beat. I could count on one hand the number of times he'd asked after my well-being. "Why?"

Theo's eyes skimmed over my face. "You seem on edge."

"I'm fine," I said, forcing a smile.

"As long as you're sure."

I nodded. *Great. Why does he have to pick now to pay attention?*

"Have fun. I'll be home early tomorrow, so I'll see you then."

That happy feeling I'd had as I'd gotten ready for the big night out had all but disappeared. My friends, my beautiful and carefree friends, were enjoying another night of their youth and I felt like I was living a lie. Theo wanted me to be some prim and proper wife, at home in the kitchen, and I was desperately trying to hold onto some semblance of myself.

I could have a night off from my life as often as I liked. But wherever I went, I was still me.

* * * *

I closed my eyes and leaned against the back of the booth, wanting to disappear with the waves of the music that washed over me. Still on edge from my encounter with Theo, which really, hadn't been an encounter at all...to him at least. I was left at half-mast.

"Are you okay?" Hayley asked.

"I'm great, why?" I asked before gulping down my Cosmo.

"You're practically vibrating."

I arched an eyebrow.

"Are you stressed about the wedding?"

"No."

"That guy from Vegas?"

Though my pulse spiked, I'm sure my face or tone didn't change. Yeah right. I was probably doing a hell of a good impersonation of Porky Pig. "Wh-what guy from Vegas?"

Hayley nudged me with her elbow. "Look, I'm not stupid, okay? I know something happened out there and something has definitely been going on with you since you got back. You don't have to fill me in on the details, but you know you can talk to me, right?"

I smiled. "Nothing to talk about."

Hayley narrowed her eyes and gave me a look that made me drop my eyes. "I figured out who Blake was. I know it was him you were with in Vegas," Hayley said. Her tone suggested she was more annoyed that I hadn't thought she could have figured it out, not pissed for not telling her in the first place.

I'm going to be sick.

Hayley's sigh made me glance up at her face, which had thankfully softened. "I'm not going to say anything, not to anyone."

"Nothing to tell." *I think I'm becoming a pathological liar.*

She placed a hand on her hip. "You know, one of these days I'm going to read about you in the paper."

"What?" I asked, laughing.

Hayley gestured at me with her hand. "All this stuff you're keeping repressed is one day going to make you snap and take out a mall with a semi-automatic."

I rolled my eyes. "You watch too much TV."

Hayley laughed. "Are you kidding? I don't need to! Your life is all the drama and scandal I need! It's like watching your favorite soap and knowing there are all these secrets floating around and trying to piece together the puzzle before the season finale."

"You *definitely* watch too much TV."

"Maybe. But I'm still dying to see how it all ends," Hayley said.

I followed her out onto the dance floor where I closed my eyes and let the music do its job and steal me away.

* * * *

There was a drastic shortage of cabs at the end of the night. The others all lived near each other so they shared the one cab waiting out front. We were drunk enough not to be worried about me waiting alone and so kissed each other goodnight with promises to go out again soon.

It was about two and a half minutes later that I wished I'd shared the cab with them and made the driver double back to take me home. A cold chill swept through my thin dress, which provided no warmth. I wasn't drunk enough to think wandering around the neighborhood looking for a cab was a good idea so I did something I'd never done before. I called Theo and got him to send his car and driver.

Sometimes a girl just needs to be rescued.

The back seat was empty when the car showed up an agonizing forty minutes later. Of course it was empty. Theo wouldn't have got out of bed for anything other than one of his precious clients.

When I got home I was shivering too violently to negotiate my key into the lock. My Cosmo buzz had long since worn off and all that kept me going was the thought of warm pajamas and a hot drink.

I jumped back as the door swung open. A thousand apologies and excuses escaped my lips. It wasn't wise to wake Theo up unless being throttled was a favorite kinky pleasure.

My apologies were pointless. It was Blake standing in front of me, not an irate fiancé.

"Oh, it's you. What are you doing here?" I asked, as I brushed past him and padded barefoot down the hall to the lounge, ignoring how stunning he looked in his suit, even if it was crumpled as though he had slept in it.

"Theo's dinner was canceled at the last minute so he asked if I wanted to watch the game with him since you were going out. We had a few beers and it got late so he told me just to crash," Blake said as he followed me into the room. "You look freezing."

"That might be because I am," I said, shivering.

Blake smiled and tossed a comforter from the couch at me. "Sit."

For once I did as I was told. I wrapped the soft fabric around my freezing body and sank into the couch. Blake returned a few minutes later with a steaming mug of tea. I wrapped my hands around it and tried to absorb every bit of heat.

"Did you have a good night?"

I nodded, lowering my face to inhale the steam rising from the tea.

"It's late. Won't you be exhausted at work tomorrow?"

"I don't sleep much."

"Oh."

That old saying, 'you could cut the tension with a knife'? Boy, did I get it now. And because the cold had frozen most of my brain cells, I decided to try to hack the tension to pieces instead of skirting around the edges like I always did. "What were you thinking the other day at the tux fitting, saying those things to Theo?"

Blake didn't drop his eyes from mine. "What do you mean?"

"That wasn't fair. You made him look really stupid."

"Only to you. No one else." His voice hardened.

All at once I felt exhausted. "It isn't fair, Blake." Neither was the way I had eye-fucked him, but I wasn't mentioning that.

"To who exactly? You? Me? Or Theo?"

I sighed. "If you want us to be friends, you have to stop doing this. Nothing is ever going to happen with us, not again."

Blake snorted. "We certainly think highly of ourselves, don't we?" He fished inside the breast pocket of his suit jacket and pulled out a quarter.

"You have to start thinking of me as one of the guys."

"I don't get how you can do that," Blake said, rolling the coin across his fingers.

I blinked, having been entranced by his coin trick. "What?"

"Change your mind so damn fast. First you want me, then you don't. Oh but, yeah you do. No, actually, you'll take a pass."

I rolled my eyes. "You know, for a guy, you can be such a girl."

"Oh yeah? Well, for a girl you can be such a pain in the ass!" Blake hissed through clenched teeth.

I loved arguing with Blake. He got me riled up and on edge so quickly. He was just as highly strung as I was, and wouldn't back down from a fight. But tonight I didn't have the energy to rise to the bait.

"Have you thought about a date for the wedding?" I asked abruptly—and unexpectedly, if Blake's face was anything to go by. "Hayley is one of the bridesmaids, I don't think she has a date yet. Want me to set it up?"

Blake watched my face carefully. I knew this was a test and he did too. There was no emotion in my voice, face or eyes. If I convinced him that I truly saw him as a friend, maybe I could convince myself while I was at it. His green eyes narrowed.

It was Blake's eyes that had first stood out to me. They were so soft yet penetrating, dazzling and kind all at the same time. I could get so wrapped up in his eyes that the rest of his face would blur and become unfocused. Only when it re-focused did I remember just how devastating that face was.

I need a cold shower.

Almost as if a light bulb had pinged inside my head, the answer stared me right in the face. Blake was a gorgeous guy and he had paid attention to me. No wonder I'd developed a little attachment. I could have hugged myself with glee as I realized it was only a crush. Just a teeny, tiny insignificant little crush that would fade with enough perseverance and time. *I hope.*

He looked at the coin in his hand and shook his head. "I can find my own date, thanks."

My heart gave a pang, but I didn't let it show. I shrugged. "Suit yourself."

Chapter Eight

"I hope you aren't working tonight," Theo announced when he came home.

"Why?" I ran an itinerary of wedding arrangements in my head. We had nothing planned, no details to check on. I couldn't believe there was only a little under three months left.

"We have dinner plans."

News to me. "Oh. I'll go get ready." I chose my black Armani dress and pushed the images of the last time I'd worn it out of my mind.

I was ready before Theo—no surprise there—and waited patiently like the good little wife-to-be that I was. He didn't look up from his Blackberry when he met me in the hall, and continued to pay it more attention in the car. "What's the occasion?" I asked, as we walked into Theo's favorite restaurant in Midtown.

He waved to someone at the bar. Theo chuckled. "It's a double date actually."

My stomach dropped. Oh, God. "With who?"

"I set up Blake with a girl from my office. He has no idea. Thinks it's just me and him."

My pulse quickened as I imagined having to endure sitting across from Bake for an entire meal. I would really have to work on not staring at him like he was a giant fat-free chocolate cake. He was waiting at the bar. A brief look of shock flitted across his handsome face before regaining control. Did he have to look so good? He was wearing a well-cut black suit. It flattered his shape and made him look even more amazing.

"I didn't realize Marley was coming." Blake looked directly at Theo. "I would have brought my own date had I known."

Theo grinned. "Taken care of."

Blake glanced at me.

Theo scanned the bar. "Ah! There she is!" He waved over Simone, a stunning blonde woman. She was as thin as a rail and had legs for days. I'd met her once or twice at a few office parties Theo had taken me to. She was nice enough. Not terrifying or intimidating. Not at all.

We were seated at one of the best tables, a large square affair on the upper level with views of the restaurant below and the city beyond the tall arched windows. A flair of panic rang through my body as I reached to pull out a chair. I glanced at Blake and saw a look that was probably all over my face, too.

Where the hell do I sit?

There was no solution to this ridiculous problem. Not one I liked, anyway. Blake and I would either end up right beside each other, or right in front of each other. Which was worse? Being so close we could touch? Or being unable to escape his gaze that seemed to cut through to my very core.

"Are you going to sit down?" Theo pulled me from my dilemma with a jolt.

"Uh, of course. Yes." *But where?*

Simone took the chair to my right, Theo to my left. Blake and I exchanged an uncomfortable look and with a sigh, I resigned myself to my fate. *Unable to escape those eyes...that face...those lips it is, then. Awesome.*

"Thank you for coming, Simone. I know it was last minute," Theo said, accepting the menu that our server handed him.

"Not a problem," Simone said with a coy smile.

Coy my ass. She'd be wearing a shit-eating grin if she could have gotten away with it. Who the hell went on a blind date and ended up with Blake Hamilton?

Theo clapped his hand on Blake's shoulder. "My old friend here has been a recluse since coming back to his homeland."

Simone eyed Blake. "What a shame for the rest of us. Maybe we can change that?"

It took everything in me to not snort at that blatant come-on.

Blake cleared his throat. "So you work with Theo?"

"Very closely," Simone said, glancing at Theo. "He's a slave driver. But I'm hoping all my long hours in the office will pay off soon and he'll come to his senses and realize he desperately needs me as a partner."

Theo gave her a tight-lipped smile. "All in due time."

Her eyes hardened but the curve of her lips tried to say she wasn't affected by his brush-off. She wasn't fooling anyone, especially Theo. He met her stare for a long moment before he turned to look at me.

"Do you know what you want?"

Isn't that the million dollar question? I gave him a stiff nod, and Theo signaled the waiter.

Einstein's theory of relativity could not have been truer that night. The time I'd spent with Blake in Vegas felt like a heartbeat — barely any time at all. But this meal? Christ, it went on for days.

I had no idea how a simple dinner could be so intense, with half the party squirming uncomfortably and the other half completely oblivious. For the most part, I fidgeted with my napkin and drank my wine too quickly. It earned disapproving glares from Theo, who never made it a secret that he detested my inability to sit still.

When the main courses arrived, I ate slowly, meticulously. Anything to keep my attention from the warped reality playing out around me.

After the plates had been cleared, I had nowhere else to go but the warped reality we seemed to be stuck in. And, maybe I should have been playing closer attention because during the mental vacation I'd taken, Simone had been utilizing the time to get closer to Blake.

She had angled her chair nearer to him, and hung on every word that fell from his lips. He and Theo were discussing a problem one of Theo's clients was having in acquiring a property in Soho for development. Simone chimed in, offering her two cents. Mostly their words floated over me, but Blake ensnared my attention.

I couldn't tear my eyes away from him. I was enraptured as he spoke with clarity and thought-out answers. The furrowing of his eyebrows imprinted in my mind when he tried to think of a solution and spoke his ponderings. Everything, it seemed, that Blake did, he did carefully and concisely.

"I hope you will both overlook Marley's slack-jawed expression."

I glanced at Theo, frowning in confusion at his words.

Theo smiled at Blake and Simone. "All this intelligent talk tends to go over her pretty little head. Isn't that right, sweetheart?" He winked at me, smirking at his own joke.

He nearly got a fork in his hand. *Ass.* My heart thumped with angry adrenaline and I swallowed back what would have taken this awkward dinner into a whole other ball game. Folding my hands in my lap, I gave him a saccharine-sweet smile.

Simone leaned closer to Blake and murmured something I couldn't make out.

I remembered the pinch of jealousy I felt when Hayley had gotten along with Blake, and that had all been innocent enough. That jealousy was nothing compared to the white-hot hatred that ran through me when I watched Simone drape herself all over Blake.

Okay, so she didn't 'drape' over him, but I bet she would have if the restaurant hadn't been quite so public. Instead she leaned in to whisper in his ear, her hair falling in front of her face, so I had no idea what she was whispering. *Slut.*

Is it normal to feel this jealous over someone you only have a crush on? Every time he smiled at her, or leaned a little closer, my eyes tightened. The rational part of my brain told me he was only being polite. The rest, well, wasn't happy.

"So, Marley."

I tore my eyes from the salad Theo had ordered for me. Apparently I was looking a little bloated. Simone was smiling a very friendly smile.

"How's life in PR?" she asked.

"Fine."

Theo laughed. "She's only an assistant. I don't think we'll be seeing her name on the letterhead just yet."

Simone swatted Theo's hand and tutted. She turned back to me and tilted her head. "Must be fun, working the clubs."

I glanced at Theo. Just how much had he told her about me?

Simone chuckled. "I know I would love the excuse to go out three nights a week and get paid for it!"

I glared and couldn't keep the ice from slipping into my tone. "It's work. It's not meant to be fun."

"It must be better than being stuck in an office all day long."

"Yeah." I laughed. "I get to be stuck in an office all day long and then stand outside *all night long*."

Simone shifted in her seat, an uncomfortable look on her face. "You get to go inside at some point, surely?"

"Oh, yes. I get to go in and check on the private parties, make sure everything is all right. It's especially wonderful when yuppie bitches have too much to drink and I have to take care of them."

"Yes, I can imagine that would be unpleasant."

"Makes a nice change from the usual condescending tripe they insist on speaking." I felt Blake's eyes on me but I refused to look at him.

Simone cleared her throat and attempted a different approach. "I really love that dress. You must get a lot of attention when you wear it. It suits you perfectly."

Feeling bolder than normal — probably had the rage to thank for that — I didn't take my eyes off Blake when I answered. "Like you wouldn't believe."

"You'll have to excuse Marley, Simone. She can act fairly petulant at times," Theo apologized.

I took a deep breath but could still feel my temper mounting. Theo ignored me and started another long-winded conversation, in which I was not included. The final straw on the disastrous double date was when I dropped my phone. I was sending a harsh text message to Hayley complaining about the meal. I bent to retrieve it and saw Simone's hand on Blake's leg. Not knee, thigh. Within dick grabbing range. Jerking up, I banged my head on the table, making me curse. Theo grabbed my elbow and righted me so quickly I got a head rush. I grasped my aching head and glared at him.

"Will you stop embarrassing me," he whispered in my ear.

Blake quietly excused himself. His departure was barely registered through the anger that now radiated toward Theo.

My cheeks burned. "I. Bumped. My. Head," I said through clenched teeth.

"Go splash some water on your face and cool off." Theo dismissed me with a flick of his hand.

I rose from the table and stomped toward the hallway that led to the restrooms. In the ladies' room, I leaned over the sink and tried to rein in my anger. I had never felt this sick with jealousy before in my entire life. Blake brought out such extreme reactions in me. It was hard to identify my feelings properly.

My head was so confused. Seeing Simone with her lecherous hands on Blake made me want to rip the hair from her scalp. I was pretty sure this wasn't normal for someone you only had a crush on. The attraction was there all along with me and Blake. Obviously, or we wouldn't have hooked up in Vegas. But now it was different. I couldn't tell if it was a physical thing or with real emotions. *How can you differentiate in the beginning?*

One last deep breath and I felt ready to return. I pulled open the bathroom door and when I saw Blake waiting in the hallway and glaring at me, not even attempting to hide *his* anger, I knew what I felt for him was real. This was nothing close to having a crush.

My breath left me in a rush. I was an utter fool to have denied what I was feeling for so long.

"What the hell is wrong with you?" he demanded. I had never seen Blake so angry. His eyes were hard but I didn't drop my gaze from his. "You're sitting across from me looking like I just spat in your face."

I gasped. "I am not!"

"You are, Marley. You've been sending bitchy signals all night." Blake's voice was cold and unforgiving. "Ignoring everyone while we were eating, and I don't know how Simone hasn't noticed the looks you've been shooting her. Not to mention, what was it you said, 'yuppie bitches'? You think anyone missed the fact that was aimed for her?"

Adrenaline pumped through me, and I took a step toward him. I folded my arms across my chest. "I guess you must really like her, huh?"

Blake frowned. "What?"

"Well, the fact that she was thirty seconds from jerking you off under the table was a good indication that you're hot for her." My guts chewed with the raw intensity of my anger.

Blake held his hands up and stepped closer. "Wait a minute. *Her* hand was on *my* leg. Not the other way around. I kept trying to move it but she kept putting it back."

I rolled my eyes. Such a guy response.

This seemed to annoy him even more. He shoved his hand through his hair, the frustration pouring out of him. "What does it matter to you? It doesn't change anything."

"What's that supposed to mean?" A useless question, because I already knew the answer.

He narrowed his eyes, fully intent on spelling out the obvious to show just how unfair my jealousy was. "You're still with Theo. So what if Simone does want me? So what if we do hook up tonight? It's got nothing to do with you."

A hard lump formed in my throat but I didn't change my angry glare.

"So, what? You're the only one who gets to be happy?" There was a note of sorrow in Blake's voice as though all at once his anger had drained from him.

"No! I—"

"Then what do you want, Marley? *What do you want?*"

I gave a little groan before throwing myself onto him. I grasped handfuls of his suit jacket and smashed my lips against his. For a moment he kissed me back. His kiss manifested his anger. My lips felt bruised under their pressure.

Blake pushed me away. He grasped my wrist and pulled me around a corner. There was a door marked 'Staff Only' and a stack of crates. We stood on the other side of them, shielded from view should anyone turn the corner.

I pressed my back against the wall and Blake trapped me there, placing his palms either side of my head. My heart pounded. Blake hung his head, and I touched his hot cheek, lifting his face so he would look at me. His eyes were tortured. I ran a fingertip across his lips.

Blake sighed. "You're only doing this because you're jealous."

"No."

He gave me a look.

"Okay, yes, I was jealous." I forced down the rise of anger I felt when remembering Simone. "I've been telling myself for weeks that you're my friend, just my friend. I'm attracted to you and I thought it was just on a physical level, a crush that I would get over. But seeing her with her hands on you..."

"What are you saying?" Blake asked, his voice low and intimate.

"I wanted to scream that she was touching something that was mine. That you are mine and I belong to you and she had no fucking right." I panted, unable to catch my breath.

Blake's eyes searched my face for a long second before he dipped his head and caught me in a deep kiss. I knotted my hands in his hair, pinning his face to my own. Blake pulled my greedy cries into his mouth and his fingers bit into my hips. He ground his hips against me, and I moaned.

He broke the kiss, his chest rising and falling with heavy breaths. "You're sure about this?" Blake whispered.

I smiled but it felt wobbly, my body swimming with both relief that I was finally telling him the truth in my heart, and the overwhelming emotional connection that we were cementing. "More than anything."

His kiss was gentler this time. Blake snaked his arms around my back, holding my small body against his. I wanted to melt into his touch. Before, there had been white-hot passion fueling every kiss. But now...there was tenderness.

I could feel his lips curling into smiles as they moved over my own. I ran my fingers through his thick dark locks, the edge of his jaw and down his throat, drunk on the feel of him. Blake held me tighter, almost lifting me off my feet. Sliding my hands into his jacket, I tugged at his shirt, desperate to touch his skin.

Blake laughed breathily. "Marley…"

"Mmm?"

"Remember where we are."

Shit. I only needed reminding once before I was brought crashing back to reality.

Blake pulled back and stroked my face.

"Do I look like I've been doing what we've been doing?"

Blake chuckled. "A little. You're just flushed." He raised his head and cupped my cheek. "I've done nothing but think about kissing you again for weeks now."

I grinned and stood on my tiptoes to reach his lips. Blake would only let me have soft kisses, no dizzying passion for us right now. He gave my hand a little squeeze and kissed me once. Twice. Thrice.

With a sigh, I forced myself away from him.

Simone and Theo barely glanced at me as I dropped back down into my seat. I watched Theo carefully, looking for any sign of suspicion.

Blake returned a few minutes later, carrying a tray of drinks. He, also, paid little attention. Goodbyes said soon after. Simone tried in vain to persuade Blake to share a cab with her. He politely, but firmly, declined and walked back to his hotel instead. We hadn't arranged when we were to meet again, but we didn't need to. An unspoken promise passed between us when our eyes locked, right before Theo tugged me away.

* * * *

The following morning, Theo told me he was going out of town for a few days. That huge case again. He didn't go into details...and I didn't ask.

My first, and only thought, was Blake.

At eleven that night I knocked on his hotel room door. In the few seconds it took for him to answer, I had a fleeting moment of doubt.

In Vegas I had been impulsive and was taking something for myself. One night that I could remember and look back on when I was living out the rest of my stifling days. The kiss when we'd been drunk was a slip in judgment.

But this...this was a conscious decision to cheat on my fiancé.

With his best friend, who would be best man at our wedding.

Blake opened the door and any apprehension fell away with his surprised smile. He took my hand and pulled me inside. "What are you doing here?"

"Would you like me to go?" I teased.

Blake answered by giving me a wicked look. He tugged on my collar until our bodies were flush together and kissed me.

"Theo's out of town and I only had to work a half-night," I mumbled against his lips.

He slid my coat from my shoulders. "So...you thought you would come visit?"

I nodded. "Something like that."

"I'm glad you're here."

Any guilt that had chewed at my stomach evaporated at the sound of his gruff voice. He led me through the suite to his bedroom and my nerves disappeared.

It was just him and me.

In Vegas we'd been strangers. We'd acted on an immediate connection and mutual attraction...and had been fueled by passion.

We knew each other better now. I knew what made him smile, what would provoke a deep, throaty laugh and how to kiss him so he made a growl low in his chest. This time there was no need to rush. The tension had been building between us for weeks and now I could finally have him again.

I pushed Blake to sit on the edge of the bed and stood between his knees. Blake's eyes were locked with mine as I stepped out of my heels and unbuttoned my silk blouse. The soft fabric fluttered to the floor and Blake finally reached out to touch me. I shivered as he pressed his large, warm palm to my stomach and stroked my sensitive flesh. He moved his hand to my hip and Blake reached around to pull me a step closer. He unzipped my skirt and pulled it down.

His eyes roamed over me, and I felt like a million bucks in another La Perla black lace set with stockings. When Blake lifted his gaze to mine and I saw his heated look, a rush of pride coursed through me. He made me feel precious. He made me feel revered. He made me feel like I was his.

I pulled his undershirt over his head. Blake stood up and tossed the item aside. He grazed my cheek with his fingertips as I moved my hands to his pants. I unsnapped the button and finally managed to unzip them and let them drop to the floor. Blake grinned and grasped the backs of my thighs, lifting me into his arms. I gasped as my back hit the mattress. Blake knelt between my legs and unclasped each stocking, a shiver making its way down my spine as he eased them off. I sat up, and he unhooked my bra. I itched for his hands to be on me, to touch me everywhere.

But he went achingly slow — driving me to the brink of madness.

I thought I would combust as Blake slid my panties off. He kept his eyes on mine as he inched the material down my legs. By the time he reached my toes, my body was a live wire of excitement. With a cry, I reached for him and brought him down on top of me. I wrapped my legs around his waist, trying to bring him closer still. There was a glint of amusement in his eyes as Blake bent his head to finally kiss me, like he knew exactly what he was doing to me. But there was nothing funny in the way that man could kiss.

His lips molded to mine like they had been created in perfect harmony, and, as I sighed in either relief or pleasure, Blake eased his tongue inside, massaging my own. I loved his mouth, the feel of his soft lips…the rough scratch of a day's worth of stubble, but most of all the rumble of pleasure that I could feel in his chest.

Blake broke the kiss, both of us breathing heavily. He cupped my breasts and teased a nipple with the tip of his tongue, making the flesh feel full and heavy. He seemed to savor me and lingered with every touch, every taste. Blake roamed his fingers over every inch of me. My cunt throbbed, and I ached to feel his hands there.

Blake set my skin on fire. Each place he touched scorched and burned, and it felt like agony and bliss all at once. And finally, I felt him where I craved him most. Blake teased my slit, pushing his fingers back and forth and working me into a frenzy. My back arched off the bed as Blake circled my clit with his thumb and pushed a long finger deep inside me, pumping me with his hand. I was perilously close to climax when Blake moved his hand away and I cried out from the loss of contact.

"Not yet," Blake murmured, his voice rough and thick.

I threw a leg over his hip and used the momentum to roll him onto his back and straddle him. Stretching my body out over his, I understood why he'd taken so long with me. He hadn't gone slow to bring me to bursting point. He'd simply adorned every inch with the right amount of attention. I wanted to lie on top of him for eternity and map out every single piece of him.

I kissed his eyelids, his earlobe, his jaw, his throat. His pulse quickened under my lips. Shifting down him, I trailed my lips over his chest, tasting the flat disc of his nipple with my tongue. Blake knotted his hands in my hair and his breathing grew more labored as I inched south.

Sitting up, I hooked my fingers into his boxer briefs to tug them down. Before I could even touch him once they were gone, Blake clutched my wrist and pulled me back to him, rolling me onto my back.

My breath caught in my throat and I closed my eyes for a second, almost overwhelmed with the sensation of being skin to skin with him again.

Blake pushed the hair back from my face. "How does someone not fall in love with you?" he whispered before claiming my mouth. Blake shifted his hips, and I felt his hard cock at my entrance.

Our eyes locked as he eased inside and filled me. I gasped and wondered how I had denied myself this for so long. It felt like forever and yet I remembered the feeling of him like it was yesterday.

Blake pulled his hips back then slammed once again into me, filling me to the hilt. I cried out as he palmed my breast. He lowered his head to claim my lips.

Blake made love to my mouth, his tongue hitting mine with the same rhythm as his dick.

I lifted my hips to meets his thrusts, and Blake grunted, pounding into me harder, harder. I lost myself, submitting completely to him. My body, my everything, belonged to him.

My orgasm built and I clenched my muscles around him as it rippled through my body. Blake gritted his teeth and thrust into me one last powerful time, and held it there as he came with me.

We lay like that, connected, together, as we fought to catch our breaths and wait for the fireworks to fade.

He kissed me — slow, gentle kisses that I felt all the way down to my toes — and I knew, without a doubt, that he owned me, body and soul.

* * * *

I slept for a few hours before I had to get up for work. Blake lay sleeping beside me and I wouldn't make the same mistake twice. Hovering above him, I ran my fingers across his cheek. He stirred, but didn't open his eyes.

"Blake..." I whispered.

He turned his head toward my voice. I ran my fingers through his short, dark locks, and Blake clasped my wrist, pulling me into his body. I smiled and kissed him, lightly, and just enjoyed the feeling of his mouth. Blake made a sleepy, contented noise. He rolled toward me and stretched. A sleepy grin broke out over his lips. "Morning."

"Morning," I whispered. "I have to go."

Blake moved me under him and nuzzled my throat. "No."

I laughed but shimmied closer somehow. "Yes."

"Play hooky," Blake whispered in my ear.

God, I want to… "I can't."

At last Blake cracked his eyes open, and my stomach fluttered as they locked with mine. He grinned, a wicked gleam in his eyes. "Bet I could change your mind."

Easy bet. I giggled and kissed him. "I'm going."

"Go then," Blake murmured against my lips. He caught my leg and hitched it across his hip.

More than anything I wanted to have this just be one of a million mornings I got to wake up beside him. But it wasn't, and this bubble we were in would burst, which made it all the harder to leave him. "I only woke you because I didn't want to leave without saying anything again."

Blake's body tensed. *Is he thinking about waking up in Vegas in an empty bed?*

I ran my thumb over his stubble. "Even then, I hated leaving you."

Blake raised himself onto his elbow to peer down at me. "Can't say it was fun being left. Why did you?"

I shrugged and dropped my eyes. "I figured it would be easier. I didn't want to have to do the whole 'last night was great, see you around' thing with you."

"A goodbye would have been nice. But I get it. I understand."

I glanced back up at him. "Was it bad? Waking up to find me gone?"

"It was confusing." Blake dropped onto his back and chuckled. "That kind of thing just doesn't happen to me. I don't get blown off, especially not after a night like that."

My forehead creased with a frown. The mental pictures I was getting were not fun. Not in the least.

Blake reached up to stroke my cheek and smirked. "I'm not saying I was a big man whore who had hookups night after night. I wasn't even thinking of our night together as a one-time thing. Not until I realized you were gone, at least. I knew I was coming out here and wanted to see you when I did. That morning I concocted a thousand different excuses for what might have happened to you. You had to leave to get your flight, that kind of thing. I was even going to try to find you."

"What?" I asked, unable to keep the smile from my lips.

Blake smirked. "Well I do have a fair amount of power in the hotel. I asked at reception, fully aware that I was acting like a chick. The only information I had was the room number we stopped at the night before and your first name."

My stomach sank at the realization that there would have been no record of me at all. "Hayley arranged everything. It was all in her name."

"I know. I could have gotten her details from the system and found you through her."

"Why didn't you?" I asked.

Blake shrugged. "Ethics, mainly. I didn't want to find you that way."

The thought of Blake trying to find me had never occurred to me before. It gave me a little boost to think he'd wanted to. But I still felt bad for leaving him in the first place.

He smirked. "That day was a long one. I could barely concentrate on anything."

"I'm sorry," I said, desperate to move away from the painful topic. "Meet me tonight."

"Where?" Blake's lips twitched in amusement.

I smiled. "Well, what do you feel like doing?"

He grinned before capturing my mouth.

What was the use in resisting?

Surprisingly I made it on time to work and sported a very happy smile. A relaxed and satisfied buzz took over my body as I completed the day's tasks, safe in the knowledge that later that night I was awaited by a gorgeous specimen of a man with takeout and a movie.

* * * *

"What are we watching?" I asked, sinking into the luxurious couch with a carton of Chinese food and chopsticks.

Blake held up a DVD case.

I beamed. "It's my favorite."

He rolled his eyes. "I thought as much. You really are a twisted little freak, aren't you?"

I threw a pillow at him, which he dodged with little effort. He put the movie on, and I was soon lost in John Carpenter's intense thriller with Michael Meyers on a murderous rampage.

Blake jumped beside me when Jamie Lee Curtis stumbled upon her murdered friends.

I couldn't help it. I turned to face him and laughed. "Are you scared?"

He scoffed. "No."

"Are you?"

"I don't get how you can enjoy people getting hacked up by a psycho. That's not entertainment in my book." Blake scowled.

"Why? Because you're scared?"

He pounced and knocked me onto my back, tickling me mercilessly.

When the tears were streaming down my face and I gasped for air, Blake stopped his cruel torment. He didn't shift away from me, instead studied my face before taking my breath away in a different way. A better way.

I wrapped my legs around his waist as his kiss deepened. Blake pushed my skirt up around my waist and shoved my underwear aside. He teased my cleft before pushing a single finger inside me. My breath caught as he pumped me with his hand, and I reached for his belt buckle.

There was a frenzy to our actions that I hadn't experienced before — not with Blake, not with anyone. I needed him like I needed food or water and I needed him *now*.

Blake kissed me harder as I slipped my hand inside his pants and took his hard-on in my hand. He groaned as I stroked him, and he slid another finger inside my cunt.

"Blake," I whispered, stroking up his impressive length faster and faster.

He pushed his pants down, and in a heartbeat I felt him poised at my entrance. Blake held my eye as he eased inside, inch by inch until he filled me. I lifted my hips as he withdrew and pushed back inside.

I clutched his biceps, the muscles corded under my hands. The strength of his body poured out of him and I wanted everything he was capable of giving me until I felt bruised and sated.

"Blake," I whispered, pleading.

He grunted his response and slammed into me, again, again, again, and I clung onto him tighter as the beginnings of my orgasm swirled. Blake lunged for my throat, sucking on my hammering pulse. I cried out and threw my arms around his neck, his breath hot against my skin.

Blake took me faster. He was frantic, passionate. He fucked me quickly, hard and thoroughly. "Fuck, Marley. I need you," he growled.

"Then take me," I said, my voice rough and labored.

He grasped my thigh and threw my leg over his shoulder, hitting me deeper with his cock. My back arched with the new way he filled me, once again straddling that delicious line between pleasure and pain. I wrapped my other leg around his lower back, holding onto him as he fucked me harder.

I panted as my orgasm built, my nails scoring the flesh of his back, as it ripped through my body, unflinching and all-consuming. Blake barked out a cry as my inner muscles clenched and rippled around his dick. He gave one last thrust and spilled his seed inside me.

Blake dropped his head to my shoulder, and I stroked his face, his back, as we lay there in various states of undress. Blake's dick softened inside me but he didn't move, seemingly content to lie with me.

After a time, Blake pulled the rest of our clothes off. We lay naked on the couch, barely an inch of our skin not touching. The blue screen from the TV cast a soft glow over our bodies. Blake kissed everywhere his lips could reach and his fingers touched the areas his lips couldn't.

It was blissful and perfect. I never wanted it to end. I sighed, hating myself already for what would come next. "I should go."

"Why?" Blake murmured, nibbling my earlobe.

I squeezed my eyes shut. "I don't know when Theo comes home. He knows I don't work tonight and would have too many questions if I'm not there when he gets back."

Blake's body had tensed the instant I'd mentioned his best friend. He pulled away from me, which wasn't easy, even on a couch as large as this. Though the majority of our bodies still remained pressed together, he felt a million miles away from me. I itched to pull him back into me, to tell him to forget what I'd said. It didn't matter. *Kiss me again. I'll stay.*

But I didn't.

Blake searched my face. "You're staying with him."

I looked down. *God, I was a disgusting human being.* "I have to."

He sighed and scrubbed a hand over his face. "You don't have to do anything, Marley."

My stomach knotted. "You don't understand."

"Then tell me." It almost sounded like a plea. Like all he wanted was to understand. And damn it, I wanted to give it to him.

"I — Theo has done a lot for me. More than I can say. I can't leave him." And I wouldn't. Not even for Blake.

"Do you even love him?"

No. "Yes."

Blake narrowed his eyes. "And you think he loves you?"

I answered carefully. "I think he loves me the best he can."

Blake arched an eyebrow. "And what would you do, if you found out he had cheated?"

I rolled my eyes, trying to lighten the atmosphere. "Please, Theo barely has time to be with me. In what life would he have time for his job, me and a mistress?"

Blake remained silent.

"Did you think I was leaving him?" I placed a hand to his cheek.

He smiled though it held no warmth. "Of course not. It was just strange to hear you talk about going home to him. That's all."

My heart squeezed. If only he knew. If only he realized how hard I was falling for him, how I wished it was just him and me with no complications.

Chapter Nine

The wedding inched closer day by day. I viewed it with impending doom rather than eternal bliss. Blake didn't mention the ticking clock hanging over our heads and neither did I. It seemed stupid to ruin what time we had by talking of the one thing that kept us from being together. Sometimes it was unavoidable, like when Blake had come over to the apartment as I'd been trying to figure out the seating arrangement. He'd gotten all weird and stuttery and had made his excuses to leave. Theo had arched an eyebrow at him but hadn't commented on his friend's behavior. Instead of acknowledging the situation, I ignored it completely and hoped if I avoided it long enough, everything would work out the way it was supposed to. Won't hold my breath on that one.

A week after the seating arrangement incident, I left the office for the day and found Blake leaning against the building wall.

"Oh! Hi," I said, grinning from ear to ear.

"Afternoon."

"Not that I'm not pleased to see you, but what are you doing here?"

Blake smiled. "I left my jacket at your apartment the other week. I was passing by and thought it might be nice to walk you home."

"It would be very nice."

As always, I itched to kiss him and lace my fingers with his. But I couldn't do any of that. To the rest of the world we were nothing more than friends and it would be disastrous to behave otherwise.

We fell into step with each other, swapping little nuggets of information about our days. It was a real struggle to walk with a little distance between us. My insides felt like metal and Blake was a high-powered magnet. My list of favorite things about Blake grew day by day. It ranged from his arms, his bottom lip, to the small ways he liked to surprise me. Though he had the cash to splash around, he wasn't extravagant and knew it was the little things that meant more to me than expensive gifts or meals.

And a surprise walk home was one of those things.

As we stepped inside the apartment, the round table in the middle of the hall was adorned with a huge bouquet of mixed roses. No doubt one of Theo's lackeys had let themselves in to leave the gift.

"Seems someone else decided to surprise you today," Blake murmured. "I didn't think Theo had this kind of romance in him."

I snorted a laugh. "He doesn't. When Theo sends flowers, it's either because he's let me down or is about to."

Blake arched an eyebrow. "So what's he done?"

I plucked the small white card nestled among the flowers. "We had dinner plans for tonight. I'm guessing I'm about to be blown off." I read the card and smirked. "'Marley, can't make it tonight. I'm sorry. Theo.' Told you."

Blake nodded but remained silent.

I wanted to ask him if he'd like to do anything, but I couldn't bring myself to. Not because I didn't want to spend time with him—I did, more than anything. But I was worried he would think that I thought him to be second best.

Blake disappeared farther into the apartment and came back moments later clutching his jacket.

"Are you going already?" I asked. *God, why am I such a pussy?* I was always too scared of the repercussions of everything to ever take the Big Step and sort out all my messes. I was too scared of hurting Blake's feelings to ask him to stay with me for a little while. I was too scared of upsetting Theo and damaging everything I cared about by leaving him and being with the man I wanted to be with. *Pussy! Pussy! Pussy!*

"Yeah, I have some things to do." Blake hesitated at the door. He turned back around to face me and glided his thumb down my cheek. It was the most contact either of us would allow inside the apartment. It was a rule we never discussed but both knew it existed. It seemed worse somehow, to fool around with Blake in the place Theo owned and lived in— well, if you could call it that.

"I'll see you soon?" I asked, panic starting to rise in my throat.

He gave me a smile that was barely even there. "Of course." Blake ducked out of the apartment and closed the door behind him.

I took a step toward the door, to where Blake had stood mere moments before. I squeezed my eyes shut and prayed he would come back.

I couldn't chase after him. He'd closed the door to himself when he'd closed the door to the apartment. I would only be allowed back in when he opened it, not when I charged after it.

I had the awful feeling down deep in the pit of my stomach that something serious had just happened. It needed to be fixed before it was irreparable, I just didn't know how. Duh! Of course I knew how, I just couldn't. *I wonder if I go for a nap will everything be better when I wake up?*

* * * *

"What is with you tonight?" Angela asked, as I rewrote another wrongly crossed off name.

"Nothing. I'm fine." *Fine.* I'd said that so many times today it didn't even sound like a word anymore.

My mind was sidetracked, and no matter how hard I tried, I just could not focus on work. The thing with Blake the day before still had my head reeling. The steady pounding of music from inside did nothing to help me concentrate. If anything, it made it harder.

A couple made their way toward me and gave me their names. I searched and searched but couldn't see them on my list. Just as I was about to accuse them of trying to gatecrash, Angela ripped the clipboard from my clutches.

"Here you are. Go on in, guys. Have a great night." Angela beamed at the couple before turning her smile into a quizzical look at me.

"Sorry," I rushed before she could say anything. "I didn't see their names."

Angela sighed. "You're no use to anyone tonight. Do us all a favor and go home."

I opened my mouth to argue back, but thought better of it and closed it again.

"Better still, aren't your friends inside?" Angela asked.

I nodded.

Angela gave me a little push toward the club doors. "Then go get a drink. I'll see you tomorrow."

I definitely wasn't going to argue with that. I felt lighter as I pushed my way through the throng of people to get to the bar for a much needed Cosmo. I felt lighter still when I finally got to Hayley's table and the girls gave a little cheer when they saw me.

"Awesome. Do you have the rest of the night off?" Hayley asked.

"Yes, thank God! I can't make my brain work right."

Beth laughed. "I don't think mine ever did."

I let the chatter wash over me, taking more of my worries away. I really should have made more of an effort to socialize with the girls. It was amazing what girl time could do for me. Before long I was laughing with them and finding the gossip fascinating, and after a few cocktails and shots, my worries weren't gone, but in that protective pink girlish bubble, I felt more at ease than I had in days.

"So...any reason for your malfunctioning brain?" Hayley inquired as we got a fresh round of cocktails at the bar.

I arched an eyebrow. "Why?"

"Because I think the reason is over there." Hayley nodded behind me.

I turned and saw Blake talking to someone. I strained as the lights pulsed and saw he wasn't talking, he was yelling. The lights shifted and I saw he was with Simone.

What the hell is Lawyer Barbie doing here?

Jealousy surged through me. She was here with him. Of course she was. I couldn't get mad. I was hardly the poster child for fidelity. The only thing that gave me comfort was the look of sheer rage on Blake's face. He was definitely mad at her for something.

I turned back to Hayley and grabbed the tray of drinks.

"You okay there?" she asked.

"Peachy."

"Okay, Miss Regression," Hayley muttered, as I brushed past her.

We fought our way through the thick crowd to get back to our seats. The calm that had worked itself through my body was shot to hell now I knew Blake and I were under the same roof. Having Simone here definitely didn't help any, and though my curiosity was damn near killing me, a huge part of me didn't want to know what they were arguing about. Ignorance is bliss and all that jazz.

"You gone and got a new lifestyle choice on us, Marley?" Beth asked, snapping my attention back to the present.

"What?"

"That chick over there is totally staring," Beth said.

I turned to where they were looking and sure enough, Simone was staring at me with an expression I couldn't quite read. As soon as my eyes met hers, her lips twisted into a smile. *Shit.*

"She works with Theo." I sighed. "I should go and say hi."

Hayley and I shared a look before I rose from my chair and made my way toward Simone. With each stride, my game face became more realistic.

"Simone! Hi!" I said. "I didn't know you come here."

"Sometimes." Simone smiled.

"Next time let Theo know. He can make sure I get you on the list."

Simone's eyes widened. "No, no. That's all right. I don't get to come out much and when I do, it tends to be last minute."

I nodded and smiled. *Suit yourself, you stuck-up bitch.*

"Aren't you working tonight?" Simone asked.

"I was. They let me off early since my girlfriends are here." *Damn, now I'm going to have to remember to tell Theo before Blondie here tattles on me.*

"How nice."

I nodded again. There wasn't really a whole lot I could say to this woman. Well, nothing that she wouldn't take offense to, anyway. "I should get back to my friends," I said.

"Of course."

"I'll see you around."

"I'm sure."

I breathed a sigh of relief once I was walking away from her. I scanned the room for Blake but I couldn't see him anywhere. The second I thought of him, I ached to be near him. Even if it was uncomfortable and awkward I didn't care, I just had to be near him. Back at the table, I swallowed the rest of my drink. "Guys, I think I'm gonna take off."

"Marley, you are so boring! It's still early," Eve said.

I laughed. "It's almost two."

Eve rolled her eyes. "Whatever. You never come out to play. You should stay longer."

I grinned at her and her face brightened. *Huh, I must have one of those faces.*

"Hello," Eve said in her most charming and seductive voice.

I narrowed my eyes—she wasn't looking at me.

Blake's almost timid response came from behind me. "Uh, hello."

As I spun around, the rabbit caught in the headlights look on his face was unmistakable. I should have been pleased by Blake's obvious discomfort under Eve's hungry stare, but right now I was just so happy to see him again. "Hi," I breathed.

"I thought I saw you. Can I get you a drink?" Blake asked.

"She was just leaving, but I'm parched," Eve said.

Some girls just have no shame.

Blake didn't even look at her. "Let me walk you."

I nodded and mumbled my goodbyes to the girls. I was really glad shooting daggers from one's eyes is a metaphor, otherwise my back would have been a bloody mess, thanks to Eve. It would take her, oh, all of five minutes to forget about the delectable dish that was Blake.

"I saw you arguing with Simone," I blurted the moment we were walking in the night air and free from the noise of the club.

Blake searched my face and seemed to choose his words carefully. "She was…being a little forthcoming and it was hard to get the message through to her."

I nodded again. *Poor girl.* It must be heartbreaking to want Blake and not get to have him. I laughed ruefully—damn, I could have been talking about myself there.

Blake arched an eyebrow but didn't question my out of place laugh.

"I missed you," I said in a rush before I had time to talk myself out of admitting my feelings.

One corner of his lips pulled up. "You only saw me yesterday."

Crap. Does he think I'm being too clingy?

I shrugged. "It felt weird when you left, like something major had happened, but I didn't know what."

Blake placed a hand on my arm to stop me. "Something did happen, Marley. I felt like I was intruding on someone else's life. You and Theo have a life together. It may not be perfect, but it's still there and I have no right forcing myself into it."

My heart pounded so fiercely I was sure it would explode from my chest. The fear that coursed through me seemed to mock me, taking pleasure in my pain. This couldn't happen, not now. I couldn't say goodbye to him. I couldn't not have him in my life, no matter how disastrously this all might end.

"You *do* have a right! I'm giving you that right!"

Blake looked down.

"It doesn't feel like you're the outsider," I rushed. "When I'm with you, it's like coming home."

Slowly, Blake lifted his eyes to mine. He seemed to consider my declaration for a moment. "You have to know that this... It can't—"

"Shh..." I stepped toward him and silenced him with my finger on his lip. God, I loved that lip. I focused on it as I stepped forward again so I was pressed right up against his body. I traced his lip with my finger and he shuddered under my touch. Blake's breath was uneven as it wafted over my face. With the faintest amount of pressure, I brushed my lips against his.

Without breaking our kiss, Blake maneuvered us into the dark alleyway behind me. The fact that anyone at all could have been watching didn't even register with me. His body against mine was pretty much all I could think about.

Blake dug his fingers into my hips as he held me. I wound my hands in his hair, forbidding him to move his face even a millimeter away. This kiss wasn't like our others. Normally they were so fueled with passion I could think of nothing but my burning desire for him. But this kiss? This kiss belonged in a box so I could take it out and relive it over and over again forever.

I could feel the frantic thrum of Blake's heart, its tempo matching my own. With every breath I took, the harder I fell for him. Blake's words rang in my ears and I tried to force them away, I wouldn't let them ruin this beautiful kiss.

Of course I knew what he was going to say. 'This can't last forever.' One day—who knew when?—this would all have to come to a close. This kiss told me we both knew this, but right now we didn't care. I would gladly trade the pain of having to say goodbye someday over not needing to say it at all.

Blake's lips curved into a smile, his breath tickling me as he chuckled. "You know, they have a name for girls who make out in alleys," he mumbled against my lips.

"Shut up and kiss me."

* * * *

There was a new purpose in my life. Before Blake, I'd focused on work as a means of distraction, but I now had a more…pleasurable distraction. I hated working nights and being away from him.

It grew harder to spend time together. At work I managed to drop a full night and make my half-night a regular occurrence. Theo still worked all the hours God provided him with, but he questioned every move I made. I told him I'd started a late-night yoga class and didn't tell him about my reduced hours at work. But even with those allotted times to spend uninterrupted with Blake, it was never enough.

I could see how much Blake hurt when I left his suite to hurry home to my fiancé. I'd created a world of mess but couldn't see an escape, a way off the merry-go-round. Round and round we went in a circle, never moving forward and never breaking the pattern.

Blake would often appear at the office to take me out for lunch. A lot of people knew we were friends, so we didn't arouse suspicion. The only thing I did notice was how Blake stopped spending as much time with Theo. It crushed me to imagine how immense Blake's guilt must have compared with my own. I felt like a disgusting person, but with an addiction that I couldn't get my fill of.

The differences between Theo and Blake became too obvious to ignore. One day Theo took me out for brunch and ordered me a bacon, lettuce and tomato baguette. *Hello!* Didn't he know anything about me at all? And the following day Blake took me to the theater where the new slasher movie was showing. He sat through it—well, grimaced through it was a more accurate description—all because he knew I was dying to see it, even though he was terrified the entire time.

Blake was edgy as we walked back to his hotel after the movie. I giggled when he jumped at yet another shadow.

He turned to glare at me. "I'm glad *you* find it funny."

"I'm sorry. I just can't believe you're so scared." I smirked.

"Yeah, well," Blake mumbled.

"Well, rest easy. Look—you can see your hotel, all nice and bright, no scary shadows."

Blake mumbled something incoherent, but I was pretty sure there were some unrepeatable words in there somewhere. It was a job not to laugh at him. He was silent all the way up in the elevator then even when he unlocked his door and stalked into the suite. I closed the door behind me and went off in search of him.

Damn. The movie must have scared him worse than I'd thought, if the full Scotch glass he was drinking from was anything to go by.

"Want to watch TV?" I asked, dropping onto the couch and searching for the remote. What was it about couch cushions that made such appealing homes for paraphernalia like remotes, cell phones, change and keys?

Blake shook his head and took another gulp of his Scotch.

I frowned. "Are you okay?"

"Yeah, I'm fine."

I resisted the urge to roll my eyes. Instead I got up and slowly made my way across the room. There were few times I agreed with pandering to the fragile male ego. But this time was deserving. "You know, that has to be one of the most romantic things anyone has ever done for me."

Blake twisted around to look at me. He searched my face, trying to tell if I was being serious. "What?"

"I know you don't really like horror movies, but the fact that you took me anyway, it was really sweet. Definitely makes the top five."

"Don't really like horror movies?" Blake repeated slowly. "Marley, I feel the same way about horror movies as you do about tomatoes."

My eyes widened. "Seriously? You don't just prefer not to see them?"

He laughed. "Oh I definitely prefer not to see them, but there's just something about watching them that turns me into a five-year-old. Girl. With pigtails."

I felt like I was looking into the innermost workings of his soul. There was something beautiful about seeing him so vulnerable and honest. I'd never been more attracted to someone in my entire life as I was to Blake in that very moment.

My heart gave a little pang and I inched closer. "And you still took me? Even though it was so hard for you?"

Blake smiled crookedly. "I knew you wanted to see it."

"Then forget what I said. It doesn't make the top five. You just broke the record." I kissed his cheek, which reddened almost instantly.

Blake took another gulp of Scotch. "So did you say something about watching TV? I think I could use the distraction right about now."

I clutched his shirt collar and tugged him closer before grinning wickedly. "I can think of a better one."

He raised his eyebrows. "Oh, yeah?"

Nodding, I clasped my hands behind his neck and pulled him down so I could reach his lips. Just as Blake parted his mouth to deepen our kiss, I broke away. I caught his hand and led him into his bedroom.

"I really like your shirts. Have I ever told you that?" I asked, unbuttoning it.

Blake cleared his throat. "No, I don't think you have."

"They look like they were made for you. They fit like a glove." I unsnapped the last button and ran my hands up his chest to his shoulders, pushing the shirt off him.

His lips twitched. "Is this the part where you say you like them, but prefer them on the floor?"

I smiled. "Something like that. But seeing you in your shirts? Instant turn-on."

Blake dipped his head to kiss me. "Well, I'm glad I have so many then."

After pulling his undershirt over his head, I dropped his pants and boxer briefs then ushered him onto the bed. Blake's eyes never left me as I slowly unzipped my dress and let it pool at my feet.

He settled himself in the middle of the bed, lounging against the pillows with his hands tucked beneath his head. "You may like my shirts...but I fucking love your taste in underwear. And this set looks familiar."

Glancing down, I realized he was right. This was the set I'd worn the night we met. I smiled again and reached around to unhook the bra. It fell to the floor and I shimmied out of my panties. "I'm more fond of what happens when they come off."

Blake's eyes roamed over me as I crawled onto the bed and swung a leg over his hip, straddling his beautiful body. His hands found my hips, his fingers kneading the flesh and his eyes were so hot and fierce they seared into me.

I leaned over, my breasts brushing his chest as I kissed him, softly at first—gentle, teasing kisses that slowly burned us until the fires roared in our veins. Blake's hands drifted around my hips, his thumb rubbing circles over my clit.

Swallowing a gasp, I rocked against his hand. Blake increased his pressure, and I cried out. Before he could finish what he was expertly starting, I lifted off his lap to position his hard-on at my entrance. Blake swallowed as I eased myself onto him, taking all of him inside.

My body stretched to accommodate the size of him. Blake teased one of my nipples before pushing upright to take it in his mouth. I clutched his shoulders as I lifted off his length to then plunge back down.

Blake gripped my hips as I increased my speed, desire fueling my every thought.

We came together, both of us panting and grasping at the other.

He kissed my shoulder, flickering his tongue out to taste a bead of sweat. "That was one hell of a distraction."

Chapter Ten

Theo knew. Either that or an alien parasite had taken over his body and turned him into a different non-Theo-type person. It wasn't just that he was acting weird. It was that he was acting really weird. He'd arrived home from work not long after me and announced that we were doing something. He hadn't told me what, just frog marched me into the bathroom and started filling the tub with hot water. He'd added different scents and bubble bath, kissed me on the forehead then told me to take my time and not show my face until I was well and truly relaxed.

I'd planned on spending the evening with Blake. Was that what all this was about? Had Theo somehow found out and was now monopolizing my time so I couldn't get the chance to see Blake? Logic told me this was doubtful. There was no way on this earth Theo would be capable of acting calm and collected if he knew. Cold and calculating, yes.

My cell phone was in the living room, along with Theo. I couldn't even call Blake to let him know I'd be late, or that I wouldn't be there at all since I had no clue what Theo was plotting. The best I could hope for was a quick text when Theo wasn't looking.

I spent an hour in the tub and only got out because I began to wrinkle beyond repair. My stomach twisted in knots and I sat on the lip of the tub chewing my fingernails—a mixture of worry over what to do about Blake and what Theo had up his sleeve. But I couldn't hide forever and finally plucked up the courage to leave the safe confines of the bathroom.

There was nothing scary to greet me. No furious Theo ranting in my face and demanding explanations. What did greet me was perhaps eerier than my erratic wonderings. Lying flat out on the bed was a stunning black dress. Upon closer inspection, I discovered it was from the new Chanel spring-summer line—black dress with jacquard organza and vinyl lace—and a gorgeous pair of pumps to match. Huh.

Was Theo lulling me into a false sense of security before he ripped the rug out from under me? Maybe…maybe not. Theo wasn't known for his patience. But whatever it was he had in store for me, I knew it was major.

I took my time getting ready. I figured if I was going down, I may as well do it looking good. I scooped my hair up and piled it on top of my head, leaving my neck bare. This kind of dress didn't need accessories— a pair of diamond studs was enough. Anything more would have been overkill.

I slid my feet into the shoes and stood up, brushing invisible lint away. With a deep breath, I walked into the lounge where Theo awaited me. He wasn't underdressed, that was for sure. He wore a classic tux with white scarf, his hair slicked back.

Theo smiled and walked to my side. He took my hand and kissed the back of it. "Come on. We're going to be late."

"For what?"

"You'll see."

Theo remained secretive in the car and refused to give in to my mounting curiosity. I arched an eyebrow at him as he helped me out of the car on Columbus Avenue in front of the David H. Koch Theater at Lincoln Center, Plaza but all he did was smile knowingly. I'd always loved the Lincoln Center at night. It looked beautiful with its golden lights highlighting the huge arched windows. It didn't matter what I was there for—the moment I stepped onto the burgundy red carpet in the lobby, the night just felt magical. The lobby at the David H. Koch Theater was more modern with its marbled floor and huge statue behind the information desk. The sheer size was awe-inspiring. The levels that spanned the place seemed to go on forever, beautiful prints of ballerinas in motion lining the walls.

It wasn't a surprise anymore that Theo had taken me to the ballet. His firm had season tickets, so they could take important clients and wow prospective ones. Luckily for me, Theo had been allowed the use of the fifth ring seats that night. But the fact that he'd brought me at all was a shock.

Only minutes into the performance, I was lost to the story. I didn't get to go to the ballet very often, so this was a rare treat for me. Theo retrieved more champagne during intermission and chatted about his day. I was much too distracted to listen. Half my brain was swirling with the images of beautiful dancers and eager for the rest of the story. The other half was still wondering what he was up to.

No force could have swayed my eyes as Giselle and Albrecht danced their last dance. Childlike, I wanted a different ending. I wanted a way for them to be together. I couldn't accept that there was no happy ending for them. Perhaps to others, the ending could be perceived as happy. But as long as they weren't together, it could never be classed as happy to me.

After the dancers had taken their bow and the lights had come up, Theo extended a hand to help me to my feet. Instead of dropping it when I rose, he didn't let go.

Puzzled, I looked up at him. His face looked just as bemused as mine surely did in that moment. A little crease formed between his brows and he raised his free hand to brush my cheek. "You're crying."

"It was sad."

I expected him to sneer and mock me. All he did was give my hand a little squeeze and escort me out. He didn't once drop his hold. In the car he was silent. I itched to watch him, to see if I could read his face. Of course I was too chicken. Our still interlocked fingers were all I was brave enough to look at.

Unsurprisingly, Theo headed for his office the second we were home. He must have had a lot of work to catch up on after wasting some of his valuable hours.

My head ached from having my hair up and my roots were screaming to be let loose. After slipping off my shoes, I padded barefoot across the bedroom to sit at the dressing table. I let my hair fall naturally past my shoulders after the last pin was removed. The painful relief made me shudder, and I ran my fingers gingerly through my hair.

Just as I was about to reach for my purse to get my phone, in the mirror's reflection a figure moved in the doorway. I jumped and banged my knee under the table. I groaned and massaged it, feeling my cheeks burn.

"I'm sorry, I didn't mean to startle you," Theo said, moving toward me. He sat beside me on the bench, his body still facing the door. He slowly raised a hand and ran it through my hair. "You look nice like this. Natural."

"Thank you," I said, a lump forming in my throat.

"Not that you didn't look nice before, when you were all done up, I just mean—"

"I know what you mean," I said, giving him a shaky smile.

He dropped his eyes. "I know I'm not around as much as I should be. I wanted you to know I'm sorry."

My stomach shifted, feeling unsettled, and I didn't have the faintest idea what to expect. I wasn't used to this Theo. "It's okay. I work a lot too."

"I have a feeling that's because of how much I work."

I shrugged. "Maybe a little. I'm not the kind to sit around doing nothing."

Theo nodded. "I wanted to take you out tonight and show you a good time. It seems like such a long time since we did anything, just the two of us. I shouldn't neglect you as much as I do. I can be selfish sometimes."

"You work hard," I said, struggling to find the right words.

"Yes. I wish I could say that I'll cut back on hours, but I can't. What with a promotion in the works and all the new cases we're taking on right now—"

"Theo, it's okay. I understand."

"But no matter how busy I am, I'm always thinking of you."

My heart sank, not at the words, but with the sincerity that shone through them.

Theo stood up and kissed the top of my head. "I have some work to do. Try to get a good night's sleep for once."

A new, strange sensation took over my body. My head and heart pounded so hard it made me feel physically sick. My stomach twisted in knots and all I wanted to do was flip a switch in my brain and turn everything off — my thoughts, my body, everything.

I rose from my place at the dressing table and pulled my dress off. It wasn't until I got changed for bed and slid between the sheets, finally able to rest my weary head, that I realized what the feeling was.

Guilt.

I'd felt guilty about what I was doing to Theo before, but this was different. I felt cruel and inhumane and I sickened myself. Was this how Blake felt? He had known and loved Theo a hell of a lot longer than I had so it was only logical to think that his guilt would be more powerful than mine.

My guilt was a demon growing larger inside my body, chewing through every organ and destroying all my humanity. I felt like a dirty wretch, more for one reason than any other.

This new guilt though? It wouldn't be enough to keep me from seeing Blake.

* * * *

The day after Theo had taken me to the ballet, I got a phone call from my mother. She was clearing out the garage and had found a few of my old things I might be interested in seeing. There was a strange tone to her voice and I suspected it was more a visit from her daughter she wanted, rather than anything to do with some old junk.

I took the train upstate to my childhood home with my mind still swirling. The familiar scenery passed in a blur and it did nothing to distract me. The sun shone on my back as I walked from the station toward my parents' house. They lived in a typical suburban neighborhood with white picket fences, neighbors watering their lush green lawns and children dashing through the sprinklers in their bathing suits.

It had been nice growing up here, if not a little monotonous. And if I hadn't lived in the town where nothing happened, I might not have gotten the push needed to move to the big city and live my own life.

Maybe all I'd done was trick myself into thinking I had my own life. Maybe Theo's chain was just long enough for me to forget that it was there in the first place.

Theo.

I shook his face from my mind. How could I still think badly of him after last night? Theo never showed a soft side and definitely never showed any emotion, let alone affection. There was something about the whole situation I couldn't put my finger on. It was like trying to remember something I had forgotten. It was right there on the cusp of my mind, ready to be remembered, only just out of reach.

Every time I thought of Theo and my steadily mounting guilt, Blake would push his way forward, flash me his knowing smile and make me feel guilty for different reasons. It felt like I was cheating on both of them. Before, it had been easy to separate the two factors. Theo was my reality and Blake was my fantasy, the one I really wanted to be with. With Theo being cold and closed off it was all too easy to flip a switch and forget about him. But now he had shown feelings it wasn't so easy to flip the switch anymore.

It wasn't really even like I was torn between them, but enough emotion was involved for it to be a bloody mess. I wasn't a spiteful person, and I felt so unkind for doing what I was to Theo. But then my mind would move to Blake and I felt guilty for feeling guilty. Then I would remember why I was guilty in the first place... *God, what a mess.* I hadn't even spoken to Blake yet. The second I woke up that morning I'd tried to call him but it had gone straight to voicemail. I had never stood him up before, and last night couldn't have been pleasant for him.

I walked up the short driveway in front of my parents' house. There was noise coming from the open garage but I couldn't see the cause of it. "Knock, knock," I called.

My mother's head appeared above a stack of boxes. I laughed at her frazzled and dusty appearance. "Oh, hi!" She smiled. "I wasn't expecting you for hours."

I blushed. She didn't need to know that after hanging up the phone I'd trotted on down to get the next train.

She peered around me. "Where's the car?"

"I got the train. I came myself."

"Oh. Is Theo busy?"

"He was going to the gym this morning and I think he was planning on dropping by the office this afternoon."

"That boy works too hard. He'll run himself into the ground."

I waved a hand. "Preaching to the choir, Mom."

"You hungry? I got fresh bagels this morning."

"Sure." I followed her deeper into the garage then in through the side door leading to the kitchen.

Freshly brewed coffee and that sweet bagel smell teased my nostrils, instantly making me feel at ease. My mom had such a homey kitchen. I remembered sitting with her many times after school and telling her about my day or sobbing in her arms after some teenage drama.

Most homes had a focal point. One room where everything seemed to happen, where everyone subconsciously congregated. In my parents' home, that room was the kitchen. We always sat at the island to have breakfast. Mom told us it was good to start the day as a family. Our comings and goings were forever erratic, but you could always count on us being together for breakfast. I was an only child and Mom had been desperate to cling to the family routine as long as possible, so our breakfast tradition had been rigidly held until I'd moved out.

I was sure there was something special about my parents' home and that's why Theo's apartment was such an enigma to me. Every friend I'd had growing up had wanted to hang out at my house and that was because of the atmosphere my mom set.

The outside of the house was painted a creamy yellow, the brightest on our street. Even from outside, the house beckoned. Inside was bright and airy for reasons beyond me. The kitchen was a brighter yellow than outside, but most of the other walls were cream, except for the bathroom, which was a pastel blue and my room, which was bright purple.

Ours was the freezer permanently stocked with ice pops. Ours was the oven the batch of cookies had just come from. Ours was the fridge that always housed the best snacks.

Ours was home, even to those who didn't live there.

I pulled out a stool at the island as Mom fussed around in the kitchen. I sipped the coffee she'd placed in front of me and watched her work. My mom was so interesting to watch. She was efficient and had an aura of order about her. How did moms do that? *Maybe they give you a guidebook after giving birth or something.* The only thing I was good at making was a mess. I'd never have my crap together the way Mom did.

"So...anything new?" Mom asked, sitting opposite me.

I shook my head, my mouth full of bagel.

"You sure?"

I paused in my chewing. *Okay, do I give off a pheromone when I have a troubled mind or something?* This woman always knew when something was bothering me. It was freaky. "I'm sure."

"Okay."

That right there was the biggest reason I loved my mom. She knew when to push and when to drop a subject. "How's Dad?"

"Oh, you know your father. Still scheming away. He managed to convince Hal to let him work a few mornings a week with him."

"Hal? At the hardware store?" I lowered my bagel onto the plate. "Are you serious?"

Mom sighed. "Marley, you know what he's like. He's so restless he can't sit still for more than a few seconds at a time. You don't think that trait of yours is hereditary?"

A smile pulled at the corner of my mouth. "Yeah, I guess we have that in common."

Mom dropped her gaze. "He hates not working. He's trying to get the business back."

I covered my mother's hand with my own. "You guys are doing okay, though, right?"

"Of course. It's all pride that spurs him on. The Dicksons down the street wouldn't stop bragging about their retirement home in California."

"Dad is so not ready to retire." I rolled my eyes.

Mom laughed. "Will he ever be? No, it's more like he sees what others have and can't help wishing—"

"He should be wishing for other things. Like staying healthy," I interrupted.

Mom shot me a sharp look.

"Sorry," I mumbled. "So. Where are these boxes?"

It was really only a few old yearbooks that Mom had found. For nostalgia's sake, I decided to keep them. They would occupy my time on the train. Mom gave me a ride back to the station, both of us keeping up a steady stream of cheerful chatter, neither of us saying what we really wanted to.

With my hand on the door handle, I turned to face my mother. "I don't visit enough. I should."

She smiled. "Don't worry about it. You've got your own life in the city. Don't be worrying about us old folks."

"I do, though. All the time."

Mom pulled me into a quick embrace. "Don't. We're fine—because of you."

Tears stung my eyes and I had to force myself out of her soft arms. I wanted to stay in them all day, to have her hold me and stroke my hair and sing to me in a low voice until everything was all better.

Mom chuckled. "You don't have to worry, Marley. We really are fine. You live your life. I'm so proud of you."

I prayed that my smile was genuine. "I'd better go. The train might leave without me."

She smiled. "I'll see you soon. A month and a half, perhaps?"

An invisible fist punched me in the gut, knocking the wind out of me. Where had the time gone? The wedding couldn't be that close, surely.

But it was.

* * * *

I lay staring at the ceiling until the morning light began streaming into the bedroom.

I'd tried calling Blake when I'd gotten back from seeing my mom. No answer. Not surprising. I'd tried again after dinner and before leaving for work. Still nothing.

The idea of going by his suite on the way home had been tempting, but I'd talked myself out of it. We were sure to have a fight of some kind and doing it when we were both dog tired was not the best idea.

It was agonizing, not being able to talk to him.

A run would help clear my mind. If I had to lie next to Theo while I was thinking about another man for one more second, I would lose my mind.

How could people do this to each other? I knew I was doing it, but my situation was unique, wasn't it? Other people sought out this kind of drama intentionally. I had never planned on falling like this for Blake. Sure, I had been of sound mind in Vegas and I'd known what I was doing. I guessed I'd just never banked on seeing him again.

During my run I let myself be drawn toward Blake's hotel. The fact that I looked like shit didn't even occur to me until I was knocking on his door. I tugged on my messy ponytail, wishing I had a comb or something.

The wait was excruciating. I bounced on the balls of my feet trying to figure out what had compelled me to do this. I was such a coward and hated people being mad at me. I wouldn't be able to rest until the air was cleared between us.

I knocked again, allowing myself another few minutes to wait.

My heart leaped into my throat as the door opened. Blake looked devastatingly handsome in a pair of boxer briefs with his hair disheveled and eyes barely open.

"Were you sleeping?" I asked, trying not to stare.

"I was. I heard a banging. It wouldn't go away."

I cringed. "Sorry about that."

"That's okay."

God, he's going to make me ask. "Can I come in?"

Blake moved aside, and I stepped into the suite. He padded into the lounge and dropped down onto the couch, scrubbing a hand over his face.

"I'm sorry," I said, swallowing the sudden lump that rose in my throat.

He yawned. "I already said it's okay."

"No, about Friday night."

Blake blew out a breath. "Can't say that was fun."

I sat beside him, wanting more than anything to reach out and touch him, but for the first time was unsure if I was welcome. "I'm so sorry, Blake. Theo blindsided me and I didn't get a chance to call you."

"Mar, it's fine." Blake chuckled. "I thought as much."

"I felt awful. I kept imagining you here, hating me."

He raised his hand to stroke my cheek, and I leaned into his touch. "I could never hate you."

I snorted. "Right. I do a pretty good job of hating myself most days." Wasn't that the truth. I was so close and, at the same time, so far from what I wanted most in the world. And somehow I'd created a shit storm in the process.

Blake slid closer to me and clasped both my hands. "What's wrong?"

"He took me out," I whispered, fearing my voice would break if I spoke any louder.

"Theo? Where?"

"The ballet, to see Giselle. Afterward he...he just said some things. I think he's really sorry about being away so much."

Blake puffed out his cheeks and blew out a long breath. "On Friday night? One night has you thinking like this?"

I frowned. He was right. Did one little night make up for all the absent ones? Not even close. But something had been different, and I said as much, "Something was different about him, Blake. Something got to him, made him want to try to make amends. At first I thought he found out about us. The last few days have been awful, Blake."

"So all his dream date did was make you feel guilty?"

That was an understatement. I dropped my head. "I feel so bad about this situation already without him turning into Mr. Nice Guy. And the fact that I couldn't get in touch with you to apologize... It all made me feel sick."

"Hey." Blake lifted my chin. "Forget about it. You didn't do it on purpose. And by the sounds of it, you don't need me to chew you out over this. You've done a good enough job yourself."

I let out a shaky breath, feeling the familiar stinging in my eyes. "It's all such a mess."

"You can walk away, you know. I wouldn't chase you."

Raw desperation coursed through my body. "*No. No.* Blake—"

He grabbed my wrist and hauled me onto his lap, banding his arms around my back. I burrowed my face into his neck, and Blake held me all the tighter.

"Marley." Blake's voice was rough and full of emotion.

"I know," I said, my own voice just as thick.

It was the closest we had ever got to defining our relationship. I wanted reassurance from him, but more than anything, I wanted to be able to give it to him. Neither of us was naïve enough to think we weren't living on borrowed time.

The minutes passed. My desperation had all but evaporated and I no longer felt quite so worked up. I enjoyed just being there in his arms, having him hold me like I was the most precious thing in his world. I sighed and tried to get closer to him.

But then it hit me.

Blake felt me go rigid in his arms. He tightened his grip and ran a hand down my hair. "What's wrong?"

"I'm sorry."

He chuckled. "What for now?"

"Hugging you."

"Think I can forgive you."

"No, I'm sorry for hugging you when I smell so bad. I've been running."

Blake's laughter rumbled in his chest. "Can't say I noticed." He shifted my ponytail to the other side, giving him access to kiss my neck.

I closed my eyes as the heat tore through me. "Blake—I'm disgusting."

His lips curved into a wicked smile. "Then by all means, let's get you in the shower."

Chapter Eleven

There came a point in every girl's life where she would come to dread birthdays. And yes, my twenty-fourth was a little early for this to be a problem. But it wasn't my age I worried about, it was the attention. The center of attention was never a place I craved to be. I preferred to sit in the shadows and observe the goings-on around me. I was a people-watcher, not an entertainer, and I liked it that way.

Theo had marked it in his calendar and his secretary sent a lovely bouquet of flowers. And who said romance was dead? So it didn't bother me in the slightest that Henry asked me to work the night of my birthday. There was an event at Tenjune in the Meatpacking District and we all had to dress up in our finest. Though it was meant to be my night off, I had no plans anyway. Blake was in Vegas and wasn't due back until the day after tomorrow. Theo was working and Hayley and the other girls were out of town on an impromptu trip.

Dressed in my favorite Marc Jacobs little black dress with pencil skirt, and sporting my new Jimmy Choos,

I headed for work. I didn't need to be around for the setting up. Henry just wanted me to lend a hand wherever needed later on. Angela was at the front door of the club when I arrived. She squeaked and elbowed the girl beside her.

"Are you okay?" I asked as I approached.

"Yes," Angela said in a high-pitched voice. "Um, Henry needs you inside."

My stomach felt unsettled as I descended the main staircase into the club. Angela was a lousy liar and I distinctly smelled a rat. The second I pushed open the door and was greeted by the silent darkness, I knew what would happen. My nerves soared in the second it took for the lights to come up and everyone to shout, "Surprise!" I plastered a smile on my face and prayed to God that it looked authentic.

For a few seconds everyone just stared at me. What was I supposed to do, circus tricks? My mom rushed to my side to hug me and pointed everyone out who'd come. I couldn't pick out any faces but luck was with me as the lights dimmed to normal club level and the music started pumping.

"Are you surprised?" Mom asked, as she guided me toward the bar.

"There's an understatement if I ever heard one!"

"It wasn't my idea, you know."

"Then whose was it?"

"Henry's. He noticed your date of birth when filling out some employee form or something and saw how close it was. He got in touch with me and we have all been in cahoots with each other!" Mom beamed. She looked so proud of herself.

I did have to admit, it was touching. I was a lucky girl to have people in my life who would do things like this for me. "Okay, but how the hell did you guys manage to book *all* of Tenjune?"

My mom, who was oblivious to how popular Tenjune was, looked a little puzzled. "Henry took care of it—he called in a few favors."

I snorted a laugh. There were favors and there were *favors*. Tenjune was the place to be seen in the Meatpacking District and notoriously hard to get into. I'd had more than a few girls try to befriend me because they knew I worked the PR scene and could more than likely get them on the guest list. But even for Henry, this was impressive. Normally Tenjune rented out the Purple Room for private parties. I'd never even heard of someone renting the whole place.

Not to sound like a Miserable Mary or whatever, but if I'd been in charge of the guest list then the Purple Room would have been more than enough for my guests. But obviously Theo had been included, as there were more than a few yuppie bitches present.

But still, there were worse places for a girl to have her surprise birthday party than Tenjune. It had always been one of my favorite clubs and was so stylish it hurt. It split into three different areas, all with different vibes.

The Purple Room was definitely my favorite. It was situated next to the main dance area and was tucked away behind a grand archway. It was bathed in rich purple hues, hence the name. The walls were padded and sparkled with chrome buttons while the floor underfoot felt plush. Curtains could be drawn, completely separating it from the other rooms and there was even the option of private staff. The whole room just screamed intimacy and luxury.

People congratulated me and offered to get me drinks too many times to count. Mom made me do the rounds and I mingled among my guests, thanking everyone for coming. It took a while for my nerves to settle, but once they did, I was able to take everything in better.

Hayley and the girls were here, the trip all a clever ruse to lower my suspicions. No sooner had I reached their sides though, than I was snatched away from them. Theo guided me to a different crowd of people. *His* crowd of people.

"No need to thank me," he whispered in my ear. "I could see they were boring you."

Helen beamed when she saw me and pulled me in for a pathetically weak hug. "Happy birthday."

"Thanks. And thank you for coming."

"It's my pleasure! You need your girlfriends around you on your birthday."

I glanced back at my real ones. "Yes, you do."

"Your mother took the gift I got you. I think she is putting them all on a table or something."

"Oh, you didn't have to get me a gift." I dreaded how ridiculously expensive it would be.

"Of course I did! We all did, didn't we, girls?" Helen consulted her flock. The mini Helens nodded their confirmation.

This sparked off a debate about who had had the best birthday to date. The women exchanged stories of retreats to Rome, being presented with jewelry under the Eiffel Tower and apartments bought for them on the Upper East Side.

Theo managed to sneak away from the group, who closed his place shut, leaving me no room for escape. For more than an hour, their inane drivel drove me to a state of catatonia. I tried all the excuses I could think of and they thwarted every single one. They fetched me drinks and snacks and put in my requests to the DJ.

When things were looking desperate, my glorious mother rescued me. I could have dropped to the floor and kissed her feet in gratitude.

"You haven't been dividing your time very well," she scolded.

"I know. I couldn't get away. But look, I'm going to see my other friends right now." I kissed her cheek and damn near threw myself between Hayley and Eve in their booth in the Purple Room.

Eve laughed. "I see you escaped."

"That was terrifying! You all know what I think of those women. Why did none of you come and help me?"

Hayley pushed a Cosmo under my nose, which disappeared down my throat at record speed. "We tried. They have a great defense."

I pulled a face at her. Sighing, I leaned back in my seat. I was where I needed to be.

My twenty-fourth birthday would go down in the books as my favorite birthday yet. I had a great network of friends around me, and the usual pressure was not present. It was probably because I was actually letting myself relax and hadn't had any preconceived ideas about what this birthday would hold.

After the few cocktails had begun to take effect, I put up no fight when the girls dragged me onto the dance floor. We sang along to the words and danced like no one could see us. I felt free—free and happy, like I might burst at any second and shower everyone with glitter.

A tap on my shoulder made me start. Turning around, I looked into the happy face of my father. "Hi, Dad," I said, hugging him.

"Happy birthday, baby. Are you having a good party?"

"The best. Where have you been hiding?"

"In a few corners. I don't like big productions."

I laughed. My father and I were too similar for our own good. "So what made you quit lurking?"

"Your mother. She said I had to dance with you."

"Well, she was right."

With perfect timing, the music slowed to a softer beat, and I stepped into my father's arms.

"Don't worry. No one is watching," I assured him.

"And it had better stay that way," he murmured.

Oh yeah, we were definitely two of a kind. "So. What's this I hear about you going back to work?"

He rolled his eyes. "She told on me, huh?"

"Yes. Why didn't you tell me?"

"Hey, I'm the parent here. Isn't it supposed to be you who tells me things?"

I giggled. "I suppose. But I still appreciate being kept in the loop."

"You don't need to keep worrying about me, Marley. I'm fine."

I frowned. There was every reason to keep worrying about him. "I'm your daughter. Of course I'm going to worry about you."

"Hey now," Dad said, detecting the tiny break in my voice. "None of this on your birthday. Smiles only."

I smiled and nodded, but my throat felt closed off.

"That's better. Now, where's that man of yours? I haven't seen him all night."

Now that I thought of it, I had barely seen Theo myself. I scanned the room and clocked him in a corner talking to someone. A blonde someone. "Oh, there he is. Want me to get him?"

"Yeah. I'll be at the bar. Tell him I'm buying him a drink."

I grinned. "Dad, it's a free bar."

"Then this round is on me." He winked, and I left to get Theo.

The closer I approached, I could see how rigidly Theo held himself. A feeling of unease unfurled in my belly. "Theo?"

He spun around with the speed of a tornado sweeping through a valley, blocking his companion from sight.

"My dad has been looking for you. He's at the bar."

Theo nodded, looking really agitated. "Great, let's go find him."

A low chuckle came from behind him. "What's the rush, Theo? I have a gift for the birthday girl."

I peered around Theo to see Simone leaning against the wall. *Who the hell invited her?* "Oh hi, Simone. I didn't realize you were here. I would have said hello."

"I got here late."

I nodded. I never knew what to say to this woman. She always looked at me like she was in on some joke and I was the idiot who didn't get it.

"I got you a gift. I hope you like it." She thrust a small gift bag into my hand. "It's perfume. The receipt is in the bag if you hate it."

It felt like I was slapped with a get-out-of-jail-free card and an insult all at once. I hated opening gifts in front of people—I never knew how to act and just felt awkward, but this felt even worse.

"Oh, wow, thanks, Simone. I'm sure it's...you know, great or something." I cringed. *Really?*

Theo caught my elbow. "Come on. I thought you said your dad was looking for me."

I managed to flash Simone a smile before Theo dragged me across the room. I arched an eyebrow at him, but he wasn't even looking at me.

"Mr. Jacobs! It's been too long!" Theo said, louder than normal, when he reached my father who was stationed at the bar, no doubt trying to avoid attention, just like me.

My dad shook his outstretched hand and grinned. He twisted to face me. "One of your friends was looking for you."

"Okay," I said, nodding.

The bartender stopped in front of me.

"Water, please."

After he'd handed me one, I figured now would be a perfect time for a break. The party was awesome but I really needed some air.

This club was used a lot in events we covered, so I knew it inside out. I disappeared out of the main room and down a few service corridors before arriving at the fire escape. I sat down on the iron steps, relishing the cool air on my skin.

The one thing I disliked about New York was the lack of stars. At my parents' house I used to sit out on the roof late at night and just stare up at them. Whatever problems I had paled in comparison to the immense workings of the universe. I closed my eyes and imagined I could see them. I saw my favorite constellations behind my closed lids, twinkling brightly.

"Penny for 'em."

I damn near jumped out of my skin. I'd know that voice anywhere — even a whisper among shouts.

Blake chuckled and joined me out on the fire escape, lowering himself to sit beside me. "When were you going to tell me it was your birthday?"

"Never." I cracked a smile. "I thought you were in Vegas."

"Just got back. Had an interesting message on my machine from Theo telling me to get my butt down to a surprise party if I got back in time." He scanned my face. "Do you mind me being here? I can go."

"Don't you dare," I threatened. "How could I mind you being here? You just made my night."

Blake flashed me a dazzling smile. He stroked the underside of my arm. "Are you enjoying your party?"

"Yes, actually."

He laughed. "You sound surprised."

"I am. I normally hate birthdays. This one is good, though." I leaned into him as though the heat from his body beckoned me.

He wrapped an arm around my shoulders, pulling me even closer to him. I dropped my hand into his lap and Blake's fingers traced up and down my arm, making me break out in delicious shivers.

I pressed closer to him. "I wish we could leave right now. Go someplace, just the two of us."

There was a smile in Blake's voice. "Me too."

"Ahem."

Blake and I leaped apart so fast the fire escape rocked.

Hayley wore an amused expression as she glanced between us. "Your mother is looking for you, Marley. She wants you to cut the cake."

"Right, yeah, of course," I said, stumbling over my words.

"Hope I wasn't interrupting anything," she said, grinning.

I shot her a glare as I marched past her.

No one had missed me in my absence. Well, apart from my mother, who was panicking that the candles would burn all the way down before I got to them, but they didn't. They even lasted through a deafening chorus of 'Happy Birthday'. I held my hair back as I blew out my candles.

There was only one thing I had to wish for.

* * * *

The morning after my party I sat among a sea of presents. Hayley was on her way to help me open them, though I suspected her reasons for coming by had nothing to do with present opening. The gentle *ding-dong* of the doorbell interrupted me prodding a few gifts. I rose from my spot on the floor, stretched and padded down the hall to let Hayley in.

"Morning," I said.

Hayley grunted and pushed past me into the apartment. She was a far cry from the club-loving girl she'd looked last night, dressed up to the nines. This morning she wore leggings, boots and an oversized sweater that had probably come from her last boyfriend. With long, caramel hair pulled into an unintentionally messy bun and no makeup, she was like a whole other girl. One that could, apparently, pull off any look she threw on. She collapsed in a heap onto one of the couches in the lounge, her arm draped across her face.

"Hayley, why are you here if you're so tired?" I asked. "How much sleep have you had?"

"Sleep? I haven't been to sleep yet. After we left your party, Eve and I found an after-hours thing. I pretty much went home to shower and then came here." She removed her arm to give me a look. "I knew *you* would be up."

I rolled my eyes. "You want a coffee?"

"God, yes," Hayley said past a yawn.

When I came back with two mugs of coffee, Hayley was sitting cross-legged on the floor examining a lavishly decorated present. "Good haul, huh?"

"Yeah," I said. "Open some. I know you're dying to."

Hayley didn't need telling twice. She tore through the wrapping at a pace that would have impressed any child on Christmas morning. "Those lawyer wives may bore the hell out of you, but they sure give good gifts," Hayley commented as she opened another brightly colored Hermès silk scarf.

I laughed. "What, so I'm supposed to befriend them because they give good gifts?"

"Nah, it's not worth the trade off," Hayley said. "So where's Theo this morning?"

I shrugged. "Tore out of here like a bat out of hell first thing. No doubt working."

Hayley arched an eyebrow and went back to her furious unwrapping. She was efficient in making piles of clothes, bath salts and edibles. A few people had given me expensive Belgian chocolates.

Opening presents was thirsty work. I dumped a box of cookies in her lap after handing her a fresh mug of coffee once she'd finished all her unwrapping. We fell into silence, only interrupted by the rustle of the cookie box and Hayley's weirdly loud chewing. *Oh my God, can she chew any louder? Seriously. Girlfriend's got a problem.*

"What?" Hayley asked past a mouthful of half-chewed cookies after she'd caught me staring.

I gave her a look. "You wonder why you don't have a boyfriend?"

She flipped me off.

"So ladylike." I sighed.

Hayley rolled her eyes and washed her cookies down with a mouthful of coffee. "Whatever. Not all of us are greedy like you are."

I laughed. "What's that supposed to mean?"

She narrowed her eyes at me. "You know what it means."

"I'm not being greedy." Hayley and I seemed to have come to an unspoken agreement to drop all pretenses. I knew she knew. And she knew I knew she knew.

"Then what are you being?" Hayley asked. "Seriously, Marley, where do you see this all going?"

I dropped my eyes. "I can't see where it's going. I can't imagine breaking it off with Blake and I definitely can't imagine telling Theo."

"You have to do something. You think Blake will hang around forever? Or that Theo won't tell you where to get off if he finds out you're screwing his best friend?"

I frowned. "Okay, I'm gonna pass this off as tired and hungover Hayley, instead of just plain bitchy Hayley."

Hayley laughed. "I'm not being bitchy! I'm just talking to you. You're the one getting her panties in a bunch."

"Am not," I mumbled.

Hayley moved to sit beside me. "Look, I'm your friend and friends tell each other the truth. What's the point in sugar-coating anything? You know the score."

"Yeah I know," I whispered. "And I know I have to do something. I just—"

"You don't want to hurt anyone," she guessed. "And I bet it would be a hell of a lot easier to do something if you weren't so utterly head over heels, disgustingly in love with Blake."

"This is you trying to help?"

"I'm good, aren't I?"

"Not really."

Chapter Twelve

I made sure I got to work bright and early Monday morning. As a thank you for throwing me such an awesome birthday party, I left a cup of Henry's favorite coffee from Starbucks and a donut with glaze and sprinkles on his desk. He caught up with me in the copy room.

"What have I done to deserve an assistant like you?" Henry asked, planting a sugary kiss on my cheek.

I laughed and wiped the glaze he'd so kindly left behind on my face.

"So, was someone pleased about the party?"

"Yes! Henry, it was awesome. Why weren't you there?"

Henry laughed. "I wish I had been. From the way the girls are talking in the break room, it was some party. But the boss's work is never done and I had a meeting that night."

"You did?" Panic mounted in my stomach. "I don't remember seeing anything in your diary —"

Henry raised his hands to interrupt me. "It was impromptu and a very relaxed version of a meeting over drinks. You didn't drop the ball. I don't think it would be possible for you to screw up."

I smiled uneasily. At least that was true in my work life. "So what was the meeting for? Are you getting a new client?"

Henry grinned. "It's just a future project. Nothing that you need to worry about."

I frowned.

"Hey, it's you leaving us, not the other way around."

Sighing, I turned away from him. "Fine. Don't tell me."

Henry laughed and left me to my copying.

I spent the rest of the day stuffing envelopes with invitations and bits of sparkly confetti for an event. *Glamorous, huh?* I was tired and irritable from the stupid paper cuts all over my fingers, one really sore one on the flappy bit of skin between my thumb and index finger. So for once when it was time to call it a day, I was relieved.

I turned off my computer and tidied the paraphernalia away before grabbing my bag from under the desk. The office was unusually quiet as I made my way down the corridor. People here worked such odd hours. There was always someone hanging around.

Turning the corner, I saw everyone huddled around Kelly's desk. "Marley!" Kelly cried, spotting me.

Every single one of them looked like they would burst with excitement at any second. "What's going on?" I asked, glancing between them all.

"Happy birthday!" Kelly cried.

I laughed. "Uh, thanks, Kelly. But you said that already. On Saturday, at my party."

She giggled. "Yeah, but now we have your birthday gift! Come see!"

I crossed the room to her desk where she shoved a wide white box into my arms. Kelly tore the top of the box off, impatience winning. Nestled among lilac tissue paper was a purple hardback book. In a little window on the front cover was a picture of me. I was smiling, happier than I'd ever thought possible for me. Who had I been looking at to provoke that smile?

"Do you like it?" Kelly asked.

"What is it?"

She lifted the book from the tissue paper and let the box drop to the floor. Kelly opened the front page. Written in beautiful calligraphy was my name and Saturday's date. I flipped through a few more pages, startled and moved by what I saw. There were photographs from my birthday party. In boxes dotted around each page, people had written little sentiments about me.

Tears swam in my eyes as I looked into the expectant faces of my colleagues. "I don't know what to say... This is beautiful."

"You like it?" Kelly asked, her eyes wide.

I hugged her with as much fierceness as I could with one arm. "I love it."

"Good. It took forever to put together. I was printing the pictures off all day and Angela and Irene were decorating the book after everyone from the party wrote in it."

"I can't believe you all did this for me."

Angela grinned and looked like she herself would dissolve in a puddle of girly mush at any moment. "Aw, come on, Marley. We had to give you a good gift since this is your last birthday with us."

I placed the album on the desk and went around every person and hugged them. How had I ever doubted I didn't belong here?

* * * *

With no work or plans for the evening, I crashed out on the couch with a beer and lost myself in the album. More than a few times I was brought to tears by the tenderness of someone's words, or laughter over some photos. At the time, I hadn't noticed the album being circulated, and I knew it must have been during the party and not before. I distinctly recognized Hayley's drunken script a few times.

The best photos of me were the ones I hadn't been prepared for — no posing or trying to get my best side or smile just right. I always looked my prettiest when I didn't know the camera was on me. And I loved the 'caught in action' pictures of other people.

There were a few hilarious pictures of me and the girls dancing and a few when the person realized at the last second that they were about to be immortalized. One of my favorites was a picture of me and my dad dancing. I would have to remember to talk to Kelly and see if she could get a copy for my parents.

Another picture that stood out was one of me and Theo. He was frowning at something in the distance and I stood, hand on hip, with my eyes raised toward the heavens. I remembered this. I had been trying to talk to Theo and he'd been so distracted he had barely heard a word I'd said. But this wasn't why it stood out. It was because I'd never realized how opposite we looked.

Theo had blond hair, was stern-faced and more or less always looked impeccable. I, on the other hand, had dark chocolate hair and was very slight in build with a mouth that always looked like it was trying to twist into a smirk.

Underneath the picture of Theo and me was one of me and Blake. The image of us made my breath catch in my throat. I looked like I had been made for him. Blake's head was dipped to whisper in my ear and I was clutching my cocktail glass, wearing the biggest smile in the history of smiles.

Blake was so much bigger than me, but his frame was tall and lean. Whenever he leaned over or looked down at me, it felt like he was protecting me, rather than intimidating—unlike Theo. Damn, that guy had invented looming menacingly over a person.

I ran a fingertip over Blake's face. He'd made me laugh so much the night of the party. Was it only because we relied on stolen moments together that all the extra ones we got seemed even more special? Theo was a big, dull dud at parties and chose to remain professional at all times. Blake's spirit was more relaxed and fun to be around when he unwound. I thought Theo and I were opposites. The biggest opposite of all was the men I divided my time between.

The ringing of the doorbell broke my train of thought. I placed the album on the coffee table in front of me and got up to answer the door.

"Oh!" A jolt coursed through me, and Blake flashed me a crooked smile. "I was just thinking about you."

Blake arched an eyebrow. "Really?"

I rolled my eyes and swatted his stomach. "Come and see what my work friends did for me. Wait. You already know, right? Do you want to see it anyway?"

"Of course." Blake stepped into the apartment. "Theo's downstairs in the lobby on his cell. Didn't want to get in the elevator and lose reception."

I sighed. Sounded like Theo all right.

Blake spotted the album and bent to look at the open page. "Is it meant to be ironic that right under the picture of you and Theo is one of you and me?"

I nudged him with my elbow. "Hey, I didn't make it."

"Sorry," Blake mumbled. He straightened himself and turned to face me.

There was something off about Blake today. I couldn't put my finger on it. "Are you okay?"

"Yes, why?"

I frowned. "I don't know. Seems like something is bothering you."

"The only thing bothering me is how little I've seen you lately." Blake reached out slowly to touch the tips of my fingers.

It was frustrating to have him so close, to be able to smell him and feel the heat from his body and not be able to do anything about it. With my spare hand I lightly touched his chest to feel the thrum of his heart under his soft charcoal sweater.

A hint of a blush crept up and stained my pale cheeks. We were barely touching, yet it felt sensual and almost erotic. I let out a breathy laugh and looked up into Blake's heated eyes, which burned into mine. A thousand silent words swam around us, weaving and hovering in the background. None of them needed to be said aloud.

"What are you doing tomorrow?" Blake asked throatily.

I smiled. "Seeing you." With a quiet laugh, I shook my head to clear the fog. "Beer?"

"Yes, thank you."

No sooner had I walked into the kitchen, than I heard the front door open and close. My heart pounded at the closeness of the timing. I wondered if Blake was feeling just as rattled. I brought an extra beer for Theo and handed it to him. He accepted it without looking at me and didn't break his conversation with Blake.

"You're welcome," I mumbled. As I handed Blake his, our fingers brushed, making my skin tingle.

"What's this?" Theo asked, snatching my attention away from Blake. He bent to pick up the album.

"Oh, the girls at work made it for me. Don't you remember it?"

"Should I?"

"You signed it."

"Oh, right, yeah. Of course."

Liar. "It's really cool. Have a look," I said. "There's a good picture of you and Simone."

Theo's head snapped up. He searched my face for a moment. "There is?"

I motioned for him to hand me the album. Flicking through the pages, I found the one I was looking for. Theo and Simone stood in the same dark corner I'd found them in before she'd given me the perfume. In the picture Theo was running a hand through his hair and smiling at Simone. His eyes looked almost pleading, like he was trying to convince her of something. She looked smug as always.

"What were you talking about?"

"Jesus, Marley, it's a picture, not a fucking video clip," Theo barked, his face twisted with a snarl. "How the hell should I know what we were talking about?"

I stepped back as though he had struck me. "I only asked, Theo."

He muttered something and turned away from me.

If I had to spend one second more under the same roof as him, I was going to scream. Dangerous words had pooled on my tongue and if I wasn't careful, I could lose everything if they were spoken. "Well. I'll leave you two to your boys' night."

"Where are you going?" Theo asked.

"Out." I grabbed my keys from the dish on the hall table, pulled on my jacket then stormed from the apartment without look back.

It was Blake I felt bad for. He was the one who would have to put up with Theo in his bad mood. In my rush to get away and piss off Theo, I'd forgotten to grab any cash. I didn't have a dime on me. Nursing a coffee or going to a movie were out. It was a long walk to Hayley's neighborhood. I just prayed she was home.

* * * *

It had been well over a week since I'd dropped in on Hayley—the night Theo had bitten my head off. On opening her door, she'd hugged me then crossed her arms and told me to pull my head out of my ass and stop being such a stranger.

I'd never been the kind of girl who dropped her friends the minute she found herself with a boyfriend. But it had become very apparent that my time was dominated mostly by men. I couldn't remember the last time I'd met the girls for a drink or had been dragged to the movie theater to watch a ridiculous romantic comedy.

I guessed the problem was there weren't enough days in the week. I still worked a few nights at the club or an event if we had one on. I tried to see Blake the nights I wasn't working and also had to put in some Theo-hours, lest he become suspicious about what I did in my spare time. And what with working all day in the office, there was a serious lack of space in my schedule for my girls.

'The best times together were the spontaneous ones, but every now and then a little planning was needed to get everyone together. So I cleared my schedule for the night, told Theo and Blake—separately, of course—that I had been neglecting my girlfriends and they could live without me for the night. Hayley was renting a bunch of old movies, Eve was bringing the food and Beth and I were bringing the wine.

I adored Hayley's apartment. She was the kind of girl who didn't care how things were meant to look— if she liked it, then that was all that mattered—and her apartment definitely showed off that side of her personality. Actually, it showed off every side of her personality.

It could have been described as kitchy-glam. In her lounge was a TV set, a totally busted orange couch, a big fat red armchair and a black with white cushioning sixties ball chair. It spun on its own axis and I shamelessly bogarted it whenever I visited.

Hayley hung different fabrics from the walls whenever she felt like it with twinkly fairy lights strung around everywhere. Stacks of books and DVDs were resting against any given wall and picture frames were strewn across every plausible surface.

If Theo wasn't into clutter, then Hayley was his extreme opposite.

We lazed on the floor of Hayley's lounge, eating out of Chinese cartons and salivating over the deliciousness that was James Dean. Eve kept up a running commentary of the movie, most of which consisted of 'what a damn waste'.

Beth left around eleven, complaining of a wine headache. Hayley announced she wanted to watch *Bonnie and Clyde*—girl had a serious crush on the young Mr. Beatty—which sent Eve running for the hills after twelve. She said she was in the mood for a 'late run' and an old friend from high school was in the city.

Hayley popped in the DVD and wrapped a blanket around her legs. "Want to know something really depressing?" Hayley asked. "He could have been mine."

"Who?"

"Warren."

I swallowed a laugh. "Okay."

Hayley sighed. "He could have been. And you know the one thing that got in the way?"

"Annette Benning?"

She rolled her eyes at me. "Timing! If he was a born a few years later—or me a few years earlier—our timing would have been perfect. He would have met me and the rest, as they say, would have been history."

"Yeah, okay."

Hayley tossed a pillow at me and it bounced off the top of my head. "You should be on my side for the whole timing thing. It's the only thing in your way too."

I swiveled around to face her. "What?"

"Timing. It all comes down to timing." Hayley sat up straighter, as if she were on the brink of an epiphany. "Imagine for a second that we took the trip to Vegas a few years ago. You would have met Blake *before* you met Theo. Voilà! Problem solved."

"But *we* wouldn't have gone to Vegas a few years ago. We haven't been friends that long."

Hayley rolled her eyes. "Okay… But you see what I mean, don't you? Blake makes you so happy—it's obvious you guys belong together. It's just bad timing."

"Bad timing," I murmured.

"I'm a genius, right?"

"Hardly. A genius would have seen a way out of this predicament for me by now."

She dropped her eyes. "Doesn't take a genius to see the way, Marley."

"What do you mean?"

"Well… It's all about making a choice. You can't have them both forever. Make the choice. Who's going to win?"

There only was one winner…and only one option. The wedding was getting closer every day and it felt like the clock that was ticking wasn't just for my lifelong commitment to Theo, but for the end of things with Blake, too. "It's not that simple, Hayley."

"Yes it is!" Hayley exploded. "God damn it, Marley! You're my best friend and I love you, but come on! It *is* that simple. Blake or Theo? And before you launch into your defense, I get it, okay? I get that you feel like you owe Theo and you should honor your commitment to him. But don't you think that's shot to hell now? And I get that you're all in love with Blake, whatever. Doesn't matter if you love the guy or not. All that means is it will hurt more when this whole fucking mess is done."

I blanched from Hayley's words. There wasn't a damn thing I could say in my defense.

"I'm not apologizing for that. You need a good dose of tough love right about now. You know I'm here, no matter what you choose."

I nodded. "I'm not mad. Because you're right. I needed to hear that. I just— Ugh, you know what? Forget it. Let's just watch the movie. Is there any more wine?"

"There's my girl." Hayley grinned, handing me the bottle.

Chapter Thirteen

Early morning sunlight streamed into the room. It took a moment to realize that I hadn't woken naturally — a noise had pulled me out of sleep. My cell vibrated, jittering across the nightstand. My heart gave an uneven thump and an instant goofy smile broke across my face when I saw Blake's name on the screen. A quick glance over my shoulder confirmed I was alone.

"Hi," I answered.

"Hi," Blake said. "How are you?"

"I'm okay. I just woke up."

"Any plans for the rest of your day?"

"No," I said, excitement building at the thought of potentially spending all day with him.

"Great." There was a smile in Blake's voice. "I'm coming to pick you up. I'll see you soon."

After placing the cell back on my nightstand, I gave a little squeal and ran into the bathroom.

I showered quickly and dressed in my short green floaty dress with thin little straps, and my lemon

Mary-Janes. It was the first week in May and I was feeling very spring.

* * * *

Blake took me to Coney Island for the afternoon. He was devastated when I told him I had never been and was hell bent on educating me in all its wonders. We went to the Coney Island Museum and the New York Aquarium where he happily trailed behind me as I admired all the colorful fish. We watched the seal performance with their trainers and, bless his heart, he didn't mock me when I grinned and laughed with glee at their tricks.

We mooched around the Coney Island Beach Shop, trying on novelty sunglasses and hats. Blake insisted on buying me a souvenir T-shirt and I wore it over my dress with pride. I bought a disposable camera and took pictures of us acting nowhere near our ages and goofing around in the store.

Next on Blake's itinerary was a hotdog at Nathan's Famous. I'd never been a big hotdog fan, but these were out of this world. I got a great picture of Blake stuffing his face, but then the jerk got one of me. *Maybe this whole camera thing is a bad idea…*

Blake took me for a walk down the boardwalk so I could see all the sights and wonders this little pocket of heaven held. The sun was still bright but the colors in the sky were more rich and vibrant, indicating the day was slowly drawing to a close. Midway along the boardwalk, Blake paused and took off his socks and shoes. He stepped onto the beach, flexing his toes in the sand. He strolled off toward the water and motioned for me to follow him.

I was about to reach him when I realized he was standing in the surf, the water lapping at his feet, soaking the bottom of his jeans.

Blake turned and saw me watching him. "Come on. What are you waiting for?"

"I'm not getting my feet wet. That water must be freezing."

"It's not."

I arched an eyebrow.

He rolled his eyes. "Quit being so stiff. Come on."

I sighed and took a reluctant step forward. Glancing up at Blake's face, I saw he wore a peculiar expression. His eyes were closed and he had the tiniest hint of a smile on his face. It was like he was trying to soak every element into his skin. "What are you doing?"

"Nothing."

"Then—"

"Shh." Blake opened his eyes.

He really dazzled me when he did things like that. His eyes were pretty devastating the majority of the time anyway, but when they were hidden from sight for more than a few seconds then once again revealed, the full force of them knocked the breath out of me. He smiled. God, I was probably drooling.

"Close your eyes."

"What?"

Blake sighed. "Marley..."

"Fine." I closed my eyes. "Now what."

"Walk forward until you feel the water."

I did. Even though it was early May, the water was nothing close to unpleasant like I'd imagined.

"Can you feel how amazing that is?"

"Not really. Mainly my feet feel wet."

"Okay, just let everything go, all your thoughts, everything. You are a shell, a sponge, waiting to soak everything up."

I sighed but did as I'd been told. I forced every thought out of my head and just listened to everything around me. I could hear the older children playing in the distance, desperate to get as much time on the beach as possible. The crash of the waves and call of the seagulls rang out in front of me. Chatter from the boardwalk was behind me, and the screams from the rollercoaster rose and dove as the car made its way along the tracks.

All of this was present with the sea tickling my feet and the sun kissing my face. He was right. It was amazing.

"You feel it?"

I nodded. "It feels like I'm standing on the edge of the world."

"I used to come here a lot as a kid. Never failed to calm me down, or help find a solution if I had a problem."

I opened my eyes and turned to face him. Taking a step toward him, I placed both hands on his chest and stood on my tiptoes to plant a soft kiss on his lips.

It was dangerous, but I didn't care. I also knew that this was not the typical haunt for any of Theo's friends or co-workers, so I doubted there was any risk of getting caught. It was dangerous because Blake and I were crashing down boundaries and becoming less concerned with keeping our feelings hidden away from sight.

Blake's eyes searched mine. I don't know what he was trying to find. Everything I felt for him was plain on my face, there for the taking. He framed my face with his hands before dipping his head and kissing me right back.

It wasn't a passionate kiss and we didn't need it to be. For those few moments, I gave myself more to Blake than I'd ever given myself to anyone. I was his. I belonged to him. We were together and there was no one else.

When we walked back along the beach, we walked right in the surf. I laced my fingers with Blake's, allowing myself just a little bit more of that connection. "It's so beautiful here," I commented when we paused again.

Blake nodded and dropped down onto the sand. He lay down and stretched himself fully, folding his hands underneath his head.

"Blake?"

"Hmm?"

"Your pants are getting wet."

"They're already wet."

I sat down beside him, drawing my knees up to my chest, sneaking glances at his body. His T-shirt rode up, revealing a thick stretch of his stomach. It made my heart flip-flop and I couldn't make myself look away. I reached out and traced a line across the visible patch of skin.

Blake shivered under my touch. I grinned and lay down beside him. He tucked me into his chest.

"Thank you," I whispered.

"For what?"

"Being you. This afternoon has been perfect. I don't want it to end." I let out a breath. "We'll always have this, forever. We'll always have Coney Island."

We were silent for a long time after that. I closed my eyes and let the sounds wash over me. I desperately tried to etch every detail of this afternoon into my mind, determined not to lose a single second of it.

"Are you ready to leave?" Blake asked.

"Not yet."

Chapter Fourteen

I was walking on clouds after my beautiful afternoon at Coney Island. I took off my souvenir shirt and hid it at the bottom of a drawer, safe from wandering eyes. No sooner had I shut the drawer than the front door slammed closed.

In the kitchen, I found Theo emptying a tray of ice cubes into a dishtowel.

"What's going on?" I asked.

"Nothing." He rolled the towel up and held it to his jaw. "Some crazy jerk hit me on the way home, okay?"

"I guess the city is full of crazies after all." I walked around the counter to get to Theo. He let me remove the home-made icepack so I could see his face. A nasty bruise had formed on his jaw. I whistled softly. "The guy put some weight behind this. You say the attack was unprovoked?"

Theo snorted. "Damn right it was."

"You'll live." I pushed the icepack back in place.

He made a noncommittal noise, his forehead creased with annoyance.

Let him sulk. I shook my head and picked up his discarded suit jacket and folded it over my arm as an excuse to have something to do.

Theo pushed off the counter. "I can get that."

"It's fine, Theo," I said. "I've got it." I felt his eyes on me as I left the kitchen and headed for the hall closet. I hung it up inside, smoothing out the fabric. Theo would pack it away for dry cleaning soon enough.

As I brushed over the jacket, my hands bumped something in the inside pocket. Thinking it was his wallet or keys, I fished the item out knowing that Theo would lose his shit if he couldn't find his stuff.

It wasn't his wallet or keys.

It was a little blue Tiffany's box.

Swallowing a sigh, I opened the box to see a platinum diamond bracelet nestled inside. Whatever I was about to be let down about, it would be a big one. Had to be, for him to splash out this much.

I hated myself as the first thought that crossed my mind was that maybe it would give me some more time with Blake.

* * * *

My heart felt light and there was a distinct bounce in my step. Blake had called and invited me over, and I couldn't wait to get out of the apartment. Theo entered the apartment just as I was pulling on my jacket to leave.

"Are you going somewhere?"

"Yeah. I'm meeting a friend for dinner."

"Which friend?"

"Hayley." My stomach twisted. "I'll probably be out late."

Theo nodded, seeming to accept my lie. "What restaurant are you going to?"

I wasn't a natural at deception, but it was becoming increasingly easier to do. "I'm not sure. She arranged the booking."

"Why don't you stay home for once? You're barely here anymore." Theo betrayed nothing in his ice-cold blue eyes. I couldn't tell if he was being difficult for difficulty's sake, or if he truly wanted me to stay home.

"It's rude to cancel, Theo." And not that I'd tell Theo, but I hadn't seen Blake since Coney Island. We had talked on the phone, but I needed to see him. Needed him. And that trumped any fear I might have had in making Theo suspicious.

For a fleeting moment I thought Theo would refuse to let me leave. His jaw hardened and he gave me a tight smile. "Enjoy your night, then," he said, before stepping out of the way.

I let out a slow breath once I'd closed the apartment door behind me. The uneasiness I'd felt inside around Theo disappeared with each step away from him. I was heading toward Blake, where in my heart of hearts, I knew I truly belonged, though the tether between me and Theo would never let me stay for long.

* * * *

I'd barely laid a knock on the door before it wrenched open. Blake stepped back to let me into the suite. He pulled me into a tentative embrace before dipping his head and planting a soft kiss on my cheek. I frowned as he pulled away and led me toward the lounge.

"I got some food for you—and a movie." Blake fussed around the TV, getting the movie ready. *Urban Legend* started, and he disappeared into the kitchen to retrieve a steaming plate of pasta carbonara, my absolute favorite.

"Aren't you eating?" I asked, noting only one plate.

"I'm not hungry."

Blake sat on the couch as I folded my legs under me and sat on the floor. Not before long, I was engrossed in the movie. When my plate was empty and the movie almost over, I drummed my fingers on my knee. The evening wasn't quite what I'd had in mind.

I twisted around and leaned an elbow on the edge of the couch. Blake was bent over a notebook, his eyebrows pinched together as he focused. The knuckles on his right hand were red and angry looking. "What did you do to your hand?"

Blake jerked his head up, as if suddenly aware of my presence. He glanced at his hand. "Nothing. It's fine." He reached over and squeezed my shoulder. "Enjoy your movie. It's almost over."

Fifteen minutes later, the movie was finally finished and I was bored. I stretched and stood up. Blake didn't notice my movement. Walking around the side of the couch, I crouched down and leaned on the armrest by Blake's head. On the page he had been scribbling on all night was a beautiful sketch of a house. A mansion, more accurately.

"Wow," I breathed.

Blake twisted around to look at me. A faint blush touched his cheeks and he placed the notebook face down on the couch.

"What's the matter? You can't be embarrassed. Blake, that was amazing," I said, nodding toward his notebook. "I'm sorry. I didn't mean to upset you."

Blake shook his head. "No, I'm just...a little distracted, that's all."

"So I noticed." I stood up and adjusted his arm so I could perch on his lap.

He moved his arms around me, barely even touching me at all. "I'm not going to break, you know."

He chuckled and kissed my shoulder. But his hold tightened, and I melted into his chest, letting the drum of his heart soothe and relax me.

"This is better," I murmured. "Can I see that picture now? Please?"

Blake groaned and reached for his notebook, dropping it in my lap. "You, woman, are insufferable."

"This is amazing," I said as I ran a fingertip over the page. "What is it? I mean, I know it's a house and everything but—"

"It's my house. At least, one day it will be."

"Have you... Is this your design?"

Blake nodded.

"Wow." To say I was impressed would have been a severe understatement. "Wow."

"It's not that great. It isn't finished. There are lots of problems with it."

"I can only see one."

"What? Where?" Blake asked, surprised.

I grinned. "You can't get to the roof out of any of the windows."

Blake chuckled. "Oh. I'll have to fix that then, huh?"

"Yup."

"I couldn't just sit out on a terrace?"

I shook my head. "To enjoy the stars, you have to be on the roof."

"Okay."

"You'll fix it?"

"I'll fix it."

A smile teased my lips and I pushed myself away from him. I caught his eye and felt my heart give an uneven thump before I lowered my mouth onto his.

Blake stood up with me still in his arms. He carried me into his bedroom and laid me down softly on the bed. Blake hovered above me, gently peeling away the layers of clothing until I was bare to him. I pulled his shirt over his head, running my fingers down the firm planes of his chest.

Blake touched my mouth with his thumb, back and forth over my bottom lip as though memorizing the shape. His eyes drifted over my face, scanning every dip and curve.

"Blake?" I whispered. I felt more on display than I ever had before. Blake made me feel cherished, something that had to be protected and treasured.

His hand left my mouth, and he drifted his fingertips across the bridge of my nose and along my cheekbones. "I love your freckles. You can't even really see them unless you're up close. So it's like a secret you only share with someone close to you."

Growing up, I'd hated those freckles. There weren't many, just a little spattering, but enough to make me seriously self-conscious in my early teen years. But right now...I'd never been more proud to have them.

Blake lowered his head to kiss my cheek, trailing his lips down until he met my lips. His kiss was soft, lingering. As he deepened it, he cupped my face and slowly touched my tongue with his. He settled himself between my legs, and when I felt his hard length at my cleft, I was more than ready for him.

My breath caught in my throat as he pushed inside so slowly I ached. He filled me and, not for the first time, I felt like I'd been made for him because we fit together so perfectly. Blake held my eyes as he made love to me, stoking a low burning fire in my body. His gaze never faltered as he rocked into me.

There was something different about this time with Blake — something sweet and bittersweet all at once. The world had shrunk to just the two of us. Nothing else existed outside this bed. Blake and I were connected, so in tune with each other. It was easy to forget the troubles that awaited us outside this room.

I clutched him tighter, held him closer as my release hit. Blake thrust into me, hard and firm, staying there as he came.

He brushed light kisses across my face, my throat, my collarbone. I felt worshiped and sated — full, content, adored.

* * * *

It was late. I'd stayed far longer than I'd planned. But it was getting harder and harder to leave him, leave the warmth of his bed and the security of his embrace.

"Stay," Blake murmured. He could always tell when I was about to pull a Cinderella.

I slid to the side of the bed and began pulling on my clothes. "I wish I could."

"Marley, come on." Blake slid his arm around my waist and tugged me back into bed.

"I can't," I said, avoiding his eyes. He had joked before about wanting to keep me forever, but he was usually understanding when I made my exit. Having him ask me in all seriousness to stay... It made leaving a hundred times harder.

He laced his hand with mine and planted a kiss to my palm. "Stay. I want to wake up with you beside me."

"You know I can't." As a rule, I never stayed the whole night. Theo wouldn't care if I called and said I was staying with Hayley, if he even noticed at all. But I needed to keep some things constant, otherwise... How long would it be before I didn't care anymore? If I started spending the night with Blake, how long would it be before Theo realized something was going on?

I knew what I was doing to Theo was terrible and inexcusable, but having him find out didn't scare me. A huge, colossal part of me was achingly close to breaking down and telling Theo myself, just so I could finally be with Blake — really be with him.

But a promise was a promise.

Theo and I might not love each other the way we were supposed to, but I owed him my life.

Blake sighed and dipped his head to my shoulder.

"Hey." I touched his cheek.

Blake lifted his pained eyes to read my face and my throat tightened.

"You know I want to," I said, keeping my voice soft.

"Bullshit!" Blake exploded. He dropped my hand and leaped from the bed. He paced back and forth as his anger mounted. "It's all bullshit!"

My heart pounded in fear of what he would say next. I slid off the bed and tried to stop his furious pacing. "It's not bullshit," I said. I tried not to feel hurt as he spurned my attempt to touch him. I knew there had been something wrong with him. He had been acting strange all night.

"Yes it is! You spout all this shit to me and whisper how much you want to be with me. But it's all bullshit."

A lump formed in my throat and tears stung my eyes. "No it isn't. You know how I feel about you."

"Yeah, you claim to have feelings for me, yet you won't spend one lousy night with me. Once I have woken up with you in my arms. Once."

"You know I can't stay the night! How many times have we been through this? I can't hurt him, Blake," I cried, throwing my arms out to the sides then letting them smack off my thighs.

"But you can hurt me?" Blake shouted. "You get the best of every world in this arrangement. You have me when you want me and him to run home to."

A tear slid down my cheek. "That's not fair."

"Isn't it?"

"No! How can you think I like anything about this mess?" I screamed through my tears. "How can you think I like lying in bed at night beside Theo wishing more than anything in this life that it was you I was with? That it's your face I see when we have sex?" My voice trembled and broke as the raw emotion came out. "That more than anything I wish it was you that was marrying me."

The anger faded from his eyes but was replaced with bitter pain. "It doesn't change the fact that it isn't. He has the best of you, Marley. He has all of you, every single piece. The world knows you're together. He's a selfish bastard and he doesn't deserve what he has. I wish you knew how true that is."

I stepped forward and placed my hands on his chest. This was it. The end I'd known was coming but had tried desperately to ignore. All these weeks I'd known it would come. It had to. There was no fairytale ending for us.

"The world may know Theo and I are together, but" —I let out a shaky breath—"he will never have the best of me. That belongs to you—only you."

"I can't do this anymore." Blake's voice was coarse. "I can't take seeing you run back to him after being with me. I can't stand the way he treats you. I-I can't be a part of this anymore."

I squeezed my eyes shut. My heart couldn't take the strain of seeing his extraordinary face so broken. Jesus, why hadn't I just said I would stay? The consequences of not going home to Theo were nothing in comparison to what I was losing.

"There are some things in the city I need to take care of but after that, I'll leave. I don't think we should be around each other," he said, low and gravelly.

I rested my head against his bare chest.

Blake wrapped his arms around me and pressed his face into my hair. "I won't come to the wedding. I'll find a believable enough excuse."

I took a breath to speak.

"Don't." Blake's voice broke. "This is hard enough."

He trembled as he kissed my hair. I had to leave while I still could. I wrenched myself out of his arms and fled from the suite as though the hounds of hell were snapping at my heel.

* * * *

"Marley?" Theo called from his office.

"I'm going for a shower," I choked out. I locked myself in the en-suite bathroom and turned on the shower. The room filled with steam and the pounding water was loud enough Theo would never hear me.

I cried and cried until there was nothing left and I was exhausted and spent. I felt like my best friend had died. In a way, he had. I loved Blake so purely. I knew there would be a gaping hole in my heart that could never be filled.

I scrubbed my body with the painfully hot water, leaving my skin red and sore. I pulled on sweats and climbed into bed, praying to God that Theo would keep working in his office and leave me in peace with my aching heart.

He did.

As I waited for sleep to snatch me from this dreadful pain, all I could think about was how I had never told Blake I loved him.

* * * *

Everyone noticed my zombie impression as I trudged my misery-ridden body from place to place. No one enquired, and I volunteered no information.

Work became my place of solitude again. I threw myself into the task at hand and stayed late most nights, only going home to change for working the clubs and events.

It struck me as odd that Henry never advertised my job. No one came for interviews, and should someone call on the off chance a position was going, they were always told there was nothing available. This hurt, actually. I figured I must not be very good at my job if they weren't even going to replace me.

Or maybe it was because they still hoped I would change my mind.

A flicker of excitement rumbled in the pit of my stomach. I could talk to Theo. I could explain to him how much my job meant to me. I could carry on my life here...

The more I thought about it, the more excited I became. I flounced into Henry's office and asked, if wasn't too late, how he would feel about me retracting my resignation? Henry grinned and hugged me, confirming my suspicion that this was what he had been holding out for all along.

I raced home that evening, no work to look forward to but eager to see Theo and lay down my law.

Unusually, he was home by eight.

"Hi," I said, the second he was inside.

"Hello," Theo said absently as he shrugged out of his jacket.

"I have to talk to you."

Theo arched an eyebrow but let me lead him into the lounge. He sat and I remained standing. I paced back and forth and fidgeted with my hands as I spoke in a rush. "I told Henry I was taking back my resignation. I mean, Theo, come on. I love my job. I don't want to give it up! I'm really good at it and there is a promotion opening up soon. I could apply for it and further my career! You're hardly ever here anyway. You wouldn't even miss me!"

Theo pinched the bridge of his nose before standing. "Have you lost your mind?"

That made me pause. "No."

He stalked toward me, his face a mask of undisguised anger. "Are you kidding me with this? I told you to quit. A job is fine for a single girl. A married woman should be at home. I need a boy to continue my family name. How are you going to have a career and be a good enough mother?"

I gasped. "Theo, we've never even talked about—"

"It will still be happening!" Theo screamed in my face. "You will be my wife and the mother of my children! And you will give me the respect I deserve! I have given you everything and you cannot even bring yourself to bend to my will?"

"It's a ridiculous request! I don't want kids, for years at least!" The truth was, I hadn't ever been able to picture myself with kids…especially kids with Theo.

Theo sneered. "We try on the wedding night."

My mouth fell into a little 'o' of shock. "Are you serious?"

"Marley, you knew what you were getting into with me. You know I'm a respectable man and my demands are not outrageous. You will be a traditional wife and mother. That is your career plan."

I folded my arms across my chest, defiance giving me the confidence I needed. "And if I refuse?"

"You won't. You'll tell Henry tomorrow you made a mistake. And if you don't, I will. Don't underestimate me, Marley."

I marched away from him and stormed from the apartment. My feet raced me toward the only place I needed to be. Half of me wanted comfort, the other half wanted to sneer in the face of Theo and show him *exactly* how much I respected him.

Chapter Fifteen

My pulse raced with adrenaline as I pounded on the door, the seconds ticking by endlessly slow.

Blake opened the door, his eyes widening. "What—?"

With a little cry I forced myself into his arms, cutting off his words with a forceful kiss. Blake kicked the door shut and pinned me against the wall, kissing me back every bit as hard.

Our teeth knocked and our tongues collided. This kiss was full of desperation and need. It became almost a battle of wills and neither of us was prepared to back down.

I'd dreamed about kissing Blake again since the night he'd ended things. My emotions were already so heightened, being with him again made me dizzy, which was why it took a few moments to notice that he wasn't kissing me back anymore. He pulled back and wiped my face, and it was then I realized that I was crying.

"What happened?"

The second his voice reached my ears, I dissolved in a puddle of stupid girlish sobs. Blake supported me and led the way to the couch where I spilled out the whole argument I'd had with Theo.

Blake squeezed my shoulders. I swung a leg over his lap and wrapped myself around him, wanting to disappear into his chest and hide where it was safe forever. Maybe it was because I hadn't seen Blake for a week. Maybe it was because I would never be fully immune to him. Maybe it was because I was feeling so vulnerable. But the instant my body was flush against his, a rush of wanting coursed through me, fierce and powerful. His scent intoxicated me and drowned my senses. His neck was hot against my cheek – the very nearness of him threatened to send me into a frenzy.

I lifted my face to press my cheek against his. Blake's warm breath teased my hair, and before I could talk myself out of it, I tightened my hold on him and clamped my mouth over his. Blake jolted from my sudden move before surrendering himself to me. The intensity of my kiss heightened as the urgency for him grew. In my haste I fumbled over the buttons on his shirt.

Blake curled one hand over mine and gently pried them from his shirt. "Marley, no. Not like this. Not because of him."

I was too emotionally spent and exhausted to feel embarrassed. I rested my forehead against his and let out a tiny sob when I felt him brush the hair from my face.

Blake pushed me away from him. His long fingers cupped my chin and raised it so I had to look at him. Like this wasn't hard enough already. He stared at me for a long time before speaking. "Why are you with him, Marley, when he treats you this way?"

"He isn't that bad. He just doesn't communicate well."

"I don't get it. He has a hold on you, I know it, but I can't figure it out." Blake stood up from the couch. "You have this amazing spirit, and he is killing it."

I shrugged. "I'm not so great."

Blake groaned. "Yes you are! You have so much passion and energy inside you, but day by day he is crippling you, making sure you will never have anything except for him."

"He just has ideals on how his life is meant to be."

"And that means you have to bend to how he sees things? When you're with someone, they should slot into your life, no matter what. Not break and distort you till you fit the mold they've had ready for years."

Blake's words hit me like a freight train. He was right, of course. Theo had known all along what his wife would be like. I was nothing close to his dream and so he'd molded me accordingly. "Theo's your best friend. How can you talk like this about him?"

Blake frowned. "Yeah, he was a good *friend*. As a fiancé, he sucks. I have a lot of respect for Theo and the name he's made for himself. But I did a disgusting thing to him, something no one deserves. And even though I should be full of repentance, I can't help but want to shake him to make him realize what he has right in front of him."

I couldn't even look at Blake. All I'd achieved in coming here was refreshing the wounds still raw between us. We were never meant to see each other again and I had only lasted a week.

"You're miserable," he said. It wasn't a question.

I looked up at Blake's tired face. "Don't look so chirpy yourself."

"I don't mean you're miserable because of us. You're miserable every day because of him. Why are you with him? I want a direct answer, Marley."

It wouldn't help, once he knew. But I owed him the truth, at least. "He saved my parents."

"What does that mean?" Blake asked. He sat on the coffee table opposite me, slouching forward to lean his elbows on his thighs.

"I had just started seeing Theo when my dad got sick. Cancer. My parents have never been wealthy. They owned a hardware store and did pretty well from it, enough so that money wasn't tight but nowhere near Theo's financial standing, if you know what I mean. When Dad got sick, his insurance company wouldn't cover the costs for the kind of treatment he needed. They were going to lose everything. They sold the business and were about to sell the house when Theo stepped in.

"He got my dad the best damn doctor in the city and covered the costs for all his treatment. Theo managed to sue the health insurance company for emotional damages and misleading information or something, and got Dad a big fat compensation check. Dad hates owing people, and tried to pay Theo back. Theo would hear none of it. He wouldn't take Dad's money. Told him to put it away for a rainy day."

"How is your dad now?"

"He's okay. They did a really aggressive treatment and the cancer went into remission. We got really lucky, more than a lot of people. He's been healthy for almost a year now, but we still worry. My mom told me he's even gone back to working mornings for a friend of his. They haven't touched the compensation. I think they're too scared to. They were so unprepared when Dad got sick, didn't really think about the 'what ifs' of the world." I let out a morbid laugh. "They sure are now."

"I'm so sorry, Marley."

I finally looked into Blake's eyes. "We're all okay now, thanks to Theo."

Blake sat up. "I don't want to sound disrespectful, but... Marley, are you with him because he did one humane act? You think that one act counters all the shitty things about him?"

"Not in the least. You're not getting this, are you?" And here it came—my ugliest truth. "I'm with him because I feel obligated."

"What, a life for a life?" Blake asked.

I stiffened. "Seems a fair trade to me. He saved my dad's life. I gave him mine."

"He didn't save your dad's life, Marley. The doctor did. The drugs did. Theo just footed the bill."

I looked down. "How can I leave him after all he's done for my family?"

Blake sighed and moved to sit beside me. He took my hands in his lap. "This isn't your burden to shoulder. Do you really think your parents would want you doing this if they knew how you felt?"

I shook my head. *Of course they wouldn't.*

"I can't influence you here, Marley. This has to be all you." Blake stared at me, long and hard.

There was a knock on the door, and Blake pulled his gaze from me. He rose to answer it and my stomach dropped when Theo's frame filled the doorway. The look on his face as his eyes traveled around the suite before landing on me was furious.

"What are you doing here?" Theo asked, storming across the suite. "Why are you always running to him? Every time I turn around, you're with him!"

I stood up to face him. "Why wouldn't I be? He's my friend. He's actually nice to me, Theo."

Theo sneered. "Nice. Whatever. He's only nice because he wants in your pants."

"Leave her alone, Theo," Blake warned from where he stood across the room.

Slowly, Theo turned to face him. "Oh, that's right. The white knight doesn't like the lady being hurt, does he?"

Blake's face clouded over. "Don't be a jackass. You're bullying her."

"Bullying her? I do not bully her. Besides, she can stick up for herself. You just want to make yourself look good in front of her," he sneered, inching toward Blake. "Won't do you any good, Blake. She'd never touch you."

My breath caught in my throat but Blake remained silent.

"She doesn't like you, Blake. What you're doing is pathetic." Theo reached out and grabbed my hand, tugging me forward. His tight grip bruised my soft flesh, the bone and muscle aching. "We're going."

An involuntary cry of pain clawed up my throat as I tried to free my arm. Theo tugged once again, apparently not even realizing the painful hold he had on my arm. Blake flew across the room. He pushed Theo from me, who stumbled backwards and tripped over the coffee table.

"Stay the hell away from her!" Blake roared, standing guard in front of me.

Theo jumped up and grabbed Blake by the shirt, his arm raised ready to hit him. Theo looked him dead in the eye for a second before slamming his fist into Blake's face.

Blake stumbled then regained his balance. Theo was on him in an instant, grabbing him again and swinging his fist to land another sickening punch on his face.

Terror held me prisoner. The second the attack had started, I was frozen with fear. I wanted to cower and hide away from the violence. *This is my fault... This is my fault.*

"Fucking hit me!" Theo screamed in Blake's bloody face, who hadn't once tried to defend himself.

"No," Blake said. "Look at her, Theo. She's terrified."

Theo ripped his eyes away from Blake and saw me shaking. He dropped his hold on Blake and walked toward me. For every forward step he took, I retreated.

"Marley—" Theo started.

"Get away from me," I whispered.

"I'm sorry I lost my temper. I didn't mean to hurt your arm."

"Get away from me," I repeated, my voice shaking.

Theo stepped back. "I'm going for a walk to cool off. I'll expect you home later." He turned and headed for the door, pausing at Blake. "I'm only leaving because she's scared. Do not think you have won here. You will never win. Do you understand me?"

The air in the suite was charged, even after Theo had removed himself. Blake didn't move. He watched me as though looking for cues, like it might be him I was afraid of. Inhaling a shaky breath, I unrooted myself and crossed the room to him. I pushed Blake gently toward the couch. "Sit."

My heart still pounded as I walked into the kitchen, busying myself trying to find things to help Blake. Once I'd found everything I needed, I carried a bowl of warm water with a cloth and a dishtowel filled with ice cubes back into the lounge. I knelt on the floor in front of him and washed the blood from his face.

The water was a rosy pink once the task was done. I picked up the home-made ice pack and moved to sit beside him on the couch. Blake winced as I applied the icepack to his already swelling cheek.

"You're shaking," Blake commented.

"I'm fine," I lied.

"How does your wrist feel?"

"It kills, but I think it's okay."

Blake eyed me carefully. "You don't have to stay with me."

"I know."

The air seemed to hum around us. Before, it had sizzled with violent electricity. Now it was full of all the unanswered questions hovering around us. I wanted to tell Blake everything in my heart. But maybe it would hurt more to have the truth out there, spoken aloud. Maybe it would be better if he never knew the intensity of my feelings for him.

I wanted to say it was him my heart really chose. There was never any competition when it came to my heart. Blake won hands down. But my mind chose Theo. I owed him too much to go back on my word now. However cruel he seemed sometimes, it was nothing really.

"Why didn't you fight back?" I asked.

"I knew it would upset you."

"Simple as that, huh?"

"Yeah, simple as that."

Blake knew me so well. A part of me wished he didn't. I could see just how easy it would be, to be with him. It wouldn't be complicated, it wouldn't hurt and it would be as natural as breathing.

"When do you leave?"

Blake's eyes widened so briefly if I hadn't been watching his face, trying desperately to etch every line, every plane into my mind, I would have missed it.

It was cruel of me to ask, and I truly hated myself for it. Maybe my question wouldn't have seemed so hurtful if I hadn't been trying to get into his pants a little while ago. But I needed to let him know I still expected him to leave—that my choice was still Theo. Also, though I hadn't seen him all week, it comforted me to think that he was still close by. I needed to know exactly when that comfort would expire.

"In the morning."

My heart skipped a beat. "So soon?"

Blake's eyes hardened. "I told you I was leaving as soon as I had everything in order. There's nothing else keeping me here, is there?"

"No," I whispered.

Blake took a deep breath then let it out slowly, like he was getting ready to make a speech or something. But he never spoke.

"I should go."

The words, while necessary, hurt more than a thousand knives.

Blake caught my hand, but it was his eyes that held me prisoner. "Promise me something?"

"Anything," I vowed.

"Open your eyes."

"I don't understand."

Blake sighed. "Just...start paying attention. Don't ignore things the way you have been. Ask the right questions." His eyes pleaded with me. They told me there was so much more he wanted to say to me but couldn't—or wouldn't.

"I promise."

Blake released my hand and slowly let it drop in my lap. "I know it's better to make a clean break, but if you ever need anything, please call me," Blake said hoarsely. "Take care of yourself."

I stood up and moved to the door. I turned to face him and greedily drank him in one final time.

It was now or never.

"Goodbye, Blake."

Chapter Sixteen

I didn't know where Theo was when I got home. I didn't know if he was even in the apartment. Grief had racked my body the last time I'd returned home after a hideously painful farewell with Blake. Now...all I felt was empty. It was as though someone had attacked me with a carving knife and picked my bones clean from muscle and tissue. I was left with no soul...no heart.

I took a few painkillers after peeling off my clothes before bed. I knew they would bring relief to both my aching wrist and unconsciousness.

* * * *

Though it was raining come the morning, I walked to work. I was protected from the spring drizzle with my sixties-style drooping umbrella, and had always found that the smell of warm rain relaxed me.

Losing myself in the ever constant crowded sidewalk — the only thing that could be counted on in this city to stay the same — my mind drifted here and there, not really stopping long to ponder over anything properly. One thought, more of an image really, that popped up with expected frequency was Blake. He haunted every corner of my mind — his easy smile, those gorgeous eyes that could penetrate my very soul and hold me his willing prisoner. His infectious laugh that never failed to make me smile. The way he would look at me, almost as an art student studies a magnificent piece by a master.

My promise to Blake rang in my ears like a ghostly echo. What did he mean, 'Open your eyes'?

There was something that kept bothering me. Last night things had escalated with barely any provocation, suggesting that their friendship was on the rocks... But why? What had happened to them? Well, I guessed I could summarize it in one word. Me. Blake obviously found it hard to be around Theo knowing he was screwing him over. But why would Theo be mad at Blake? He didn't know anything. *Oh God, I hope he doesn't know anything.* Something must have happened... A fight or something.

Okay, so safe to say something had come along and set a fire underneath their friendship. Did it have something to do with what Blake had said? He wanted me to see something, I was sure of it. But what? Christ's sakes, why did men have to be so cryptic? Jeez, and they said *women* were the complicated sex.

I glanced at my watch. It was only seven a.m. I'd left much earlier than I'd needed to. Looking up at the street sign, I saw I wasn't anywhere near my office, I had just been wandering around in the rain.

If I hurry...

As my thoughts fought a bloody war over what I should do, I raked a hand through my hair. The night before when I'd gathered the things together in Blake's kitchen, I'd happened to notice a plane ticket on the counter. The airport and time had not escaped my eyes. If I hurried, I could see him before he checked in.

Even before I subconsciously started looking for cabs, I knew the part of my brain all for going to the airport would win. The need to see him one last time... It was too great to ignore.

I hailed a cab, jumping in when one stopped. I tapped my feet as we lurched forward, the rain pounding on the windows making my beautiful city gray and bleak. When we finally arrived, I think I overpaid the driver, but I didn't care.

People jumped out of my way as I raced blindly into the airport. A small part of my mind told me the searching was too wild, my eyes would never spot him this way. Forcing myself to a stop, I squeezed my eyes shut and focused. My heart slowed and my thoughts settled.

I stood on the high walkway, looking down at the people below. The check-in desk lines were busy like always, but it only took a heartbeat to find the man I wanted.

He stood at a check-in desk, his back facing me. The woman behind the desk was flirting with him — her coy smile gave it away. Whether he participated in the flirting, I didn't know.

Blake placed his bags on the conveyor belt and took his boarding pass. The finality of it made my breath catch in my throat. Why had I decided to come here? All it had achieved was showing me how truly done all this was. But at the same time, it showed me the last chance I had to be with him. I could run down to him, go with him. I wouldn't need any stuff, I could buy new stuff. There was bound to be a job in Vegas for me. I could make a new life out there with him... It would be easy. It would be simple. It would be perfect.

Yes, I'd got to see my last chance...the chance I knew I wouldn't take.

For a brief and horrifying moment, Blake turned in my direction. He frowned and turned away. I let out a breath. He dropped his head and knocked his fist against the counter for a beat or two before holding his head high and striding toward his old life with no complications.

His beautiful face was bruised and a little swollen, despite my best efforts last night. I itched to kiss each one, to heal his perfect features.

With every step he took, Blake carried himself farther away from me. How I stood rooted in that spot until he disappeared from sight, I'd never know. It seemed to take all my strength not to run screaming after him and beg him to steal me away.

* * * *

Hayley opened her door. She took one look at me, turned on her heel then marched into the kitchen. I stepped into the apartment and closed the door. I could hear the chink of glasses, then Hayley reappeared and motioned for me to follow her into the living room.

She carried with her two mismatched wine glasses and two bottles of wine. Hayley filled the glasses and turned to face me.

Her eyes searched my face for the longest time, and I could feel my brick wall being chipped away piece by piece. She reached out for me and crushed me in a bear hug, moments before the river of tears began its descent down my face. Hayley shushed me and stroked my hair. She didn't even loosen her grip till she knew I had it together.

I gulped down my glass of wine and sank into Hayley's couch.

"Better?"

"No."

She slid the other full glass in front of me. I took my time with this one and didn't throw it down my throat. I sighed.

"It's over, isn't it?"

Though I had never intended to pour my heart out to Hayley, I ended up spilling out every last morbid detail from the night at the hospital, to Coney Island and the two awful departure scenes. I told her what Blake had said the night before. "Hayley, if you knew anything, would you tell me?"

She frowned. "Like what?"

I shrugged. "Anything. Blake wants me to find something out, something important. But I don't know what."

"I don't know anything. I barely spoke to either of them."

She refilled the empty glasses then picked up her phone. She ignored my protests as she placed an order for an enormous Chinese delivery. Despite my lack of interest before, I ate like a pig once the food arrived. Hayley chatted more to herself than me as we ate.

With both our bellies at bursting point and unable to face wine for the time being, Hayley flicked on the TV, settling on some reality show. After a few minutes of silence, I felt her eyes on me. That was all it took for what control I'd mustered to begin to crumble.

Hayley reached for me, wrapping her arms around my shoulders. "It's going to be okay, Marley. You'll see," she said softly.

"Is it?" I mumbled into her hair.

"Yes."

"Promise?"

She laughed. "Promise."

"Liar."

* * * *

Whoever said absence makes the heart grow fonder was talking out of a hole in their ass. With every day that passed, Blake felt farther and farther away from me. My heart was wretched and torn apart. There was nothing fond about the agony in my chest that seemed intent on crushing me. Hayley helped when she could, but mostly I kept my misery locked away and out of sight. My misery didn't love company. It craved isolation and darkness.

Theo never commented on the black, thunderous cloud that stalked my every step. Either he didn't see it or he chose to ignore its presence. Instead of fighting past the aching pain and moving on, I let it consume me. I didn't have the strength to try to get over Blake...and part of me didn't want to. In the long run, we'd barely had a whisper of time together. A few mere months as opposed to the years that faced me without him. When I was eighty years old, I wanted to remember exactly how he'd made me feel. If that meant enduring this pain, then so be it. I wanted to remember.

With less than three weeks to go before my wedding to Theo, I couldn't ignore my reality any longer. I guessed all along that I had been hoping some freak accident would intervene and I wouldn't have to marry him. A hurricane would destroy the church. The chef would fall and bump his head and forget to make the food. A blistering heat wave would consume the city at the same time that the florist's air conditioning would break, causing the flowers to wilt and die.

A girl could dream...

But dreaming didn't work, nor did wishing or praying if this week was anything to go by. Someone had once said if you wanted something bad enough, the universe would make sure you got it. *Yeah, right.*

The uneasy knot that formed in my stomach tightened as the bridal store came into view. It started as a niggling feeling when I began my walk toward the destination, and it heightened until I felt I was on the edge of a full-blown panic attack. With everything going on in my head, a trip to the dominatrix dress fitter was not what I wanted to be doing.

She gave me the same thin-lipped smile, sending a jolt of fear through my body. So yes she was still scary, yes she tightened the corset to within an inch of my life, and yes, she definitely enjoyed inflicting pain.

Once she had damn near squeezed the life out of me, she left to answer the phone ringing at the front of the store. I let out a cautious breath, unsure if anything would burst if I did. At least this was the last fitting. I never had to see the sadistic woman ever again. I let this thought comfort me for a moment. A moment was all it lasted before, with sickening dread, I realized that the next time I wore this dress, I would be facing Theo.

I leaned back against the fitting room wall and tried to catch my breath. Tears pricked my eyes and I was dangerously close to losing it. *Don't be stupid! Get it together...*

Closing my eyes, I tried to visualize the day. The church filled with people I didn't know. *Okay, that's worse. Look for the people you do know.* Hayley would be ahead of me, like a lighthouse guiding the ship to safety. But she wouldn't be leading me to safety! She would be tossing me into the lion's den! *Okay, worse again. Look for Mom. Ahh...there she is. Mom's crying, bless her heart. Dad... Where is Dad? Oh, beside me. Whoops!* Dad would be looking at the floor, afraid anyone would see the tears I knew would be welling up in his eyes. And at the front would be... *Wait, there's no one there.*

No matter how hard I tried, I couldn't picture Theo standing at the altar, smiling as he waited for me to reach him. I had his face at the back of my mind. I just couldn't project him into my wedding scenario. Even the space behind where he should have been was empty. A few unimportant groomsmen waited, but the spot of the best man was empty. I had no idea who Theo would get as a last minute stand-in now that Blake was...

Blake...

The very instant I thought of him, there he was. Standing in Theo's spot, grinning like an idiot who'd won the lottery and been given a puppy all at the same time. There were no nerves visible on his face and the more I pictured him standing there, all my anxiety washed away. I felt as calm as the day I'd stood on the edge of the world with him by my side. How easy it was to picture a fantasy wedding to Blake. I could see it all...as clear as if I was remembering the actual event.

Never did our eyes leave each other's. I could feel the electricity that would shoot up my hand and arm as he slid the wedding band onto my finger where it would remain for the rest of my days. In that second, I would feel whole, complete. The race was over. We had won. All that was left was forever. When he kissed me—our first official kiss as husband and wife—I would get too caught up in the moment. The priest would cough discreetly, and Blake would smile against my lips. I wouldn't care. I would let myself have a few more moments of kissing the lips of the man I would adore forever and ignore the mounting giggles behind me.

I opened my eyes and the fantasy dissolved in front of reality. The dress fitter returned, and I practically screamed for her to take the dress off. I redressed quickly and flew from the store as if my life depended on it.

What was it Hayley had once said? One night in the club she'd said I was practically vibrating. It had been because of Blake and Theo—wasn't it always?—but that had been nothing compared to the way I felt now. Storming ahead with my hair whipping around my face, I thought I was going to explode. I rattled with nerves and I needed it to stop. Right now.

People jostled into me but I was too pre-occupied to care. My body felt as though I stood in the middle of a volcano. I could feel my hair clinging to my face and I didn't know if it was some symptom of my panic attack that rose my temperature so high, or if it was merely the atrociously fast pace my legs seemed determined to maintain. Combine this with the heat from the May sun and I was a big sweaty mess. I didn't need to look to know a heat haze would hover in the distance, blurring the shapes and colors. Hell, they would be blurred without the haze to my eyes right now. I wasn't a stranger to the stifling heat in the city, but it was the first time it had felt suffocating.

I found a nearby pharmacy and raced inside. Charging around the aisles, I finally found what I was looking for. I tore the lid off and swallowed a large gulp of the pink Pepto. Barely giving it time to settle in my stomach to ease the nauseated feeling that had steadily risen since leaving the bridal store, I frantically tried to find some stress-relief pills or something. The first thing I found was some herbal stuff. I chased two down with more Pepto.

Closing my eyes, I let out a breath and willed myself to a calm state of mind. Upon opening them again, my freak-out was about over. Letting out another breath, I made my way to the counter and hoped they wouldn't be too pissed I'd tried before buying.

A familiar mass of blonde hair was in front of me in line for the check-out. I groaned internally and hoped I had on my best game face.

"Hi, Simone. Small world, huh?"

Simone gave a small jump before turning around. She wore a distinct animal-caught-in-the-headlights look. "Oh. Hi, Marley."

"How are you?"

"Fine."

I glanced down to what she clutched in her hands. Prenatal vitamins. A blush crept up my face as she noticed me snooping. "Oh!" I cried. Damn it! How do I get into these situations? "Congratulations! I mean, wow. Um, I didn't know you were seeing anyone. Not…not that you need to be, damn, I didn't mean it like that! Um, congratulations."

Simone's eyes were hard and her lips thin. I thought she was going to hit me. Instead she turned around and paid the clerk. When it was my turn, I practically threw the money at the poor guy then charged after Simone, because I just couldn't leave well enough alone.

"Simone! Wait!" I caught up with her a little outside the pharmacy.

She wordlessly turned to face me.

"I'm really sorry. I didn't mean to snoop, and I won't say anything to Theo, if you don't want colleagues to know yet. It's none of my business and...sorry again."

To my surprise, and complete horror, Simone burst into tears. "It's not your fault. It's just this guy. He's just so, ugh! He really gets to me, and I just can't... And now this— I thought he would be happy, but he got so mad, like I did this on purpose? We should be so happy, and we're not. You want to know why? Fucking timing! I can't believe my own damn bad luck that somebody else met him first!" Simone shouted through her tears.

"I'm sorry, Simone. You want to go somewhere to talk?"

She shook her head. "I'm sorry for unloading on you, I didn't mean to. Please don't say anything—"

"Of course not." I watched her carefully—she seemed a bit more in control. "I have to ask—and tell me to butt out if you don't want to talk about it—but, this guy? Is he married?"

She flinched. "Not yet. But he's going to be."

I nodded. Poor Simone. I should give her Blake's number. He managed to find a way to leave me, maybe he could help Simone. "I don't know what to say."

"You don't need to say anything. It's not your problem." And she was back. Hard, cold Simone.

"And it's not just yours either. Tell this guy he has to face up and take responsibility."

"Oh, he will. Trust me. I have this all figured out. One way or another, he will be mine."

Gulp. I laughed breathily. "Damn, I feel sorry for the woman up against you."

Simone smiled. "You should. I feel sorry for anyone who gets in my way."

I no longer wanted to be having this conversation with Simone. There was a black fire in her eyes that I knew not to mess with. *Damn. If I'm this shaken up by Simone, I'd sure hate to be the woman in her way.*

Chapter Seventeen

A few days after my exchange with Simone and exactly two weeks before the wedding, I paid an unexpected visit to my mom. She was standing by the sink, rinsing out a glass when I snuck up behind her. She jumped and nearly dropped the glass. Spinning around to face me, her expression was priceless — annoyed and happy, all rolled into one.

She pulled me into a hug, getting my back wet in the process. Apologizing profusely, Mom ushered me to a stool at the island and made us some coffee.

"So, any reason for your impromptu visit?" Mom asked as I blew on my coffee.

I shook my head. I could feel her eyes on me, but I couldn't face them. Not yet anyway. She must have sensed my reluctance, and let out a stream of unimportant chatter. Little by little, she engaged me in conversation, until, without even realizing it, she brought me out my funk. Moms are superstars, truly.

"There's a flea market today that I was going to go to. Feel like coming?" Mom asked.

I smiled. "Sure."

* * * *

We wandered around the flea market with our arms linked, looking at the knick-knacks for sale. Mom picked up a few steals. I couldn't concentrate enough to focus on anything. Mom nudged me in the ribs with her elbow.

"What?" I asked her.

Mom smiled and nodded her head. "Mrs. Wheeton was asking about the wedding."

I turned toward the woman Mom had indicated, realizing that we had paused in our browsing and I was being extremely rude. "Oh. Sorry, I was miles away."

She nodded and smiled kindly. "It will be a little hectic now, is it? Taking care of last minute details. How long is it now? Three weeks?"

"Two," I corrected, wishing she wasn't wrong.

Her smile widened. "How excited you must be!"

I nodded, ignoring that sick feeling rising in my throat.

"I hope you will send me a few pictures of the big day? I'd love to see one of you and your new husband!"

Oh, God, I'm going to throw up. "Of course," I whispered.

"I'll make sure of it," Mom said, tugging me away.

She didn't say anything on the drive home but I could see her mind turning. Once I was back in the safety of her kitchen, I sat again at the island and Mom made us some lunch. She pushed a plate of sandwiches under my nose along with a glass of water. After ten minutes of silence and untouched sandwiches, Mom sighed and got back up. She placed a carton of Ben and Jerry's in front of me, which I dug into with vigor.

"You can talk to me, Marley. You know that, right?" Mom asked.

"Yes," I said past a mouthful of ice cream.

"What's on your mind? And remember, I'm your mother. I know when you're lying."

I sighed and placed my spoon down. "I really don't want to talk about it."

She covered my hand with her own. "It's not too late if you have changed your mind about Theo."

I snapped my head up to look at her. "Why do you think I've changed my mind?"

She shrugged. "Just the way you act. You're miserable."

"I'm not."

"What did I say about lying?"

I groaned. "Mom, seriously, I'm not talking about this."

"Marley, this isn't like taking a new job that you're not sure about. This is *marriage*. This is a decision that you will live with for the *rest of your life*. Think about it. Do you want Theo for the rest of your life? Even if you aren't sure about the answer, it's not fair on either of you to make the commitment anyway. Speak up, before it's too late."

"And were you sure? About Daddy?"

Mom's face was deadly serious when she answered me, "More sure than I have been about anything."

"How did you know?" A part of me knew she was about to describe everything I felt with Blake. I was very sure she wasn't about to say because she felt obligated and was trying to repay a debt.

She shrugged. "I just did. It was just a feeling he gave me. I can still remember our first date, our first kiss, how I felt when he proposed…everything."

I leaned my elbows on the table and cupped my chin, torn between morbid curiosity and loving hearing about this side of my parents. "How did you feel?"

"Dizzy. I was so happy that I felt dizzy."

My God they were cute. "When did you know you wanted to be with him forever?"

"I'm not sure. After our first kiss, I knew I was onto something pretty amazing."

There was a faraway look in Mom's eyes, and I knew she was in another time entirely. In that moment I loved my parents for showing me the kind of love to aspire to. Even if I wasn't choosing to claim it for myself. Growing up, I'd had a few friends whose parents had separated, divorced or had daily screaming matches. It wasn't something I ever worried about for Mom and Dad.

I arched an eyebrow. "That good, huh?"

Mom's grin widened. "There were fireworks."

I laughed. "Wow. Never knew Dad had it in him."

Mom laughed. "Oh, I wouldn't read too much into that. It was the fourth of July."

My smile fell. And there I had been thinking we were all capable of finding the fireworks with someone.

Mom caught my expression. "The real fireworks came later, when I knew I was in love with him."

"Do you still see them now?" I asked quietly.

Mom smiled, soft and reassuring. "Not as fiercely, but yes."

I focused on the little beads of condensation running down the side of the carton of ice cream.

There was a heavy pause before Mom spoke again. "Marley, I'm not too sure how to say this, but, I truly hope you aren't marrying Theo in some misguided attempt to repay him for what he did for Daddy."

I sighed. There were two options open to me. Tell the truth and get her valuable wisdom on what to do — or lie. "Of course not."

I felt more alone than ever when I left my mom. I wanted to tell her the truth and have her make everything okay again, but she couldn't. Only I could do that. And the right thing for me to do was to continue down my chosen path. After all, I'd chosen it and I'd given my word. As Frost said, *'I have promises to keep, and miles to go before I sleep'*.

* * * *

I was not having a good day. It had started as I'd walked into the office and Kelly had looked at me like I'd forgotten my skirt. Normally I wouldn't have thought anything about it, but not two minutes later the same thing had happened with the girl who sat opposite me. And the mailroom guy and everyone else. They all kept staring at me. The insecure little girl in me wanted to run from the room and hide where their suspicious eyes couldn't find me. But, I was a big girl and I would grin and bear it.

I turned my computer on and it churned to life. I entered my username and password and 'unknown user' flashed on the screen. *Huh.* I tried again. Same thing. No one else seemed to have any trouble with their computers. Just me.

Henry chose that moment to walk past my desk. He did a double-take when he saw me. *Jesus, him too?*

"Marley, can I see you in my office?" he asked, his normally cheerful face pulled into an angry frown.

My hands shook as I followed him into the office. He even shut the door behind me. Henry never shut his office door.

"What are you doing here, Marley?"

"I don't understand," I whispered. I didn't know what was going on. It was like everyone was in on the joke but me. A dull panic rose in my stomach.

"I mean, why are you here?"

"Um, I came to work?"

Henry sighed, his eyes still tight with anger. "So, you decide to get your boyfriend to quit for you, then decide you want to come back again? This is a job, Marley! You can't just quit and pick it back up when you feel like it!"

Henry had never in his life shouted at me like he did then. I had to say, it was pretty terrifying. "Seriously, Henry, I have no idea what you're talking about."

"You hurt a lot of people, Marley. Everyone here was so excited you were staying. None of them would say it to your face, but it was so backward what you were doing. Quitting to be a full-time wife, to do nothing but sit around and stroke that asshole's ego. When you came to your senses and decided to stay, they were freaking ecstatic!

"You really hurt their feelings when you couldn't even say goodbye. You couldn't even say goodbye to *me*. I thought more of you, Marley. Really I did."

Tears stung my eyes. "Henry, I don't know what you are talking about. I don't know how else to say that!"

Henry frowned. "You really don't, do you?"

I shook my head.

"Theo called here after you left on Friday. He told us you wouldn't be coming back."

His words knocked the breath out of me. "He did what?"

Henry's eyes softened and he was back to being the caring boss I knew and loved. "I thought you were too much of a coward to tell me yourself. I shouldn't have doubted you."

"I can't believe he did that," I whispered.

"Of course, if you want to come back, you're more than welcome. It was just a shock seeing you, that's all."

"Um, I better go fix this. I'm so sorry, Henry. I never wanted my personal life to affect my work or your company." I shook my head, overwhelmed and so, so confused. "I don't know where my head is right now."

Henry pulled me into a hug. "Do whatever you need to do. Take some time off. I think you need it. We'll all be here for you. A family, remember?"

I nodded. "Will you explain to Kelly for me? I can't talk about it."

"Sure thing."

"Thank you. For everything, Henry." I pulled away from him and fled from the building.

Disbelief and shock rang through me. How could Theo have done this? In his defense, he had warned me. Either I was to quit on my own or he would handle it. He'd told me so himself. But still... What an asshole! To go behind my back like that! I wanted to get my hands around his neck and throttle the life right out of him!

Before I could change my mind, I stormed toward his office. I was having this out with him, and I didn't care where. My conversation with Henry played on a loop in my head, all the way to Theo's floor in his office building.

A bell chimed when the elevator reached my chosen floor. The steel doors slid open, revealing the bustling office before me. My face burned with anger as I stepped out into the room. Though the office floor teamed with people, I couldn't make out a single voice. The blood rushed in my ears and my heart pounded too loud to hear anything. With my eyes focused on Theo's closed office door, I marched forward.

A hand touched my arm and I jerked around. A small red-haired woman smiled at me. "Can I help you?"

"What?" I asked, frowning.

"I asked if I can help you? I'm Karen, the receptionist—I spoke to you when you got out of the elevator. You seemed miles away!" She smiled.

"Right. Sorry, yeah, miles away," I agreed. "I'm just going to see Theo."

"Do you have an appointment?"

"I'm sure he will see me. I'm Marley. His fiancée," I bit out. "I need to see him. Now." It had to be now. I needed all of this pent up frustration out right this very second or I was going to implode.

"He's in a meeting," Karen said. "Would you like to wait at my desk? Have a coffee?"

"No," I said. "I can't. I need—"

"Oh!" Karen cried. "Looks like his meeting is finished after all."

I glanced toward Theo's office. Simone walked from the room, a sly smile on her full lips. Theo's head popped out and he whispered something to her. Simone giggled and placed a hand on his chest. It was brief but it screamed intimacy.

If I were standing any farther away, I probably would never have noticed. But because I wasn't, the piece of jewelry on Simone's wrist was plain as day. I'd seen it before—in a Tiffany's box I'd found in Theo's jacket pocket.

So he wasn't going to let me down, then, because it had never been for me.

It had been for Simone.

Why the fuck was Theo giving Simone a Tiffany's bracelet?

The room spun around me. My eyes lost their focus. I felt like I was on a merry-go-round, traveling way too fast. My conversation with Simone zoomed through my mind.

'I have to ask, and tell me to butt out if you don't want to talk about it, but, this guy? Is he married?'

'Not yet. But he's going to be. One way or another, he will be mine. I feel sorry for anyone who gets in my way.'

She'd all but told me herself she was sleeping with Theo. Jesus Christ.

"Would you like me to let him know you are here? Or do you just want to go in?" Karen asked.

"No!" I cried, my attention zeroing in on her. "I have to go. Don't— Please don't tell him I came."

She frowned. "Of course."

"Thanks." I moved as quickly as I dared, almost running into the elevator. The journey down took too long. I paced back and forth in the tiny metal prison until the doors opened and I lurched outside.

Chapter Eighteen

My thoughts went round and round in my head. Faces passed me by in a blur. I crashed into bodies as my feet pounded the street underfoot, racing me home. Blake's voice whispered around me the way wind teases the branches of the trees. *'Open your eyes... Open your eyes... Open your eyes...'*

I fumbled with my key, cursing aloud before I finally managed to turn it and unlock the door. Bursting it open, I then slammed it shut behind me and turned every lock. Leaning on the door, I tried to catch my breath. I closed my eyes... *Focus!*

How did I begin to piece together this catastrophic puzzle? The truth was almost within reach. I couldn't stop now. Blake had said I ignored things right in front of me, but this I couldn't ignore. I ran down the hall into Theo's meticulously kept office. Papers flew around me in a flurry as I ransacked drawers and filing cabinets. I didn't know what I was looking for... I just knew I had to find something.

There had to be some evidence in here somewhere — anything to prove what I felt in my very bones. It shouldn't be too hard. I didn't plague Theo's every step the way he did mine. He had no reason to carefully guard his secrets. I stood in front of the wall-length bookcase filled with thick law books and leather covered folders.

I picked one folder at random and scanned through it. Seemed to be a record of Theo's finances. I couldn't see anything out of the ordinary, but it was pretty old. At the opposite end of the shelf I picked up another folder. This one seemed to be the most recent.

I carried it over to Theo's desk and sat down to study it more closely. A lot of it was everyday stuff like mortgage payments, insurance and all the other luxuries Theo indulged in—his gym membership, payment for his personal nutritionist and his addiction to Prada suits.

But there was a weekend in a Vermont bed and breakfast. Checking the date, I realized it was the same weekend I'd been in Vegas.

Several other hotels and trips popped up in cities all over the country. *So much for that huge case, right, Theo?*

I stood up from the desk and backed away from the awful book that held so many of Theo's dark secrets. Racing into the bedroom, I opened a drawer in my bureau and yanked out the purple photo album with such ferociousness it made the whole bureau shake. I dropped it on the bed and flipped the pages over until I found the one I was looking for.

There they stood—unaware their moment had been frozen and remembered forever. The closer I looked at the photo of Theo and Simone, the more I seemed to uncover. The smile on Simone's face was one of superiority. She held all the cards, Theo was at her mercy. I'd noticed before how Theo's eyes seemed to plead with her. Maybe it was because now I was so close to the truth I could smell it, but he actually looked afraid.

I felt faint as all the pieces came together... How Theo had bought the bracelet for Simone...in celebration of their pregnancy? All the lies all this time... How many had he told me? I'd chained myself to him, given up Blake for him. And for what? This?

* * * *

There were hours left before Theo was due home and I had little to do to occupy my racing mind. My eyes were open and the truth was out. I couldn't believe I had been stupid enough to not realize he was seeing Simone all this time. I'd never suspected anything, and lately, I guess my eyes had been so firmly fixed on Blake everything else had fallen out of sight.

More than anything, I couldn't believe I'd actually felt sorry for Simone. When I'd run into her and she'd unloaded all her pent-up frustration onto me, I'd sympathized with her. *God, what an idiot.* She must have laughed all the way back home after that little encounter. She was a sick, twisted, hateful little bitch.

And I'm pretty sure she isn't a natural blonde.

I cursed them both as I went to work raising the cuffs on all Theo's pants. Not so much that he would notice right away — but enough that he would look like a complete douchebag with his socks showing. Next I cut out all his pockets and reset his TiVo so it would only record *Teen Mom* and *America's Next Top Model*.

The hour grew late and the sky darkened. Lights flickered on in the thousands of windows visible from the view at Theo's penthouse of secrets and lies. From my seat at his desk, I heard Theo unlock the door and enter the apartment. His footsteps echoed down the hall before he walked into the office and flipped on the light.

"Shit!" he exclaimed when he saw me.

"Welcome home, Theo."

His eyes flitted downwards before hesitantly rising to meet my steady gaze. "Marley, why do you have a gun?"

I cocked my head to the side as though I was weighing him up.

"Marley," Theo said as his voice shook. "Why do you have a gun?"

I glanced down at the steel handgun resting on the open pages of the book that bore Theo's secrets. "This gun?" I asked, picking it up and examining it curiously.

"Yes, that gun."

I shrugged. "Thought I might use it. Haven't really decided yet."

Theo raised his hands up slowly. "Now, just take it easy, Marley. You don't want to do—"

"Why are you with me, Theo?" I asked.

"What?"

"Why are you with me?" I asked more slowly.

"I— Because I love you."

"No, what's the real reason? Is it my charming personality? My brown hair? Or is it because you thought I would be easy to control?"

"Marley, baby, I don't know what you're talking about."

The word 'baby' made my temper flair. "Seems like I'm hearing that word a lot these days, Theo. It's what you want, isn't it? A baby?"

"Yes," he said nervously.

"By me?"

"Who-who else?"

"I'm just trying to figure out why you want to be with someone like me. I don't share your interests. You don't include me in anything. I don't understand your work. Wouldn't you be happier with someone like, I don't know, Simone?"

What little color Theo had left, drained from his face. "If I wanted to be with someone like that, I would. It's you I want."

I laughed ruefully. "We've established that you want me. I want to know why."

"I—I think you're good for me."

"I'm good for your image."

"No—"

"You wanted a trophy wife—one that would stand by your side and look pretty. One that wouldn't question anything. You couldn't have someone like Simone for your wife. She would be too smart for you! She wouldn't let you push her around or make her quit her job."

"Marley, I don't know what you're talking about—"

I laughed. "You know, I had some free time on my hands today. Just like tomorrow. And the day after that, and the day after that..."

Theo's eyes widened. "Is that what this is about? Your job?"

My lips curled into a sneer. "Yeah, I'm waving a gun at you because of a job. Like I'm that emotionally unstable. Sheesh." I rolled my eyes.

Theo gasped when he realized what lay open in front of me.

"I did a little reading today."

"You read my account book?" Theo asked. The jerk had the nerve to look mad at me!

"I did. Want to know what I found?" I asked, smiling. "Quite a few little romantic breaks. Except, I don't remember going on any of them, so they all must have been with Simone, right? That hurts my feelings, Theo."

A tear slid down Theo's cheek. "I'm so sorry, Marley. You were never meant to get hurt! Never. The whole thing with Simone... I'm sorry, I don't know how it happened. She's just so...so... She wouldn't let me..."

"Shut up!" I raised the gun and pointed it at his chest. "I never want to hear your lies again."

"Marley, please!" Theo choked out, his voice thick and hoarse.

"Goodbye, Theo." My voice was calm, even before I squeezed the trigger.

"No!" Theo blinked at the plastic click. He stared at me for a long moment before sinking to his knees, clasping his chest and gasping for breath.

"Realistic, huh? It's amazing what you can buy these days. Like I would do jail time over your pathetic ass!" I threw the plastic gun at Theo as he raised his hands to shield himself.

Theo turned to look at me. On any other day the look in his eyes would have terrified me. Today, I felt nothing.

"You fucking bitch," Theo whispered as he got to his feet.

"What's the matter, Theo? Scare you?"

"You're fucking crazy!" Theo screamed. Sheer undiluted rage smoldered in Theo's eyes.

Only the adrenaline that still coursed through me helped me hold my ground. I refused to drop my eyes as he stalked toward me, looking angry enough to curl his fingers around my throat. "So you know everything."

"Everything."

Theo watched as I repositioned myself closer to the door. He paused his slow predatory pursuit to close the open account book on his desk. He lowered his frame into the chair, keeping his eyes on me the entire time.

I folded my arms across my chest. "Tell me why, Theo."

He arched an eyebrow at my demand, the fire still burning in his pale blue eyes. "Which part?"

"All of it," I demanded.

"Where would you like me to start? When I started fucking Simone, or when I chose you to be the one for me to marry?"

I felt my cheeks burn as I tried to control my vicious hate for the man.

Theo chuckled. "The Simone story isn't too long. You know how she is. She's a predator and was never shy about her intentions. One night at a function, I gave in to her efforts."

"When?"

Theo shrugged. "Months ago."

"Before or after you proposed?"

"Before."

I blanched. "Then why did you ask me? Why not just have her?"

"For the reasons you stated earlier. Simone isn't the kind of girl I could marry. She's too opinionated and far too much trouble to control. You, on the other hand, were perfect."

I couldn't believe he was talking so calmly, as though this were any other conversation. Theo stood up and turned to face the window, looking out over the city. "It was all perfect timing really. When we met at that party, it was easy to see how everyone responded to you. It's interesting how you yourself never see it, but I did. You have an innocent charm and I knew you would make me look good. It was only afterward that I saw just how beneficial you could be. And your dad getting sick? A stroke of perfection. When the senior partners found out about that charity donation, the promotion was mine."

Angry tears stung my eyes. For a brief moment, I wished that gun had been real.

"So." Theo turned back to face me. "Who told you?"

"What?"

"All this," Theo said, gesturing vacantly with his hand. "Who told you?"

I narrowed my eyes at him. "No one told me, you asshole! I figured it out for myself."

"You mean it wasn't Blake?"

My stomach dropped. "Blake?"

Theo watched me for a moment before his lips curled into a sly smile. "You mean your little boyfriend didn't tell you? I thought you two were close."

"More than you will ever know."

"He fucked you, didn't he?"

My cheeks flushed with chagrin.

Theo smiled. "And you think I'm the cruel one. He really did a number on you, huh?"

My heart pounded and the sick feeling returned to my stomach.

Theo shook his head. "Thought you were smarter than that, Marley. To fall for a guy like that. Blake's a player, always has been."

"You're lying."

He smiled. "I'm not. Why do you think he was so interested in you when he came to the city? I asked him to keep you out of my way so I would be free to see Simone, but I didn't expect him to do such a good job. I thought he had a crush on you, never thought he would do anything about it. Guess he couldn't help himself. He's not one for morals, you know?"

"Shut up," I whispered. The rage that flooded my veins drained from me, leaving only despair and a sliver of doubt which I clung to.

"What really surprises me is that he didn't even care enough to tell you about the baby."

"He knew?" *It has to be lies...it has to be...*

Theo laughed. "He knew who, why—the whole shebang. He was pissed when he found out."

I felt like someone had punched me in the gut. I struggled to catch my breath and make my head stop spinning.

"You know, it makes me wonder if he cared about you at all."

"He did. He loved me."

"Then why didn't he tell you?" Theo asked, almost kindly.

I had no idea how my legs still held me up. They felt as though they would give way at any moment. Theo's hurtful words rang in my ears and as much as I wanted to ignore them and think them false, it all made too much sense.

"Do you want a drink?" Theo asked, moving toward the shelf he kept a few bottles of liquor on.

"No. I have to go."

"Where?" Theo asked. "When will you be back?"

I laughed, more in shock than anything else. "I won't be."

The smile fell from Theo's lips.

"You thought after everything I found out, I'd still stay with you? Jesus, Theo! And as much as I hate the psychotic bitch, what about Simone? She's having your baby, Theo."

I walked past him and marched down the hall. Opening the closet next to the front door, I pulled out two large suitcases.

"Marley, think about this," Theo called from behind me.

"What is there to think about?" I asked. "Goodbye, Theo."

I wheeled my suitcases out of the building and the doorman put them into the trunk of a cab for me. Lights washed over me in the back seat as the cab took me farther from the place that had never felt like home. The shackles Theo had locked in place so long ago now came undone. I was free.

Chapter Nineteen

Tears welled in Hayley's eyes when she opened her door to find me waiting with my life stuffed into two suitcases. She stood opening and closing her mouth for a moment, appearing at a loss as to what to do next.

Then she snatched my suitcases from my grip and wheeled them into her spare room. "It's yours, as long as you need or want it. Okay?"

My throat tightened and all I could do was nod. I dropped down onto her couch, sinking into the worn cushions. When Hayley returned, she held two glass tumblers and a bottle of tequila.

I guessed this time my drama warranted more than wine.

"You can either drink and talk, or drink—or talk. Whatever you need." Hayley poured two generous servings of tequila and left one on the coffee table.

I took it and slung the liquid straight down my throat.

"Um, okay," Hayley said. "Another, then?"

I nodded.

Hayley lifted the bottle.

"Theo's been having an affair since before he even met me. With Simone." Better to get it all out quick. Like pulling off a Band-Aid.

She jerked and tequila sloshed over the side of the glass. Hayley took a moment to carefully place the bottle back on the table. Her hands shook. "I knew I hated that fucking asshole—and that fucking slut."

"So you had no idea?"

Hayley whipped around, her eyes wide. "What? Are you serious? Do you really—fuck, Marley. I mean— Jesus Christ, like I wouldn't tell you?"

I released a shaky breath. This was good. This was good. If Hayley really didn't know then I hadn't been betrayed by everyone. Maybe there really wasn't any reason to believe Theo about Blake's involvement. I'd hurt Theo and he'd hurt me right back.

Theo wasn't the kind not to even the score.

"Did I mention she was pregnant?"

Hayley swore—in a way that would make the most seasoned of sailors blush.

A morbid laugh bubbled in my throat. "Want to know something really weird? I sort of feel like I'm the other woman. I mean, she met him first. She's carrying his child."

Hayley snorted. "Right. Even Theo isn't dumb enough to take her word. He'll get a paternity test the second she pops it out."

I leaned forward to finish off pouring our drinks. "The part I can't wrap my head around is, how the hell did he have time? Between his job and me, you're lucky if he factored in four hours a night for sleep. How did he manage to placate her?"

Hayley shrugged and accepted the glass I offered her. "Probably with money. Pretty things. Think about it. If it's really been going on for so long, she must have had a game plan. She couldn't act like a jealous wife or he'd get tired of her and move on. I'm guessing she followed his lead and gritted her teeth when she didn't get her own way. That, and the mistress gifts had to be ridiculously expensive. And I'd bet my left tit that pregnancy was planned."

That sounded like Simone. And Theo, for that matter.

"I wonder if 'that huge case' was his euphemism for 'I'm going to fuck Simone'," I thought out loud.

Hayley finished her drink. "Probably. And that weekend in Vegas must have provided them some quality time together."

"At least we were both having a good time," I mumbled into my glass before finishing the rest of the tequila.

"Here, here," Hayley folded her legs underneath her. She placed a pillow on her lap and patted it. "Come on. I'll braid your hair."

I laughed softly, not really feeling like laughing at all, and lay down with my head on the pillow. "You're so weird."

She tugged on my hair but not hard enough to hurt. "Shut up. My mom did this when I felt shitty. And if you keep drinking all my tequila like that, I'm going to end up having to drag your ass to the ER."

Hayley put on old movies and we lay sprawled out on her couch and watched them all night long. We exchanged stories of loser ex-boyfriends and I found myself laughing along with Hayley. The idea of all the work to do over the coming week was a sobering thought. So many things had to be canceled and people had to be notified. How would I manage it all myself?

"What are you going to do about Blake?"

Hayley's question stabbed my heart. "What do you mean?"

"Well wasn't the whole reason he left because you were marrying Theo? Isn't it kind of a moot point now?"

"I guess. Who's to say he would want me after everything that happened?"

Hayley squeezed my arm. "Of course he'll still want you."

I shrugged.

She sighed. "Maybe…maybe a break from them both would be good for you. Some time by yourself, time to think. Couldn't be a bad thing."

My head was so muddled right now I couldn't imagine being with anyone. Or was it Theo's words that had made me hesitant in pursuing what I really wanted?

When Hayley finally dozed off and the darkness gave way to the pale pink of the morning light, I crept from the lounge and out onto the fire escape. Below me the city was beginning to stir. I could see a few joggers, someone opening up a coffee shop, a news-stand guy with his early bird customers.

My mind reeled with everything I'd discovered. Even though I wasn't romantically in love with Theo, I still felt wounded by him. It couldn't just be karma. What I'd done with Blake didn't come close to the way Simone had mentally and cruelly attacked me. I'd betrayed Theo by falling for Blake and acting on my feelings for him, but did that mean I deserved all that had happened? I hoped not.

I just didn't understand how Theo could have been so heartless. No, not heartless. He was spiteful and sadistic. He'd said he didn't mean for me to get hurt. Yeah. Right.

The thing that got to me the most was what I'd given up for him. I was in love with Blake and though he'd never said it, I knew that love was reciprocated. I'd killed our relationship. I'd killed it for Theo. I thought I owed him because of my father. The guilt I'd felt day by day over my own betrayal was a wasted emotion. Had I known Theo was screwing around with Simone, I wouldn't have thought twice about making the commitment with Blake.

I pulled my cell from my pocket and stared at it for a while. My stomach fluttered as I worked up the courage to place the call I wasn't altogether sure I wanted to make. Did I want to know the answers? Wasn't ignorance bliss? A greedy part of me just wanted to hear his voice one more time.

Scrolling through my list of contacts, I found his name. I pressed Call and held the phone to my ear.

The butterflies in my stomach danced. Actually, jived around on jackhammers would be a better description. The line rang and rang and rang some more. No answer. Not surprising, really. Why would Blake want to talk to me? I hadn't given him a reason to stay. Why would he think there was a reason for me to talk to him?

"Hello?" Blake's voice was hoarse with sleep but it still managed to send an electric current throughout my body.

"Hi, it's me." I couldn't seem to raise my voice above a whisper.

"Yeah, I know."

Covers rustled on Blake's end. It was six-thirty in the morning, no wonder he'd taken so long to answer. A quick mental calculation told me it would only be three-thirty in Vegas—he'd probably only just got to bed. It was painfully easy to visualize him sitting up in bed, rubbing the sleep from his eyes with his hair disheveled. Just thinking about it made my heart thump even more erratically.

"I'm sorry I woke you."

"It's okay."

The understanding in his voice made my eyes sting. I bit my lip as the tears silently cascaded down my face. There were so many things I wanted to say and so many I shouldn't. I'd placed this call for a reason, and I needed answers before I crossed the point of no return.

"Marley, are you okay?"

I took a breath. "Did you know? About Theo and Simone?"

There was a moment before Blake spoke. "Yes."

"You helped him?"

"Yes."

A lump formed in my throat, but I forced myself to carry on. "Did you know about the baby?"

Blake's voice was thick. "Yes."

The pain hit me like a white-hot poker plunging into my chest. I disconnected the call, ending communication and all further contact with Blake. So he'd known everything. The three of them must have laughed so hard at my ignorance.

Blake's betrayal hurt a thousand times more than Theo's. I'd thought he was on my side. Turned out he'd only distracted me from seeing Theo's actions. They'd both used me to get what they wanted.

It was as though someone had flipped my 'off' switch. The energy drained from me. After learning the hideous truth from Blake, I climbed back into Hayley's apartment and hid in my room. Crawling onto the bed, I pulled the blankets over my head. No matter how hard I tried I couldn't make the voices stop. Over and over again they taunted me, whispering their cruel words.

I squeezed my eyes shut but all I could see was Theo's hateful sneer as he shattered my image of Blake. How long had it been going on? Had it all been a set-up from the beginning? Had Blake known who I was in Vegas? This must have been the plan all along – to distract me well enough that I wouldn't even consider what Theo was doing.

My soul burned with shame and humiliation. My love for Blake was so real and pure – and it had been nothing more than an illusion. He should consider becoming an actor. Clearly he had a talent for the performance arts.

Tender moments we had shared, the intimate post-coital whisperings – I saw them all as if from behind a two-way mirror. The veil had been lifted and I now saw nothing but lies. Why did he have to be so convincing in his act? Every touch, every kiss, every single moment we'd spent together had made me more sure of his feelings. My mind drifted back to our afternoon in Coney Island. He'd made me so freaking happy that day.

The most confusing aspect of it all was that Blake was still the person I wanted to run to. It was an automatic thing, a reflex. I craved his arms to hold me. I wanted to press my ear to his chest and hear the steady rhythm of his heart. The thought of his smile made my heart twist in agony but at the same time made me want to smile too. Worst of all was how I wanted to drown in his eyes. Those piercing eyes, which always betrayed his emotions. They laughed at me in amusement and could make me feel like my heart was bleeding every time I left him.

I never thought it possible to feel so much love and pain because of one person. I supposed the term would be bittersweet. I definitely felt bitter. I guessed remembering the things I loved about him was the sweet part. It sure didn't feel sweet.

Chapter Twenty

Hayley ripped the covers from my body, making me feel naked and vulnerable. Luckily for her, I wasn't actually naked. The bed dipped as she perched on the edge. "Do you want anything?"

I shook my head and rolled away from her.

She sighed and replaced the covers back over me. A moment later I heard the door click shut as she left the room.

The pillow beneath my head was damp from my endlessly streaming eyes. My head pounded from the violent sobs that had racked my body for hours before slowly fading to a whisper. Eventually the tears had run dry and my breathing had slowed, and sleep snatched me into its peaceful embrace.

* * * *

Hayley let me wallow for exactly two days before she brought in the heavy artillery. I heard the door open then close again. It took only a few moments for the scent of her perfume to reach my nose. Slowly, I pulled the covers down. My mom had tears in her eyes, though she was smiling.

"Mom?" I croaked.

She reached forward to brush a lock of matted hair from my face. "Shh, it's okay."

The softness of her voice was all it took for me to crumble. In an instant she lay by my side and pulled me into a fierce hug. I didn't know how long we stayed like that. Long enough to soak a patch on her blouse. My mom embodied everything that was warm and safe. I didn't have to keep anything in around her.

"Sweetie?" Mom asked some time later.

"Mmm?"

"Are you hungry? Hayley's worried about you, says you haven't left this room in a few days."

"I'm fine."

"I brought Phish Food."

"Maybe I could try a little."

Mom chuckled and gave my arm a soft pat. She sat up and helped me to my feet. On the way out of the room, I caught sight of myself in the full-length mirror. It had to be said, I'd have fit in on October thirty-first. My hair hung in knotted clumps and my face was blotchy and swollen. It was not a look I wore well.

"About time." Hayley grinned when I walked into the lounge.

I shot her a look.

I curled up in a corner of the couch, and Mom fetched me my Phish Food, which I shamefully bogarted.

"Okay. Time to get to work." Mom sat down beside the coffee table and laid her hand on a stack of papers.

"What's all that?"

"Wedding details, guest list, things like that."

It was a hell of a stack. "Right now? I have to call them all right now?"

Mom smiled. "You don't."

"Yeah, think of us as your PAs for the day," Hayley said.

"You two are doing it?"

"Of course."

My eyes threatened to well again, but the chocolaty goodness that was Ben and Jerry's heaven helped me keep control.

Mom and Hayley were like a force of nature that afternoon. They didn't take any crap from any of the vendors or suppliers we were letting down at such short notice. They refused to give any personal details to the guests they called, despite being bombarded with questions.

A few people — like the uptight chef — refused to give the deposits back. What did I care? It was Theo's money. The still-to-call pile of papers shrank as the dealt-with pile grew. With each phone call, my heart lightened. Maybe it was relief. Maybe it was fear. The path of my life lay open and wide like a deserted highway. It had no road signs and I didn't know the way. Where am I going now?

Despite having more freedom than I'd ever been used to, the walls seemed to close in around me with frightening speed. I'd never been claustrophobic, yet I felt like I was suffocating. As humans, we tended to fear the unknown. There was an ancient and deep-rooted part of our subconscious that told us there was something lurking in the darkness, simply waiting for the right moment to snatch us away — something that told us not to take a leap of faith and keep us from making the decisions that really counted.

I'd never depended on Theo, and as young women went, I'd like to think I was fairly independent. But ever since I'd walked out on him, it had felt like I was clawing for survival, like I had been pushed out into the street, naked and vulnerable with no one around to protect me. I certainly didn't miss Theo and I definitely didn't want him back. But the fear of not knowing what I was going to do now was crippling.

Mom had gone to see Henry and explained the situation to him. He'd given me an indefinite leave of absence, which was unbelievably kind of him given all the crap he'd had to deal with because of me. I did toy with the idea of going to work anyway — for a healthy mental distraction — but it was exhausting enough to try to convince Hayley I was okay without having to do it all night and all day with co-workers too. When Hayley was at work and there was nothing but the silence of her apartment, I more or less gave in and let the pain wash me away. My pain was the ocean and the shoreline was growing distant as the waves carried me farther away from normalcy.

Theo made a half-hearted attempt at getting in contact with me. He called my cell twice, but after Hayley hissed some pretty unrepeatable cusses down the phone to him, he didn't call back. Everything was silent on the Blake front. Not a whisper from the man who'd shattered my heart and mauled my soul. The mere thought of him would reduce me to pitiful sobs and it was a downward spiral into full blown hysteria.

On what would have been my wedding night, I planned to have a hot bubble bath then hide under the covers and try in vain to stop thinking about Blake.

My skin tingled from the hot water, which did nothing to soothe my mind. Rubbing my hair dry with a towel, I walked into the lounge and found Hayley and the other girls looking suspiciously dressed up and wearing eager smiles.

"What?" I asked carefully.

"Go get dressed. We're taking you out."

My heart sank. "Oh...Hayley, I don't really feel like—"

"No buts. We're going downtown to a few dives where no one knows you, so if you end up crying into your cocktail, it doesn't matter." Hayley stepped toward me. "We all know what tonight is and none of us are prepared to leave you alone so you can sit and wallow."

"I'm really not getting out of this, am I?"

"No—and the sooner you give in, the sooner you can have a drink."

"Fine," I mumbled.

I knew I couldn't hide away from the world forever, but I had hoped for a few weeks of peace before having to face it again. But true to her word, Hayley took us to a dirty little Irish bar in a neighborhood where we knew no one. Though I didn't say so the bar was my kind of place. It was a little like Cheers — everyone knew your name. Well, except ours. The girls were loud but the jukebox was louder. The floor was sticky and the guys were flirty and seriously cute. Eve was on good form and managed to get more than a few rounds bought for us. A circle of guys crept closer and closer to us, and it wasn't long before our groups integrated. Our table was littered with empty shot glasses and pint glasses of beer, which Hayley insisted we all drink. Beer and tequila... Not looking forward to tomorrow.

It wasn't long until I started to feel the effects of the alcohol. I no longer sat so rigidly in my chair and I'd stopped arguing when someone placed a fresh beer in front of me.

"Marley's getting drunk," Eve said. She giggled and poked me in the ribs.

I poked her back. "Says who?"

"Says the fact you've stopped complaining that we're forcing you to drink devil juice," Hayley said.

"Beer is devil juice. It's practically a food group. An evil fucking food group." I swirled the beer around in its glass. "Except this stuff. It's kind of nice. Piss water. But nice piss water."

The girls cackled. I stuck my tongue out at them.

"Your girl is a happy drunk," the guy beside Hayley said.

She nodded. "She is. Drunk Marley is awesome."

"Drunk Marley swears a lot," Beth chimed in.

"Drunk Marley likes to cuddle," Eve said, raising her glass in the air like she was toasting the fact.

"Drunk Marley likes to be drunker," I said, snagging a shot glass sitting across from one of the guys and not thinking twice about claiming it.

"Drunk Marley has no shame." Eve took the shot glass back and gave it to the guy. She gave me her own instead.

I flung my arm around her neck and almost tipped the glass into her lap. "You're a sweetheart."

"Yes, yes, now drink your medicine." Eve angled the glass toward my mouth.

Just as I was about to take the shot, a crowd of women filled the bar. I set the glass on the table a touch too hard and half the contents sloshed out.

"Marley?" Hayley asked.

Dragging my eyes to her, I pointed to the source of my annoyance.

A bachelorette party. It was a fucking bachelorette party. And I've been having such a good time... Assholes.

A few of the guys started cracking wedding jokes and I figured it would be best for me to be elsewhere. "I'm going to get some drinks!" I yelped.

One of the guys rose to help and followed hot on my heels to the bar.

"What's your name?" I asked him after giving the order to the bartender. He was seriously, seriously cute—twinkly blue eyes and dark hair with a few days' worth of stubble.

"Shane."

Whoa. And Irish to boot. "Marley."

"I remember." He smiled.

Swoon... That really is a killer smile...damn it! Like I need to be thinking about pretty Irishmen and their gorgeous smiles. Maybe that's exactly what I need to be thinking about. You know the old saying, the best way to get over a guy...

"They look like they're having fun," he said, nodding toward the bachelorette party.

And there goes my hot-guy buzz. I nodded. Like I could ever have gone through with it anyway.

Shane grinned. "I bet you have a bloke at home, eager to get you down the aisle."

A small, yet almost inhumanly high-pitched giggle escaped my throat.

He arched an eyebrow. "Something wrong?"

I beckoned him to come closer with my index finger. Leaning in, I whispered, "Tonight is supposed to be my wedding night."

Shane's face dropped a little. "What do you mean, supposed to be?"

"I left him."

"Oh. I'm sure you could work it out."

I giggled. "Nope."

Shame smirked. "Ah, I'm sure it's not that bad."

"He cheated on me and got his girlfriend pregnant."

"Oh." Shane glanced around him, no doubt trying to work out the exits. Shane laughed nervously. "You Yanks are like a soap opera. No other drama apart from that then?"

I shook my head. "Oh! Except that I was sleeping with his best friend. I totally fell for him but it was all a trick. My fiancé arranged the whole set-up."

Shane looked terrified.

"It's actually really funny when you think about it."

"Is it?" he asked.

I looked down, feeling the familiar sting in my eyes. "No. Not really."

The bartender placed a tray of drinks in front of me. Grabbing a beer, I gulped half of it down.

"Better?"

Finishing the beer, I nodded. In that moment I was convinced I'd found my kindred spirit. I threw my arms around Shane's neck. "You're nice. Nice and Irish. A nice Irish." I giggled.

Chapter Twenty-One

The sound of jackhammers pounding into concrete woke me up. The bright morning light stung my eyes. After I'd gathered my bearings, I realized the jackhammers weren't outside. They were in my skull.

I stumbled out of my room and into the kitchen. Chasing down some painkillers with a huge glass of ice cold water, I sank onto the couch. Hayley sat at the other end, watching me with far too much amusement.

"Good night?"

I made a meek attempt to kick her. "It was your idea."

She laughed. "I didn't tell you to drink your body weight in beer and tequila. Or attack some poor Irish man and unload all your drama onto him."

I groaned. "Oh, God, I forgot all about that."

Hayley laughed harder. "I doubt he will forget about you in a while."

In spite of my mortification and agony-ridden head, I laughed. "Poor guy."

"It was when you started describing Blake's hands in painstaking detail that he looked ready to throw himself off the Brooklyn Bridge."

"Shut up!"

Hayley's laugh was interrupted by the shrill ringing of my cell phone. "Ugh. That thing has been going off all morning."

It took me a few minutes to find it, finally locating it in my purse in the kitchen sink.

"Maybe it's the police!" Hayley called. "You're being charged with culpable homicide. The guy jumped after all!"

I slid my finger across the screen to answer. "Hello?"

"Marley? Baby, it's Mom."

"Hi, listen, can I call you back? I've got a monster hangover and I need to spend the morning with my head down the toilet."

My mom let out a shaky breath. "No, I can't call back. You need to come home. Now."

The nausea that had been building rose to a crescendo. "What's wrong?" Somehow, before she answered, I already knew the answer.

"Daddy's sick." Her voice broke. "Can you get the train home today?"

"I'll be on the next one." I floated back through the lounge toward my room.

"Who was that?" Hayley enquired, not tearing her eyes from the TV.

"My mom." My voice sounded distant and foreign. "I have to go home."

"Will you be back for dinner? Sunday night is movie night."

"I don't think I will be back," I whispered.

* * * *

The whole journey upstate I felt disconnected from my body. During the call to Henry on the train where I told him about the situation and that I wouldn't be back at all, my voice didn't break once. I didn't cry. I didn't feel scared, anxious or anything. I felt nothing. I was numb. I moved as if in a trance. My feet felt like lead weights as I hauled my suitcase in search of a cab.

There was nothing different about my parents' home as the cab slowed to a stop outside. There was no red cross painted on the door. The Grim Reaper wasn't lurking behind the trash cans, and a chorus of angels didn't hover above the roof. But as I pushed the front door open, something was wrong. I expected to open this door and be knocked off my feet by the grief that would surely be thick in the air. I expected to hear the racking sobs of my mother as her heart once again broke. I expected to hear someone cooking. People did that, didn't they? Something bad happened, people brought food or felt the need to hold your kitchen hostage.

Instead, there was an eerie calm. The TV played in the den and I could hear movement upstairs. It was…normal. My feet guided me into the kitchen — the first place I visited when coming into this house. Mom was sitting at the island, nursing a mug of coffee that was probably long since warm. I didn't understand. Shouldn't there be a flurry of activity? Shouldn't we be in a hospital or something?

"Mom?"

Her head snapped up at the sound of my voice. She smiled, but it wobbled. "He's upstairs in your room. I think he's been waiting for you."

"Why?" I whispered.

"You need to go talk to him, Marley." She hung her head. "Maybe he'll listen to you."

I tore myself from the room and climbed the stairs. The door to my childhood bedroom lay ajar. Pushing it open fully, I saw my dad standing in front of a cluttered shelf, home to dozens of framed pictures — some of friends, some of family... All of them good times.

A floorboard creaked under foot. Dad turned to face me. He looked the same but different. I opened my mouth to speak but no words would come. It seemed my dad was also having incoherency trouble. He turned back to the shelf of photographs.

"Do you remember the day this was taken?" Dad pointed to a picture of the two of us.

I was maybe six years old and we were at a state fair. I shook my head.

Dad smiled. "It was just the two of us, all day long. You loved this one slide, couldn't get you off it. At the end of the day you asked if we could live at the fair. You wanted us to pack up the house and live at the fair forever and ever. You said you wouldn't even mind sleeping in the haunted house, just as long as you didn't have to leave."

I smiled. "I don't remember." He turned back to the photo. "Daddy?" My voice broke.

My dad hung his head and squeezed his eyes shut.

"Mom said you were sick again. When did you...?"

"I haven't been feeling well for a few weeks. I suppose I didn't want to face the truth."

"How bad is it? When do you start chemo again?"

Slowly, my dad turned to face me. His face seemed to age a thousand years in the moment it took for his eyes to meet mine. "I'm not having chemo."

A sickening feeling pulled at my gut. "Surgery then? Some new drug?"

He took a cautious step toward me. "No."

"What do you mean no?" I asked, my voice wavering. "What kind of treatment are you having then?"

"I'm not having any."

"I don't understand," I whispered.

"The doctor said it isn't going to go away this time." His face smoothed out, like he was resigned. "I've got three, maybe four months left."

No! My body began to shake. "But, surely with some kind of treatment—"

"With some kind of treatment I would have a few more weeks, maybe a month."

"Then do it!"

My dad dropped his eyes again. "Marley, I know this is hard to hear, but in a few months I am going to die. I don't want to spend those months so ill it feels like I am dying. The docs can give me drugs to keep the pain at a bearable level, but that's all I'm doing. I'm going to make this time count. I want time with you and your mother and I will not have that time stuck in a hospital waiting for death to find me."

I shook my head, trying to stop his words. "No, no, no! It isn't fair! You have to take the treatment, please? Please?"

My dad crossed the room and flung his arms around me. "Shh, it's going to be okay. You can't be sad, okay? Not yet. We have time. Lots of time."

I tried to speak but my voice stuck in my throat. He tightened his hold around me and didn't let go until the tears had dried and the shaking stopped.

Dad was upbeat and terrifyingly cheerful when he let me go. He started rambling about taking some vacation somewhere. His ticking clock was spurring him into action to do all the things he wanted to do. And it seemed a fishing vacation was one of them. He had all the gear in the attic, enough for me and Mom too. Dad said he was in the process of hiring a boat and spending the whole week on the damn thing, including sleeping on it. In spite of everything, I smiled as I thought of Mom having to rough it on a boat. She hated the water. I remembered one fourth of July when we'd gone out on a friend's boat. Mom had complained the entire time because the water air made her hair big and poofy.

If this was what he wanted, then I would go along with it. I wouldn't make him feel guilty about his decision to leave us earlier than he had to. Even if I didn't agree with it, I understood his choice. Mom and I remembered all too clearly how ill he had been with the treatment last time. But last time it had worked! This was the part I didn't get. Why couldn't he just have a little faith that he would get better again? But he believed the doctor that this time, there was no getting better. He was dying. It was only a matter of when.

* * * *

It was still dark outside when I was shaken awake. I blinked, trying to fight off the last of sleep.

"You awake, kid?"

"Dad?" I asked, my voice groggy. "What's wrong?"

"Nothing. Get your butt out of bed. We're wasting daylight."

I looked toward my window. "It's not daylight yet."

He chuckled. "It will be soon. You can sleep in the car."

Knowing he wouldn't have woken me unless it was important, I dragged my tired ass out of bed and into some clothes that could have been on backward, for all I knew. Mom was fussing in the kitchen when I walked in. She filled the cooler with food and had a Thermos beside it.

She smiled when she saw me and nodded toward the Thermos. "Don't worry. I've already made your coffee so strong it could melt your stomach lining."

"What's going on?"

"The boat," Mom said, dropping her voice. "What else?"

I laughed. "I'll pack a bag."

"Make it a full one. Who knows how long we'll be gone."

* * * *

We drove three hours to a lake I'd never heard of. We passed the last town before it a decent forty minutes before reaching it. Dad had a thing about seclusion.

There was a man waiting on the dock when we arrived, a gleaming boat bobbing in the water beyond it. Dad got out of the car to talk to him while Mom and I started unloading our things. After a few minutes, the man left, giving a brief wave to us in parting.

Dad came to help us and grabbed most of his fishing gear. "Maybe this time you'll catch something, huh, kid?"

"I bet I catch the same thin air as always," I said with a smirk.

"Go easy on her. Besides, we don't want to eat fish every night," Mom said. She flashed me a wink on her way past me.

"What's wrong with fish?" Dad called after her.

Before long we were unloaded and had boarded the boat. Dad had really outdone himself with this one. There was a long, wide deck and perfect fishing chair to satisfy him. And below, a galley kitchen, small lounge and two cabin bedrooms.

That night we drank wine and played cards, Dad and me getting more and more competitive the longer we played. Mom resigned after two hands and disappeared between the pages of her book, leaving 'the children' to it.

I slept fitfully, whether because of the fresh air, the rocking motion of the boat or some other reason, I had no idea.

* * * *

In the morning we ate breakfast on the deck, the early sun warming our skin.

"So what's the plan for today?" I asked, placing my napkin atop my empty plate.

Dad stretched out his arms.

My eyebrows shot up. "This? Really?" I asked.

He laughed. "What else could you want to do? You city folks—always moving so fast. Take the time to slow down, kid."

"I can slow down. But, all day?"

"Try it," Dad said, his lips twitching with amusement.

I tried it—until lunch—but then I felt so antsy it was like I had fire ants in my pants. So I donned my bikini and put shorts, T-shirt and flip-flops into a plastic bag then tied it to my wrist, figuring testing the lake waters was a great way to burn off some energy.

Shore wasn't far away, but my muscles felt stretched and used after the swim.

The woodland area that surrounded the lake was quiet, peaceful. I was the only living soul on shore, as far as I could tell, anyway.

Swimming had quelled the restless part of me, but it had also served another purpose. Disappearing on my own for a while gave my parents time they deserved on their own. I knew they wanted as much family time as they could get, but their relationship was every bit as important as the one we all shared.

I turned around to look out over the lake. Our boat was there, shinning atop the sparkling water. Maybe Dad would try to teach Mom to fish. Even though it almost killed me to do it, I kept the negative thoughts at bay. I wanted to remember this trip with fondness, and if I let the dark thoughts take over then it would always be tinged with sadness. Dad would hate that.

I kept the water's edge in sight as I wandered through the woodland. My sense of direction sucked, but so long as I could see the lake, I figured I should be safe.

The swim back took longer, my muscles sore and protesting. I had a feeling by the time our trip was over, I'd be more than used to it.

When I reached the boat, I hauled myself out of the water and climbed the ladder back onto the deck. As I wandered to the front, I found my parents sitting by the edge, their legs dangling over the sides. Neither of them heard my approach. Dad had his arm around Mom and her shoulders were shaking.

The pain of seeing them that way made me want to double over, it was so severe. They didn't deserve this. They didn't deserve to be in so much pain, to have to say goodbye to each other...for one to have to go on without the other.

Retracing my steps back to the ladder I'd used, I dumped my bag on the deck, loud enough to make a resounding thump. "I'm back!" I called at a volume I hadn't used since announcing my arrival home as a child.

"Back here, kid," Dad called.

I walked to where I'd seen them moments before. This time Dad was standing, his usual smile in place. Mom twisted around, tears haunting her eyes. "Good swim, baby?" she asked.

"Yeah. It's farther than I thought, though. I'll be feeling it tomorrow." I shrugged. "Maybe I'll make it a daily thing, get back into decent shape again."

"All the fish I catch will give you plenty of energy," Dad said with a wink.

"You're going to turn us into fish, Dad."

"That's the plan."

* * * *

We spent two weeks on the lake. Once I'd gotten used to the quiet, the slower-paced lifestyle, I'd had a great time. So much so I didn't altogether want to leave. Back home, things were pretty normal, except nothing was normal. It was like this new life was super-imposed over our old one, where the actions were the same, but the motives weren't.

Dad's time was mostly spent in the garage. He was a natural born tinkerer, and he loved nothing more than whiling away hours at his workbench, fixing some contraption or other. As a kid, I'd park myself on a stool and watch him work, asking him hundreds of questions about what he was doing. It must have been irritating as hell, but he never lost patience with me. And he answered every question.

"You're not an electrician," I said, swinging my legs as I sat on the stool beside Dad's workbench. That particular afternoon, his patient was a faulty toaster Mom was tossing out until Dad had salvaged it and insisted he could bring it back to life.

I was terrified he'd electrocute himself.

It was a beautiful day outside, clear blue skies and warm sunshine. The garage door was wide open — letting in the sounds of the summer and the smell of freshly cut grass. But I wouldn't be anywhere else for all the sunshine in the world.

Dad glanced at me, a cocky look in his eyes. "What's that got to do with anything?"

"Whether or not the next time someone uses that thing it means a death sentence? Or at the very least, gravity-defying hair."

He laughed. "Ye of little faith, kid. Hand me that screwdriver, would you?"

That was the best part about hanging out with him as a child. He'd made me feel important to the job at hand, asking me to fetch him things. Because of my hours in the hardware store growing up, I was well versed in most tool-speak.

I handed him the screwdriver. "What do you think is wrong with it?"

"I have a few theories. I'll know more soon." Which could be loosely translated as 'right now, I have absolutely no idea'.

"Hey, Jacobs."

Dad and I both turned at the sound of the new voice.

Hayley stood in the entrance to the garage, vintage sunglasses pushed up to the top of her head and wearing a pretty white sundress. "My hairdryer broke this morning. I knew I should have brought it with me."

"Next time," Dad said, waving his screwdriver at her.

"Definitely," she said with a grin.

I hopped off my stool and rushed to wrap my arms around her. "It's good to see you."

"You, too," she said, squeezing me tight.

"What are you doing here?" I asked, letting her go.

She hitched her thumb at the blue hatchback parked across from the house. "I brought your stuff from my apartment. I figured you must be running low on outfit choices by now."

A laugh rose in my throat. "Thanks for your consideration."

Hayley grinned. "You know how seriously I take fashion."

"Oh, God, how much did you bring?"

She furrowed her brow. "Just the essentials."

I let out a breath. "We'd better start unloading the car now then, while we still have daylight."

Behind us, Dad snorted a laugh.

"Whose car is this, anyway?" I asked Hayley as we walked toward it.

"Tom, the guy I met last week."

"Last *week*? And he's letting you borrow his car?"

She nudged me with her elbow. "Are you trying to say I'm not trustworthy?"

"I'm saying you must have some badass moves in bed to con a guy into loaning you his car."

"A lady never tells," she drawled. We reached the car, and she unlocked the trunk.

It took a few trips, but we unloaded the car and dragged the suitcases and bags up to my bedroom in no time.

"There's more here than I remembered," I said, frowning at all the stuff that now littered my bedroom floor.

"I went to Theo's."

I whirled around to face her. "You what? Why?"

Hayley looked at me as though I'd just asked her why Cosmos were practically a staple in her diet. "Why wouldn't I? I was packing up your stuff and realized how much you must have left with the skeev. You didn't want Simone having a cleansing ritual and burning half your shit, did you?"

"You're kind of awesome, Hayley."

She sighed. "I kind of know."

"I hope you're not tired from the drive, because I need help putting all this crap away."

With a look of horror on her face, Hayley scooped up a pile of dresses—mostly all designer, and I was doubtful I'd have a reason to wear them here. "Ssh! They'll hear you." She stroked the fabric, cooing as though she held her first-born.

I've no idea how she did it, but Hayley managed to condense my current wardrobe contents to maximize the space and fit everything she'd brought with her in too. *When there's a fashion will, there's a way.*

"Oh, I almost forgot," Hayley said, digging around in her purse. She pulled out a thick stack of mail. "I've been collecting your mail for you."

I accepted the pile from her. The first few were junk mail and a college newsletter. I carried them all over to my desk and shoved the whole bunch in the top drawer. "Mostly garbage. I'll deal with them some other time."

"What if there's something important?" Hayley asked.

I looked out of my bedroom window, out onto the immaculately kept front lawn. "Nothing is more important than where I am right now."

"How is he doing?"

Turning away from the window, I saw Hayley lounging on my bed. I crossed the room and lay down beside her. "It's hard to tell. I don't think he shows us what he's really feeling. Apart from a few times when it's been obvious he's in pain, he's mostly just been like the same old Dad."

"Probably doesn't want you and your mom to worry. And to keep things as normal as he can for you guys."

"Probably." I agreed. "I hate this—caught in this weird limbo where everything is the same and yet it's all so different."

"I wish I could say it'll get easier, but that's the biggest lie anyone could ever tell."

"I wish I wasn't here at all," I said quietly. "I wish I was in the city, living out of your spare room and you were bugging me to go out every night. I wish I was there because if I was then Dad wouldn't be sick again."

Hayley reached for my hand and laced our fingers.

My eyes burned. "It's just so fucking unfair. He doesn't deserve this. He's a good person. There are so many assholes in the world, so why does it have to be him?"

"Life doesn't work that way. It isn't fair, but it's what you've got," Hayley said.

"Well it sucks," I said, biting the words out. "Jesus, it sucks."

"It sucks." She squeezed my hand.

"It really fucking sucks," I whispered as the first tear rolled down my face.

Hayley stayed for dinner that night. She chatted away like her usual self and I think everyone was grateful to her for it, for giving our family a taste of normal. Dad adored her. They'd met a few times, but had never had a chance to talk properly before. Hayley earned herself a special spot in his heart by asking how the toaster was doing and taking the time to genuinely listen to what he had to say.

"Don't be a stranger," Hayley said hugging me extra tight as we said goodbye at her borrowed car.

"You, too. And I'm sorry in advance for being a shitty friend. I can't guarantee how often I'll remember to call you."

Hayley rolled her eyes. "Please. Just don't forget you know where I am if you need me. Two a.m. and you need to scream at someone, call me. Anything. Okay?"

I nodded, the lump in my throat too hard for me to reply.

She kissed my cheek and jumped into the car. I stayed on the sidewalk until her taillights disappeared.

Mom was washing up when I headed back inside, Dad nowhere to be seen.

"Where's Dad?"

"Lying down, I think." Mom glanced over her shoulder. "He fixed the toaster."

My eyebrows shot up. "He fixed it, or he fixed it and now it's worse than ever?"

Mom chuckled. "It burns on one side and barely even warms the other."

"Sounds like Dad," I said. The moment the quiet settled around us, sadness crept its way inside again. "He's starting to feel it, isn't he? He's getting tired."

She gave me a sad smile. "I think so, baby."

I hugged my mom from behind, trying my best to pass on every bit of comfort I could. She patted my arm, leaving soap on my sleeve.

The next day, Dad didn't get out of bed.

* * * *

The morning that marked my two month anniversary of coming home, Dad greeted me in the kitchen. He sat at the island nursing a cup of coffee. He grinned when he saw me, and stood up to pour me a coffee from the pot.

"About time. I swear, you weren't this bad as a teenager," Dad said, handing me the cup. "Now take your butt back upstairs and get dressed. We're going out."

"Where to this time?" More than a few times Dad had herded Mom and I into the car, only for him to drive us to some obscure tourist attraction he'd read about or had always wanted to see.

"You'll see when we get there. Don't take too long. I want to get going as soon as possible."

"Is Mom ready?"

"Mom's not coming. Just you and me today, kid." Dad pointed to the door. "Now hurry up, would you?"

I groaned like it was a mammoth task, and dragged myself back upstairs. But really, I couldn't wait to spend the day with my dad.

In the car I pestered him to the point where he yelled at me to shut up and almost veered off the road. But he still wouldn't tell me where we were going. So I huffed and shut up like I was told. For ten minutes, then I asked him again.

Two and a half hours later, I got my answer. As soon as we got near, I knew exactly where we were going. The rides loomed into the sky, tall and proud and lit up like the fourth of July.

I jumped up and down in my seat. "A state fair?"

Dad flashed me a smile. "Worth the wait?"

"Definitely," I said, grinning as Dad pulled into the parking lot. As we walked toward the entrance, it was like I was six years old again. I tugged on Dad's hand and pointed at a ride. "Look! A Slingshot!"

He visibly paled. "What's wrong with the teacups?"

I laughed. "Too extreme?"

"Light years too extreme."

We walked around the fair, taking in the rides, the games, the food and everything else it had to offer. My senses were assaulted and I tried to soak everything in, to imprint this day in my mind so I wouldn't forget a single thing. The sounds of the rides and the happy screams of the people riding them, delighted squeals of children. Stalls of food emitted the best smells on earth—fried food, sugary sweets and hotdogs filled the air. Loved-up teenagers, families, old couples still smiling... This place drew people from all walks of life.

"What's first?" Dad asked after we'd circled the fair.

"Haunted House, definitely. Then some games. No...food, then games."

He grinned. "Sounds like a plan. Let's do this."

The sun was making its slow descent toward the earth and Dad was looking tired. Before leaving, he insisted on winning a stuffed animal to take back for Mom. We stood at a ring-toss stall for what felt like hours as he tried in vain to snare a prize. A high-pitched giggle behind me made me turn. A young couple was fooling around, trying on oversized cowboy hats at a stall. The guy pulled the girl into his chest before holding up a camera to take a picture of the moment.

The scene was all too familiar for me. My afternoon in Coney Island flashed in my mind, so vivid I could feel the ocean lapping at my feet and Blake's fingers laced with mine.

The guy lowered the camera and turned to face his female companion. He touched her cheek before dipping his head to kiss her. I turned away, feeling like I was intruding on their private moment.

"You okay, kid?" Dad asked. He tucked a tiny stuffed monkey under his arm and led me in the direction of the parking lot.

I nodded, not meeting his eye.

He nudged me with his elbow.

Sighing, I switched the bag I was carrying to my other hand. I'd picked up some locally made trinkets and soaps for the girls. I hoped it would let them know that just because I wasn't in contact much, I still thought about them.

"Something's wrong."

I snuck a glance at Dad from the corner of my eye. There was a slight crease between his eyes. "Just thinking."

"What about?"

"Lots of things."

Dad sighed. "You're harder than a rock to get information out of."

I laughed. "Sorry. I don't mean to be elusive. It probably wouldn't make any sense even if I did talk about it." Two and a half months had passed since the truth had spilled to the ground like blood from a gunshot wound, nearly three months since I'd laid eyes on Blake. The time apart was almost as long as the time we'd had together. It wouldn't be long before the former overtook the latter.

As much as I hated it and wished it would go away, whenever I felt sad or if things got really hard at home, I still craved Blake. I wanted him to hold me — tell me that things would work out, that he would be by my side to walk me through the coming trials. I hated that even though I knew the truth and how deceitful and wicked he had been, a dominant part of me still wanted him.

"Lemme guess," Dad said, interrupting my thoughts. "Boy trouble?"

I blushed.

Dad smiled. "Thought so. It's okay to be sad, Marley. You called off a wedding. That isn't something you just get over."

"I know."

"So, you don't seem to mention Theo's friend much."

"What?"

"Blake, the boy from your birthday party. Theo's best man, right?"

I nodded. "You could hardly call him a boy, Dad."

Dad laughed. "I know. It's because I'm old. That's all."

"You're not old." *Far from old…*

"You two seemed close. I thought he would have visited, despite being Theo's friend."

"They aren't really friends anymore."

"I'm not surprised, considering he was in love with you."

I snapped my head up to watch Dad's face carefully. "Excuse me?"

Dad chuckled. "Trust me—it's hard to miss the look of a man in love, particularly if that man is looking at your daughter."

I lowered my eyes. "He wasn't in love with me, Dad. He was a liar. A good one at that."

"The way he watched you at the party, every move he made... If I didn't know better, I would have said he was the guy you were marrying." Dad sighed. "We owe Theo a lot, and for his kindness I will always think fondly of him. But I have never seen him look at you the way Blake did. He may have lied to you, but it wasn't about his feelings."

Dad's words hit me with the force of a punch to the gut. A lump formed in my throat and my stomach clenched. I couldn't let myself be deluded enough to believe him. Fathers would see anything when a man was talking to his daughter. But...no! No buts, no ifs and no maybes. The truth was what it was. No more, no less.

I drove us back home as Dad dozed beside me in the passenger seat. The radio played softly and the sky was an inky darkness by the time I pulled into the driveway. I shut off the engine and relaxed into my seat. The kitchen light shone like a beacon, guiding Dad and I home. I twisted around in my seat to look at my dad. He seemed more breakable than ever. He was shrinking before our eyes, disappearing a little more with every sunset. I clenched my eyes shut, determined not to let my tear ducts cast an ugly shadow over my day with Dad.

"Dad," I said quietly, touching his arm.

He stirred, opening his eyes slowly. "Oh, I'm sorry—was I sleeping for long?"

I smiled. "No. Come on. Mom will want that prize you won for her."

Dad smiled and got out from the car. I watched his movements and noticed how he tried not to wince as he straightened his tall frame. He rubbed his temples as he walked toward the front door. Dad would be tired tomorrow and in a lot of pain. He always was after big excursions, and today had been the biggest so far.

Mom helped him upstairs to bed, but not before he gave her a blow by blow description of our day. I would never forget the look that passed between my parents as he handed her the prize he'd taken so long to win. Dad looked proud, with just a hint of awkwardness. Mom blushed and reached out quickly for the small monkey. Their fingertips grazed, and if I wasn't mistaken, I thought I saw the fireworks in their eyes.

Closing the door to my bedroom with a soft click, I then walked to my closet to search for my big thick sweater. I pulled it on and opened my window as wide as it would go. Gingerly easing myself out, I found my footing on the roof and edged around to my familiar spot. I lay down on the cool shingles and laced my fingers under my head. It was the first time I'd come out there since returning home. The familiarity of it was as comforting as slipping into a warm bath. The crisp night air washed over me, cleansing my soul.

It was dawn before I returned inside.

Chapter Twenty-Two

Dad was in bed for three days after our trip to the fair. Mom arranged for a nurse to come in once a day to make sure his pain medication was at the right dosage and keep him as comfortable as possible. He, typical of any man, insisted he was fine. Even when it was excruciating for him to move, he told us he was just stiff. We played along with him. Why bruise his ego if we didn't have to?

People began visiting him more. This actually angered him. He didn't understand why, when faced with death, they wanted to see him. In life, he said, he barely saw them. Why bother making the effort now? I could see his point. Mom told him it was more for their sake than his and he should allow them to come. People felt guilt and grieved in different ways. Some would never live with themselves if they didn't get a chance to see him one last time.

The day that marked my third month at home, I woke to find myself alone in the house. Mom had left a note taped to the coffee pot saying she and Dad were out doing errands. Mom's handwriting was shakier than normal. Whatever the errands were, I doubted they would be pleasant. Sure enough, when they returned home, both were silent and downcast. Dad disappeared into the garage and Mom cleaned the bathroom until the smell of bleach permeated the entire house. I didn't ask where they had been, and I didn't want to know. A chill haunted the rooms of the house. A chill I feared. Retrieving my bike from the side of the house, I pedaled until I no longer felt its presence.

My hair whipped around my face as I pedaled faster. My high school looked exactly the same. I'd have bet Mrs. Caine was still threatening expulsion to anyone who dared chew gum in her class. On the outskirts of town lay the church we still visited every Christmas Eve as a family. I slowed to a stop and took in the building.

The gates were locked but beyond that I knew was the gravel path that led to the entrance of the church — the heavy wooden doors that creaked and groaned. In daylight, the tall and intricate stained-glass window depicting Jesus and the Virgin Mother usually felt warm, like a beacon of hope. Only now it seemed dark and distant in the overcast light.

A tall spire reached up to the heavens, or at least it had felt that way when the pastor had taken me up there when I'd thrown a fit one time after Sunday school, claiming Quasimodo was up there. Disney had a lot to answer for that day.

The grounds surrounding the church were cheerful out front — rows of wildflowers, meticulously cared for flowerbeds and carefully groomed shrubs. The rear of the church was where my thoughts dreaded to linger. The graves closest to the church were scattered, almost seeming random. The headstones were weather worn and faded, though some of the names I remembered from when I was a kid and when the graveyard had been the only cool place to hang out when your curfew was eight-thirty.

Maybe it was because the sun had disappeared behind a gloomy dark rain cloud, but the church had never felt more foreboding. No, that wasn't it. As kids we used to sneak out late at night and dare each other to run between the headstones in the cemetery. The church had never seemed menacing, even at midnight. Deep down, I knew the reason. The next time I visited this church, it wouldn't be on a dare. It wouldn't be for a wedding or a christening of the neighbor's second grandchild. It would be for my father's funeral. My eyes glided back over the cemetery. Where would he lie? Maybe that's where my parents had been today. Had Dad been choosing his new lodgings?

Hysterical laughter bubbled in my throat as I imagined my father standing in an open grave and commenting on the lack of space, maybe asking if they had something with a better view. A loud grumble of thunder bellowed from above. The sky darkened as the sun disappeared completely. I glanced at my hand as a fat drop of rain splashed on it. Another hit my head and shoulder until I was stood in the middle of a downpour. I tilted my face to the sky, drenching my skin. My laughter faded as my tears mixed with the rain. Dropping to the side of the road, I pulled my knees to my chest and burrowed my face in my hands. The sound of the rain drowned out my agonizing sobs.

It isn't fair! I wanted to scream at the heavens. And as though I had spoken aloud, my answer was a roar of thunder.

I picked myself up.
I slowed my breathing.
I lost my faith in everything good.

* * * *

Dad's face stretched into a grin as I pushed my bike into the garage. "What happened to you?" he asked. "You fall in the lake?"

"No," I mumbled.

"What's wrong?"

"Nothing." My voice broke.

Dad crossed the room and pulled me into a hug. His chin rested on the top of my head.

"I don't want you to leave," I whispered.

"Baby, neither do I." The pain in my father's voice brought back the river of tears. "It will all be okay. I promise. You and Mom will be just fine. Everything is taken care of."

I squeezed my eyes shut. I had to remember exactly how his voice sounded. Exactly how he smelled. Exactly how he felt. I had to remember everything.

"You are so strong, Marley. You don't need anyone to take care of you. You and Mom, you guys looked after me."

"Stop it! You shouldn't be comforting me. I should be comforting you!" I shouted. He was the one who was waiting for death. He was the one who should be afraid, not me.

Dad laughed quietly. "Can't help it, kid. You're my baby. I'll always try and comfort you."

"I'm getting your shirt all wet."

"It'll dry."

When Dad released me, I fled upstairs to the safe confines of my room. I dug around in the back of my closet until I found an old storage container. Dragging it out, I flipped open the lid and tossed away the contents. A few books with faded yellow pages, a program from a concert and a few movie stubs. Nothing important.

I ransacked my room, flinging pictures of me and Dad into the box. An open envelope of recently developed photos lay on my desk. I picked out the ones from our day at the fair and tossed those in. Next I ran into the bathroom. I took out a can of shaving cream and one of his deodorants and an almost empty bottle of cologne. All of these things contributed to his smell. I needed to remember them. In my parents' bedroom I found a clean, folded plaid shirt my Dad liked to wear when tinkering around with gadgets. That went in too. In a few short minutes I had packed the essence of my father into a box.

* * * *

We stopped going out. My dad stopped all the road trips and outings. He had seen enough, he said. We made breakneck speed trips to the grocery store, desperate to get back home. Sometimes Dad went by himself, a part of him still craving normalcy. Mostly we all sat around talking, drinking coffee and watching a lot of movies. Dad never understood my movie obsession and told me one afternoon he wanted to take a stroll in my world. He ordered me to find all my favorite movies so we could watch them. I chattered throughout most of them, explaining to him why I loved them so much. He tried really hard, but he didn't get them the way I did. But that didn't matter. We were spending precious minutes together as a family. It didn't matter what we were doing.

It was cruel how things snuck up on us. My father faded before us so gradually it was almost impossible to see. When he'd first told me he was going to die, he'd seemed completely normal, healthy even. When he got tired he would go to bed a little earlier at night. Then he started napping in the afternoons. Now if he got tired, he stayed in bed all day long. The days passed and slowly the light drained from him. His energy diminished day by day. He struggled to keep up a cheerful tone, even though he knew Mom and I desperately needed it. A raspy edge consumed his voice and he had a faraway look in his eyes.

I had been home for four months now. After breaking down in his arms the night I'd got caught in the rain, I didn't let my dad see me cry again. He didn't deserve to see my pain. He deserved to be surrounded by laughter and joy and love.

Dad contracted a viral infection and took to his bed for a week. He would regain some energy and make it downstairs only to return to his bed shortly after. The nurse came more frequently. It seemed every time she came, she upped the dosage of his morphine.

Passing his room early one morning, I heard a strange noise. Mom was already up, I could hear her downstairs. I stepped into the room, trying to determine the noise. It sounded like a chainsaw that wouldn't start. Standing by my father's side, I realized the noise was coming from him. His breathing was ragged and labored. Each breath seemed a colossal effort.

I sank to my knees beside the bed and took his hand in mine, careful not to wake him. I hadn't realized how thin my dad was until his wedding band slid clean off his finger onto the bedspread. I slid it back on for him. Running my eyes up his arm, I noticed how saggy and sallow the skin appeared.

Mom called me from downstairs. Her voice snapped me from my trance-like state. I bolted from the room as though it was a fearful place. The warm and familiar smell of pancakes and syrup wafted under my nostrils, instantly calming me down. I wolfed down an enormous portion. Mom took some upstairs for Dad. We both knew he wouldn't eat them. He didn't eat much of anything now.

Dad barely seemed to get over the viral infection before he was plagued with something else. The nurse told us his immune system was failing, so he was susceptible to any infections and germs. We knew this, of course, but let her get on with her job. Dad's conscious states grew few and far between. Sometimes he would sleep all day and night and I wouldn't get to talk to him at all. During those restful periods for him, I would be terrified I would never get a chance to hear his voice again. The terror paralyzed me in my bed every morning when I woke. It would be so severe I almost couldn't bear to check on him, just in case…

Mom sat with him almost all day. When it got too hard, she would clean something. But mostly she sat in the armchair by the bed, reading her magazine and telling him the gossip from the celebrity pages. She read poetry to him sometimes, usually something by Frost. He adored Frost.

Whenever Mom needed to leave, I would sit with Dad. A lot of the time I would sit outside the room with my back to the wall, listening to my mom chattering to him as if he could hear her. I almost expected him to answer her. On the odd occasions when he woke and did answer her, I would force myself to wait a minute or two before flying into the room.

It was almost frustrating to watch my father dying. He was young. He took care of himself, yet he was still so sick. This shouldn't have been happening to him. This kind of thing happened to someone else, not to people I cared about. It was wrong and it was far from fair. We had come so far with technology and science and as humans—how was it we could just let them die like this? How had we not come up with a magic cure-all yet?

Parents had a natural instinct to protect their young. They would do anything in their power to keep them from hurting, from getting sick, to keep them safe. It was like second nature. My second nature seemed to be in denial that this was the end for my dad. I just couldn't wrap my head around the fact that soon he wouldn't be here. I wouldn't be able tell him about my day and help him tinker with some contraption in the garage. He was going to be gone, rotting in a hole in the ground. Would he be watching us always from above? Or would he cease to exist, a candle extinguished in the wind? I couldn't accept that there was nothing I could do for him. After all he had done for me in my lifetime, why couldn't I help him survive? I didn't understand.

* * * *

I'd never forget the day my father died. Something lured me toward his room, a hypnotic pull. The day before, he had only been awake for a half hour. We'd known the end wasn't far. I pushed open the door to hear the familiar sound of his labored, raspy breathing. He looked like an old man surrounded by pillows. He cracked his eyes open as I paused in the doorway. Dad smiled, even though it looked like it exhausted him to do so. Mom was asleep in the armchair by the bed. I crawled onto the bed and hugged my knees to my chest. Dad was already asleep again. I stayed that way for a long time, ignoring the ache in my knees and the cramps in my calves.

Mom woke and sensed the change in the air. We shared a look, neither brave enough to talk. After a few hours of silence, Dad awoke. He didn't seem to be in any pain anymore. He looked almost happy.

"Hey, you wanna know my favorite movie?" I asked, sliding up the bed to sit beside him.

Dad smiled. "Lemme guess, something bloody and disgusting."

I rolled my eyes. "No. *The Wizard of Oz.*"

Dad's pale eyes brightened for a moment. "Really?"

I nodded.

Mom chuckled. "You own the Alfred Hitchcock collection, and *that* is your favorite movie?"

"Uh-huh."

"I took you to see that. Do you remember?"

"Yeah, at the Apollo. I remember. I've loved it ever since."

"You wanna watch it, kid?"

"Sure." I hopped from the bed and hunted down an old copy in my bedroom. My parents' voices were murmuring as I re-entered the room.

Mom had tears sparkling in her eyes. Her knuckles were white from grasping Dad's hand.

The opening credits rolled on screen. I took my spot beside Dad again. I curled up against him, making sure I wasn't putting any of my weight on him. He was asleep within seconds. His breath rattled in this throat, the fluid making it gurgle. Throughout the next hour, his breathing grew more irregular and ragged. Dorothy hadn't even made it home to Kansas when the life fled from my father's still body.

Chapter Twenty-Three

If this had been a movie, then some depressing yet meaningful song would have played as I moved in a dream-like state. It would have skimmed over the details of the next few days as though they were only seconds long. I held my mom for the longest time as she sobbed for her husband. I left the room and perched on the edge of my bed. Mom made the phone calls. Who would have to be notified? The funeral home? Would we need an ambulance? We weren't really having an emergency. He was dead, not dying.

I glanced down at the jeans and T-shirt I was wearing. Would I ever wear these clothes again? Surely I would be haunted with images of this day if I did. It seemed like an overreaction to discard them. *Why the hell am I thinking about clothes?* My father wasn't even cold in the next room and I was deciding on throwing away a pair of jeans.

My thoughts were flooded with the image of my dad, lying still with his unmoving chest. I began to shake. I didn't let the tears fall. Mom was already a mess. I couldn't take care of both of us.

Someone came to retrieve the body.

The body…

I didn't watch.

I waited until I heard the car leave before going downstairs. Mom stood at the kitchen window, watching as the vehicle carrying her husband disappeared around the corner. I placed a hand on her shoulder. She covered it with her own. I guided my mom into the den. I held her tight and stroked her hair as we sat on the couch.

* * * *

The next day, Mom and I took turns in calling people. Friends, family, anyone who needed to know about Dad. We split the list in half, but when she wasn't looking I stole from Mom's pile. Her words were getting more and more clipped with every call, a sure sign that the stress of the situation was getting to her.

I wanted to protect her from this, to shield her from the pain and take away all the horrible stuff she was feeling. So I did the next best thing, and tried to take care of us both so she didn't have to.

As I cleared away the uneaten sandwiches from lunch, the doorbell rang. Mom was upstairs, but I heard her weary steps as she came down to answer the door. I held my breath in the kitchen, knowing that whoever was here would no doubt bring a new set of challenges. Even a well-meaning neighbor had the power to dropkick us in the guts. Just sitting through a normal conversation felt like climbing a mountain that's peak was hidden in the clouds — the air too thin to breathe.

"Marley?" Mom called from the den.

I wiped my hands and let out a breath before heading in. Mom stood with the church pastor, a guy I hadn't seen for years. He wore a kind smile that was both reassuring and comforting. But Mom wrung her hands, anxious energy pouring out of her.

"Hello, Marley. It's lovely to see you again," Pastor Duncan said, reaching out to shake my hand.

I doubted it. He'd been royally pissed the day of the Quasimodo incident. I tried to smile. "You, too."

"I was just saying to your mother how very sorry I am about the passing of your father. He was a wonderful man. He will be sincerely missed in the community."

My throat tightened and I gave him a brief nod. *Get it together.*

"Can I get you some coffee?" Mom asked.

"That would be lovely. Thank you," Pastor Duncan said.

Mom squeezed my arm on her way out of the room.

"Are you here to plan the funeral?" I asked quietly, so she wouldn't overhear.

Pastor Duncan glanced at the doorway. "I can do that now, or at a later time. Most people prefer to get it out of the way so they can prepare themselves better."

"I'll go talk to her."

Mom stood in front of the coffee maker, her shoulders and back tense.

"Mom? Pastor Duncan wants to know if we'd like to start arranging the funeral," I said, leaning on the cabinets beside her.

She glanced at me, her red-rimmed eyes bloodshot. "Maybe now isn't a good time."

"It'll never feel like a good time. At least this way it's one more thing done and we don't have to worry about it anymore."

Mom released a shaky breath and gave me a smile. "You're right. Will you keep the pastor company for a few minutes while I finish the coffee?"

I squeezed her arm. "Of course."

Mom eventually joined us, some twenty minutes later, and wasted no time in getting down to business. "What do you need?"

Pastor Duncan blinked, appearing taken aback by Mom's abruptness. He recovered quickly. "I know about his life with the church, his good-standing in the community. But it would be helpful to have some familial anecdotes, any people you'd like personally mentioned. Did he have any special wishes you'd like to fulfill?"

She was quiet for a moment. "He always just said, 'Make sure I have the best seat in the house, I don't want to miss anything'."

I laughed. Sounded like Dad.

"Any particular music he wanted?"

"Gerry and the Pacemakers—*You'll Never Walk Alone*," she whispered. Mom's hands shook as she reached for a cup of coffee.

"Pastor Duncan, why don't we take our drinks into the kitchen and we can talk in there?" I stood up and moved around the coffee table to hug my mom. "I've got this," I whispered in her ear.

The pastor glanced between Mom and me, but followed me out.

"Are you sure you're up to this?" Pastor Duncan asked as we settled at the island in the kitchen.

"Absolutely. And I spent enough time with my dad to have listened to every story worth telling a hundred times. I can do this."

"It's very admirable, doing it for your mother."

I shrugged. "It's what families do—take care of each other."

Over the next few hours we hammered out the details for Dad's funeral. There was no sign of Mom when I showed the pastor out. I presumed she'd gone to lie down again. So I used the time to call old contacts from the city to arrange the flowers and food for the wake.

I arranged everything on the days leading up to the funeral, throwing myself head first into the planning. It helped, I think. It was a good distraction.

The night before the day we were all dreading, as I headed to bed the soft murmur of Mom's voice in her bedroom drifted into the hall. "I don't know what to do about Marley," she said.

I paused, not wanting to eavesdrop, but curious as to what she meant.

"I feel awful. I've abandoned her to take care of everything. At first I was so grateful, but now I think it's unhealthy for her."

"No, it's more than a distraction. I—I haven't even seen her cry. I think she's in shock."

Not wanting to hear anymore, I passed quickly into my own room and softly closed the door. As I lay in bed, preparing for another sleepless night, I wondered if Mom was right. It wasn't normal not to cry. I was numb. I felt barely anything.

Maybe I was in shock.

* * * *

My eyes opened after another sleepless night. Gentle sunlight teased the room, warming the carpet where it touched. I eased my weary frame from the bed and threw open my window. A beautiful burst of warm autumn air hit my face. Someone had mowed their lawn, and the fragrance teased my nostrils. What a beautiful day. Did one wish for a nice day when burying a loved one? Maybe this was the definition of bittersweet.

The house was quiet. Mom sat on the edge of her bed wrapped in a towel. Her shoulders were slumped and her breathing was shaky. I sat beside her and rested my head on her shoulder. I squeezed her hand. She patted my knee and rose to her feet. She told me to get ready.

I stood under the showerhead and let the water cascade over my face. I'd never felt more detached from myself. My movements felt foreign, as if something else controlled my body. I pulled the dress that I would never wear again after today over my head then smoothed down the fabric. I rolled my hair into a low bun and fixed it into place with pins that would surely give me a headache. After fastening the straps on my black Mary-Janes, I was ready. The car arrived on time to pick up me and Mom.

Hands patted our backs and squeezed our shoulders as Mom and I sat in the front row of the graveside service. Dad's best friend gave a beautiful eulogy and spoke warmly of our family. I barely heard him. My hands were locked around Mom's trembling fists. She drew the strength from somewhere deep within her to stand and speak to the crowd gathered to remember my father. She didn't say anything about him. Instead she recited his favorite poem. *Stopping by Woods on a Snowy Evening* by Robert Frost.

The priest said a few parting words. I stood by the grave, loosely clutching the white rose in my hand and watched my father being lowered into the ground. Mom dropped hers in, followed by the other mourners. A few touched me, a few whispered their condolences. Before long, I was the only one remaining. I couldn't drop the flower. It would be too final, somehow. But it had to be done. I had said goodbye and I had to let go. Except I hadn't said goodbye, not really. I hadn't said anything for days, now that I thought about it.

The sun was hot on my back, feeling more amplified through the black material of my dress, though I felt chilled to my very core. I glanced down at the innocent rose and saw myself uncurling my fingers and letting it drop in slow motion. It hit with a delicate thud on the gleaming wood, bouncing up a little before lying as still as my father inside.

* * * *

I glided through the crowd of strangers in my home. I placed trays of food on the foldout table in the lounge and filled people's drinks for them. The air in the house was stifling hot. I couldn't breathe. I shakily poured myself a large Scotch then snuck out of the back door into the yard. At the rear of the yard, surrounded by bushes and foliage, grew a decent-sized oak tree. Dad had hung a swing from its strong branches when I was little and it had survived. I pushed through the foliage and perched on the swing, holding onto the rope with one hand and keeping a tight grasp on my glass with the other. My bare calves were scratched and began to sting, but I didn't care. I closed my eyes, a shiver going through me. The shaded area was a lot cooler and it chilled my skin.

"Should have known I would find you out here."

I jumped. That was the last voice I'd expected to hear today. Slowly opening my eyes, I turned my head to face Theo. His face didn't show the usual sneer or sarcastic smile. The coldness in his eyes I was so accustomed to seeing was no longer present. Instead I saw a hint of the man I'd once known—the man who'd showed me so much kindness, before turning into a world-class creep.

He shoved his hands in his pockets and walked toward me. He crouched in front of me. "How are you?"

I looked down, unable to even comprehend that question.

"Right. Stupid question."

"Why are you here?" Was that really my voice? It sounded so disconnected and unemotional.

Theo sighed. "Your father was a good man. I had a lot of respect for him. I cared about him—and you."

I lifted my eyes to meet his. They seemed sincere. Which of course meant nothing now that I knew exactly how good a liar he was. Just like me, really. Maybe Theo and I were two sides of the same coin after all. "How long have you been here?"

"All day. I came to the service and stood in the back. You were busy inside. I guess you didn't see me." Theo straightened himself. "I wasn't sure how you would react to me being here."

I pinned him with a look. "I'm hardly going to cause a scene at my father's wake, Theo."

Theo gave a slight shake of his head. "I just didn't want to upset you. That's all."

This was exhausting. Everything about Theo, Blake, Simone and the baby was exhausting. I was tired of being tired. Losing Dad had put things into perspective. What a waste of energy it all was. "Theo, I don't have it in me to hate you. Life's too short to bear grudges. Isn't forgiveness what humanity is all about?"

Theo took a step toward me. "You forgive me?"

I scoffed. "I didn't say we were about to become best friends forever. I just mean I'm not angry anymore."

"Thank you, Marley. It's more than I ever expected." Theo's face took on an almost peaceful look like maybe this situation had taken its toll on him, too.

"What did you expect?"

Theo shrugged. "I came with intent to make amends. My therapist said—"

I barked a laugh, sudden and loud in the quietness of the garden. "You're in therapy?"

He blushed, and it was the first time I'd ever seen him less than absolutely cool and confident. "Yes. Simone and I are trying to make a go of things. She said I was carrying around baggage because of us, so she made me see a therapist."

I tossed my head back and laughed with such vigor I almost fell from the swing. "I'm sorry. I don't mean to laugh, but, seriously? She wants *you* to go for therapy? Shouldn't she have been first in line to get the craziness cured?"

Theo's lips twitched but he didn't give in to his obvious mirth. "She's in therapy with me."

Oh, wait, this is too perfect. "Couples counseling?"

He nodded.

A fresh bout of laughter bubbled in my throat. "What I would give to be a fly on the wall…"

"Anyway, my therapist said that I had to admit fault to everything that happened. In order to move on, I had to at least try and make amends for what I did."

I nodded. "I appreciate the intent. I'm glad you're facing up to everything. Sounds like this therapist is good for you."

"She is. Despite what you might think, so is Simone."

I arched an eyebrow but remained silent. Now was not the time to list all the ways Simone could not be linked, in any way, shape or form, to the word 'good'.

"She feels bad too. I know she wants to apologize for everything — I could arrange for you two — "

I held up a hand. "I don't think my forgiveness stretches that far. Not yet at least."

He smirked and moved to lean against the thick tree trunk. "So...how long have you been home?"

"Since I found out Dad was sick again. Four months."

Theo's eyebrows drew together. "Why didn't you tell me?"

I flinched and raised my chin a notch higher. "We didn't need your help."

There was a pinch of hurt in Theo's voice. "I didn't mean for money reasons, Marley. Despite what you think, I do still care about your family."

"How did you find out anyway? About the funeral today, I mean." I needed a conversation change. Whether he meant his words or not, I didn't need Theo Lorimer messing with my head again.

"Your mom called me."

I twisted to face him. "She did?"

Theo nodded. "How come none of your friends are here?"

"Told them not to come. I don't think I could stand them comforting me right now." Hayley hadn't taken the news very well. She was very much the kind of friend to call you on your bullshit, and she hadn't liked being overruled.

"It's not healthy to shut people out."

"Well, it helps right now, okay?" I said, scowling.

"Okay." Theo kicked up some dirt with the toe of his expensive shoe. "I'm a little surprised someone else isn't here."

"Who?" I asked, frowning.

"Blake."

I ignored the unpleasant twist in my stomach at the sound of his name. "Why would he be here?"

"Figured he would want to be here for you. I thought if I was coming, he definitely would be."

I swirled the Scotch around the glass before taking a gulp.

"Have you spoken to him?" Theo asked.

Shut up, shut up, shut up. "And why would I do a stupid thing like that?"

"It wouldn't be stupid. Avoiding him, that's stupid."

I laughed in disbelief. "You've changed your tune. Now you're all for me and Blake to be together?"

"He made you happy. Something I never did."

I turned away from him.

Theo reached for one rope, moving as though to push me on the swing before restraining his motion. "How can you find it in your heart to forgive me, but you won't even consider forgiving him?"

Was he really asking me that right now? "What he did was so much worse."

"No it wasn't. It just feels that way," Theo said, as though it was the simplest thing in the world.

A hard lump lodged in my throat. Not now... Another gulp of Scotch helped to remove it.

"He misses you, you know."

"Have you spoken to him?" I asked when curiosity got the better of me.

"Not recently."

"Then how can you think he misses me?"

He gave me a cocky smile. "You're a hard one not to miss."

I chuckled softly. "Simone's really thawed your heart out, huh?"

He nudged me, and I heard him laugh under his breath.

"Marley?"

We both turned as my mom called me from the back door.

"I should go and help her. Thank you for coming, Theo. It would mean a lot to my dad." I gave him a smile, small in size but the most genuine I'd mustered for Theo in a long time.

"No trouble," Theo said.

I rose to my feet and pushed my way through the foliage.

"Hey, Marley?"

Turning to face him, I kept quiet.

"Give him a call. This—everything that happened— Blake was never the bad guy."

My heart squeezed. "He knew about your affair. He made me fall in love with him. It was all a lie."

Theo shook his head. "No it wasn't. I saw what was developing between you two. I'm not proud to admit it hurt my ego. I guess... I couldn't stand that I gave you everything, but it was only him who could make you really smile."

"It doesn't matter now."

"Yes it does," Theo insisted. "You deserve to hear the truth."

"I've heard it."

"Have you? Did Blake defend himself?"

"He told me all I needed to know."

"Then he told you how I asked him to distract you?"

I folded my arms, staring coldly at Theo.

"I asked him twice to take you out, to distract you. I didn't need to ask any more than that because you were always with him anyway. In the end, he was only trying to protect you, Marley. He hated what I was doing, he told me so himself. I've never seen Blake so angry. He did what he did because he didn't want you to get hurt."

"But I did," I choked. "Because of him! He hurt me so much more than you ever did! Everything he ever told me was a lie!"

"No it wasn't, Marley."

All the emotion I'd tried to keep bottled down was fizzing dangerously close to the surface. "Yes it was! He didn't even try and deny it. He doesn't care about me. He never did."

"That's not true."

"Then where the hell is he, Theo? You said it yourself. If you could come, then surely he could too. Take a look around. He isn't coming."

"He did once."

I raised my eyes to meet Theo's mournful gaze. He took a step toward me.

"Right after you left, he came to the apartment looking for you. I wouldn't tell him where you were."

"That's it? Once he tried to clear his conscience? He makes one half-hearted attempt to get in contact with me, big deal. He didn't even try and call."

"Would you have answered?" Theo asked.

"Don't be ridiculous. Of course I wouldn't have answered."

Theo's lips pulled into a small, sad smile. "You see? He knows you, Marley. He never called because he knows you, and he knew you wouldn't have answered his calls. One more piece of evidence that he was so much better for you than I ever was. You should see him — really. This whole mess is my fault, not yours, and not his."

"All the things you said —"

Theo shook his head. "I said a lot of things I didn't mean, made them sound worse. Marley, that night...the night you left me, I would never have thought it possible. I was arrogant enough to think I'd snared you for good. When I realized you might leave me, it hurt. I wanted to hurt you back."

I took a deep breath and felt my body begin to shake. Not now — this couldn't happen now. I wasn't ready to break down. Turning away from him, I said, "Thanks again for coming, Theo."

He didn't try and stop me again as I walked toward the house.

A lot of the guests had already left by the time I made it back indoors. An intimate group sat in the lounge, sharing anecdotes about my dad. It was good they were being cheerful. When the last of the mourners left, I set to work removing all traces of the wake. I didn't know when Theo left. I never saw him again.

Once our house was empty, and it was just Mom and me again, we sat at the island, eating toast that was burned on one side and barely warm on the other.

* * * *

The gate was locked but that didn't stop me. As a child I'd scaled the outer wall hundreds of times. I wasn't quite as limber as I had been in those childhood years. The jump down the other side was farther than I remembered. I landed awkwardly and swore colorfully when I realized nothing was broken.

My sneakers crunched leaves and snapped twigs underfoot as I maneuvered around the different obstacles. It took longer than expected to find what I was looking for. Everything always looks different in the darkness. The moonlight cast a silvery glow over the smooth stone. I ran my fingers over the gold indented writing. Dad had bought a new grave — the headstone had been fixed in place right away.

"Hi, Dad."

I dropped to the ground and folded my legs under me, leaning against the side of the hard stone. Sighing, I plucked at the grass next to me.

"I don't know why I'm here. I guess I needed someone to talk to. I know, I know…little ironic, isn't it? Theo came today. He seemed sincere. I think he's really cut up about you. Who knew, right? Theo Lorimer has a heart." I rolled my eyes. "Sorry. I know. That was harsh. You know, there can be fun in trash-talk sometimes. You shouldn't look down on it so much."

I twirled a blade of grass between my fingers. "He really got to me today. Said some things I wish he hadn't — things about Blake. You remember Blake. You had some pretty crazy theories about him. I wish I could believe you — even Theo. You know what I hate? When people babble about the head and the heart wanting two different things. Well mine sure don't! Deep down in my heart I've always hoped all this was some twisted mix up, and Blake really was the man I thought he was. And now my head is full of all the stuff Theo said today. It's like on one hand there's what I *do* believe, and on the other, what I *want* to believe. What do I listen to? I wish you were here to tell me what to do."

My eyes stung. "You always say the right thing. You always know exactly what I need. Not many dads are like that, but you are. Were. I don't know how to do this without you."

The silence of the cemetery rang in my ears. I took a deep breath, trying to slow my racing heart.

"I wish you knew Blake better." I laughed. "You would have sniffed him out in a second, were he a liar. I swear you were a police dog in another life, Dad. You had this sense—just knew when something wasn't right or when someone was lying to you. I wish I had that. Although, it was a pain in the ass when I was a teenager. *Nothing* got past you."

I lay down on the damp grass beside my father's grave and curled up into a ball, tucking my hands under my cheek. "Tomorrow's going to be really hard. Up until now Mom's had stuff to keep her mind busy. Everything is done now. She has the rest of her life without you and it all starts tomorrow. We really need you around, Daddy. We're lost without you."

A hot tear splashed onto my hand—and another, and another until my body was racked with gut wrenching sobs.

* * * *

I woke a little before dawn. I sat up and rubbed my arms. The sky was pink and bright—it would be another beautiful day. My damp jeans clung to my legs as I stood up. I trailed a hand over the top of Dad's headstone and said goodbye. I shivered as I walked home, unable to make my legs take me any faster.

The house was still silent as I quietly made my way upstairs. Mom's bedroom door was firmly shut. I didn't expect her up anytime soon. Peeling off my damp clothes, I tossed them in the hamper then started the shower. I waited until the water was scalding hot before climbing inside.

Tears fell freely down my face as I scrubbed my body. When I wiped the foggy mirror, I saw some color had returned to my cheeks. Since Dad's passing, they had taken on an unhealthy gray tone. I rubbed my hair dry and pulled on a pair of shorts and a holey T-shirt. I climbed into bed, which felt like heaven after a night in the cemetery. For the first time in days, I felt almost normal. I felt human. I felt alive. My eyelids drooped. I could keep them open no longer.

* * * *

The bed dipped. Something touched my face and I stirred from a deep, boneless slumber. Rolling onto my side, I curled into a ball and kept my eyes squeezed shut. The weight on the mattress lifted.

"Marley," his voice whispered.

It penetrated the sleepy fog still clouding my brain and pulled me awake, the whole world clearer like Dorothy stepping into Oz in a Technicolor rainbow. My heart picked up speed and I hadn't even opened my eyes yet. Because I knew, without looking, exactly what I would see.

He brushed my cheek with his fingertips, and it was reflex that made me lean into his touch. When I blinked my eyes open, Blake's face was full of sorrow. Blake cupped my face and there were a thousand things written all over him that he didn't have to say out loud.

I pushed up onto one elbow. "You came," I said, my voice hoarse with sleep and thick with emotion.

"Did you think that I wouldn't?"

A fat tear rolled down my face and he wiped it away with the pad of his thumb. I leaned forward to press my forehead to his, our breaths mixing.

"Marley —"

Sitting up fully, I grasped his belt buckle and tugged him closer. "Don't talk."

Blake kicked off his shoes and shoved his jeans down, his T-shirt following his pile of clothing on the floor. I scooted over in my small, narrow childhood bed and he climbed in beside me. He slid his arm around my shoulders to hold my head against his chest.

I breathed in the scent of him, which hurt and healed all at once.

"What do you need?" Blake asked, his voice cautious.

"You. Just you," I whispered, pulling the long T-shirt I'd slept in over my head.

Blake rolled me onto my back, covering me with his large, strong body. When he finally kissed me, I moaned into his mouth. His grip on my hips tightened as he slipped his tongue inside my mouth. He broke the kiss, pressing his lips to my throat, my collarbone, until he met my breasts and he pulled one hardened nipple into his mouth.

I arched into his touch, my fingers knotting in his hair as he worked me into a frenzy. His hands drifted down my body, reaching my soaking slit. He pushed a finger inside, stroking my inner walls and reaching the sweet spot that made me buck against his hand.

Wrapping my legs around his waist, I urged him closer. Despite the limited space, he was still too far away. Blake removed his hand and his hard length nudged my cleft. He lunged for my mouth, kissing me with a fervent plea.

Blake thrust inside, and I cried out, his mouth muffling the sound. He pounded into me hard and fast, too much time, too much everything between us to even think about taking things slowly. My desperation to find some kind of relief with him fueled my release and I came quickly. Blake increased his pace, pounding into me while the orgasm ripped through my body. He came with a violent thrust, pinning me to the bed with his hips.

Blake rolled us to the side and pulled me into his arms, his hold never faltering.

"I miss you," I whispered.

* * * *

The first smile in ages curled the corners of my mouth and I searched with my foot for his. All I was met with was cool sheets and an empty bed.

It took half a second to realize that I'd been dreaming.

Pain lanced my chest. It had felt so real. Was it because I refused to let him die from my memory that recalling him was so vivid? It would be a kindness to forget—or to forget the bad, and only remember the good.

Waking up that morning, I had never felt so lonely.

* * * *

The week following the funeral, Mom and I both resembled a train leaving the station—moving slowly at first, before gradually picking up speed. Mom spent a lot of time alone, disappearing for hours at a time into the bathroom, even the garage. I spent a lot of time on the roof late at night that week. I thought about everything, getting no closer to untangling my web of thoughts. But mostly I thought about my dad. I wondered if it was easier to grieve for the passing of a loved one if you were forewarned. It had to be easier than if it happened suddenly. It almost felt like we had done our grieving over the last four months. The hardest thing to get used to now was the silence. Sports statistics didn't blare from the den. Hammering and the radio couldn't be heard from the garage. It was an odd feeling—like I had forgotten something, like I was looking at a room and something was out of place. I just couldn't figure out what.

All I wanted to do was fuse to the mattress. Sleep still wasn't any easier, and it seemed that after finally drifting off, I woke mere minutes later. It didn't help that dreaming of Blake seemed to open the floodgates, and he was always on my unconscious mind.

But that morning, as I scrubbed my gritty, tired eyes after a night of tossing and turning, something familiar probed my senses. The smell of bacon sizzling in the pan tickled my nostrils and coaxed me further awake. She's back... I swung my legs out of bed and sleepily walked downstairs.

Mom smiled when I entered the kitchen. "I had a feeling the bacon would wake you."

"Does every time." I perched on a stool at the island as Mom filled a coffee mug in front of me. "Any reason for the bacony-goodness?"

Mom dished me up a plate, along with eggs and toast. My mouth watered and I greedily tucked in.

"I woke up this morning and I realized your father would be disgusted with me. It's been so long since I cooked you breakfast. The funeral was four weeks ago. It's time I got back into Mom-mode."

I smiled uncertainly. "You don't have to rush anything on my part, Mom. You should take your time in getting over things."

"I know. But I do feel ready. I can't hide away forever."

I arched an eyebrow. "Sounds like you've got a game plan."

She dropped a dozen or so pamphlets beside me. "Yup."

"What is all this?" I spread them out, seeing the major sights and cities of Europe staring back at me.

"Daddy always wanted to take a trip around Europe. We never got around to it. Before he died he made me promise I would make the trip. I think it's time to do it."

"Good for you, Mom. You should go." I took a bite of toast. "When are you planning on going?"

"Soon. Next week."

I choked. "Next *week*? Seriously?"

She nodded. "I was on the Internet all night. I've got it all planned."

"Do you really though? Flights, hotels, cash, everything?"

Mom frowned. "Who is the parent here? Everything is taken care of."

"So. Guess that means I'm heading back to the city then."

"You have to do it sometime, sweetie."

"I know." I looked up. "Don't you want me to wait here for you? Look after the house?"

"The neighbors have a key. The house will be safe." Mom sat beside me. "If I have to move on, so do you."

I nudged her with my elbow. "Meanie."

Chapter Twenty-Four

Mom drove me and my two suitcases to the city. Hayley awaited me with open arms, eager to have me back. She said I could have my room again for as long as I needed. The goodbye with my mom was quick, like pulling off a Band-Aid. She kissed my cheek and promised to send a postcard from Paris. I was so proud of her. It was hard enough to even go through the motions of everyday life and here she was about to embark upon an adventure.

* * * *

I woke late the morning after my homecoming hungover but perky, an ache to my bones that had come from hours of dancing.

Almost the second I was unpacked, Hayley had called Beth and Eve, picked me out an outfit and poured the first round of cocktails. I hadn't realized how much I'd missed my usual crowd until I was in the heart of it again at our usual table in the club. It was odd how easily I'd slipped into my old life. The girls had been perfect. None of them had asked how I was holding up. None asked any invasive questions. They'd simply welcomed me home.

After a long, hot shower and a giant cup of strong coffee, I decided to get proactive. I threw on some clothes and bolted from the apartment. Excitement fueled my steps as I made the familiar journey to my old office.

Kelly gave a little screech and rushed from her desk to hug me. I sat with her to have a coffee while we caught up, even though it was someone else I was dying to see. She kept up a babble of chatter, saving me from engaging too much.

As I drained the last of my coffee, Henry walked into reception. He did a double-take when he saw me standing before him, grinning.

"Marley, good to see you. What are you doing here?"

"I came to see you, actually."

"Oh. Do you want to come through, then?"

I nodded and followed Henry into his office. He closed the door behind us and sat beside me on the long couch in the corner. I tucked my legs underneath me.

"How are you doing? I heard about your father. I'm sorry."

I dropped my eyes. "I'm okay. Dealing, I guess."

"When did you get back to the city?"

"Yesterday. Mom's doing this trip around Europe, so my time at home ended."

Henry nodded.

"I want to get back to normal, as much as possible anyway." I took a deep breath. "I'm really sorry for everything that happened, Henry. I know I messed you guys around. I never meant to. But all that drama is over now. No more Theo, no more distractions — just me."

Henry gave me a small smile. "I'm glad to hear it. He was no good for you."

"I know I have absolutely no right in asking this, but, is there any chance you would have me back?"

He sighed. "Marley, a lot's happened around here since you left. Things aren't what they used to be. Stuff has changed."

"I'd work really hard," I whispered. "Any hours you want."

"It isn't that simple. Your job isn't available anymore."

"You hired someone else?"

Henry shook his head. "There isn't a job to fill."

I frowned. "I don't understand."

Henry stood up. "Right after you left, I was in talks with another firm similar in size to ours out West. We both wanted to take our companies to the next level and invest in a new project. We decided to merge to make that possible."

"What's the new project?"

"We bought a hotel. I'm going to be running it on location. That's why your job isn't available anymore. As of the end of this week, I won't be here. The office out there is already set up and waiting for me. I've hired someone to take over here, and they're bringing their own assistant."

"Oh. Wow, Henry, that's amazing. I'm really happy for you."

"Thanks. I'm nervous, but a good nervous."

I grinned. "You'll do great." Disappointment and pride rushed through me. I really was happy for Henry. He deserved success. I had been naïve to think

I could just slot back in here after all this time. I stood to leave.

Henry opened the door for me. "Hey, you ever get tired of New York and want to relocate, give me a call."

I laughed. "I will. Thanks again for everything, Henry. Can I use you for a reference?"

Henry chuckled. "Absolutely."

Something made me pause before leaving. "Do you mean that? I should call if I ever feel like leaving the city?"

Henry frowned slightly. "Yes, I do. I guessed with everything that has happened this year, moving would be the last thing you would want."

"Right. I just… I don't know." I shook my head and laughed. I took a step out of his office before turning back. "I didn't even ask. Where is the hotel?"

"Vegas."

I'd never been more confused in my entire life. When I left the office, I made myself accept that I couldn't be a part of their world anymore. My job wasn't there. I couldn't go back—simple. So why, when I walked home with my head in the clouds, did I have a bubble of excitement in my stomach? I deluded myself into thinking it wasn't the location of the hotel, but the thought of a new adventure.

The night before I'd come back to New York, I had wondered why I was. Why come back? Yes, it was home for me now, as it had been for years, and my friends were here. But what else? I had no fiancé awaiting me, no job, no prospects. What was the point? But I'd come back anyway. It was the only logical option. I couldn't stay at home with my mom gone.

I turned the key in the lock and opened the door to Hayley's apartment. *Hayley's* apartment. I didn't even have anywhere that was mine. Hayley would have me stay forever, but I would have to venture out on my own eventually. Part of me actually wanted it to be sooner rather than later. After five months of living at my parents' place again and Theo's for over a year before that, I was beginning to crave my independence.

Sometimes at the end of the day it was really nice to come home and see no one. To have cereal for dinner instead of cooking. To not have to talk at all. I missed the silence of living alone. I missed having long baths without someone screeching on the other side of the door that they needed to use the bathroom. I missed being able to sleep with my bedroom door open. I missed, well, a lot.

So if I was going to leave Hayley's apartment and look for my own, I needed a reason to still be in the city. My head was way too full for this kind of thinking. I needed to get some of it out.

I tossed my purse on the couch and knelt in front of the coffee table.

"What are you doing?" Hayley asked through a yawn as she padded into the lounge.

"I'm going to think on paper."

She arched an eyebrow.

"Have you only just got up?" I asked with a grin. "Dude, it's almost five in the afternoon."

Hayley rolled her eyes and dismissed my teasing with a wave of her hand. "Yeah. You been out already?"

"I went to ask for my old job back."

"And?"

"Henry doesn't work there anymore. So my job isn't there."

"Wow," Hayley said, flopping onto the couch. "Can't he take you wherever he is going?"

I chuckled.

"What?"

"Henry's firm merged with another. They bought a hotel in Vegas."

"Shit, seriously? Damn. Why not go there?"

"Go to Vegas?"

"Yeah, why not? What's stopping you?"

I would have given anything to have Hayley's outlook on life. She saw something she wanted? She went right ahead and took it. She got a job opportunity in a different state? The hell with everything, she went. Hayley lived life right. She didn't torment herself with over-thinking. Everything had a yes or no answer. There was no gray area, no ifs, buts, or maybes.

"That's what I'm trying to figure out."

Hayley rolled her eyes. "You take things way too seriously."

I tossed a cushion at her. She was right, of course. I hunted around for a notepad and a pen.

"Are you seriously making a list of reasons to stay or go?"

"Do you want to help me or not?" I asked, flashing her a look of warning.

She winked then disappeared into the kitchen, before reappearing with a bottle of wine. "Okay. Reasons to stay. Me, of course. The girls. Fifth Avenue. Your favorite Chinese restaurant is right down the street."

I jotted everything down. Placing the pen down, I looked at the list. Wow. Didn't think it would be that short. "Reasons not to stay," I said, picking the pen back up. "No job prospects. No man tying me down. No real reason to stay."

"And reasons to go?"

I laughed. "I'll have a job if I do."

"Vegas has some awesome shopping opportunities. It's hot almost all year round. You would never be bored somewhere like that. Um, a fresh start?"

"Which sounds really good right now." And it did. I had been afraid coming back to New York would feel like starting over. But now I was faced with an actual fresh start. Yes it was scary and yes I would be terrified. But it might be kind of amazing.

"Reasons not to go?" Hayley asked softly.

"I would miss you."

"I could visit."

"It's farther from my mom."

"She could visit. Your Mom is jet-setting right now anyway. And you know both she and your dad would be all for this adventure." Hayley glanced at me cautiously. "And, hey, Vegas is a big city full of busy, busy people. I wouldn't be surprised if you never run into any old faces."

When I got back to the city I'd told Hayley everything—the whole sordid and twisted tale of Blake, Theo and I. And bless her heart, she'd listened earnestly and had never mentioned it again. I didn't know if it was because she knew me well enough that it was something I needed to think through on my own, but I was grateful to her nonetheless.

I looked around at her. My heart swelled with love for my friend who knew how to reassure me without even doing it directly. Of course my biggest reason not to go was Blake. I didn't want to see him or talk to him until I'd muddled through everything that spun in my head. If I saw him then everything would be forgotten. Those eyes would make me forgive him and I would forget how he'd hurt me. No. I needed to figure out what was truth and what was fiction before I saw him. But the job was now. If Henry was serious about me going with him, this would need to be a fast decision.

The words on the paper swam before my eyes. I read my reasons dozens of times. I was no further forward. In the end, it was Theo who made my mind up for me. On the run up to our wedding, he'd become more and more overbearing. His outrageous demands had made me swear I would never again let a man stop me from doing something. If I didn't go with Henry to Vegas then I would be doing just that. I would be letting Blake stop me from pursuing something I wanted to do. It didn't even really make sense to me—and Hayley definitely didn't get it when I told her—but it helped me make up my mind. I was going to Vegas.

I didn't have much by the way of personal effects. Theo hated things cluttering up his apartment, so when I'd moved in with him, I'd sent most of my books and things to my parents' house. The move would be simple. Clean. Easy.

It had to be now or I'd change my mind. So for the second time that day, I rushed to my old office. Henry was in reception this time and saw me coming.

"Marley? What—?" he started.

"Tell me you were serious," I said, trying to catch my breath.

"Serious?" Henry frowned for a second before his eyebrows shot up into his hairline. "About the job? Coming to Vegas?"

I nodded.

"Well, Christ, Marley, of course I was serious but... Really? Is this the time to be making such an upheaval in your life?" Henry asked. He cupped my elbow and steered me into his office.

"I couldn't think of a better time to do it," I said, unable to stop the excited smile. "There's nothing keeping me here, Henry. And I need to do something. I need a reason to get up in the morning."

He let out a heavy breath. "I need your word that you're committed to this. That after a week or a month you won't turn around and say you miss the city and the girls, or you've run into someone and now you can't face seeing them again, and you want to come back. I appreciate everything that you had going on before you left, but this is a new chapter in my life and in my business. I can't be bringing a ton of baggage with me."

"Henry," I said, taking a step toward him and keeping my face as solemn as I could manage. "I swear to you that my reasons for wanting to do this are pure. I'll be the girl you knew when you first hired me. And if I do run into...someone, then I can also swear that it will never affect my work and it will never affect your business. I learned my lesson, Henry."

He raked his eyes over my face for a long moment. Then his mouth stretched into a wide smile and he took two quick steps toward me and pulled me into a huge hug. "Then pack your bags. We leave in one week."

I left Henry in a flurry of activity as he arranged for my suite in his new hotel, which would be my temporary lodgings until I found somewhere permanent. He promised to have my plane ticket messengered over to Hayley's apartment within the next few days.

Hayley was bouncing on the balls of her feet outside the office building when I emerged. "Well?" she asked, clasping her hands together under her chin.

"It's a good thing you like Vegas, because you're going to visit me at least once a month," I said, laughing.

She squealed and threw her arms around me. "Oh my gosh! I'm so happy for you, but I also kind of hate you... I just got you back. How long do I have you for?"

"A week."

"A week?" Hayley looked as though she could faint. "I hope you're wearing comfortable shoes, because we're about to have a marathon shopping expedition."

"What?" I asked.

She looped her arm with mine and dragged me in the direction of Fifth Avenue.

"Hayley, what on earth do I need to go shopping for?"

She looked at me as though I'd just sprouted horns. "A new work wardrobe, what else? New city, new clothes. That's the rule."

"I don't need a new work wardrobe."

"I couldn't agree more." Hayley grinned. "You also need a new summer wardrobe, a new autumn and winter wardrobe...not including shoes, of course."

I rolled my eyes. "Of course."

"You're a New Yorker, girlfriend. You need to let those showgirls know you're the hot shit in town."

Chapter Twenty-Five

The dry heat of Vegas hit my face the second I stepped off the plane. Henry wanted me to meet his new business partner for lunch, so he'd arranged for our luggage to be taken to our individual suites. What I really wanted was a shower, but that would have to wait an hour or so.

Max Airman, Henry's new business partner, seemed a nice guy. Not someone I could imagine Henry spending a great deal of time with. But then, I supposed both men would be busy enough to not need to spend too much time together. Max looked a few years younger than Henry, maybe late thirties with already graying brown hair and a waistline that would soon be bordering chunky.

He was full of energy and a little too loud. The minute we had finished lunch, he insisted on giving me a guided tour of the hotel. The Oasis, the hotel Henry and Max had purchased, wasn't as large as one I'd stayed in before. But just because it wasn't as big, didn't mean it was small. It was still home to over two thousand guest rooms, a good size casino, a small movie theater, three restaurants and a night club—and a pool with its own bar. So the tour took almost three hours. And that was with Max moving at the pace of a six-year-old on crack.

"Well…herein lies the end of the tour!" Max grinned as he stopped in front of the fountain in the lobby.

"Already?" I asked, hoping the sarcasm wasn't apparent.

"Yes, time did fly, didn't it?"

"Mmm."

"I know we looked in the three restaurants, but dining in one of them would give you a better feel for the place, I think!" Max leaned slightly closer. "Would an hour suit you?"

"For dinner?" I squeaked.

"Of course."

I could have broken down in tears. All I wanted to do was crawl upstairs and collapse in my bed. Instead I slapped on a surprised smile and said, "I'd love to."

I turned to Henry, who let out a comically faux yawn. "I'm dog tired. You two go, have fun."

Damn…if I'd known that excuse would fly, I would have used it myself.

* * * *

Max insisted on taking me for a drink in the hotel's nightclub after dinner. After a few glasses of champagne, he began looking at me with a familiar look in his eye.

"So do you think you will like Vegas, Marley?" Max asked, standing a little closer than I would have liked.

"I'm sure I will."

"Any sights you're particularly keen on seeing?"

A blush stained my cheeks. "I'm not one for sightseeing."

"Oh come on," Max said, nudging me in the ribs. "There must be something that would catch that eye of yours."

I shook my head.

"Hmm. I'll have to find a way to tempt you."

Looking up, I saw Max drink me in with his eyes. I cleared my throat and his eyes snapped upward to my face.

"You would find I'm an excellent tour guide. Perhaps after work one evening I could show you a few of my favorite spots."

Oh, crap. "Um, that's okay. I really wouldn't be terrific company."

"I doubt that," Max murmured.

Jeez, if this guy were a dog, he would be humping my leg right about now. Actually, if Max had his way, he wouldn't need to be a dog to be doing a bit of humping. I shuddered. "No, really. I'm the kind of girl who looks the wrong way when something is pointed out. Attention isn't my strong point."

"So what does it take to get your attention?" Max asked, taking a step closer, if that was possible.

"Oh, um, you know, lots of things."

"Such as?"

"Um…I always pay attention at work. I like working. I like it a lot."

"I'm glad I've found such a dedicated worker then. Long, dark nights in the office appeal to you?"

Can this guy turn anything dirty? "Technically Henry found me. I work for Henry and him alone."

Max nodded. "And if I need anything?"

"You should ask your own assistant to help you."

"What if only you can help me?"

My stomach shifted uneasily. However, kneeing my boss's new partner in his crown jewels before I'd even officially started working probably wasn't the best idea.

Max didn't wait for me to answer. "You know, we're a very relaxed group here in Vegas. I mean, I don't know what it was like in New York, but here we tend to keep things in the family."

Before I could stop myself, I gasped.

He grinned. "Something wrong?"

"Me? No, nothing at all." Okay, I was going to have to nip this in the bud. "I just don't approve of inter-office relations."

Max frowned. "Any particular reason?"

"Um, distractions?"

He leaned closer. "Aren't distractions good things?"

"No!" I said a little too loudly. "No. I give one hundred and ten percent when I'm working. There's no way I could do that if I had that kind of distraction around me all day."

"Shame," Max whispered in my ear.

I stepped away from him and smiled in a way that, hopefully, told him I was drawing a line under the conversation. He seemed to take it in good stride and accepted my response. Good, because I was just shy of screaming at him that I wasn't interested. But it didn't get rid of the look in his eye, the perv.

It was after one a.m. before my head landed on a soft, plump pillow.

* * * *

My sleep had been dreamless, but I found I wasn't well rested the following morning. When my alarm beeped at six-thirty, I could have thrown it out of the window. Despite having had five hours' sleep, more than I was used to, all I wanted to do was close my eyes and drift off again, but things had to be done. Henry was showing me around our office, somewhere in the hotel. We needed to get things set up, and sleeping late wouldn't help anyone.

Henry and I had arranged to meet in the lobby at eight so we could head into the office together. He was already waiting for me when I arrived, two takeout coffees in his hand.

"Ready?" Henry asked, handing me a coffee and smiling.

"As I'll ever be."

We entered a door near the reception desk, which Henry accessed by a keycard and ID number.

"You'll get your keycard and ID later today," Henry said as we stepped inside a small elevator, once again using his card. "It's a pain in the ass, but I guess it's called for out here."

When we exited the elevator, we were on a bustling office floor, a long row of separate offices and a main bullpen area filled with desks already occupied by workers dominating the space.

"This is the main hub of communications. Anything done at any time in this place comes through here," Henry said as we passed through, heading down a long hallway, the noise and commotion of the main area fading behind us. "We're in here." Henry once again used his key card to enter a new area. This place was luscious and opulent, intricate moldings and high-end furniture. Big, leafy plants and Grecian statues decorated surfaces and huge windows showcased the best views Vegas had to offer. Two platinum blondes sat at a huge curved desk in the center, three separate hallways spanning out behind them.

"Good morning, Henry," one of the blondes greeted him.

He nodded his head. "Sally. Theresa."

I smiled at the two women and was relieved when they both smiled back, seemingly genuine. I followed Henry as he continued down the hallway on the right.

"And this," Henry said, stepping through an open doorway, "is us."

Two gleaming black lacquered desks stood in the middle of the room facing each other. State-of-the-art computers sat atop them, along with phones, small desktop filing systems and Rolodex.

"You'll be out here with Chelsea, the other assistant."

"The other assistant?" I asked. "Is she, like, my boss or something?"

Henry laughed. "No, more like the other way around. I want you to do most of what you did in New York, answering my messages, dictation, that kind of thing. But, if you're game, I'd like you to be more hands-on with the PR side of things. Most of our events will be in-house now, and you could use that opportunity to really learn the ropes. It will mean roughly four nights a week at the club. Chelsea can handle the admin in the office so you can come in late the mornings after."

Okay. That was a lot to process. My stomach fluttered at the new opportunity. "Wait. I wouldn't have to tell her what to do, would I?"

"I hope you'll help guide her, but no. I'll give her instructions but you may have to delegate some menial work her way from time to time." Henry crossed the room and opened yet another door. "This is my room. Little bigger than New York, huh?"

I followed him inside. *I'll say...* Henry's desk was gargantuan. Tall filing cabinets stood against one wall, and behind the desk were floor-to-ceiling windows, letting in a flood of light. "Is it? I hadn't noticed?"

He laughed. "Well, this concludes the tour. Let's show these guys how New Yorkers do things."

We got straight to work. A little after nine, a slim redhead took up the desk opposite me. She blinked when she first spotted me, a smile spreading across her face a short moment later.

"Oh, hi. You must be Marley. I'm Chelsea," she said, coming around the desk to shake my hand.

"Yes, Marley. Nice to meet you," I said.

"How are you enjoying Vegas so far?"

"I only flew in yesterday."

Her smile widened. "I'll get some of the girls together for drinks after work one night. We'll show you how it's done here."

I laughed. "Sounds dangerous."

"Only for the faint hearted."

Lord.

That day was backbreaking. Henry leaped in at the deep end, organizing a huge bash at the club to celebrate the new partnership between himself and Max. I spent most of the day on the phone organizing additional staff, a guest DJ and building a star-studded guest list—plus answering Chelsea's never ending stream of questions. That girl was more curious than Hayley, which said a lot.

I returned to my suite that night utterly exhausted, my mind aching with tiredness. But I felt satisfied and hard worked—and content that I got to do it all over again the next day.

It took most of that first week to really find my footing. I completely re-organized the filing system so it was more or less the same as we'd worked with in New York, to make things that bit easier for Henry. Once it was done, things flowed more smoothly and I was able to relax into the swing of things.

And I eventually got around to sorting out my things. Despite Hayley's overly enthusiastic shopping persuasions that had made my wardrobe explode in size, it didn't take that long to unpack, which went some way to adding a sense of peace to my mind.

By the time I opened the final case, I almost felt at home. The last case had more knick-knacks than clothes. I put a picture of me and my dad on the nightstand. At the bottom of the case was a pile of envelopes grouped together with an elastic band. Written on a big pink Post-it was a message from Hayley. *Letters are for opening!* I checked the postmark on the first one, dated more than six months ago. I frowned before remembering that Hayley had brought me a pile of mail when I'd first returned home. Guess I still hadn't gotten around to it. I tossed the pile on the coffee table. They waited this long, they could wait a little longer.

Chapter Twenty-Six

After work the following day, a few of the girls I worked alongside invited me out for dinner and drinks. I happily agreed, longing to see more than the walls of my suite. We went to a little restaurant just off the Strip. It was good to be back in the company of girls. I relaxed more than I normally would, but that might have been because of the four Cosmos rather than their company. When we headed back onto the Strip, one of the girls suggested going to Vault. Fear struck my heart. I couldn't face going there, just in case. I told them I had a headache and would see them in the morning.

I watched them go, cackling as they walked into the lobby of the hotel that once upon a time I'd wished I'd had the courage never to leave. The fountain sprays started, rows of water weaving and flowing in time to the music blasting from the speakers all around. Folding my arms across my chest, I became entranced as I watched, wondering how music, water and a few lights could seem so magical.

Later, as I dropped onto the couch in my suite, I felt an utter coward for not going to Vault. What did it matter if I did go and bumped into a familiar Tall, Dark and Handsome? God, I was so mad at myself! My first chance to prove none of this shit mattered to me and I'd bailed. I didn't cower around in New York terrified I would run into Theo. Why should Vegas be any different? Maybe because I didn't actually care if I saw Theo. And I definitely *did* care about seeing a certain Tall, Dark and Handsome.

With nothing better to do, I sorted through my pile of mail. It was bigger than I remembered. Checking the envelopes nearer the back, I saw the postmark was more recent. Hayley must have added to the pile.

Most of it was junk. Credit card and phone bills. Who'd want that? I came across a thick cream envelope. Curiosity tugged at me and I tore it open. My face twisted into a smile before I doubled over with laugher. Theo and Simone's wedding invite. I couldn't decide what was funnier — them getting married or them inviting me.

Another envelope nestled among the junk mail sparked my interest. It was handwritten and dated almost seven months ago. I didn't rip it open as I had done with Theo's invite. Instead, I took my time. As I unfolded the small sheets of paper, a coin fell from between them, spinning as it landed on the table. I stilled it with my finger, pulling back to see that it was a quarter. An odd flutter unsettled my stomach and a chill cooled my fingertips.

Marley,
I've tried to write this letter a dozen times now and every time I try to it comes across phoney and insincere. So, I'm

just going to say what I'm thinking and pray you know me well enough to trust the words.

I couldn't sleep for days after you called. I kept hearing your broken voice in my head. I knew it would come. I knew one day you would ask me to tell you the truth and I swore I wouldn't lie anymore. I wish I could change things, but I can't. I don't know what Theo told you, but I'm going to tell you what happened from my perspective. I need you to hear it from me.

A few days after I came to New York, Theo asked me to take you out. He wanted you 'distracted' for the evening. At first he didn't tell me why – that came later, when it was too late to stay away from you. I'd be a liar if I said I didn't at least suspect. But how could I tell you the truth? Would you have believed me? It was hard enough getting you to trust me after coming back into your life without throwing something like that at you. So, I did as he asked. I was curious about you. To be perfectly honest, I don't think I could have stayed away from you if I tried. Maybe a week later he asked me to do the same thing. So I did. After that second time, Theo never asked me to take you anywhere. After that, we were making our own plans. I did what I did for my own selfish reasons. I wanted to know everything about you. You were a complete mystery to me. I wanted to know exactly what made you tick, what made you smile, what made you sad. I wanted everything, Marley.

So is this how Theo described my input? Did he tell you I helped him cheat because I quite simply couldn't stay away from you?

And yes, I knew about Simone and the baby. I hated him for that, for being so careless and flippant with his relationship with you. He had no idea what he was throwing away, but then, being Theo, I suppose he was arrogant enough to believe he could get away with anything.

So why didn't I tell you any of this? Why did I hide it? I honestly don't know. At first, I suppose it's because I felt my loyalty lay with Theo. He asked me for a favor and I felt obligated to comply. I've known him for years. He was my best friend. In the end, I guess it was because I couldn't stand to be the one to hurt you. I was terrified you would react exactly as you did. I was also scared because Theo is a damn good lawyer. How easy would it be for him to worm his way out of everything and blame someone else for his own actions?

Most selfishly, I just wanted to be the one you wanted. For you to walk toward me of your own free will. I chose you – over and over it was you I chose. Nothing else mattered and I'm not proud to say I didn't care what it took or who got hurt, I wanted you. I suppose, for once, I wanted to feel like you chose me too.

So there you have it – my part in this awful mess. What you believe now is up to you. I know Theo has planted the seed of doubt in your mind about me and I don't blame you for hating me. It's nothing less than I deserve. I'm not too sad. The only thing I'm happy about is that you are finally away from him. He holds no influence over you. You're free from his twisted world of games and deceit. And for that I'm happy.

After this letter I can promise you won't hear from me again. I won't pester you for forgiveness and demand you hear me out. What happens now is up to you. All I can hope for is one day, I can earn your trust again.

Blake.

The paper shook in my hands as I finished reading. Everything Blake had said in his letter was exactly what I wanted to believe. It was everything I'd dreamed he would say to me – which is exactly why I didn't trust it.

I must have read that letter a dozen times before I moved from the couch. I stepped out onto the balcony for some air, letting the noise of the Strip below wash over me. For some reason, it was Theo I couldn't get out of my head. When he'd turned up at the wake, he had seemed more sincere then than he ever had. What would he gain now by lying? I couldn't see anything. He was marrying Simone. He didn't have anything to lose. His words also seemed to back up Blake's letter. I checked my watch. Just after twelve. I had to do this now, before I lost my nerve.

* * * *

My heart pounded in my ears as I walked down the hallway I'd traveled only once before. The door I'd fled out of so long ago loomed into view. How odd it was. I had been here once what felt like years ago, yet my feet guided me here as if it were a familiar street I walked every day.

I raised my shaking hand to knock timidly on the door. *Maybe he won't even be here. He's probably still working.* The door started to open. *Oh, crap. I bet a heart attack feels just like this.* As I tried not to throw up, I took a deep breath and summoned up enough courage for a meek smile. The smile soon fell as a blonde knockout wearing a bikini stepped into view.

"Hi, can I help you?" she asked, leaning against the door jamb.

"I'm looking for Blake?" *Oh my God! Does my voice have to sound so pathetic?*

"Sorry, he's not here. I can get a message to him."

"Oh, no, that's fine," I said in a rush as I started to back away.

"What's your name? I'll tell him you stopped by."

"No! No, that's okay. Don't tell him I came. Really."

She gave me a quizzical look, probably wondering why my eyes were so wide. I backed away farther before turning on my heels and fleeing.

My cheeks burned with chagrin as I stomped back to my hotel. I hadn't seen Blake for nearly seven months. What had I expected? To find him knee deep in Kleenex, waiting for me to turn up to pull him out of a pit of depression? I shouldn't have gone looking for him. God, I really hoped she didn't tell him I'd showed up... Because of course he would be able to tell exactly who the moron the leggy blonde described. What an embarrassment.

* * * *

"You definitely need to see a show. I totally recommend Zumanity," Chelsea said.

Sally, who sat on my other side at the in-pool bar, shook her head. "Whatever, Chelsea. Not everyone likes erotic dances like you do."

I choked on a mouthful of Cosmo. "Erotic dances? In a show? Seriously?" The girls had lived in Vegas all their lives and were all too eager to familiarize me with all it had to offer.

That particular Sunday afternoon, we'd all found ourselves on the same schedule and they'd insisted I joined them down at the hotel's pool, swearing I'd love it. So I'd donned the leopard print bikini Hayley had made me buy, and after ten minutes of sitting on a stool in the water and sipping a Cosmo, I knew it would be a frequent haunt of mine.

Chelsea giggled. "It's not that bad! It's the adult side of Cirque du Soleil. Just more sensual and raunchy."

I was pretty sure I was blushing.

"Forget the show," Sally said. "Go to a comedy club. The Improv at Harrah's is really good, and they do dinner packages. We should all go, make a night of it!"

"Yeah." I nodded. "Definitely."

"You *have* to check out the Fashion Show Mall, it's to *die* for," Chelsea emphasized.

"Will you give the girl a break?" Sally scolded. "Anyway, the best thing about Vegas is the clubs. Stocked full of guys just looking for a good time."

"Don't you get sick of hooking up with tourists?" Chelsea asked her. "It's like it has a time limit before you even get started."

"That's why I like it." Sally grinned.

"What about you, Marley? Seeing anyone?"

I shook my head, praying they'd let the subject go and not start digging.

I'd barely slept the night before. I'd kept seeing the blonde woman. She'd been in a bikini. I could only guess she had been going to use the hot tub. *Bitch.*

Sally raised her glass as though to toast my single status. "Then we have to find you a nice Vegas guy. We're going out tonight. Want to come?"

"Yeah, come!" Chelsea exclaimed. "You should have come to Vault the other night. It was awesome."

"Ugh, I *love* Vault," Sally said. "You ever been?"

"Once."

"So? What did you think?"

"Um, yeah. It uh, definitely left an impression."

A loud splash from the other end of the pool made me jump. A few startled shrieks followed. We three girls craned our necks toward the commotion. People dove out of the way, clearing a path up the center of the pool straight toward us.

"What the hell?" Chelsea murmured.

I pushed my sunglasses on top of my head, trying to figure out what was fast approaching us. All I could make out was that it was smaller than a human and gray.

"Is that a —?" Sally said, disgustedly.

"*Dog?*" Chelsea finished.

I grinned as the dog paddled beside us. I reached out and ruffled its head, and I swore the thing grinned at me.

"Where the hell is its owner?" Sally asked.

I laughed. "Who knows?"

"You like it?" Chelsea asked.

"Sure, why not? I think he's beautiful." The dog was a husky and absolutely gorgeous.

Sally shuddered.

Damn, it's only a dog. What's her problem?

I slid off my stool and stood in the waist-high water. "Come on," I called to the dog.

It followed me out where the pool beached. The dog stopped to shake off the excess water, creating another wide space around us as he showered the surrounding people. I laughed and grabbed him by the collar, leading him away from everyone. I stopped at the lounger the girls and I had left our towels and things on. I towel-dried my hair and the dog sat patiently by my feet.

"Where's your boss?" I asked him.

The dog turned to look at me and I reached out to scratch his ears. A laugh bubbled in my throat as he twisted into my hand and leaned heavily against my leg, letting out a weird groan of pleasure.

As the dog turned, I noticed he had a tag hanging from his blue leather collar. I tried to get a hold of it but he wouldn't keep still. The dog jerked his head and backed away from me, leaving the collar in my hands. A sharp whistle pierced the air and the dog took off. My leg was covered with wet dog hair and I still had his collar.

I groaned and stood up, pulling on my halter top and short denim cut-offs. I shoved my feet into my thong sandals and started in the direction that the dog had run off in. There was no sight of the dog anywhere. I read the tag on the collar. No name was listed, just a cell phone number. Huh. It looked familiar. I scrolled through the memory in my cell until I found the corresponding number. A jolt went through me. Of course. When was I going to stop being surprised when stuff like this happened?

The woman who greeted me at the reception desk inside the Marebello eyed me up and down. I was no longer all drippy. The Las Vegas sun had taken care of that for me. However my hair was knotted and I didn't exactly match the high-class clientele of the famous hotel.

"Can I help you?"

I tugged at the hem of my halter, wishing there was more fabric. "Yeah, I found this and wondered if you could return it to its owner?" I held up the collar.

Her eyes widened. I glanced at the collar then back to her face.

"Oh! No! It's nothing like that! Oh God, I didn't mean anything kinky—" Why could I not stop talking? I laughed nervously. "It fell off a dog. The owner of the dog lives here."

"Oh!" The woman laughed. "Of course. Who is the owner?"

"Blake."

"Blake," she repeated.

"Yes, Blake Hamilton."

Her face was blank.

"The manager?"

She frowned and held up a finger. "Wait one moment."

I turned to lean on the desk as she picked up the phone by her computer.

Ten agonizing minutes later, the woman from the night before approached me, looking absolutely fabulous in an Armani suit with her hair pulled into a high glossy ponytail. And I looked the definition of white trash. God, I really wished I had been wearing more clothes. My hair clung damply to my back, but was pushed back from my face with my sunglasses. At least they were designer.

She gave me a puzzled look before smiling. "Hello. I'm Natasha Evans. Can I help you with something?"

My face burned. "I was looking for Blake."

A flicker of recognition crossed her perfect face. "What was it regarding?"

I held up the collar.

She arched an eyebrow.

I sighed and looked at the ground for a moment. Did I look like the kinky type or something? "His dog dropped this. Can you make sure it gets to him?"

"I'm really not sure when I would see him." She took a step closer to me. "You're Marley, aren't you?"

"No," I said quickly.

Natasha reached behind the desk and pulled out a pad and a pencil. She scribbled an address and tore it off then handed it to me.

"What's this?" I asked, looking at the paper.

"You can find him there." She glanced at the clock. "He had an appointment on the Strip this afternoon, but he should be back at that address by now. He will want the collar back as soon as possible."

"Can't I just leave it here? I have a lot to do and—"

"Like I said," she interrupted, "I have no idea when I will see him." She turned on her heel and walked away from me.

Great. This is what being a Good Samaritan does for you.

* * * *

The cab drive was over way faster than I'd hoped. After screeching the address at the cabbie, I had clung to the edges of the seat wondering what had possessed me to do this. I could have just left the stupid collar on the stupid reception desk and washed my hands of the whole stupid drama. But, because it was me and I liked stupid things, I hadn't. The cab drove me away from the Strip and into a rich-looking neighborhood where the houses got bigger, were spaced farther apart and were better hidden by foliage. I had no idea where I was, but tried to remember the general way back, should I need to storm away from...anything.

The cab slowed before driving through open gates leading up a short and winding driveway. Hedges surrounded the property, concealing it from view from pedestrians.

"This okay for you?" the driver asked, watching me in his rear-view mirror.

No! Take me back! "This is fine." I shoved a fifty dollar bill through the little hatch.

"Okay."

I nodded.

The driver cleared his throat. "I have another fare..."

"Oh!" I snapped back to reality and realized I was still clinging to the seat as though my death awaited me. I took a deep breath, clutched the collar tightly then stepped out of the cab. The door was barely shut before the cabbie took off, completely abandoning me.

My feet dragged as I walked toward the front door. I knocked timidly, barely grazing the glass. Sighing, I leaned against the doorbell.

Nothing.

I cupped my eyes to the door to peer in. No sign of life. I almost sighed in relief when I realized I could leave guilt free. Wasn't my fault he wasn't here, wherever here was. I was about to turn to leave when I heard music playing.

Could be a neighbor…

I almost believed my pathetic excuse, until the sound of a dog barking at the rear of the house shattered my fragile excuse.

Closing my eyes and taking a deep breath, I readied myself. There was a path at the side of the house and since I followed it, I hoped it led to the back of the property. I hadn't realized how big the house was until I turned the corner and saw just how far back it went. It really was impressive. The yard, when I finally got to it, was amazing. A long decked area ran around the back side of the house. A wooden table and set of chairs sat next to a grill in front of tall French windows, all of them open with their sheer white drapes blowing in the breeze. I walked farther into the yard, turning another small corner, and was now facing a huge swimming pool with adjoining hot tub.

Double doors from the kitchen opened onto the pool area and still I could see no one. I could hear the music. It was louder from back here, confirming my suspicions that it did indeed come from this house somewhere.

I took a cautious step toward the open door. "Hello?" I called.

A bark answered me—and another. The dog raced toward me out of the house. Despite my sickening nerves, I smiled at the sight of my four-legged friend. Damn, he was really moving. If he didn't slow down he was going to crash right into—

At the last moment it jumped, placing both front paws on my shoulders and knocking me down. It had to be at least fifty pounds. Felt it, too.

After the initial shock of being swept off my feet by a dog, I tried to get my breath back. My eyes stung from the glaring sun and I held a hand in front of my face, trying to block it. The dog panted excitedly in my face. I groaned under its weight and tried to ignore my throbbing ass.

We both turned toward the sound of a whistle, and the dog bounced off me and sat by my side. As I was about to stand up, I was shielded from the brightness by a body standing before me, eclipsing the sun.

"Huh. Didn't expect to find you out here."

Chapter Twenty-Seven

I didn't know if it was because I hadn't seen them in so long and needed to be desensitized to those eyes again, or if it was because with the sun shining behind his head he looked like a god. Or because I might have a concussion. Either way, I was rendered incoherent.

"Um..."

Blake pulled back and extended a hand. I was tempted just to stay where I was. I stared at it before sliding my hand into his and letting him pull me to my feet. The closeness of his body to mine sparked an instant reaction right through me. My hand felt like it was sizzling. I jumped back. What had I been thinking, coming here? I could barely even form a freaking sentence!

"I found your collar," I blurted out.

Blake arched an eyebrow. I thrust the collar still clutched in my hands toward him. He took it and for the briefest second our fingers brushed. My pulse quickened.

"Thanks. You didn't have to bring this all the way out here. How did you find it?"

"I was in the pool your dog jumped in. I guess it fell off or something and he ran away." I fidgeted with my hands as I spoke in a rush. "I took it to the Marebello but they wouldn't take it."

"I'm not surprised."

For seven months I'd imagined what I would say to this man should I ever see him again. All my speeches where I let him have it and where I would cuss more than I have in my entire life, it all dribbled out of my head. All I could think about was how hot he looked. Not just regular good-looking, but hot.

He made my body awaken and every second of that seven month separation meant nothing.

Christ! Marley, get a freaking hold of yourself!

He looked different from how he normally did. I was so used to seeing Blake looking sharp in a designer suit and appearing effortlessly elegant. Today he looked...rough. Blake wore a pair of worn jeans and a white T-shirt, both splattered with paint. I had to stop myself from smiling when I noticed a smear of cream paint across his cheek.

Blake started to take a step toward me but pulled back at the last second. He jammed his hands in his pockets. "Will you stay for a drink?"

Shit... That would involve motor functions, something I wasn't confident in right now. I felt my head nod. *Oh, God, I'm so going to regret this...*

Blake smiled and motioned for me to follow him inside. Once in the large, bright kitchen, I leaned against the island, which created a barrier between us. He opened the fridge. "I've only got beer, is that okay?"

I nodded. He pulled two out and stretched across to hand me one. I placed it on the island and loosely cupped it with both hands, staring intently at the label, as though it would give me notes on what to say next.

"Don't have much in the way of groceries yet," Blake murmured. He leaned with his back against the counter opposite me, obviously liking the barrier as much as I did. He took a long, hard pull on the bottle. *Huh.* Maybe he was nervous too.

A smirk teased my lips. Of course he was nervous. He probably expected me to throw something at him. I jumped when I felt the dog lean against my leg. I hadn't even realized he had followed us inside.

Blake let out a breath of air. "Jeez, Marley, will you say something already? You're killing me over here."

I glanced up at him and saw how tortured his eyes were. "I met Natasha." Where the hell had that come from? Talk about an ice breaker. Not.

"She's my replacement."

What? "Is that a new word for girlfriend I haven't heard yet?"

Blake smiled a little. "Not that I know of. She replaced me as manager of the hotel when I quit."

"But she was in your room."

A look of surprise flickered across his face. "That suite is for the manager of the hotel. And since I'm not anymore, I don't live there. Natasha, my replacement, does."

"She said she could get a message to you."

"My dad does still own the hotel. It wouldn't be too hard for her to find me."

"But she knew who I was." Okay, was I trying to convince him or me? For every query I had, he knocked them away with a plausible explanation. So why the hell was I still trying to get him to say she was his girlfriend, or at the very least, his sex friend?

Blake dropped his eyes. "Yeah, well."

"Yeah well what?" I muttered.

He lifted his head to look at me again. "Am I on trial here or something? FBI agents don't grill as hard as you do."

I rolled my eyes and caught him smirking at me. Little beads of condensation trickled down the side of the bottle. Tracing the top with my index finger, I tried to look anywhere that wasn't Blake.

I'd been angry for so long but I just didn't feel it anymore. I still felt hurt and a little bit betrayed, but I didn't have the energy to be angry anymore. Mostly I missed him. Here he was, right in front of me, and I missed him more in that very second than I had these past seven months. It felt like I was standing in the kitchen of a stranger. I didn't know this Blake. The Blake in front of me was a harder, stonier version of my Blake. He couldn't have seemed more defensive than if he had stood behind a ten foot high brick wall. Not completely different from the one I had built around myself.

"Are you enjoying your vacation?"

Blake's random question made me snap my head up to look at him. I couldn't read his face. "Vacation?"

"Isn't that why you're here? I figured when I saw you at the club and then at the pool, you were on vacation."

"Club?"

"On Saturday night, in the hotel you were at today. You were with a guy." Once again I couldn't read him. To the casual observer, anyone would think he was disinterested. But Blake had spent years studying the best poker faces. He could be furious inside and I would never have known.

Max, right. "Oh. Yeah. Feels like forever ago. Guess it's been a long week."

"Too much partying?"

I shook my head. "Too much work."

Blake frowned. "Work? Is your firm handling an event out here or something?"

"Or something." I didn't want to tell him work had me in Vegas indefinitely. I didn't want him to think I was living in his city and hadn't cared enough to let him know I was coming. After everything, I couldn't hurt him. I didn't have it in me.

A moment's silence passed, the air seeming to sizzle and crack with electricity.

Blake cleared his throat. "So why did you go to my suite?"

"What?"

"Earlier, you said Natasha was at my old suite, so I'm guessing you stopped by." Blake lowered his eyes briefly, as though embarrassed then mumbled, "I'm just wondering why."

"Why were you at my hotel today?" I blurted, desperate to avoid answering his question.

"I was running an errand for my dad. He just sold that hotel and wanted me to drop something off to the new owners."

"Your dad used to own it?"

Blake nodded.

I laughed quietly. *The universe is totally working against me.*

"The new owner's a real douche," Blake said, his eyes intent on my face.

A frown worked its way onto my forehead. Now that I thought about it, Blake and Henry had never met. Henry hadn't been at my birthday party, so there was no reason for Blake to connect Henry to me.

"He is not."

Blake tilted his head as he spoke. "Know him well?"

Secrets, Lies and Vegas

"Very."

He nodded. "Got a thing for guys in the hotel business, huh?"

"What?" If I hadn't been so surprised I would have been pissed. Me and Henry? He was my dad's age! And...no way! Me and Henry—the idea was laughable. Not to mention gross.

"First me, now Max. I can see the pattern." Blake's voice had taken on a bitter, jealous edge.

I hadn't even heard it when we used to talk about Theo. It didn't suit him and instead of being angry at his bizarre accusation, all I wanted was to say something that would turn his voice back to the silkiness I remembered.

I straightened up. "Max as in Max Airman? Are you kidding me?"

"You were on a date with him at that club."

I snorted. "That was so not a date. That was two hours of me trying to convince him I wasn't the kind of girl who fools around with her boss."

Blake frowned and took an involuntary step toward me. "Boss? Max Airman is your boss?"

Crap. Really talked myself into a corner. Taking a deep breath, I found the courage to meet his eyes. "Sort of. He's Henry's new partner."

"Henry bought the hotel with Max? Where—where is he handling things? New York or..." Blake's voice trailed off, as though he couldn't bring himself to finish the question.

I wanted to believe it was because he didn't want to let himself hope.

"He's working on site."

"Marley, have you moved to Vegas?"

I nodded once.

Blake let out a breath, and a smile pulled at the corner of his mouth. "Didn't expect that."

"Yeah, well, neither did I." I dropped my eyes and somehow the conversation dropped with them.

Blake stepped back again and after a minute he said, "You gonna answer my question?"

"What question?"

"How come you went by my old suite?"

Shit. My cheeks flushed. "Just wanted to talk to you, I guess."

"What about?" Blake asked, throatily.

"I just finished your letter."

Blake raised his eyebrows and chuckled. "Wow. Seven months to read a letter. Didn't peg you for a slow reader."

I narrowed my eyes at him. "I only just got it."

"Mailing system not all it's cracked up to be, huh? Why'd it take you so long to get it?" Blake asked cautiously, clearly sensing my aggravated state.

"It was with a bunch of mail I shoved in drawer and forgot about."

"For seven months?"

My eyes hardened and teeth clenched. "Yeah, for seven months. We've established the time frame already. You know, sometimes real life just has to wait. Things happen and stupid things like mail don't matter."

"What happened, Marley?" Blake took an uneasy step toward me. "Did Theo—?"

"Oh my God!" I shouted. Something inside me snapped and every heightened emotion I'd felt in the last few months boiled to the surface. "Not everything is about Theo! Is that all you think can upset me? Not everything links back to him, you know. And it's because of Theo that I'm here right now, so before you get all —"

"Wait, what?"

I took a breath. "Yeah. You have Theo to thank for me being here."

"Why?" Blake took a step back and turned to face the window. "You two friends now or something? Things get rekindled again? Felt like telling me in person the wedding of the year is back on?"

God, he was lucky I didn't throw my beer bottle at his thick skull. "No, but I did get an invite to his wedding to *Simone*," I emphasized. "Theo came to talk to me, at my dad's funeral of all places —"

Blake whirled around. *Jeez, if he keeps this up I'm never gonna get my sentence out.*

"What?" I asked, unable to read the look in his eyes.

"Your… Your dad died?" Blake closed his eyes slowly and his shoulders sagged. "God, Marley, I'm so sorry," Blake choked.

I stiffened. "You didn't know?"

"How could I? Who do I talk to that knows you?" He stepped toward me. "How can you think for one second that, had I known, I would have stayed away?"

A lump formed in my throat and I shrugged my shoulders, not trusting myself to speak.

"I'm glad Theo went. Shows he still has some humanity in him. Oh, shit, he didn't bring Simone, did he?"

"No, he didn't. He was…different." I laughed quietly.

Blake eyed me carefully. "Don't take this the wrong way, but, just be careful he isn't trying to pull you back in —"

"No, he didn't try anything like that. He was sincere. It wasn't for me that he came. It was for my dad."

The dog sniffed at my hand, trying to get me to stroke him. I scratched his head and neck as I told Blake what Theo had said at the funeral and how he'd apologized for everything.

Blake chuckled. "Sounds like he's in therapy."

"He is. Simone made him go."

Blake threw back his head and laughed. It was a good few minutes before he calmed himself, and he had to clutch his sides when he did. God, it was good to hear him laugh. It didn't feel like we were strangers anymore but there was still so much unsaid.

"Theo said you came looking for me. You know, back then." I looked down at my hands.

"I did. He wouldn't tell me where you were. So I wrote you a letter and just hoped you had redirected your mail by then."

I smirked. So simple yet genius. It made me glad I had re-directed my mail to Hayley's apartment. "Theo would have tossed it if he'd found it."

"Which is why I'm glad he obviously didn't." Blake observed me for a moment. "He loves you, you know."

"What?"

He nodded toward his dog.

"Oh." I giggled. "He's pretty cool. What's his name, anyway?"

Blake shrugged. "I can't think of one. I've only had him a few days. The rescue center I got him from found him tied to a street lamp. All I've discovered about him is he really likes pools and enjoys getting his head scratched a little too much, going by the noises he makes."

I laughed. "What have you been calling him?"

He smiled. "Nothing, really. Dog, or boy—that's about it."

I crouched down so I was eye level with the dog. "That's no good. You need a name. You know, I used to call all my fish 'Bob' when I was a kid because I could never think of good names for them."

Blake laughed. "Right. I'd think of you every time I said his name."

I straightened myself up. "Why?"

He grinned. "Bob?"

"So?"

I folded my arms as Blake chuckled again. "Bob and Marley?"

"Oh! Bob Marley." I giggled, marveling at my own stupidity. "You know that's not who I'm named after."

Blake raised his eyebrows. "No? I figured your parents must have been huge reggae fans or something."

"Nope. They were fans all right, but of Dickens, not reggae."

His brows dropped into a frown. "Dickens..." Blake thought for a moment before his lips twitched. "Are you named after Jacob Marley?"

I rolled my eyes. "Yes. I know. It's weird—weirder than being named after a dead reggae singer. My dad really liked A Christmas Carol. He took a kind of twisted liking to the way Marley spooked Scrooge in the beginning. You can imagine how fun it was when my school put on a production when I was nine."

Blake chuckled. "He sounds like my kind of guy." Before the moment could turn painful, the dog jumped up excitedly between us. "I think he likes Bob," Blake said as the dog lifted its front paws for me to catch, like we were doing a little dance.

"Hi, Bob." I grinned.

He barked.

Blake rolled his eyes. "Bob it is then."

Chapter Twenty-Eight

For every moment I spent in Blake's company, a brick was removed from the wall I'd built around myself. But there were too many unanswered questions that stopped me from falling into his arms and kissing him in a way that would make me forget my name. It didn't help that Blake looked like he was trying very hard not to touch me. Even after all these months of separation, it almost felt like trying to break a habit. I'd never realized how hard it was not to touch someone. It also didn't help that I kept focusing on his hands.

I adored Blake's hands. They were smooth to the touch with long, slender fingers. It didn't take much to remember exactly how Blake's hands felt when they knotted in my hair as he kissed me so deep he could taste my soul.

I remembered looking down at our entwined hands one evening as we'd lazed together watching a movie. My hands had seemed so small and dainty in comparison with his. It seemed that every part of me slotted so easily into him, like I had been made for him. That thought opened a floodgate of memories. A shiver crept down my back as I recalled the feeling of Blake running his fingertips down my naked spine as I'd straddled him in the hot tub…

The force of the memory slammed into me, making me breathless.

"You all right there?" Blake asked.

I nodded and took a gulp of my beer. I needed to get a hold of myself. If I kept thinking like that… Well, I wouldn't be held accountable for my actions.

"So what is all this?" I asked, waving my arm around the kitchen. "You buy it?"

Blake gave me a small smile and looked a little abashed. "I built it."

I choked on my mouthful of beer. *"Built?"*

He nodded.

"In seven months?"

Blake chuckled. "I've owned the land and had the designs for the place for a while now. I made a few tweaks and it was ready to go. I found if you offer enough money, construction workers can be very helpful."

A frown creased my forehead. "You mean this is…the house you used to sketch…this is it?"

Blake nodded.

"Wow. Just… Wow. It's good you're putting your degree to good use." God, I was lame.

"Yeah, I always wanted to. I work for myself now and it's great."

"You started your own architecture firm?"

Blake nodded.

"Wow," I repeated.

He laughed. "Don't feel too awed yet. The only client I have is me."

"It'll come. Give it time."

Blake looked at me with such a burning intensity it was really hard to push the sex memories out of my head. He smiled and his cheeks flushed lightly, as though we caught what the other was thinking. "Do you want a look around?" Blake asked.

"Okay," I said.

His smile widened, and he led the way out of the kitchen.

"I'm still decorating a few rooms." He glanced down at his paint-spattered clothes. "Clearly."

The house was pretty much bare, not many personal touches. I absolutely adored his den. Huge, wide windows dotted along one wall, light pouring in as though coming from a source the rest of the world hadn't yet discovered. An enormous fawn colored suede couch in a U shape curved around a colossal flat screen mounted on the wall. *Jealous much.* The TV at my suite was tiny in comparison. I noticed there were four or five stacks of DVDs in the corner, each about waist high.

I arched an eyebrow at him.

"What? Someone once told me movies are the best kind of education."

It had been me, of course. It was a painful reminder of a once-happy day.

Blake sensed the drop in atmosphere and quickly moved the tour along. It was impressive. He had done well. It was one of those houses that just seemed to capture the light. It was all big and airy and made you feel right at home.

Bob trotted alongside us as Blake gave me a running commentary of each room and what he planned to do with it. He told me anecdotes of when things had gone wrong. I smiled and laughed along with his jokes, but really my heart felt heavy. The more we delved into the house, the more Blake came out of himself and I saw the man I had fallen in love with.

The light of the day was fast fading and even when darkness encroached on the house, it felt bright and warm.

Blake was showing me around the rooms upstairs when his cell phone rang.

"Great. I have no idea where that is coming from," he mumbled. "Keep looking around, I'll be right back." Blake bounded down the stairs, leaving me alone.

I wandered in and out of a few rooms, not really paying attention. The door to the farthest away room lay slightly ajar. I pushed the door open fully and walked inside. *Whoops, Blake's bedroom. Probably not a great idea to be in here.* Or maybe it was better — or safer — to look around while I was alone.

I couldn't have forced myself to leave that room. It was spectacular. First off, it was enormous. On the opposite side from the door, the room was curved like a big, fat romantic tower. The windows were huge and went right around the curve of the wall. Upon closer inspection, I saw they were French windows and opened out onto a large balcony. Before I ventured out on the balcony, I took the opportunity to snoop around a little.

Blake's bedroom was that of a typical guy. A bed, a mirror, a walk-in closet, a nightstand, a desk and an en-suite bathroom — not much else.

A blue photograph packet lying on Blake's desk caught my eye. The empty envelope was resting on top of the developed photos and I couldn't help myself. I moved the envelope to the side and picked up the small stack of photos.

A wash of agony tore through my body. The pictures from our day in Coney Island struck a pain in my heart so intense it made me want to cry out. We looked so different then…so carefree despite it being such a hard time. I traced a finger down Blake's face in the picture and wished I could go back to that day, even if just for a moment.

Before my emotions got the better of me, I replaced the photos and headed out onto the balcony. Blake had excellent views, but the way he had designed the house provided excellent coverage for privacy. I thought it was odd that he didn't have any furniture on the balcony, but then remembered that he hadn't long moved in.

At the far end of the balcony, was a winding stone staircase. I frowned. Was it normal for balconies to have stairs going up to the roof? My curiosity won again and I slowly walked up the steps.

I gasped as I reached the top. A perfect little alcove was cut into the roof. Ankle high lanterns lit up the area beautifully, casting a magical glow. There were two of those really big sun loungers that were more like double beds than loungers. Walking to the edge and leaning on the railing, I could see everything. The lights of the Strip twinkled in the distance, reminding me exactly where I was.

The sound of footsteps shuffling up the steps made me turn. Blake looked nervous as he walked toward me. "Thought you'd find your way up here."

"It's amazing," I whispered.

"Marley—"

"What is this?" I asked suddenly, producing the quarter that had fallen out of his letter from my pocket. He didn't need to know I'd been carrying it around like a strange, foreign talisman since I'd discovered it.

Blake paused in his approach, his eyes on the coin.

"It was in your letter," I said, feeling stupid. Maybe its presence had been an accident. I'd held onto it because it was easier, and more discreet, than carting around his letter. I'd kept that coin physically on me since I'd found it for the sole reason of needing something of his with me, even if it was an accident, and placing sentimental value on a simple coin was crazy.

"I know." Blake jammed his hands in his pockets, eyes finally meeting mine. "I put it in there."

"Why?"

"I wanted you to have it. Whether you knew what it was or not."

"So what is it?"

"My cut."

"Your—" I started. Looking down at the innocent coin, I felt my heart skip a beat. His cut... Surely he hadn't kept it all this time. That was... Wow. For Blake to have kept it all this time had to mean something—meaning I meant something to him. "Did you know who I was?" I asked, a small crease forming between my eyes. I had to get this out now or I never would, and I'd be stuck in this weird limbo with Blake forever. "The night we met, did you know me?"

"No," Blake said, frowning.

"So you two weren't trying to set me up from the beginning?"

Blake's expression turned from confused to horrified as he realized what I was saying. "You think I chased you because Theo told me to? How can you think that?"

"It's amazing what theories you come up with when you get a bombshell like I got."

"I know what I did was wrong, but, how could you think I could be that cruel?"

I looked down. "I didn't want to. But come on, Blake. I find out you knew about everything and helped with it all. Of course I'm going to think the worst."

Blake shook his head and turned away from me for a moment. "Marley, I'm not going to beg you to believe me. I told you my side in the letter. It's up to you what you believe."

"I felt like a fool, Blake," I said quietly. "It felt like you and Theo were laughing at me, that it was all just part of your game to make me love you."

"No," Blake said fiercely. "It was never like that."

I took a step toward him, feeling the tears sting my eyes. "Even when I wanted to hate you, it was always you I wanted around. You never stopped being the person I wanted to run to."

Blake hung his head. "I wish I could have been there for you. God, there's so much I would change if I could go back."

"I wouldn't," I whispered.

"You wouldn't?" Blake asked.

I didn't realize that was exactly how I felt until I heard myself saying the words. The heat radiating from his body made mine hum as I stepped closer toward him.

"I wouldn't change a damn thing," I said passionately. "Yeah, it really hurt and it was awful to go through. But if I hadn't, I wouldn't be here, right now in this moment."

The smallest step was all it took for me to be nearly pressed against him. Blake's eyes bore into my face.

Normally that alone would have made me self-conscious and unsure of myself, but I'd never been surer of anything than I was when I met those piercing green eyes.

I reached up to rest my fingertips lightly on his chest. Blake gave a little shiver under my touch and when his eyes met mine again, the fire in them was fierce and he made no effort to conceal it.

Blake stroked along each side of my jaw before splaying his fingers into my hair, cupping my face gently. He titled my head upward, his eyes making my heart splutter frantically. For a moment we did nothing at all, as if giving the other the chance to back away if either wanted to. *Yeah, right.*

I thought I was going to burst with anticipation. The heat from his body so close to mine, his fingers in my hair, the glorious scent of him... It all made me want to cry out for him. In the end I didn't know who closed the tiny gap between us. All I was aware of was his hot breath on my face before our lips collided with such a force I would have been knocked down had Blake not held me so tightly. My mouth exploded in a mixture of familiar tastes and feelings. Fat tears rolled down my cheeks with the sheer force of it. Tighter and tighter he held me, his hands moving from my face to my lower back to pin me to him.

Our kiss broke, both of us panting heavily. Everything I needed to know was in that kiss.

"Marley," Blake mumbled against my lips.

"Shh," I whispered, my lips moving against his.

"Wait," he said more forcefully this time. "Are you seeing anyone?"

Apparently the kiss hadn't told him everything he needed to know. With a little shove I pushed away from him. "Am I—? Are you serious? No, I'm not seeing anyone, you jerk."

Blake's lips twisted in a smile. He reached for me and pulled me back against him. "Good. Because this time, I'm doing everything right," he whispered as he brushed his lips over mine. "You feel like getting married?"

"What? Right now?" I asked, startled. Maybe I could forgive his question, then.

"'Tis the tradition in Vegas."

Every part of me screamed yes. There was nothing holding either of us back anymore. All the lies, all the sneaking, it had all been stripped away. He was just Blake and I was just Marley. We wanted each other with such a ferocity that I doubted even time could weaken it.

"I've shared you and I've lost you once. I'm not making the same mistakes again and don't want to live another second if I don't have you in my life," Blake said fiercely.

I grinned before answering him with a kiss. And I do believe I saw fireworks—and it wasn't even the fourth of July.

About the Author

Pamela has adored books since she can remember. There was no greater pleasure than discovering a new world to venture into, a new character to fall in love with…until she created her own and realized there was something even more magical.

When she isn't locked away at her computer, or scribbling in a notebook, Pamela can be found as her alter ego—namely wife to Matthew and mother to Todd. They also share their home with a schizophrenic cat and two greedy goldfish.

Pamela L. Todd loves to hear from readers. You can find her contact information, website details and author profile page at http://www.totallybound.com.

Totally Bound Publishing

Home of Erotic Romance